Books by John Barth

CHIMERA

LOST IN THE FUNHOUSE

GILES GOAT-BOY

THE SOT-WEED FACTOR

THE END OF THE ROAD

THE FLOATING OPERA

CHIMERA

CHIMERA

)CHIMERA

by John Barth

RANDOM HOUSE *NEW YORK*

Copyright © 1972 by John Barth

All rights reserved under International
and Pan-American Copyright Conventions.
Published in the United States
by Random House, Inc., New York,
and simultaneously in Canada
by Random House of Canada Limited, Toronto.

Library of Congress Cataloging in Publication Data

Barth, John.
    Chimera.

    I. Title.
PZ4.B284Ch   813'.5'4   72-3389
ISBN 0-394-49139-9
ISBN 0-394-48189-5   (lim. ed.)

Grateful acknowledgment is made
to Collins-Knowlton-Wing, Inc., for permission
to reprint material from *The Greek Myths*
by Robert Graves. Copyright © 1955 by Robert Graves.

"Dunyazadiad" first appeared in slightly different form
in *Esquire* magazine, June 1972. "Perseid" first
appeared in *Harper's* magazine, September 1972.

Manufactured in the United States of America
by The Book Press, Brattleboro, Vt.

9 8 7 6 5 4 3 2
First Edition

CONTENTS

Dunyazadiad

1

~~~~~~~~~~~~~

"At this point I interrupted my sister as usual to say, 'You have a way with words, Scheherazade. This is the thousandth night I've sat at the foot of your bed while you and the King made love and you told him stories, and the one in progress holds me like a genie's gaze. I wouldn't dream of breaking in like this, just before the end, except that I hear the first rooster crowing in the east, et cetera, and the King really ought to sleep a bit before daybreak. I wish I had your talent.'

"And as usual Sherry replied, 'You're the ideal audience, Dunyazade. But this is nothing; wait till you hear the ending, tomorrow night! Always assuming this auspicious King doesn't kill me before breakfast, as he's been going to do these thirty-three and a third months.'

" 'Hmp,' said Shahryar. 'Don't take your critics for granted; I may get around to it yet. But I agree with your little sister that this is a good one you've got going, with its impostures that become authentic, its ups and downs and flights to other worlds. I don't know how in the world you dream them up.'

" 'Artists have their tricks,' Sherry replied. We three said good night then, six goodnights in all. In the morning your brother went off to court, enchanted by Sherry's story. Daddy came to the palace for the thousandth time with a shroud under his arm, expecting to be told to cut his daughter's head off; in most other respects he's as good a vizier as he ever was, but three years of suspense have driven him crackers in this one particular—and turned his hair white, I might add, and made him a widower. Sherry and I, after the first fifty nights or so, were simply relieved when Shahryar would hmp and say, 'By Allah, I won't kill her till I've heard the end of her story'; but it still took Daddy by surprise every morning. He groveled gratitude per usual; the King per usual spent the day in his durbar, bidding and forbidding between man and man, as the saying goes; I climbed in with Sherry as soon as he was gone, and per usual we spent *our* day sleeping in and making love. When we'd had enough of each other's tongues and fingers, we called in the eunuchs, maidservants, mamelukes, pet dogs and monkeys; then we finished off with Sherry's Bag of Tricks: little weighted balls from Baghdad, dildoes from the Ebony Isles and the City of

Brass, et cetera. Not to break a certain vow of mine, I made do with a roc-down tickler rom Bassorah, but Sherry touched all the bases. Her favorite story is about some pig of an ifrit who steals a girl away on her wedding night, puts her in a treasure-casket locked with seven steel padlocks, puts the casket in a crystal coffer, and puts the coffer on the bottom of the ocean, so that nobody except himself can have her. But whenever he brings the whole rig ashore, unlocks the locks with seven keys, and takes her out and rapes her, he falls asleep afterward on her lap; she slips out from under and cuckolds him with every man who passes by, taking their seal rings as proof; at the end of the story she has five hundred seventy-two seal rings, and the stupid ifrit still thinks he *possesses* her! In the same way, Sherry put a hundred horns a day on your brother's head: that's about a hundred thousand horns by now. And every day she saved till last the Treasure Key, which is what her story starts and ends with.

"Three and a third years ago, when King Shahryar was raping a virgin every night and killing her in the morning, and the people were praying that Allah would dump the whole dynasty, and so many parents had fled the country with their daughters that in all the Islands of India and China there was hardly a young girl fit to fuck, my sister was an undergraduate arts-and-sciences major at Banu Sasan University. Besides being Homecoming Queen, valedictorian-elect, and a four-letter varsity athlete, she had a private library of a thousand volumes and the highest average in the history of the campus. Every graduate department in the East was after her with fellowships—but she was so appalled at the state of the nation that she dropped out of school in her last semester to do full-time research on a way to stop

Shahryar from killing all our sisters and wrecking the country.

"Political science, which she looked at first, got her nowhere. Shahryar's power was absolute, and by sparing the daughters of his army officers and chief ministers (like our own father) and picking his victims mainly from the families of liberal intellectuals and other minorities, he kept the military and the cabinet loyal enough to rule out a coup d'état. Revolution seemed out of the question, because his woman-hating, spectacular as it was, was reinforced more or less by all our traditions and institutions, and as long as the girls he was murdering were generally upper-caste, there was no popular base for guerrilla war. Finally, since he could count on your help from Samarkand, invasion from outside or plain assassination were bad bets too: Sherry figured your retaliation would be worse than Shahryar's virgin-a-night policy.

"So we gave up poly sci (I fetched her books and sharpened her quills and made tea and alphabetized her index cards) and tried psychology—another blind alley. Once she'd noted that *your* reaction to being cuckolded by your wife was homicidal rage followed by despair and abandonment of your kingdom, and that Shahryar's was the reverse; and established that *that* was owing to the difference in your ages and the order of revelations; and decided that whatever pathology was involved was a function of the culture and your position as absolute monarchs rather than particular hang-ups in your psyches, et cetera—what was there to say?

"She grew daily more desperate; the body-count of deflowered and decapitated Moslem girls was past nine hundred, and Daddy was just about out of candidates. Sherry didn't especially care about herself, you understand—wouldn't have even if she hadn't guessed that the King was sparing her out of respect for his vizier and her own accomplishments. But beyond the general awfulness of the situation, she was particularly concerned for my sake. From the day I was born, when Sherry was about nine, she treasured me as if I were hers; I might as well not have had parents; she and I ate from the same plate, slept in the same bed; no one could separate us; I'll bet we weren't apart for an hour in the first dozen years of my life. But I never had her good looks or her way with the world—and I was the youngest in the family besides. My breasts were growing; already I'd begun to menstruate: any day Daddy might have to sacrifice me to save Sherry.

"So when nothing else worked, as a last resort she turned to her first love, unlikely as it seemed, mythology and folklore, and studied all the riddle/puzzle/secret motifs she could dig up. 'We need a miracle, Doony,' she said (I was braiding her hair and massaging her neck as she went through her notes for the thousandth time), 'and the only genies *I've* ever met were in stories, not in Moormans'-rings and Jews'-lamps. It's in words that the magic is—Abracadabra, Open Sesame, and the rest—but the magic words in one story aren't magical in the next. The real magic is to understand which words work, and when, and for what; the trick is to learn the trick.'

"This last, as our frantic research went on, became her motto, even her obsession. As she neared the end of her supply of lore, and Shahryar his supply of virgins, she became more and more certain that her principle was correct, and desperate that in the whole world's stock of stories there was none that confirmed it, or showed us how to use it to solve the problem. 'I've read a thousand tales about treasures that nobody can find the key to,' she told me; 'we have the key and can't find the treasure.' I asked her to explain. 'It's all in here,' she declared—I couldn't tell whether she meant her inkstand or the quill she pointed toward it. I seldom understood her any more; as the crisis grew, she gave up reading for daydreaming, and used her pen less for noting instances of the Magic Key motif in world literature than for doodling the letters of our alphabet at random and idly tickling herself.

" 'Little Doony,' she said dreamily, and kissed me: 'pretend this whole situation is the plot of a story we're reading, and you and I and Daddy and the King are all fictional characters. In this story, Scheherazade finds a way to change the King's mind about women and turn him into a gentle, loving husband. It's not hard to imagine such a story, is it? Now, no matter what way she finds—whether it's a magic spell or a magic story with the answer in it or a magic anything—it comes down to particular words in the story we're reading, right? And those words are made from the letters of our alphabet: a couple-dozen squiggles we can draw with this pen. This is the key, Doony! And the treasure, too, if we can only get our hands on it! It's as if—as if the key to the treasure *is* the treasure!'

"As soon as she spoke these last words a genie appeared from nowhere right there in our library-stacks. He didn't resemble anything in Sherry's bedtime stories: for one thing, he wasn't frightening, though he was strange-looking enough: a light-skinned fellow of forty or so, smooth-shaven and bald as a roc's egg. His clothes were simple but outlandish; he was tall and healthy and pleasant enough in appearance, except for queer lenses that he wore in a frame over his eyes. He seemed as startled as we were—you should've seen Sherry drop that pen and pull her skirts together!—but he got over his alarm a lot sooner, and looked from one to the other of us and at a stubby little magic wand he held in his fingers, and smiled a friendly smile.

" 'Are you really Scheherazade?' he asked. 'I've never had a dream so clear and lifelike! And you're little Dunya-zade—just as I'd imagined both of you! Don't be frightened: I can't tell you what it means to me to see and talk to you like this; even in a dream, it's a dream come true. Can you understand English? I don't have a word of Arabic. O my, I can't believe this is really happening!'

"Sherry and I looked at each other. The Genie didn't seem dangerous; we didn't know those languages he spoke of; every word he said was in *our* language, and when Sherry asked him whether he'd come from her pen or from her words, he seemed to understand the question, though he didn't know the answer. He was a writer of tales, he said—anyhow a *former* writer of tales—in a land on the other side of the world. At one time, we gathered, people in his country had been fond of reading; currently, however, the only readers of artful fiction were critics, other writers, and unwilling students who, left to themselves, preferred music and pictures to words. His own pen (that magic wand, in fact a magic quill with a fountain of ink inside) had just about run dry: but whether he had abandoned fiction or fiction him, Sherry and I couldn't make out when we reconstructed this first conversation later that night, for either in our minds or in his a number of crises seemed confused. Like Shahryar's, the Genie's life was in disorder—but so far from harboring therefore a grudge against womankind, he was distractedly in love with a brace of new mistresses, and only recently had been able to choose between them. His career, too, had reached a hiatus which he would have been pleased to call a turning-point if he could have espied any way to turn: he wished neither to repudiate nor to repeat his past performances; he aspired to go beyond them toward a future they were not attuned to and, by some magic, at the same time go back to the original springs of narrative. But how this was to be managed was as unclear to him as the answer to the Shahryar-problem was to us—the more so since he couldn't say how much of his difficulty might be owing to his own limitations, his age and stage and personal vicissitudes; how much to the general decline of letters in his time and place; and how much to the other crises with which his country (and, so he alleged, the very species) was beset—crises as desperate and problematical, he avowed, as ours, and as inimical to the single-mindedness needed to compose great works of art or the serenity to apprehend them.

"So entirely was he caught up in these problems, his work and life and all had come to a standstill. He had taken leave of his friends, his family, and his post (he was a doctor of letters), and withdrawn to a lonely retreat in the marshes, which only the most devoted of his mistresses deigned to visit.

" 'My project,' he told us, 'is to learn where to go by discovering where I am by reviewing where I've been—where we've *all* been. There's a kind of snail in the Maryland marshes—perhaps I invented him—that makes his shell as he goes along out of whatever he comes across, cementing it with his own juices, and at the same time makes his path instinctively toward the best available material for his shell; he carries his history on his back, living in it, adding new and larger spirals to it from the present as he grows. That snail's pace has become my pace—but I'm going in circles, following my own trail! I've quit reading and writing; I've lost track of who I am; my name's just a jumble of letters; so's the whole body of literature: strings of letters and empty spaces, like a code that I've lost the key to.' He pushed those odd lenses up on the bridge of his nose with his thumb—a habit that made me giggle—and grinned. 'Well, *almost* the whole body. Speaking of keys, I suspect that's how I got here.'

"By way of answer to Sherry's question then, whether he had sprung from her quill-pen or her words, he declared that his researches, like hers, had led him to an impasse; he felt that a treasure-house of new fiction lay vaguely under his hand, if he could find the key to it. Musing idly on this figure, he had added to the morass of notes he felt himself mired in, a sketch for a story about a man who comes somehow to realize that the key to the treasure he's searching for *is* the treasure. Just exactly how so (and how the story might be told despite all the problems that beset him) he had no chance to consider, for the instant he set on paper the words *The key to the treasure is the treasure*, he found himself with us—for how long, or to what end, or by what means, he had no idea, unless it was that of all the storytellers in the world, his very favorite was Scheherazade.

" 'Listen how I chatter on!' he ended happily. 'Do forgive me!'

"My sister, after some thought, ventured the opinion that the astonishing coincidence of her late reveries and his, which had led them as it were simultaneously to the same cryptic formulation, must have something to do with his translation to her library. She looked forward, she said, to experimenting whether a reverse translation could be managed, if the worst came to the worst, to spirit me out of harm's way; as for herself, she had no time or use for idle flights of fancy, however curious, from the gynocide that was ravaging her country:

remarkable as it was, she saw no more relevance to her problems than to his in this bit of magic.

" 'But we know the answer's right here in our hands!' the Genie exclaimed. 'We're both storytellers: you must sense as strongly as I that it has something to do with the key to the treasure's being the treasure.'

"My sister's nostrils narrowed. 'Twice you've called me a storyteller,' she said; 'yet I've never told a story in my life except to Dunyazade, and her bedtime stories were the ones that everybody tells. The only tale I ever invented myself was this key-to-the-treasure one just now, which I scarcely understand . . .'

" 'Good lord!' the Genie cried. 'Do you mean to say that you haven't even *started* your thousand and one nights yet?'

"Sherry shook her head grimly. 'The only thousand nights I know of is the time our pig of a king has been killing the virgin daughters of the Moslems.'

"Our bespectacled visitor then grew so exhilarated that for some time he couldn't speak at all. Presently he seized my sister's hand and dumbfounded us both by declaring his life-long adoration of her, a declaration that brought blushes to our cheeks. Years ago, he said, when he'd been a penniless student pushing book-carts through the library-stacks of his university to help pay for his education, he'd contracted a passion for Scheherazade upon first reading the tales she be-guiled King Shahryar with, and had sustained that passion so powerfully ever since that his love affairs with other, 'real' women seemed to him by comparison unreal, his two-decade marriage but a prolonged infidelity to her, his own fictions mere mimicries, pallid counterfeits of the authentic treasure of her *Thousand and One Nights*.

" 'Beguiled the King with!' Sherry said. 'I've thought of that! Daddy believes that Shahryar would really like to quit what he's doing before the country falls apart, but needs an excuse to break his vow without losing face with his younger brother. I'd considered letting him make love to me and then telling him exciting stories, which I'd leave unfinished from one night to the next till he'd come to know me too well to kill me. I even thought of slipping in stories about kings who'd suffered worse hardships than he and his brother without turning vindictive; or lovers who weren't unfaithful; or husbands who loved their wives more than themselves. But it's too fanciful! Who knows which stories would work? Especially in those first few nights! I can see him sparing me for a day or two, maybe, out of relief; but then he'd react against his lapse and go back to his old policy. I gave the idea up.'

"The Genie smiled; even *I* saw what he was thinking. 'But you say you've read the book!' Sherry exclaimed. 'Then you must remember what stories are in it, and in which order!'

" 'I don't have to remember,' said the Genie. 'In all the years I've been writing stories, your book has never been off my worktable. I've made use of it a thousand times, if only by just seeing it there.'

"Sherry asked him then whether he himself had perhaps invented the stories she allegedly told, or would tell. 'How could I?' he laughed. 'I won't be born for a dozen centuries yet! You didn't invent them either, for that matter; they're those ancient ones you spoke of, that "everybody tells": Sinbad the Sailor, Aladdin's Lamp, Ali Baba and the Forty Thieves . . .'

" 'What others?' Sherry cried. 'In which order? I don't

even *know* the Ali Baba story! Do you have the book with you? I'll give you everything I have for it!'

"The Genie replied that inasmuch as he'd been holding her book in his hand and thinking about her when he'd written the magic words, and it had not been translated to her library along with him, he inferred that he could not present her with a copy even if the magic were repeatable. He did however remember clearly what he called the frame-story: how Shahryar's young brother Shah Zaman had discovered his bride's adulteries, killed her, abandoned the kingdom of Samarkand, and come to live with Shahryar in the Islands of India and China; how, discovering that Shahryar's wife was equally unfaithful, the brothers had retreated to the wilderness, encountered the ifrit and the maiden, concluded that all women are deceivers, and returned to their respective kingdoms, vowing to deflower a virgin every night and kill her in the morning; how the Vizier's daughter Scheherazade, to end this massacre, had volunteered herself, much against her father's wishes, and with the aid of her sister Dunyazade —who at the crucial moment between sex and sleep asked for a story, and fed the King's suspense by interrupting the tale at daybreak, just before the climax—stayed Shahryar's hand long enough to win his heart, restore his senses, and save the country from ruin.

"I hugged my sister and begged her to let me help her in just that way. She shook her head: 'Only this Genie has read the stories I'm supposed to tell, and he doesn't remember them. What's more, he's fading already. If the key to the treasure is the treasure, we don't have it in our hands yet.'

"He had indeed begun fading away, almost disappeared; but as soon as Sherry repeated the magic sentence he came back clearly, smiling more eagerly than before, and declared he'd been thinking the same words at the same moment, just when *we'd* begun to fade and his writing-room to reappear about him. Apparently, then, he and Sherry could conjure the phenomenon at will by imagining simultaneously that the key to the treasure was the treasure: they were, presumably, the only two people in the history of the world who had imagined it. What's more, in that instant when he'd waked, as it were, to find himself back in the marshes of *America*, he'd been able to glance at the open table of contents of Volume One of the *Thousand and One Nights* book and determine that the first story after the frame-story was a compound tale called 'The Merchant and the Genie'—in which, if he remembered correctly, an outraged ifrit delays the death of an innocent merchant until certain sheiks have told their stories.

"Scheherazade thanked him, made a note of the title, and gravely put down her pen. 'You have it in your power to save my sisters and my country,' she said, 'and the King too, before his madness destroys him. All you need to do is supply me from the future with these stories from the past. But perhaps at bottom you share the King's feelings about women.'

" 'Not at all!' the Genie said warmly. 'If the key trick really works, I'll be honored to tell your stories to you. All we need to do is agree on a time of day to write the magic words together.'

"I clapped my hands—but Sherry's expression was still cool. 'You're a man,' she said; 'I imagine you expect what every man expects who has the key to any treasure a woman needs. In the nature of the case, I have to let Shahryar take me first; after that I'll cuckold him with you every day at sunset if you'll tell me the story for the night to come. Is that satisfactory?'

"I feared he'd take offense, but he only shook his head. Out of his old love for her, he gently declared, and his gratitude for the profoundest image he knew of the storyteller's situation, he would be pleased beyond words to play any role whatever in Scheherazade's story, without dreaming of further reward. His *own* policy, moreover, which he had lived by for many nights more than a thousand, was to share beds with no woman who did not reciprocate his feelings. Finally, his new young mistress—to whom he had been drawn by certain resemblances to Scheherazade—delighted him utterly, as he hoped he did her; he was no more tempted to infidelity than to incest or pederasty. His adoration of Scheherazade was as strong as ever —even stronger now that he'd met her in the lovely flesh—but it was not possessive; he desired her only as the old Greek poets their Muse, as a source of inspiration.

"Sherry tapped and fiddled with her quill. 'I don't know these poets you speak of,' she said sharply. 'Here in our country, love isn't so exclusive as all that. When I think of Shahryar's harem-full of concubines on the one hand, and the way his wife got even with him on the other, and the plots of most of the stories I know—especially the ones about older men with young mistresses—I can't help wondering whether you're not being a bit naïve, to put it kindly. Especially as I gather you've suffered your share of deceit in the past, and no doubt done your share of deceiving. Even so, it's a refreshing surprise, if a bit of a put-down, that you're not interested in taking sexual advantage of your position. Are you a eunuch?'

"I blushed again, but the Genie assured us, still unoffended, that he was normally equipped, and that his surpassing love for his young lady, while perhaps invincibly inno-

cent, was not naïve. His experience of love gone sour only
made him treasure more highly the notion of a love that time
would season and improve; no sight on earth more pleased
his heart, annealed as it was by his own past passions and
defeats, than that rare one of two white-haired spouses who
still cherished each other and their life together. If love died,
it died; while it lived, let it live forever, et cetera. Some
fictions, he asserted, were so much more valuable than fact
that in rare instances their beauty made them real. The only
Baghdad was the Baghdad of the *Nights*, where carpets flew
and genies sprang from magic words; he was ours to command as one of those, and without price. Should one appear
to *him* and offer him three wishes, he'd be unable to summon
more than two, inasmuch as his first—to have live converse
with the storyteller he'd loved best and longest—had already been granted.

"Sherry smiled now and asked him what would be the
other two wishes. The second, he replied, would be that he
might die before his young friend and he ceased to treasure each other as they did currently in their saltmarsh
retreat. The third (what presently stood alone between him
and entire contentment) would be that he not die without
adding some artful trinket or two, however small, to the general treasury of civilized delights, to which no keys were
needed beyond goodwill, attention, and a moderately culti-
vated sensibility: he meant the treasury of art, which if it
could not redeem the barbarities of history or spare us the
horrors of living and dying, at least sustained, refreshed, ex-
panded, ennobled, and enriched our spirits along the painful
way. Such of his scribblings as were already in print he did
not presume to have that grace; should he die before he woke
from his present sweet dream of Scheherazade, this third

wish would go unfulfilled. But even if neither of these last was ever granted (and surely such boons were rare as treasure keys), he would die happier to have had the first.

"Hearing this, Sherry at last put by her reserve, took the stranger's writing-hand in her own, apologized for her discourtesy, and repeated her invitation, this time warmly: if he would supply her with enough of her stories to reach her goal, she was his in secret whenever he wished after her maiden night with Shahryar. Or (if deception truly had no more savor for him), when the slaughter of her sisters had ceased, let him spirit her somehow to his place and time, and she'd be his slave and concubine forever—assuming, as one was after all realistically obliged to assume, that he and his current love would by then have wearied of each other.

"The Genie laughed and kissed her hand. 'No slaves; no concubines. And my friend and I intend to love each other forever.'

" 'That will be a greater wonder than all of Sinbad's together,' Sherry said. 'I pray it may happen, Genie, and your third wish be granted too. For all one knows, you may already have done what you hope to do: time will tell. But if Dunyazade and I can find any way at all to help you with *your* tales-to-come in return for the ones you've pledged to us—and you may be sure we'll search for such a way as steadfastly as we've searched for a way to save our sex— we'll do it though we die for it.'

"She made him promise then to embrace his mistress for her, whom she vowed to love thenceforth as she loved me, and by way of a gift to her—which she prayed might translate as the precious book had not—she took from her earlobe a gold ring worked in the form of a spiral shell, of which his earlier image had reminded her. He accepted it joyfully,

vowing to spin from it, if he could, as from a catherine-wheel
or whirling galaxy, a golden shower of fiction. Then he
kissed us both (the first male lips I'd felt except Father's, and
the only such till yours) and vanished, whether by his will or
another's we couldn't tell.

"Sherry and I hugged each other excitedly all that night,
rehearsing every word that had passed between the Genie
and ourselves. I begged her to test the magic for a week before offering herself to the King, to make sure that it—and
her colleague from the future—could be relied upon. But
even as we laughed and whispered, another of our sisters
was being raped and murdered in the palace; Sherry offered
herself to Shahryar first thing in the morning, to our father's
distress; let the King lead her at nightfall into his fatal bed
and fall to toying with her, then pretended to weep for being
separated from me for the first time in our lives. Shahryar
bid her fetch me in to sit at the foot of the bed; almost in a
faint I watched him help her off with the pretty nightie I'd
crocheted for her myself, place a white silk cushion under
her bottom, and gently open her legs; as I'd never seen a
man erect, I groaned despite myself when he opened his robe
and I saw what he meant to stick her with: the hair done up
in pearls, the shaft like a minaret decorated with arabesques,
the head like a cobra's spread to strike. He chuckled at my
alarm and climbed atop her; not to see him, Sherry fixed her
welling eyes on me, closing them only to cry the cry that
must be cried when there befell the mystery concerning
which there is no inquiry. A moment later, as the cushion
attested her late virginity and tears ran from her eye-corners
to her ears, she seized the King's hair, wrapped about his
waist her lovely legs, and to insure the success of her fiction,
pretended a grand transport of rapture. I could neither bear

to watch nor turn my eyes away. When the beast was spent and tossing fitfully (from shame and guilt, I hoped, or unease at Sherry's willingness to die), I gathered my senses as best I could and asked her to tell me a story.

" 'With pleasure,' she said, in a tone still so full of shock it broke my heart, 'if this pious and auspicious King will allow it.' Your brother grunted, and Sherry began, shakily, the tale of the Merchant and the Genie, framing in it for good measure the First Sheik's Story as her voice grew stronger. At the right moment I interrupted to praise the story and say I thought I'd heard a rooster crowing in the east; as though I'd been kept in ignorance of the King's policy, I asked whether we mightn't sleep awhile before sunrise and hear the end of the story tomorrow night—along with the one about the Three Apples, which I liked even more. 'O Doony!' Sherry pretended to scold. 'I know a dozen better than that: how about the Ebony Horse, or Julnar the Sea-Born, or the Ensorcelled Prince? But just as there's no young woman in the country worth having that the King hasn't had his fill of already, so I'm sure there's no story he hasn't heard till he's weary of it. I could no more expect to tell him a new story than show him a new way to make love.'

" 'I'll be the judge of that,' said Shahryar. So we sweated out the day in each other's arms and at sunset tried the magic key; you can imagine our relief when the Genie appeared, pushed up his eyeglasses with a grin, and recited to us the Second and Third Sheiks' Stories, which he guessed were both to be completed on that crucial second night in order, on the one hand, to demonstrate a kind of narrative inexhaustibility or profligacy (at least a generosity commensurate to that of the sheiks themselves), while, on the other hand, not compounding the suspense of unfinished tales-within-tales at a time when the King's reprieve was still highly tentative. Moreover, that the ifrit will grant the merchant's life on account of the stories ought to be evident enough by daybreak to make, without belaboring, its admonitory point. The spiral earring, he added happily, had come through intact, if anything more beautiful for the translation; his mistress was delighted with it, and would return Sherry's embrace with pleasure, he was confident, as soon as the memory of her more contemporary rivals was removed enough, and she secure enough in his love, for him to tell her the remarkable story of the magic key. Tenderly then he voiced his hope that Scheherazade had not found the loss of her maidenhood wholly repugnant to experience, or myself to witness; if the King was truly to be wooed away from his misogyny, many ardent nights lay ahead, and for the sake of Scheherazade's spirit as well as her strategy it would be well if she could take some pleasure in them.

" 'Never!' my sister declared. 'The only pleasure I'll take in that bed is the pleasure of saving my sisters and cuckolding their killer.'

"The Genie shrugged and faded; Shahryar came in, bid us good evening, kissed Sherry many times before caressing her more intimately, then laid her on the bed and worked her over playfully in as many positions as there are tales in the Trickery-of-Women series, till I couldn't tell whether her outcries were of pain, surprise, or—mad as the notion seemed—a kind of pleasure despite herself. As for me, though I was innocent of men, I had read in secret all the manuals of love and erotic stories in Sherry's library, but had thought them the wild imaginings of lonely writers in their dens, a kind of self-tickling with the quill such as Sherry herself had fallen into; for all it was my own sister I saw doing such incredible things in such odd positions, it would be many nights before I fully realized that what I witnessed were not conjured illustrations from those texts, but things truly taking place.

" 'On with the story,' Shahryar commanded when they were done. Unsteadily at first, but then in even better voice than the night before, Sherry continued the Merchant-and-Genie story, and I, mortified to find myself still moistening from what I'd seen, almost forgot to interrupt at the appropriate time. Next day, as we embraced each other, Sherry admitted that while she found the King himself as loathsome as ever, the things he did to her were no longer painful, and might even be pleasurable, as would be the things she did to him, were he a bedpartner she could treasure as our Genie treasured his. More exactly, once the alarm of her defloration and her fear of being killed in the morning began to pass, she found abhorrent not Shahryar himself—undeniably a vigorous and handsome man for his forty years, and a skillful lover—but his murderous record with our sex, which no amount of charm and tender caressing could expunge.

" 'No amount at all?' our Genie asked when he appeared again, on cue, at sunset. 'Suppose a man had been a kind and gentle fellow until some witch put a spell on him that deranged his mind and made him do atrocious things; then suppose a certain young lady has the power to cure him by loving him despite his madness. She can lift the spell because she recognizes that it *is* a spell, and not his real nature . . .'

" 'I hope that's not my tale for tonight,' Sherry said dryly, pointing out that while Shahryar may once upon a time have been a loving husband, even in those days he gave out virgin slave-girls to his friends, kept a houseful of concubines for himself, and cut his wife in half for taking a lover after twenty years of one-sided fidelity. 'And no magic can bring a thousand dead girls back to life, or unrape them. On with the story.'

" 'You're a harder critic than your lover,' the Genie complained, and recited the opening frame of the Fisherman and the Genie, the simplicity of which he felt to be a strategic change of pace for the third night—especially since it would lead, on the fourth and fifth, to a series of tales-within-tales-within-tales, a narrative complexity he described admiringly as 'Oriental.'

"So it went, month after month, year after year; at the foot of Shahryar's bed by night and in Scheherazade's by day, I learned more about the arts of making love and telling stories than I had imagined there was to know. It pleased our Genie, for example, that the tale of the Ensorcelled Prince had been framed by that of the Fisherman and the Genie, since the prince himself had been encased (in the black stone palace); also, that the resolution of the story thus enframed resolved as well the tale that framed it. This metaphorical construction he judged more artful than the 'mere plot-function' (that is, preserving our lives and restoring the King's sanity!) which Sherry's Fisherman-tale and the rest had in the story of her *own* life; but that 'mere plot-function,' in turn, was superior to the artless and arbitrary relation between most framed and framing tales. This relation (which to me seemed less important than what the stories were *about*) interested the two of them no end, just as Sherry and Shahryar were fascinated by the pacing of their nightly pleasures or the refinement of their various positions, instead of the degree and quality of their love.

"Sherry kissed me. 'That other either goes without saying,' she said, 'or it doesn't go at all. Making love and telling stories both take more than good technique—but it's only the technique that we can *talk* about.'

"The Genie agreed: 'Heartfelt ineptitude has its appeal, Dunyazade; so does heartless skill. But what you want is passionate virtuosity.' They speculated endlessly on such questions as whether a story might imaginably be framed from inside, as it were, so that the usual relation between container and contained would be reversed and paradoxically reversible—and (for my benefit, I suppose) what human state of affairs such an odd construction might usefully figure. Or whether one might go beyond the usual tale-within-a-tale, beyond even the tales-within-tales-within-tales-within-tales which our Genie had found a few instances of in that literary treasure-house he hoped one day to add to, and conceive a series of, say, *seven* concentric stories-within-stories, so arranged that the climax of the innermost would precipitate that of the next tale out, and that of the next, et cetera, like a string of firecrackers or the chains of orgasms that Shahryar could sometimes set my sister catenating.

"This last comparison—a favorite of theirs—would lead them to a dozen others between narrative and sexual art, whether in spirited disagreement or equally spirited concord. The Genie declared that in his time and place there were scientists of the passions who maintained that language itself, on the one hand, originated in 'infantile pregenital erotic exuberance, polymorphously perverse,' and that conscious attention, on the other, was a 'libidinal hypercathexis'—by which magic phrases they seemed to mean that writing and reading, or telling and listening, were literally ways of making love. Whether this was in fact the case, neither he nor Sherry cared at all; yet they liked to speak *as if it were* (their favorite words), and accounted thereby for the similarity between conventional dramatic structure—its exposition, rising action, climax, and dénouement—and the rhythm of sexual intercourse from foreplay through coitus to orgasm and release. Therefore also, they believed, the popularity of love (and combat, the darker side of the same rupee) as a theme for narrative, the lovers' embrace as its culmination, and post-coital lassitude as its natural ground: what better time for tales than at day's end, in bed after making love (or around the campfire after battle or adventure, or in the chimney corner after work), to express and heighten the community between the lovers, comrades, co-workers?

" 'The longest story in the world—' Sherry observed, *The Ocean of Story*, seven hundred thousand distichs—was told by the god Siva to his consort Parvati as a gift for the way she made love to him one night. It would take a minstrel five hundred evenings to recite it all, but she sat in his lap and listened contentedly till he was done.'

"To this example, which delighted him, the Genie added several unfamiliar to us: a great epic called *Odyssey*, for instance, whose hero returns home after twenty years of war and wandering, makes love to his faithful wife, and recounts all his adventures to her in bed while the gods prolong the night in his behalf; another work called *Decameron*, in which ten courtly lords and ladies, taking refuge in their country houses from an urban pestilence, amuse one another at the end of each day with stories (some borrowed from Sherry herself) as a kind of *substitute* for making love—an artifice in keeping with the artificial nature of their little society. And, of course, that book about Sherry herself which he claimed to be reading from, in his opinion the best illustration of all that the very relation between teller and told was by nature erotic. The teller's role, he felt, regardless of his actual gender, was essentially masculine, the listener's or reader's feminine, and the tale was the medium of their intercourse.

" 'That makes me unnatural,' Sherry objected. 'Are you one of those vulgar men who think that women writers are homosexuals?'

" 'Not at all,' the Genie assured her. 'You and Shahryar usually make love in Position One before you tell your story, and lovers like to switch positions the second time.' More seriously, he had not meant to suggest that the 'femininity' of readership was a docile or inferior condition: a lighthouse, for example, passively sent out signals that mariners labored actively to receive and interpret; an ardent woman like his mistress was as least as energetic in his embrace as he in embracing her; a good reader of cunning tales worked in her way as busily as their author; et cetera. Narrative, in short— and here they were again in full agreement—was a love-relation, not a rape: its success depended upon the reader's consent and cooperation, which she could withhold or at any moment withdraw; also upon her own combination of experience and talent for the enterprise, and the author's ability to arouse, sustain, and satisfy her interest—an ability on which his figurative life hung as surely as Scheherazade's literal.

" 'And like all love-relations,' he added one afternoon, 'it's potentially fertile for both partners, in a way you should approve, for it goes beyond male and female. The reader is likely to find herself pregnant with new images, as you hope Shahryar will become with respect to women; but the story-teller may find himself pregnant too . . .'

"Much of their talk was over my head, but on hearing this last I hugged Sherry tight and prayed to Allah it was not another of their *as if*'s. Sure enough, on the three hundred eighth night her tale was interrupted not by me but by the birth of Ali Shar, whom despite his resemblance to Shahryar I clasped to my bosom from that hour as if I had borne instead of merely helping to deliver him. Likewise on the six hundred twenty-fourth night, when little Gharíb came lustily into the world, and the nine hundred fifty-ninth, birthday of beautiful Jamilah-Melissa. Her second name, which means 'honey-sweet' in the exotic tongues of Genie-land, we chose in honor of our friend's still-beloved mistress, whom he had announced his intention to marry despite Sherry's opinion that while women and men might in some instances come together as human beings, wives and husbands could never. The Genie argued, for his part, that no matter how total, exclusive, and permanent the commitment between two lovers might turn out to be, it lacked the dimensions of spiritual seriousness and public responsibility which only marriage, with its ancient vows and symbols, rites and risks, provided.

" 'It can't last,' Sherry said crossly. The Genie put on her finger a gift from his fiancée to her namesake's mother—a gold ring patterned with rams'-horns and conches, replicas of which she and the Genie meant to exchange on their wedding day—and replied, 'Neither did Athens. Neither did Rome. Neither did all of Jamshid's glories. But we must live as if it can and will.'

" 'Hmp,' said Sherry, who over the years had picked up a number of your brother's ways, as he had hers. But she gave them her blessing—to which I added mine without reservations or *as if*'s—and turned the ring much in the lamplight when he was gone, trying its look on different hands and fingers and musing as if upon its design.

"Thus we came to the thousandth night, the thousandth morning and afternoon, the thousandth dipping of Sherry's quill and invocation of the magic key. And for the thousand and first time, still smiling, our Genie appeared to us, his own ring on his finger as it had been for some forty evenings now —an altogether brighter-looking spirit than had materialized in the book-stacks so long past. We three embraced as always; he asked after the children's health and the King's, and my sister, as always, after his progress toward that treasury from which he claimed her stories were drawn. Less reticent on this subject than he had been since our first meeting, he declared with pleasure that thanks to the inspiration of Scheherazade and to the thousand comforts of his loving wife, he believed he had found his way out of that slough of the imagination in which he'd felt himself bogged: whatever the merits of the new work, like an ox-cart driver in monsoon season or the skipper of a grounded ship, he had gone forward by going back, to the very roots and springs of story. Using, like Scheherazade herself, for entirely present ends, materials received from narrative antiquity and methods older than the alphabet, in the time since Sherry's defloration he had set down two-thirds of a projected series of three *novellas*, longish tales which would take their sense from one another in several of the ways he and Sherry had discussed, and, if they were successful (here he smiled at me), manage to be seriously, even passionately, *about* some things as well.

" 'The two I've finished have to do with mythic heroes, true and false,' he concluded. 'The third I'm just in the middle of. How good or bad they are I can't say yet, but I'm sure they're *right*. You know what I mean, Scheherazade.'

"She did; I felt as if I did also, and we happily re-embraced. Then Sherry remarked, apropos of middles, that she'd be winding up the story of Ma'aruf the Cobbler that night and needed at least the beginning of whatever tale was to follow it.

"The Genie shook his head. 'My dear, there are no more. You've told them all.' He seemed cruelly undisturbed by a prospect that made the harem spin before my eyes and brought me near to swooning.

" 'No more!' I cried. 'What will she do?'

" 'If she doesn't want to risk Shahryar's killing her and turning to you,' he said calmly, 'I guess she'll have to invent something that's not in the book.'

" 'I don't invent,' Sherry reminded him. Her voice was no less steady than his, but her expression—when I got hold of my senses enough to see it—was grave. 'I only recount.'

" 'Borrow something from that treasury!' I implored him. 'What will the children do without their mother?' The harem began to spin again; I gathered all my courage and said: 'Don't desert us, friend; give Sherry that story you're working on now, and you may do anything you like with me. I'll raise your children if you have any; I'll wash your Melissa's feet. Anything.'

"The Genie smiled and said to Sherry, 'Our little Dunyazade is a woman.' Thanking me then for my offer as courteously as he had once Scheherazade, he declined it, not only for the same reasons that had moved him before, but also because he was confident that the only tales left in the treasury of the sort King Shahryar was likely to be entertained by were the hundred mimicries and retellings of Sherry's own.

" 'Then my thousand nights and a night are ended,' Sherry said. 'Don't be ungrateful to our friend, Doony; everything ends.'

"I agreed, but tearfully wished myself—and Ali Shar, Gharíb, and little Melissa, whom-all I loved as dearly as I loved my sister—out of a world where the only *happy* endings were in stories.

"The Genie touched my shoulder. 'Let's not forget,' he said, 'that from my point of view—a tiresome technical one, I'll admit—it *is* a story that we're coming to the end of. All these tales your sister has told the King are simply the middle of her own story—hers and yours, I mean, and Shahryar's, and his young brother Shah Zaman's.'

"I didn't understand—but Sherry did, and squeezing my other shoulder, asked him quietly whether, that being the tiresome technical case, it followed that a happy ending might be invented for the framing-story.

" 'The author of *The Thousand and One Nights* doesn't invent,' the Genie reminded her; 'he only recounts how, after she finished the tale of Ma'aruf the Cobbler, Scheherazade rose from the King's bed, kissed ground before him, and made bold to ask a favor in return for the thousand and one nights' entertainment. "Ask, Scheherazade," the King answers in the story—whereupon you send Dunyazade to fetch the children in, and plead for your life on their behalf, so that they won't grow up motherless.'

"My heart sprang up; Sherry sat silent. 'I notice you don't ask on behalf of the stories themselves,' the Genie remarked, 'or on behalf of your love for Shahryar and his for you. That's a pretty touch: it leaves him free to *grant* your wish, if he chooses to, on those other grounds. I also admire your tact in asking only for your life; that gives him the moral initiative to repent his policy and marry you. I don't think I'd have thought of that.'

" 'Hmp,' said Sherry.

" 'Then there's the nice formal symmetry—'

" 'Never *mind* the symmetry!' I cried. 'Does it work or not?' I saw in his expression then that it did, and in Sherry's that this plan was not news to her. I hugged them both, weeping enough for joy to make our ink run, so the Genie said, and begged Sherry to promise me that I could stay with her and the children after their wedding as I had before, and sit at the foot of her bed forever.

" 'Not so fast, Doony,' she said. 'I haven't decided yet whether or not I care to end the story that way.'

" 'Not care to?' I looked with fresh terror to the Genie. 'Doesn't she *have* to, if it's in the book?'

"He too appeared troubled now, and searched Sherry's face, and admitted that not everything he'd seen of our situation in these visions or dreams of his corresponded exactly to the story as it came to him through the centuries, lands, and languages that separated us in waking hours. In his translation, for example, all three children were male and nameless; and while there was no mention of Scheherazade's *loving* Shahryar by the end of the book, there was surely none of her despising him, or cuckolding him, more or less, with me and the rest. Most significantly, it went without saying that he himself was altogether absent from the plot— which, however, he prayed my sister to end as it ended in his version: with the double marriage of herself to your brother and me to you, and our living happily together until overtaken by the Destroyer of Delights and Severer of Societies, et cetera.

"While I tried to assimilate this astonishing news about myself, Sherry asked with a smile whether by 'his version' the Genie meant that copy of the *Nights* from which he'd been assisting us or the story he himself was in midst of inventing; for she liked to imagine, and profoundly hoped it so, that our connection had not been to her advantage only: that one way or another, she and I and our situation were among those 'ancient narrative materials' which he had found useful for his present purposes. How did *his* version end?

"The Genie closed his eyes for a moment, pushed back his glasses with his thumb, and repeated that he was still in the middle of that third novella in the series, and so far from drafting the climax and dénouement, had yet even to plot them in outline. Turning then to me, to my great surprise he announced that the title of the story was *Dunyazadiad;* that its central character was not my sister but myself, the image of whose circumstances, on my 'wedding-night-to-come,' he found as arresting for taletellers of his particular place and time as was my sister's for the estate of narrative artists in general.

" 'All those nights at the foot of that bed, Dunyazade!' he exclaimed. 'You've had the whole literary tradition transmitted to you—and the whole erotic tradition, too! There's no story you haven't heard; there's no way of making love that you haven't seen again and again. I think of you, little sister, a virgin in both respects: All that innocence! All that sophistication! And now it's *your* turn: Shahryar has told young Shah Zaman about his wonderful mistress, how he loves her as much for herself as for her stories—*which he also passes on*; the two brothers marry the two sisters; it's your wedding night, Dunyazade . . . But wait! Look here! Shahryar deflowered and killed a virgin a night for a thousand and one nights before he met Scheherazade; Shah Zaman has been doing the same thing, but it's only now, a thousand nights and a night later, that *he* learns about Scheherazade— that means he's had two thousand and two young women at the least since he killed his wife, and not one has pleased him enough to move him to spend a second night with her, much less spare her life! What are you going to do to entertain *him*, little sister? Make love in exciting new ways? There are none! Tell him stories, like Scheherazade? He's heard them all! Dunyazade, Dunyazade! Who can tell your story?'

"More dead than alive with fright, I clung to my sister, who begged the Genie please to stop alarming me. All apologies, he assured us that what he was describing was not *The Thousand and One Nights* frame-story (which ended happily without mention of these terrors), but his own novella, a pure fiction—to which also he would endeavor with all his heart to find some conclusion in keeping with his affection for me. Sherry further eased my anxiety by adding that she too had given long thought to my position as the Genie described it, and was not without certain plans with respect to our wedding night; these, as a final favor to our friend, she had made written note of in the hope that whether or not they succeeded, he might find them useful for his story; but she would prefer to withhold them from me for the present.

" 'You sense as I do, then,' the Genie said thoughtfully, 'that we won't be seeing each other again.'

"Sherry nodded. 'You have other stories to tell. I've told mine.'

"Already he'd begun to fade. 'My best,' he said, 'will be less than your least. And I'll always love you, Scheherazade! Dunyazade, I'm your brother! Good night, sisters! Fare well!'

"We kissed; he disappeared with Sherry's letter; Shahryar sent for us; still shaken, I sat at the bed-foot while he and Sherry did a combination from the latter pages of *Ananga*

Ranga and *Kama Sutra* and she finished the tale of Ma'aruf the Cobbler. Then she rose as the Genie had instructed her, kissed ground, begged boon; I fetched in Ali Shar, walking by himself now, Gharíb crawling, Jamilah-Melissa suckling at my milkless breast as if it were her mother's. Sherry made her plea; Shahryar wept, hugged the children, told her he'd pardoned her long since, having found in her the refutation of all his disenchantment, and praised Allah for having appointed her the savior of her sex. Then he sent for Daddy to draft the marriage contract and for you to hear the news of Scheherazade and her stories; when you proposed to marry me, Sherry countered with Part Two of our plan (of whose Part Three I was still ignorant): that in order for her and me never to be parted, you must abandon Samarkand and live with us, sharing your brother's throne and passing yours to our father in reparation for his three-years' anguish. I found you handsomer than Shahryar and more terrifying, and begged my sister to say what lay ahead for me.

" 'Why, a fine wedding-feast, silly Doony!' she teased. 'The eunuchs will perfume our Hammam-bath with rose- and willow-flower water, musk-pods, eagle-wood, ambergris; we'll wash and clip our hair; they'll dress me like the sun and you the moon, and we'll dance in seven different dresses to excite our bridegrooms. By the end of the wine and music they'll scarcely be able to contain their desire; each of us will kiss the other three good night, twelve goodnights in all, and our husbands will hurry us off toward our separate bridal-chambers—'

" 'O Sherry!'

" '*Then,*' she went on, no tease in her voice now, 'on the very threshold of their pleasures I'll stop, kiss ground, and say to my lord and master: "O King of the Sun and the Moon and the Rising Tide, et cetera, thanks for marrying me at last after sleeping with me for a thousand and one nights and begetting three children on me and listening while I amused you with proverbs and parables, chronicles and pleasantries, quips and jests and admonitory instances, stories and anecdotes, dialogues and histories and elegies and satires and Allah alone knows what else! Thanks too for giving my precious little sister to your brute of a brother, and the kingdom of Samarkand to our father, whose own gratitude we'll hope may partially restore his sanity! And thanks above all for kindly ceasing to rape and murder a virgin every night, and for persuading Shah Zaman to cease also! I have no right to ask anything further of you at all, but should be overjoyed to serve your sexual and other interests humbly until the day you tire of me and either have me killed or put me by for other, younger women—and indeed I *am* prepared to do just that, as Dunyazade surely is also for Shah Zaman. Yet in view of your boundless magnanimity Q.E.D., I make bold to ask a final favor." If we're lucky, Shahryar will be so mad to get me into bed that he'll say "Name it"—whereupon I point out to him that a happy occasion is about to bring to pass what a thousand ill ones didn't, your separation from me till morning. Knowing my husband, I expect he'll propose a little something *à quatre*, at which I'll blush appropriately and declare that I'm resigned after all to the notion of losing you for a few hours, and wish merely thirty minutes or so of private conversation with you before you and your bridegroom retire, to tell you a few things that every virgin bride should know. "What on earth is there in that line that she hasn't seen us do a hundred times?" your delicate brother-in-law will inquire. "Seeing isn't doing," I'll reply: "I myself have pretty intensive sexual experience, for example, but of one man only, and would be shy as any virgin with another than yourself; Shah Zaman has the widest carnal acquaintance in the world, I suppose, but no long and deep knowledge of any one woman; among the four of us, only you, King of the Age, et cetera, can boast both sorts of experience, having humped your way through twenty years of marriage, a thousand and one one-nighters, and thirty-three and a third months with me, not to mention odd hours with all the concubines in your stable. But little Dunyazade has no experience at all, except vicariously." That master of the quick retort will say "Hmp" and turn the matter over to Shah Zaman, who after bringing to it the full weight of his perspicacity will say, in effect, "Okay. But make it short." They'll withdraw, with the grandest erections you and I have ever shuddered at—and *then* I'll tell you what to do in Part Three. After which we'll kiss good night, go in to our husbands, and do it. Got that?'

" 'Do *what?*' I cried—but she'd say no more till all had fallen out as she described: our wedding-feast and dance; the retirement toward our chambers; her interruption and request; your permission and stipulation that the conference be brief, inasmuch as you were more excited by me than you'd been by any of the two thousand unfortunates whose maidenheads and lives you'd done away with in the five and a half years past. You two withdrew, your robes thrust out before; the moment your bedroom doors closed, Sherry spat in your tracks, took my head between her hands, and said: 'If ever you've listened carefully, little sister, listen now. For all his good intentions, our Genie of the Key is either a liar or a fool when he says that any man and woman can treasure each other until death—unless their lifetimes are as brief as our murdered sisters'! Three thousand and three, Doony

—dead! What have you and I and all that fiction accomplished, except to spare another thousand from a quick end to their misery? What are they saved for, if not a more protracted violation, at the hands of fathers, husbands, lovers? For the present, it's our masters' pleasure to soften their policy; the patriarchy isn't changed: I believe it will persist even to our Genie's time and place. Suppose his relation to his precious Melissa were truly as he describes it, and not merely as he wishes and imagines it: it would only be the exception that proves the wretched rule. So here we stand, and there you're about to lie, and spread your legs and take it like the rest of us! Thanks be to Allah you can't be snared as I was in the trap of *novelty*, and think to win some victory for our sex by diverting our persecutors with naughty stunts and stories! There *is* no victory, Doony, only unequal retaliation; it's time we turned from tricks to trickery, tales to lies. Go in to your lusty husband now, as I shall to mine; let him kiss and fondle and undress you, paw and pinch and slaver, lay you on the bed; but when he makes to stick you, slip out from under and whisper in his ear that for all his vast experience of sex, there remains one way of making love, most delicious of all, that both he and Shahryar are innocent of, inasmuch as a Genie revealed it to us only last night when we prayed Allah for a way to please such extraordinary husbands. So marvelous is this Position of the Genie, as we'll call it, that even a man who's gone through virgins like breakfast-eggs will think himself newly laid, et cetera. What's more, it's a position in which the woman does everything, her master nothing—except submit himself to a more excruciating pleasure than he's ever known or dreamed of. No more is required of him than that he spread-eagle himself on the bed and suffer his wrists and ankles to be bound to its posts

with silken cords, lest by a spasm of early joy he abort its
heavenly culmination, et cetera. Then, little sister, then, when
you have him stripped and bound supine and salivating, take
from the left pocket of your seventh gown the razor I've hid
there, as I shall mine from mine—and geld the monster! Cut
his bloody engine off and choke him on it, as I'll do to Shahryar! Then we'll lay our own throats open, to spare ourselves
their sex's worse revenge. Adieu, my Doony! May we wake
together in a world that knows nothing of *he* and *she*!
Good night.'

"I moved my mouth to answer; couldn't; came to you as
if entranced; and while you kissed me, found the cold blade
in my pocket. I let you undress me as in a dream, touch my
body where no man has before, lay me down and mount to
take me; as in a dream I heard me bid you stay for a rarer
pleasure, coax you into the Position of the Genie, and with
this edge in hand and voice, rehearse the history of your
present bondage. Your brother's docked; my sister's dead;
it's time we joined them."

2

~~~~~~~~~~

"That's the end of your story?"

Dunyazade nodded.

Shah Zaman looked narrowly at his bride, standing naked
beside the bed with her trembling razor, and cleared his
throat. "If you really mean to use that, kindly kill me with it

first. A good hard slice across the Adam's apple should do the trick."

The girl shuddered, shook her head. As best he could, so bound, the young man shrugged.

"At least answer one question: Why in the world did you tell me this extraordinary tale?"

Her eyes still averted, Dunyazade explained in a dull voice that one aspect of her sister's revenge was this reversal not only of the genders of teller and told (as conceived by the Genie), but of their circumstances, the latter now being at the former's mercy.

"Then have some!" urged the King. "For yourself!" Dunyazade looked up. Despite his position, Shah Zaman smiled like the Genie through his pearly beard and declared that Scheherazade was right to think love ephemeral. But life itself was scarcely less so, and both were sweet for just that reason—sweeter yet when enjoyed as if they might endure. For all the inequity of woman's lot, he went on, thousands of women found love as precious as did their lovers: one needed look no farther than Scheherazade's stories for proof of that. If a condemned man—which is what he counted himself, since once emasculate he'd end his life as soon as he could lay hands on his sword—might be granted a last request, such as even *he* used to grant his nightly victims in the morning, his would be to teach his fair executioner the joys of sex before she unsexed him.

"Nonsense," Dunyazade said crossly. "I've seen all that."

"Seeing's not feeling."

She glared at him. "I'll learn when I choose, then, from a less bloody teacher: someone I love, no matter how foolishly." She turned her head. "If I ever meet such a man.

Which I won't." Vexed, she slipped into her gown, holding the razor awkwardly in her left hand while she fastened the hooks.

"What a lucky fellow! You don't love me then, little wife?"

"Of course not! I'll admit you're not the monster I'd imagined—in appearance, I mean. But you're a total stranger to me, and the thought of what you did to all those girls makes me retch. Don't waste your last words in silly flirting; you won't change my mind. You'd do better to prepare yourself to die."

"I'm quite prepared, Dunyazade," Shah Zaman replied calmly. "I have been from the beginning. Why else do you suppose I haven't called my guards in to kill you? I'm sure my brother's long since done for Scheherazade, if she really tried to do what she put you up to doing. Shahryar and I would have been great fools not to anticipate this sort of thing from the very first night, six years ago."

"I don't believe you."

The King shrugged his eyebrows and whistled through his teeth; two husky mamelukes stepped at once from behind a tapestry depicting Jamshid's seven-ringed cup, seized Dunyazade by the wrists, covered her mouth, and took the open razor from her hand.

"Fair or not," Shah Zaman said conversationally as she struggled, "your only power at present is what I choose to give you. And fair or not, I choose to give it." He smiled. "Let her have the razor, my friends, and take the rest of the night off. If you don't believe that I deliberately put myself in your hands from the first, Dunyazade, you can't deny I'm doing so now. All I ask is leave to tell you a story, in exchange for the one you've told me; when I'm finished you may do as you please."

The mamelukes reluctantly let her go, but left the room only when Shah Zaman, still stripped and bound, repeated his order. Dunyazade sat exhausted on a hassock, rubbed her wrists, pinned up her fallen hair, drew the gown more closely about her.

"I'm not impressed," she said. "If I pick up the razor, they'll put an arrow through me."

"That hadn't occurred to me," Shah Zaman admitted. "You'll have to trust me a little, then, as I'm trusting you. Do pick it up. I insist."

"You insist!" Dunyazade said bitterly. She took up the razor, let her hand fall passively beside the hassock, began to weep.

"Let's see, now," mused the King. "How can we give you the absolute advantage? They're very fast, those guards, and loyal; if they really *are* standing by, what I fear is that they'll misconstrue some innocent movement of yours and shoot."

"What difference does it make?" Dunyazade said miserably. "Poor Sherry!"

"I have it! Come sit here beside me. Please, do as I say! Now lay that razor's edge exactly where you were going to put it before; then you can make your move before any marksman can draw and release. You'll have to hold me in your other hand; I've gone limp with alarm."

Dunyazade wept.

"Come," the King insisted: "it's the only way you'll be convinced I'm serious. No, I mean right up against it, so that you could do your trick in half a second. Whew, that gooseflesh isn't faked! What a situation! Now look here: even this advantage gripes you, I suppose, since it was given instead of taken: the male still leading the female, et cetera. No help for that just now. Besides, between any two people, you know—what I mean, it's not the patriarchy that makes you take the passive role with your sister, for example. Never mind that. See me sweat! Now, then: I agree with that Genie of yours in the matter of priorities, and I entreat you not only to permit me to tell you a story, but to make love with me first."

Dunyazade shut her eyes and whipped her head from side to side.

"As you wish," said the King. "I'd never force you, as you'll understand if you'll hear my story. Shall I tell it?"

Dunyazade moved her head indifferently.

"More tightly. Careful with that razor!"

"Can't you make it go down?" the girl asked thickly. "It's obscene. And distracting. I think I'm going to be sick."

"Not more distracting than your little breasts, or your little fingers . . . No, please, I insist you keep hold of your advantage! My story's short, I promise, and I'm at your mercy. So:

"Six years ago I thought myself the happiest man alive. I'd had a royal childhood; my college years were a joy; my career had gone brilliantly; at twenty-five I ruled a kingdom almost as prosperous as Shahryar's at forty. I was popular with my subjects; I kept the government reasonably honest, the various power groups reasonably in hand, et cetera. Like every king I kept a harem of concubines for the sake of my public image, but as a rule they were reserved for state visitors. For myself I wanted nobody except my bride, never mind her name, whom after a whole year of marriage I still loved more than any woman I'd ever known. After a day's work in the durbar, bidding and forbidding et cetera, I'd rush in to dinner, and we'd play all night like two kittens in a basket. No trick of love we didn't turn together; no myth of gods and nymphs we didn't mimic. The harem girls, when I used them, only reminded me of how much I preferred my wife; often as not I'd dismiss them in mid-clip and call her in for the finish.

"When my brother summoned me here to visit that first time, much as I longed to see him it was all I could do to leave my bride behind; we made our first goodbyes; then I was as overjoyed as I imagined she'd be when I discovered that I'd forgotten a diamond necklace I'd meant to present to Shahryar's queen. I rushed back to the palace myself instead of sending after it, so that we could make love once again before I left—and I found her in our bed, riding astride the chief cook! Her last words were 'Next time invite *me*'; I cut them both in two, four halves in all, not to seem a wittol; came here and found my sister-in-law cuckolding my brother with the blackamoor Sa'ad al-Din Saood, who swung from trees, slavered and gibbered, and sported a yard that made mine look like your little finger. Kings no more, Shahryar and I left together by the postern gate, resolved to kill ourselves as the most wretched fools on earth if our misery was particular. One day as we were wandering in the marshes, far from the paths of men, devouring our own souls, we saw what we thought was a waterspout coming up the bay, and climbed a loblolly pine for safety. It turned out to be that famous ifrit of your sister's story: he took the steel coffer out of its casket, unlocked the seven locks with seven keys, fetched out and futtered the girl he'd stolen on her wedding night, and fell asleep in her lap; she signaled us to come down and ordered us both to cuckold the ifrit with her then and there. Who says a man can't be forced? We did our best, and she added our seal rings to the five hundred seventy she'd already collected. We understood then that no woman on earth who wants a rogering will go unrogered, though she be sealed up in a tower of brass.

"So. When I'd first told my brother of my own cuckolding, he'd vowed that in my position he'd not have rested till he'd killed a thousand women: now we went back to his palace; he put to death his queen and all his concubines and their lovers, and we took a solemn oath to rape and kill a virgin a night, so as never again to be deceived. I came home to Samarkand, wondering at the turns of our despair: how a private apocalypse can infect the state and bring about one more general, et cetera. With this latter motive, more than for revenge on womankind, I resolved to hold to our dreadful policy until my kingdom fell to ruin or an outraged populace rose up and slew me.

"But unlike Shahryar, I said nothing at first to my vizier, only told him to fetch me a beautiful virgin for the night. Not knowing that I meant to kill her in the morning, he brought me his own daughter, a girl I knew well and had long admired, Samarkand's equivalent of Scheherazade. I assumed he was pandering to his own advancement, and smiled at the thought of putting them to death together; I soon learned, however, from the woman herself, that it was her own idea to come to me—and her motive, unlike your sister's, was simple love. I undressed and fell to toying with her; she wept; I asked what ailed her: it was not being separated from her sister, but being alone at last with me, the fulfillment of her lifelong dream. I found myself much touched by this and, to my surprise, impotent. Stalling for time, I remarked that such dreams could turn out to be night-mares. She embraced me timidly and replied that she deplored my murdering my wife and her paramour, both of whom she'd known and rather liked, for though in a general way she sympathized with my disenchanted outrage, she believed she understood as well my wife's motives for cuckolding me, which in her view were not all that different, essentially, from the ifrit's maiden's in the story. Despite my anger, she went on bravely to declare that she herself took what she called the Tragic View of Sex and Temperament: to wit, that while perfect equality between men and women was the only defensible value in that line, she was not at all certain it was attainable; even to pursue it ardently, against the grain of things as they were, was in all likelihood to spoil one's chances for happiness in love; *not* to pursue it, on the other hand, once one had seen it clearly to be the ideal, no doubt had the same effect. For herself, though she deplored in-justice whether in individuals or in institutions, and gently affirmed equality as the goal that lovers lovingly should strive for, however far short of it their histories and tempera-ments made them fall, yet she knew herself personally to be unsuited for independence, formed by her nature and up-bringing to be happy only in the shadow of a man whom she admired and respected more than herself. She was anything but blind to my faults and my own blindness to them, she declared, but so adored me withal that if I could love her even for a night she'd think her life complete, and wish nothing further unless maybe a little Shah Zaman to devote the rest of her years to raising. Or if my disillusionment with women were so extreme (as she seemed uncannily to guess from my expression) that I had brought her to my bed not to marry her or even add her to my harem, but merely to take her virginity and her life, I was welcome to both; she only prayed I might be gentle in their taking.

"This last remark dismayed me the more because it echoed something my late wife had said on our wedding night: that even death at my hands would be sweeter to her than life at another's. How I despised, resented, missed her! As if it were I who was cut in two, I longed to hold her as in nights gone by, yet would have halved her bloody halves if she'd been restored to me. There lay my new woman on the bed, naked and still now; I stood on my knees between hers, weeping so for her predecessor's beauty and deceit, my own blindness and cruelty—and the wretched state of affairs between man and womankind that made love a will-o'-the-wisp, jealousy and boredom and resentment the rule—that I could neither function nor dissemble. I told her of all that had taken place between my departure from Samarkand and my return, the oath I'd sworn with my brother, and my resolve to keep it lest I seem chicken-hearted and a fool.

" 'Lest you *seem!*' the girl cried out. 'Harems, homicides —everything for the sake of seeming!' She commanded me then, full of irony for all her fears, to *keep* my vow if I meant to keep it, or else cut out her tongue before I cut off her head; for if I sent her to the block without deflowering her first, she would declare to any present, even if only her executioner, that I was a man in seeming merely, not in fact, and offer her maidenhead as proof. Her courage astonished me as much as her words. 'By Allah,' I vowed to her, 'I won't kill you if I can't get it up for you first.' But that miserable fellow in your left hand, which had never once failed me before, and which stands up now like an idiot soldier in enemy country, as if eager to be cut down, deserted me utterly. I tried every trick

I knew, in vain, though my victim willingly complied with my instructions. I could of course have killed her myself, then and there, but I had no wish to seem a hypocrite even for a moment in her eyes; nor, for that matter, to let her die a virgin—nor, I admitted finally to myself, to let her die at all before she was overtaken like the rest of us by the Destroyer of Delights et cetera. For seven nights we tossed and tumbled, fondled and kissed and played, she reaching such heats of unaccustomed joy as to cry out, no longer sarcastically, that if only I would stick her first with my carnal sword, she'd bare her neck without complaint to my steel. On the seventh night, as we lay panting in a sweat of frustration, I gave her my dagger and invited her to do me and Samarkand the kindness of killing me at once, for I'd rather die than seem unable to keep my vow.

" 'You *are* unable to keep it,' she told me softly: 'not because you're naturally impotent, but because you're *not* naturally cruel. If you'd tell your brother that after thinking it over you've simply come to a conclusion different from his, you'd be cured as if by magic.' And in fact, as if by magic indeed, what she said was so true that at her very words the weight was lifted from heart and tool together; they rose as one. Gratefully, tenderly, I went into her at last; we cried for joy, came at once, fell asleep in each other's arms.

"No question after that of following Shahryar's lead; on the other hand, I found myself in the morning not yet man enough after all to send word to him of my change of heart and urge him to change his. Neither was I, after all, in love enough with the Vizier's daughter to risk again the estate of marriage, which she herself considered problematical at best.

" 'I never expected you to marry me,' she told me when I told her these things, 'though I'd be dishonest if I didn't say I dreamed and prayed you might. All I ever really hoped for was a love affair with you, and a baby to remember it by. Even if I don't have the baby, I've had the affair: you truly loved me last night.'

"I did, and for many nights after—but not enough to make the final step. What your Genie said concerning marriage could have come from my own mouth if I had the gift of words: to anyone of moral imagination who's known it, no other relation between men and women has true seriousness; yet that same imagination kept me from it. And I dreaded the day my brother would get word of my weakness. I grew glum and cross; my mistress, intuitive as ever, guessed the reason at once. 'You can neither keep your vow nor break it,' she told me: 'Perhaps you'd better do both for a while, till you find your way.' I asked her how such a contradiction was possible. 'By the magic words *as if*,' she replied, 'which, to a person satisfied with seeming, are more potent than all the genii in the tales.'

"She then set forth a remarkable proposal: legend had it that far to the west of Samarkand was a country peopled entirely with women, adjoining another wholly male: for two months every spring they mated freely with each other on neutral ground, the women returning home as they found themselves pregnant, giving their male children to the neighboring tribe and raising the girls as members of their own. Whether or not such a community in fact existed, she thought it a desirable alternative to the present state of affairs, and unquestionably preferable to death; since I couldn't treasure her as she treasured me (and not for a moment did she *blame* me for that incapacity), she proposed to establish such an alternative society herself, with my assistance. I was to proclaim my brother's policy as my own, take to bed a virgin every night and declare her executed in the morning; but instead of actually raping and killing them I would tell them of her alternative society and send them secretly from Samarkand, in groups of a hundred or so, to organize and populate it. If, knowing their destiny, they chose to spend their last night in Samarkand making love with me, that was their affair; none, she imagined, would choose death over emigration, and any who found their new way of life not to their liking could return to Samarkand if and when I changed my policy, or migrate elsewhere in the meanwhile. In any case they'd be alive and free; or, if the pioneers were captured and made slaves of by barbarians before the new society was established, they'd be no worse off than the millions of their sisters already in that condition. On the other hand, separate societies of men and women, mingling freely at their own wills as equals on neutral ground, might just make possible a true society of the future in which the separation was no longer necessary. And in the meantime, of course, for better or worse, it would be as if I'd kept my dreadful vow.

"At first hearing, the plan struck me as absurd; after a few nights it seemed less so, perhaps even feasible; by the end of a week of examining passionately with her all the alternatives, it seemed no less unreasonable than they. My angel herself, in keeping with her Tragic View, didn't expect the new society to *work* in the naïve sense: what human institutions ever did? It would have the vices of its virtues; if not nipped in the bud by marauding rapists, it would grow and change and rigidify in forms and values quite different from its founders'—codifying, institutionalizing, and perverting its original spirit. No help for that.

"Was there ever such a woman? I kissed her respectfully, then ardently a final time. After one last love-making in the morning, while my hand lingered on her left breast, she declared calmly her intention, upon arriving at her virgin kingdom, to amputate that same breast for symbolic reasons and urge her companions to do the same, as a kind of initiation rite. 'We'll make up a practical excuse for it,' she said: ' "The better to draw our bows," et cetera. But the real point will be that in one aspect we're all woman, in another all warrior. Maybe we'll call ourselves The Breastless Ones.'

" 'That seems extreme,' I remarked. She replied that a certain extremism was necessary to the survival of anything radically innovative. Later generations, she assumed, established and effete, would find the ancestral custom barbaric and honor its symbolism, if at all, with a correspondingly symbolic mammectomy—a decorative scar, perhaps, or cosmetic mark. No matter; everything passed.

"So did our connection: with a thousand thanks to her for opening my eyes, a thousand good wishes for the success of her daring enterprise, and many thousands of dinars to support it (which for portability and security she converted into a phial of diamonds and carried intravaginally), I declared her dead, let her father the Vizier in on our secret, and sent her off secretly to one of my country castles on a distant lake, where she prepared for the expedition westward while her companions, the ostensible victims of my new policy, accumulated about her. Perhaps a third, apprised of their fate, chose to remain virginal, whether indignantly, ruefully, or gratefully; on the other two-thirds who in whatever spirit elected to go hymenless to the new society, I bestowed similar phials of jewels. Somewhat less than fifty per cent of this number found themselves impregnated by our night together, and so when the first detachment of two hundred pioneers set out across the western wastes, their actual number was about two hundred sixty. Since I pursued this policy for nearly two thousand nights, the number of pilgrims and unborn children sent west from Samarkand must have totaled about twenty-six hundred; corrected for a normal male birth rate of somewhat over fifty per cent, a rather higher than normal rate of spontaneous abortion, and infant as well as maternal mortality owing to the rigors of traveling and of settling a new territory, and ignoring—as one must to retain one's reason —the possibility of mass enslavement, rape, massacre, or natural catastrophe, the number of pioneers to the Country of the Breastless must be at least equal to the number of nights until Shahryar's message concerning your sister arrived from the Islands of India and China.

"Of the success or failure of those founding mothers I know nothing; kept myself ignorant deliberately, lest I learn that I was sending them after all to the Destroyer of Delights and Severer of Societies. The folk of Samarkand never rose against me; nor did my vizier, like Shahryar's, have difficulty enlisting sacrificial virgins; even at the end, though my official toll was twice my brother's, about half the girls were volunteers—from all which, I infer that their actual fate was an open secret. For all I know, my original mistress never truly intended to found her gynocracy; the whole proposal was perhaps a ruse; perhaps they all slipped back into the country with their phials of gems for dowry, married and lived openly under my nose. No matter: night after night I brought them to bed, set forth their options, then either glumly stripped and pronged them or spent the night in chaste sleep and conversation. Tall and short, dark and fair, lean and plump, cold and ardent, bold and timid, clever and stupid, comely and plain—I bedded them all, spoke with them all, possessed them all, but was myself possessed by nothing but despair. Though I took many, with their consent, I wanted none of them. Novelty lost its charm, then even its novelty. Unfamiliarity I came to loathe: the foreign body in the dark, the alien touch and voice, the endless *exposition*. All I craved was someone with whom to get on with the story of my life, which was to say, of our life together: a loving friend; a loving wife; a treasurable wife; a wife, a wife.

"My brother's second message, when it came, seemed a miraculous reprise of that fatal first, six years before: I turned the kingdom over to my vizier and set out at once, resolved to meet this Scheherazade who had so wooed and yarned him back to the ways of life that he meant to wed her. 'Perhaps she has a younger sister,' I said to myself; if she does, I'll make no inquiries, demand no stories, set no conditions, but humbly put my life in her hands, tell her the whole tale of the two thousand and two nights that led me to her, and bid her end that story as she will—whether with the last goodnight of all or (what I can just dimly envision, like dawn in another world) some clear and fine and fresh good morning."

Dunyazade yawned and shivered. "I can't imagine what you're talking about. Am I expected to believe that preposterous business of Breastless Pilgrims and Tragic Views?"

"Yes!" cried Shah Zaman, then let his head fall back to

the pillow. "They're too important to be lies. Fictions, maybe—but truer than fact."

Dunyazade covered her eyes with her razor-hand. "What do you expect me to do? Forgive you? Love you?"

"Yes!" the King cried again, his eyes flashing. "Let's end the dark night! All that passion and hate between men and women; all that confusion of inequality and difference! Let's take the truly tragic view of love! Maybe it *is* a fiction, but it's the profoundest and best of all! Treasure me, Dunyazade, as I'll treasure you!"

"For pity's sake stop!"

But Shah Zaman urged ardently: "Let's embrace; let's forbear; let's love as long as we can, Dunyazade—then embrace again, forbear and love again!"

"It won't work."

"Nothing *works!* But the enterprise is noble; it's full of joy and life, and the other ways are deathy. Let's make love like passionate equals!"

"You mean *as if* we were equals," Dunyazade said. "You know we're not. What you want is impossible."

"Despite your heart's feelings?" pressed the King. "Let it be *as if!* Let's make a philosophy of that *as if!*"

Dunyazade wailed: "I want my sister!"

"She may be alive; my brother, too." More quietly, Shah Zaman explained that Shahryar had been made acquainted with his brother's recent history and opinions, and had vowed that should Scheherazade ever attempt his life, he'd manage himself somewhat similarly: that is (as he was twenty years older, and more conservative), not exactly granting his wife the power to kill him, but disarming and declining to kill *her*, and within the bounds of good public relations, permitting her a freedom comparable to his own. The harem was a royal tradition, necessarily public; Scheherazade could take what lovers she would, but of necessity in private. Et cetera.

"Did you really imagine your sister *fooled* Shahryar for a thousand nights with her mamelukes and dildoes?" Shah Zaman laughed. "A man couldn't stay king very long if he didn't even know what was going on in the harem! And why do you suppose he permitted it, if not that he loved her too much, and was too sick of his other policy, to kill her? She changed his mind, all right, but she never fooled him: he used to believe that all women were unfaithful, and that the only way to spare himself the pain of infidelity was to deflower and kill them; now he believes that all *people* are unfaithful, and that the way to spare oneself the pain of infidelity is to love and not to care. He chooses equal promiscuity; I choose equal fidelity. Let's treasure each other, Dunyazade!"

She shook her head angrily, or desperately. "It's absurd. You're only trying to talk your way out of a bad spot."

"Of course I am! And of course it's absurd! Treasure me!"

"I'm exhausted. I should use the razor on both of us, and be done with it."

"Treasure me, Dunyazade!"

"We've talked all night; I hear the cocks; it's getting light."

"Good morning, then! Good morning!"

3

~~~~~~~~~~~~~~~~

Alf Laylah Wa Laylah, The Book of the Thousand
Nights and a Night, is not the story of Scheherazade, but the
story of the story of her stories, which in effect begins:
"There is a book called *The Thousand and One Nights,*
in which it is said that once upon a time a king had two
sons, Shahryar and Shah Zaman," et cetera; it ends when
a king long after Shahryar discovers in his treasury the
thirty volumes of *The Stories of the Thousand Nights and
a Night,* at the end of the last of which the royal couples—
Shahryar and Scheherazade, Shah Zaman and Dunyazade—
emerge from their bridal chambers after the wedding night,
greet one another with warm good mornings (eight in all),
bestow Samarkand on the brides' long-suffering father, and
set down for all posterity *The Thousand Nights and a Night.*
If I could invent a story as beautiful, it should be about
little Dunyazade and her bridegroom, who pass a thousand
nights in one dark night and in the morning embrace each
other; they make love side by side, their faces close, and go
out to greet sister and brother in the forenoon of a new life.
Dunyazade's story begins in the middle; in the middle of my
own, I can't conclude it—but it must end in the night that
all good mornings come to. The Arab storytellers understood
this; they ended their stories not "happily ever after," but
specifically "until there took them the Destroyer of Delights
and Desolator of Dwelling-places, and they were translated

to the ruth of Almighty Allah, and their houses fell waste and their palaces lay in ruins, and the Kings inherited their riches." And no man knows it better than Shah Zaman, to whom therefore the second half of his life will be sweeter than the first.

To be joyous in the full acceptance of this dénouement is surely to possess a treasure, the key to which is the understanding that Key and Treasure are the same. There (with a kiss, little sister) is the sense of our story, Dunyazade: The key to the treasure is the treasure.

Perseid

1

~~~~~~~~~~

Good evening.

Stories last longer than men, stones than stories, stars than stones. But even our stars' nights are numbered, and with them will pass this patterned tale to a long-deceased earth.

Nightly, when I wake to think myself beworlded and find myself in heaven, I review the night I woke to think and find myself vice-versa. I'd been long lost, deserted, down and out in Libya; two decades past I'd overflown that country

with the bloody Gorgon's head, and every drop that hit the
dunes had turned to snake—so I learned later: at twenty
years and twenty kilometers high, how could I have known?
Now there I was, sea-leveled, forty, parched and plucked,
every grain in my molted sandals raising blisters, and beleaguered by the serpents of my past. It must have been that
of all the gods in heaven, the two I'd never got along with put
it to me: sandy Ammon, my mother-in-law's pet deity,
who'd first sent Andromeda over the edge, and Sabazius the
beer-god, who'd raised the roof in Argos till I raised him a
temple. Just then I'd've swapped Mycenae for a cold draught
and a spot of shade to dip it in; I even prayed to the rascals.
Nothing doing. Couldn't think where I'd been or where was
headed, lost track of me entirely, commenced hallucinating,
wow. Somewhere back in my flying youth I'd read how to
advertise help wanted when you're brought down: I stamped
a whopping *PERSEUS* in the sand, forgot what I was about,
writing sets your mind a-tramp; next thing I knew I'd printed
PERSEUS LOVES ANDROMED half a kilometer across
the dunes. Wound up in a depression with the three last
letters; everything before them slipped my mind; not till I
added *USA* was I high enough again to get the message, how
I'd confused what I'd set out to clarify. I fried awhile longer
on the dune-top, trying to care; I was a dying man: so what
if my Mayday had grown through self-advertisement to an
amphisbane graffito? But O I was a born reviser, and would
die one: as I looked back on what I'd written, a fresh East
breeze sprang from the right margin, behind, where I'd been
aiming, and drifted the *A* I'd come to rest on. I took its cue,
erased the whole name, got lost in the vipered space between
object and verb, went on erasing, erasing all, talking to myself, crazy man: no more *LOVES*, no more *LOVE*, clean

the slate altogether—me too, take it off, all of it. But I'd forgot by that time who I was, relost in the second space, my first draft's first; I snaked as far as the subject's final S and, frothing, swooned, made myself after that seventh letter a mad dash—

"And that's all you remember?" asked Calyxa.

"That was it, till I woke up here in heaven, in the middle of the story of my life. Would it please you if I kissed your navel once again?"

"Take a chance!" I blushed and did. Here's how it was: some lost time since I'd died as I imagined with my name, I opened eyes upon a couch or altar, a velvet gold rectangle with murex-purple cushions, more or less centered in a marble chamber that unwound from my left-foot corner in a grand spiral like the triton-shell that Dedalus threaded for Cocalus, once about the bed and out of sight. Upon its walls curved graven scenes in low relief, each half again and more its predecessor's breadth, to the number of seven where the chamber wound from view—which scenes, when I had come fully home to sense, I saw depicted alabasterly the several chapters of my youth, most pleasing to a couched eye. The first, no wider than the bed from whose sinistral foot it sprang, showed Mother Danaë brazen-towered by vain Acrisius my grandfather for contraceptive reasons, lest she get the son predestined to destroy et cetera; Granddad himself, with Grandmother Aganippe, stroked horses fondly in the court, unaware that up behind them Zeus in golden-showerhood rained in upon their frockless daughter, jack-potting her with me. A pillar divided this mural from the next, as it were on my port quarter: Acrisius had judged Mom's story counterfeit, called me his twin-brother's bastard, and set suckler and suckled adrift in a brassbound box;

the scene itself was the beach of Cycladean Seriphos: there was young Dictys with his net; he'd fished us in, opened the chest, and stood agape at the sight of sweet-nursing Danaë, in mint condition despite her mal-de-mer. In the background was fairly copied the palace of Dictys's brother, King Polydectes. The third relief, a-beam of and as long as my altarcouch, was set in Samos: twenty years were passed with the fluted pillar; back in Seriphos the King lusted after Mother, and had rused my rash late-teenhood with a pledge to marry someone else instead if I'd contrive to bring him Medusa's head as a wedding gift.

"You're sure it was Zeus and not your uncle up in that tower?" I'd asked Danaë one last time—for she'd admitted an early defloration by Proetus, Acrisius's twin.

"I was sixteen," she replied, "but I knew a slug from a shower of gold." My father, she reassured me, was a lap-deep drench of drachmae.

"And you don't want to marry King Polydectes?"

"Small change."

So, banking on Dictys to safekeep her, I'd set out for Samos on a tip from half-sister Athene, to learn about life from art: for represented in her temple murals there (and so reditto'd here in mine) were all three Gorgons—snakehaired, swinetoothed, buzzardwinged, brassclawed—whereof, as semiSis was pointing out, only the middle one, Medusa, was mortal, decapitable, and petrifacient. Already holding the adamantine sickle Hermes had lent me and Athene's polished shield, I stood listening, a handsome auditor I was then, to her hard instructions. Sword and shield, she said, would not suffice; one thing depended on another; just as Medusa was prerequisite to Mother's rescue, so to kill Medusa required not only the Athenian strategy of indirection but other gear:

namely, Hermes's winged sandals to take me to Gorgonsville in far-off Hyperborea, Hades's helmet of invisibility to escape from the snake-girl sisters, and the magic *kibisis* to stow her head in lest she petrify all posthumously. But these accessories were in the care of Stygian nymphs whose location was known not even to my canny sister: only the grim gray Graeae could tell it, and they wouldn't.

My first task, then, clear-cut in the fourth panel, had been to hie me from Samos to Mount Atlas, where sat the crony trio on their thrones, facing outward back to back and shoulder shoulder in a mean triangle. Some way off from its near vertex (which happened to be between terrible Dino and Pemphredo the stinger), I hid behind a shrub of briar to reconnoiter and soon induced, concerning the single eye and tooth they shared, their normal mode of circulation. Right to left things went around, eye before tooth before nothing, in a kind of rhythm, as follows: Pemphredo, say, blind and mute, sat hands in lap while Dino, on her right, wore the eye just long enough to scan her sector and Enyo, on her left, the tooth just long enough to say "Nothing." Then with her right hand Pemphredo took the eye from Dino's left, clapped it in place, and scanned, while Dino with her right took tooth from Enyo's left, popped it in to say "Nothing," then passed it on to Pemphredo, who passed the eye round to Enyo, put in the tooth, and said "Nothing." Thus did report follow observation and meditation report, except that (as I learned some moments later) at the least alarum any gray lady could summon by a shoulder-tap what either other bore. For, having grasped the cycle, I moved closer in a cautious gyre, keeping ever abaft the eye, at the vertex between speaker and meditator; but when I rustled a pebble underfoot, then-blank Enyo, her right hand out for the eye from Pemphredo, whacked Dino into reverse and fetched the tooth as well! I lunged to her right, Pemphredoward, just as she clapped the organ in; by the time she was toothed to cry "Something!" Pemphredo had eared me at her feet and tapped Enyo for the eye, at the same time reaching right for the her-turn tooth. Dino, unable to reply that she'd returned the tooth to Enyo, swatted back both ways; twice-tapped Enyo got her hands crossed, giving Pemphredo the eye and Dino tooth; I dived through thrones to the center; all clapped all; eye and tooth flipped round in countercircles but could be by none installed before doubly summoned. By deftly interposing at a certain moment my right hand between Dino's ditto and Enyo's left I shortstopped eye; no problem then, as Pemphredo made to gum home their grim incisor, simply to over-shoulder her and excise it. The panel showed me holding both triumphantly aloft while the grieving Graeae thwacked and flopped and croaked in vain, like crippled herons.

Its Stygian successor in my judgment was less successful, artistically speaking, for while it curved some thirteen meters round behind my bedhead to the Graeae's eight, both the task and its representation were much simpler: having learned from the furious trio where the Stygian Nymphs abode (perforce returning tooth for angry Pemphredo to speak with, but retaining eye by way of insurance against Gray-Lady-bites) it was simply a matter of going there, holdig by dose thus agaist the biserable sbell those girls gave off, ad collectig frob theb the helbet, wallet ad wigged saddles.

"What did they smell like?" asked Calyxa.

"Your opposite," I said. "But if, immortal that you are,

you'd perspired through all eternity rank sweat here where I ab bost fod of kissig, dor ever washed id all that tibe—"

"I'm twenty-four," Calyxa said, "until next week. That feels okay."

But I couldn't tell her where took place that easy feat upon the wall, for just as Lethe's liquid is a general antidote to memory, the Styx-girls' stench proved specific against recollection of its source. All Pemphredo said was to shut my eyes and follow my nose, not opening the former till I was obliged to close the latter. No time at all till I had lapped the team of toolwardens there depicted and winged off, don't ask me whence.

"If she hasn't anyone to wash herself for her," primly declared Calyxa, "a girl should wash herself herself."

The penultimate panel, on my entire right hand, was most eventful and my favorite. Itself septuple in proportions similar to the whole's of which it was sixth episode, its first scene, Hyperborean, showed me holding aloft the Gorgon's dreadful head, which, catching her napping, I'd snuck in shielded to cut from her reflected neck; the second, Hesperidean, my petrifaction of inhospitable Atlas; the third, fourth, and fifth, all Joppan, respectively my backhand slaying of sea-beast Cetus, threatening Andromeda on the cliff; the post-rescuary nuptials, held over Cassiopeia's protest, whereat I'd recited to the wedding guests my history thus far; and the splendid battle in the banquet hall when my rival Phineus, who lusted after Andromeda as had Proetus Danaë, broke up the reception; the mural showed me turning into stone with all his company that avuncular nepophile. In the heptatych's sixth panelet, climax of the climax, back in Seriphos, I had once again called my enemy to my aid, rescuing

Mother and ending my tasks by the petrifaction of taskmaster Polydectes. The seventh represented a mere and minor mishap some time later, at the Larissan track-and-field meet, where a zephyr slipped my straight-flung discus into a curve and frisbee'd down to Hades Granddad Acrisius in the stands; it was as overlong for its substance as was its grand counterpart in the whole heptamerous whorl, which for all its meters (thirty-three and then some) showed but my wife and me throned in Argos, surrounded by our gold bright children, a shower of *Perseidae*.

Daily, hourly, since first waking on my Elysian couch, I reviewed those murals, wondrous, as faithful to my story and its several characters as if no chiseling sculptor, but Medusa herself, had rendered into veined Parian, from her perch in the great sixth panel, our flesh and blood. That image was of the lot most welcome to me: all golden muscle, hard as marble, I stood profiled on the Gorgon's corpse in the model glory of twenty years; the magic sandals were strapped to just below my calves; my left knee bent to bound me next moment skyward; held back at right mid-thigh was Hermes's falchion, declined from horizontal as were my knee, my penis (see below), and my eyes—not to meet, through the golden locks that curled from under Hades's helmet, those of Medusa, whose dripping head I held aloft in my left hand. Despite two small departures on the heavenly sculptor's part from classic realism (though I grant it was a moment far from aphrodisiac, he had, I'm certain, undersized my phallus; and Medusa's face, unaccountably, was but for the herpetine coiffure a lovely woman's!), it was a masterpiece among masterpieces, that panel: it it was my eye first fell on when I woke; it it was I was still transfixed by muchwhile later when my radiant nurse-nymph first entered from beyond the seventh mural to kneel smiling at my bedside as if before an altar.

My voice still scratchy from the dunes, I said: "Hello."

She whispered: "Hi," and on my asking who she was, responded: "Calyxa. Your priestess."

"Ah, so. I've been promoted?"

She raised to me brighter eyes than any I remembered having seen on Earth and said enthusiastically: "Here you've always been a god, Perseus. All my life I've worshipped you, right along with Ammon and Sabazius. You can't imagine what it means to me to see and speak to you like this."

I frowned, but touched her cropped dark hair and attempted to recall the circumstances of my death. Calyxa was neither white, like most other nymphs of my acquaintance, cinnamon-dark like Ethiopish Cassiopeia, nor high-chrysal like my handsome widow of panels Six-C through -E and Seven, but sun-browned as a young gymnasiast through her gauzy briefs—which showed her too to be lean-hipped and -breasted like an adolescent Artemist, as against Andromeda's full-ripe femalehood, say, or the cushy amplitude of—there, my memory, with my manhood, stirred, giving the lie to elsewise-marvelous Six-A.

"Is this Elysium, Calyxa, or Olympus?"

"It's heaven," she replied, brow to my hip.

I'd never heard, from Athene or the several accounts of fellow-heroes which I'd studied in the past decade, of erections in Elysium, whereas the Olympians seemed as permanently tumesced as the mount they dwelt on: I *was* elevated, then! Still stroking as I considered this rise my nice nymph's nape, I noticed that while the mural began at my bedpost, the spiral it described did not, but curved on in and upward in a golden coil upon the ceiling to a point just above where my head would be if I moved one headswidth left; when I raised me up to watch whither hot Calyxa now, I saw the same spiral stitched in purple on the bed. And—miracle of miracles!—when the sprite sprang nimbly aspread that nether spiral and drew to her tanned taut tummy dazzled me, I perceived that her very navel, rather than bilobular or quadrantic like the two others I best knew, was itself spiriferate, replicating the infinite inward wind both above and below the finite flesh on which my tongue now feast.

Godhood was okay. However, I was twice disturbed to find myself impotent: twice in that, one, I twice tried Calyxa then and there, that "afternoon" (I'd not supposed the sun set on us immortals), and despite or owing to her own uncommon expertise was twice unmanned; two, it was the second time in as many weeks and women (so it came back to me the second time) I had thus flopped, after never once failing done Andromeda in seven thousand nights—an alarming prospect for the nymphed eternity ahead.

"It doesn't *matter*," insisted sweet-sweat Calyxa, several times in each of the days and nights that followed. "It's just *being* with you I love, Perseus; it really is one of my dreams come true."

There was another thing: used as I was, as king and mythic hero, to a fair measure of respect, I was unused to reverence: I could not make water without my votary's adoring view (I had not known gods pissed like mortals); she literally licked clean the plates she fed me back to strength from (not ambrosia after all, but dates, figs, roast lamb, and retsina, as at home) (I insisted she wash them after); licked *me* clean too, like a cozy cat, in lieu of bathing, and toweled me with her hair (too short for the job): sport enough when one was in the sportive mood, as Calyxa seemed more or less continuously to be; a mere embarrassment when one was not. Truly I believe she would have reliquaried my stools if I'd allowed her (I hadn't guessed gods shat).

"You divinities take sex too seriously," she chided when I swore at that second slump. I supposed to her, not unbitterly, that nymphs like herself were accustomed to a rounder rogering from the deities they attended, and made clear, perhaps overprotested, that I myself was unused entirely to impotence, could not account for it.

"O, you'll be heavenly once you're aroused, I can see that," she soothed. Not her fault at all, I assured her; indeed, never since my first nights with Andromeda, so long years past, had I couched so lively, lean, and tight a miss; moreover, Andromeda and I, I fondly recollected, had begun as equal amateurs and learned love's lore together, whereas Calyxa's skill bespoke much prior experience . . .

Gaily she enjoined me from pout. "Believe it or not, I was a virgin till twenty-two." Cheerfully she acknowledged then that all her girlhood she'd so adored myself, Sabazius, and horny Ammon, and had in addition been so preoccupied with sports and studies, she'd let no ordinary mortal know her (I'd not heard mortals *could* lay hands on nymphs); then one evening, as she was sweeping out the sheep-god's shrine (shrines in heaven? dust on Mount Olympus?), which she ministered along with mine and Beer-Boy's, Ammon himself had appeared and to her great delight had rammed her. Thus initiate, she'd gladly become not merely tender of our three temples but priestess-prostitute as well, holily giving herself, in the honorable tradition of her earthly counterparts, to the truest of our male admirers between tuppings by two-thirds of the deities themselves.

"Sabazius too!" I protested. Ammon I could be purely

jealous of, despite my old grievance concerning his advice to Cassiopeia, for the images I'd seen of him in Joppa showed a fine-fettled fellow with handsome ram's-horns coiling from his swarthy curls. But not only had Sabazius fermented no end of trouble for me back in Argos; I winced to picture that old priapist a-puff on my neat nymph.

She giggled. "You think *you're* impotent! But don't make so *much* of it, Perseus!" Along with swimming and foot-racing, she candidly admitted, she liked few pleasures more than the chains of orgasms Ammon and one or two of her mortal partners could set her catenating. She and Sabazius, on the other hand, made do with beery conversations, burps, and blow-jobs, which, the first being long and friendly, the last short and sweet, pleased her in their way quite as well as Ammon's frisk fierce fucks.

"You worry too much," she told me on the second night, when, flaccid once again, I'd advised her vexedly to forsake me and revert to Ammonism. "In the first place, I've never stopped *being* an Ammonite and never will—or a Sabazian, either, even though neither of them keeps in touch with me any more." I was not, she gently reminded me, the only god in her pantheon; on the other hand, it made her happy beyond imagine merely to be with me on my altar-couch; to know her deity—*any* of her private trinity—as a "warm human person," "off his pedestal," in her terms. Besides, was I really so naïve as to equate love-making, like a callow lad, with mere prolonged penetration?

Yes. "I'm a *hero*!" I indicated with a sweep of my relieved glories, whose first extension she had revealed to me that day. "Virtuoso performance is my line of work!"

She removed my dexter hand, it being an article of her

creed, even with deities, to allow no sheepish, merely dutiful clitorizing. "The more you think of sex as a performance," she advised me, "the more you'll suffer stage fright on your opening nights. Just hug up close, now, and fill me in on what I showed you today."

Sigh, I did, curled up behind my wise cute tutor as the temple's great second whorl, to which she'd noonly introduced me, enconched the first. As I'd come to hope and fancy, the Perseid reliefs and my altared view were not coterminous there where I sat regnant with Andromeda; a second series—correspondent to the first in relative proportions, but of grander breadth to fit the scale of their enormous revolution—commenced just after, at the pillar on that farther wall aligned quite with my left-foot bedpost and Calyxa's navel-point.

"You saw how it was," I said: "The kids were grown and restless; Andromeda and I had become different people; our marriage was on the rocks. The kingdom took care of itself; my fame was sure enough—but I'd lost my shine with my golden locks: twenty years it was since I'd headed Medusa; I was twenty kilos overweight and bored stiff. With half a life to go, I felt fettered and coffered as ever by Danaë's womb, the brassbound chest, Polydectes's tasks. In fact— please keep your face straight—I became convinced I was petrifying, and asked my doctor if it mightn't be the late effects of radiation from Medusa. 'Just aging of the old joints,' the fool declared, correctly, told me to forget about the Gorgon, give up ouzo, get more exercise. But hare-hunts can't hold a candle to monstermachy: I stayed up too late, drank too many, traded shameless on my authority to bore each night a captive audience with the story of my life.

'Change of scene, then,' the doctor ordered: 'bit of a sea-trip, do you oodles.' He even winked: 'Take the Missus along: second honeymoon, et cetera.' "

"Sometimes," Calyxa said, "I really wonder about doctors."

"Me too. But I proposed it, and Andromeda said sure right off: park the kids in Argos, sail down to Joppa for a visit with her folks; twenty years since she'd seen Cepheus and Cassiopeia. 'Not quite what I had in mind,' I told her; 'we'll stop off there when the time comes, but let's go the route: drop in on King Dictys in Seriphos, say hello to Samian Athene, run over to Mount Atlas, where I short-circuited the Graeae—you've never seen Mount Atlas—then a quick stop at Chemmis on the Nile, where I landed for a drink before I saved your life.' By the way, Calyxa—" I had unwound to follow with my eye those furled episodes along the wall.

"Please don't stop," she pled, and taking her to mean, despite her policy, the idle handiwork that went with my recital, I resumed.

"So, it was a battle from the outset, even though I'd dropped Styxnymphsville, Hyperborea, and Hesperia from my itinerary to give us an extra week in Joppa and time for a quick look-see at Thessalian Larissa. 'Joppa period,' Andromeda said."

"*I* think she was being unreasonable," said Calyxa.

I cleared my throat. "Well, now, perhaps it was a bit vain of me to want to retrace my good young days; but it wasn't *just* vanity; no more were my nightly narratives: somewhere along that way I'd lost something, took a wrong turn, forgot some knack, I don't know; it seemed to me that if I kept going over it carefully enough I might see the pattern, find the key."

"A little up and to your left," Calyxa whispered. But I was lost now in my story. "Ever since that run-in with your pal Sabazius," I said, "things hadn't been the same between Andromeda and me." I told her how the bellied beer-god, using his Dionysian alias, had come bingeing from Naxos into Argos with his new wife Ariadne—

"He told me about her, last time I saw him," Calyxa confessed. "At first I was mad with jealousy, but he was so happy, and she was sweet . . ."

"*Everybody* was mad," I said: "the older women especially, drink drink drink, and when I tried to close the bars he talked them into eating their babies till I gave in. Honestly. I'd've held out awhile—you've got to draw the line somewhere—but Andromeda claimed it was his fame I couldn't abide . . ." Truth was, I declared, I *did* envy the upstart god his enthusiasts, the more as my own glory had not increased since I'd given up heroism for the orderly administration of Argolis; on the other hand, though not a prude, mind, I quite believed in order, measure, self-discipline, and was opposed on principle to indiscriminate housewife orgy, not to mention pedophage. I was no less than Sabazius a son of Zeus, and if no god (owing to Mother's mere mortality), I had the *vita* of a gold-haired hard-tasked hero, whereas Sabazius so far as I could see did nothing but booze and ball all day . . .

"Better say 'guzzle and go down,' " Calyxa said comfortably. She too, she added, had no taste for orgies unless among especially valued friends—such as, say (the notion made her stretch), Ammon, Sabazius, and me—her general policy being to offer herself to others, corporeally and otherwise, to the extent of her esteem for them. Nevertheless she'd gone along with group-grope, gang-bang, daisy-chain, and other perversions for her plump pal's sake, deferring her preferences to his—just as, with Ammon, she smoked hemp and humped hind-to, although left to herself, so to speak, she'd choose light palm-wine and Position One more often than not. In both instances, her pleasure in theirs not only gratified her beyond her own preferences (a mere martyr's reward, in her view) but made distinctly pleasurable, just in those circumstances, the acts themselves. In short, she was by no means blind to Sabazius's shortcomings, but they were without effect on her worship of him. "We really used to talk, he and I."

It occurred to me to ask why, in view of the foregoing, she had removed my hand in one previous paragraph and limped me with her laughter in another when I'd asked permission to kiss her navel. Her reply was a quiet, short, and serious kiss that messaged clearly even subtless me. I stirred against her nether cheeks very near to Ammonite erection, shrank from the adjective, re-cupped her, resumed my tale:

"*I* liked Sabazius okay too," I admitted, "despite the trouble he'd caused me; once I'd agreed to build him a temple to keep the housewives happy, we drained many a goblet together before he moved on. But there was no peace after that with Andromeda: now she claimed I'd given in out of weakness, or to curry favor on Olympus: was I pandering to public opinion, yielding to the pedophagic protest groups, or kicking over my traces like a foolish forty-year-old? Fame and kingship had changed me, changed me, she declared, and not for the better, et cetera."

"Excuse me for saying so," Calyxa said, "but I don't

think I care for Mrs. Perseus. Now watch you back up and defend her."

Well, I did: none of these unpleasant accusations but had its truth, as I saw when I wasn't defending myself against them, and its contrary side, as I saw when I was. But one fact was inescapable, however read or rationalized: Perseus the Hero prevailed or perished; Perseus the King had swallowed self-respect and not even compromised with, but yielded to, his adversary.

"It was all downward after that," I concluded: "squalls and squabbles; flirtations, accusations; relovings and relapses, let's not relive it, you know the story, it's all in that pillar between the last panel yonder," where Andromeda and I shared our loveseat throne ringed by little princelets, "and the one today," in which my scold-faced queen sat throned far right and sullen I far left, our grownlings wondering between and a ship making ready in the marble foreground.

"I went weekending once with Ammon down the Nile to Pharos," Calyxa remarked. "We swam a lot. It's the only time I've fucked under water."

"It's not so great, actually, didn't you find?" I asked her in her humor, delving at the same time down to recollection. "The natural lubricants get washed off, and it sort of hurts. I knew this sea-nymph once . . ."

"I liked it anyhow," Calyxa said.

Next night, too, we made less progress with each other than with the templed exposition. "If only Medusa had petrified just *that* part!" my priestess sighed—but would not let me repeat what she declared went without saying, that what fired my bolt like a green recruit's before the issue was fairly joined was not inexperience of artful love but inexperience of novel partners. "You're like some of the holiday tourists we get," she once declared: "bold as brass back home but all tinsel and tiptoe here."

When I had been Perseus proper, I told her then, I'd flown the known world over, Hyperborea to Hesperia, yet never heard of tourists to the country of the gods. Part of every morning, afternoon, and evening Calyxa disappeared into the temple's outer whorls with strict instructions, as she said from Zeus, that I was not to follow past whichever mural she'd last laid on me. Where did she go? I asked her now. What do? Was she slipping off to Ammon and Sabazius, or tourist-tupping in my heavenly precinct?

She was not annoyed until I apologized (at once) for my impertinence. "If you're going to be quarrelsome, be quarrelsome: don't take one step forward and two back."

I apologized for my apology, attributing my too-tameness to long years of Andromeda's house-training, and that in turn to her father's domination by Cassiopeia, while at the same time admitting that, as Andromeda herself had charged in the Sabazius affair, a better man would in the first place never—

"*Stop* that!" Calyxa cried. I did, began to apologize, stopped *that*, reflected a moment, and then declared her under no obligation to attend me if she found my manner, mind, or manliness disappointing; but if she chose to stay she must accept me on my terms—which for better or worse included (unlike Sabazius's or Ammon's, I daresaid) permitting me to accept her on hers. No drachma but had its other side: Andromeda in my opinion had near henpecked me out of cockhood; but I had learned from her what few men knew, fewer heroes, and no gods: that a woman's a person in her independent right, to be respected therefor by the goldenest hero in heaven. If my pert priestess was unused to parity as was I to novelty, then we had each somewhat to teach the other.

Calyxa sat up and closed me in her lap (these conversations were all postcoitally, anyhow epiclimactically, couched); but all I could get from her was "You, you! You're leaving something out."

"No help for that."

"Those *letters*, Perseus, that she threw overboard . . ."

I groaned. Had voyage in nautic history, I asked rhetorically, ever begun so crossed as ours whose wreckage that day's mural had fixed forever? We'd set out when spring gave way to summer, neither of us yielding to the other. Andromeda stormed at me it must be Joppa without sidetrips, or she'd go it unburdened of her had-been hero; I stormed back, if she'd wanted a lackey instead of a lord, she should've stuck with her Uncle Phineus. Thus we raged and counterbaited as we cleared the port. I perhapped our problem to be mixed marriage: Argives and Ethiopians were oil and vinegar, I declared, palatable when right-proportioned but never truly mixable. Pah, she spat: all marriages were mixed, a man and a woman; but there was my insufferable ego again, proposing three parts Perseus to one Andromeda, when in truth it was her rescue from monstrous Cetus had made the reputation I'd grown so puffed upon: she had as it were laid her life on the line to make me famous! I replied, not unfairly I think, that even the bards who sang our story were wont to call her both the cause of my labor and its reward—which was but putting prettily (I went on less fairly) that had I by-passed Joppa altogether I'd've spared myself two hard battles (with Cetus and with Phineus's gatecrashers), plus the sustained one of our recent years together, and found me a more congenial princess some-

where else, whereas she'd've been fishfood. That always got
to her: she bawled back that what I'd freed her from were
but the chains in which my forebears caused her to be put
(she meant Uncle Poseidon, who'd given Ammon word to
cliff her when the jealous Nereids complained to him of
Cassiopeia's boast et cetera); she owed me nothing, more
especially since I'd manumitted her into the bondage of my
tyrant vanity, a mere bedpartner and accessory to my fame:
it was but a matter, in her view, of exchanging shackles for
shekels, or iron manacles for gold. That always got to me: I
stormed back, unfairly now, that even read as I read them
the poets were wrong: freeing Mother Danaë, not Andromeda, had been my mission; regaining my lost kingdom;
resolving, by the death of both, the twinly old feud between
Acrisius and Proetus, which dated from the womb. To this
end Medusa, not fishy Cetus, had been my true adversary
and chief ally; I hadn't even employed her in the Cetus
engagement, to dispatch which wanted but my trusty sickle
and a bit of shadow-feinting. In short, the whole Joppan
adventure, charming as it was, could be regarded as no more
than a couple of sub-panels, as it were, in the mural of my
life: an interlude in, indeed a diversion from, my hero-work
proper.

"Danaë Danaë!" then had shouted Andromeda. "You
should have married your mother!"

Calyxa clucked her tongue. "You two really went at it,
didn't you?"

I agreed, my face burning afresh. "That's when she
pounced upon the brassbound sea-chest on the poop," I said.
"We had lots of traveling-bags, but I'd decided to do the trip
right—*my* trip—and had packed my things in the same old
trunk that Granddad had shipped me off in, forty years past.

For one thing, I thought Seriphean Dictys would be pleased to see it again, so I'd kept in it all my souvenirs: a piece of the net he'd fished us ashore with, the crescent scabbard of Hermes's sickle, couple of rocks from giant Atlas after I'd stoned him, fern-corals from Joppa (I'd laid Medusa's head on seaweed while I skewered Cetus), Andromeda's leg-irons, the Larissan discus, and the letters."

"Those letters, Perseus . . ." I was left-flanked on the couch; naughty Calyxa, propped on her elbows at my hip, amused herself as I spoke by scribing capitals on her forehead with my flopped tool as with an infirm pen. *R*, *S*, Something, *P*: the scrambled uncials of my name.

"Fan letters, mostly," I said. "Nut mail, con letters, speaking invitations, propositions from women I never heard of— sort of thing every mythic hero gets in each day's post. I swear I didn't save them out of vanity, as she claimed; I almost never answered them."

"Mm."

"It was partly habit, I'm afflicted with orderliness, they were even alphabetized, starting with *Anonymous*. Partly for amusement, to pick me up when I was feeling down, remind me I'd once got a few things done worth doing. But mainly, I swear, it was for a kind of *research*, what I mentioned once before: certain letters especially I read and re-read: half a dozen or so from some dotty girl in Chemmis, Egypt. They were billets-doux, I admit it—but along with the hero-worship was a bright intelligence, a lively style, and a great many detailed questions, almost as if she were doing a dissertation. How many had been the Stygian Nymphs? Had Medusa always been a Gorgon? Was it really her reflection in Athene's shield that saved me from petrifying, or the fact that Medusa had her eyes closed; and if the latter, why'd

I need the shield? How was it I'd used the helmet of invisibility only to flee the other Gorgons and not to approach them in the first place? Did everything that saw Medusa turn to stone, or everything Medusa saw? If the former, how explain the sightless seaweed? If the latter, how came it to work when she'd been beheaded? Was my restriction to the adamant sickle and the shadow-trick in the Cetus episode self-imposed or laid on by Athene, and if the former, was my motive to impress Andromeda with skill and valor rather than with magic? And if the latter, why? Considering the crooked sword, the Graeaean subterfuge, the rear-view approaches to Medusa and Cetus, the far-darting Hermean sandals, even the trajectory of the discus that killed Acrisius, would it be fair to generalize that dodge and indirection were my conscious tactics, and, if so, were they characterological or by Athenian directive? Similarly, considering Danaë's brass tower, the sea-chest, the strapping tasks of Polydectes, Danaë's bondage to him, and Andromeda's manacles on the one hand, and on the other, my conquests of Atlas, Phineus, Polydectes, and the rest by petrifaction, could not one say that my goal for myself and gift to others was typically release from immobility, and my punishment—of both my Medusa'd former enemies and my latterly tied-down self— typically its opposite? O Calyxa, this nameless girl, she had no end of insightful questions! Which I pondered and repondered as I've done these murals, to find if I could their meaning, where they pointed, what it was I'd lost. One question alone—whether I felt my post-Medusan years an example of or an exception to the archetypal pattern for heroic adventure—set me to years of comparative study, to learn what that pattern might be and where upon it I currently was. Thus this endless repetition of my story: as both protagonist and author, so to speak, I thought to overtake with understanding my present paragraph as it were by examining my paged past, and thus pointed, proceed serene to the future's sentence. My trustiest aid in this endeavor was those seven letters, at once so worshipful and wise; I'd've given much to spend an evening with their author! Hence my fury when Andromeda, herself unhinged by wrath, tore open the chest-lid just off Hydra and threw them to the fish. For the first time in our life, I struck her."

My eyes filled at the double memory; Calyxa curled me in her way until my salt tears filled her navel. Post-swatly, I went on, I took from the chest my only correspondence with Andromeda, love letters written during my youthful trip to Larissa, and posted them with the others in the Gulf of Argolis. Then Andromeda, in a perfect tempest of outrage, fishfed the entire contents of the chest: shore me of my valiant past as a steering drover ballocks a bull.

"I could listen all night to the way you talk," Calyxa said.

"We were so busy storming at each other," I went on, "and the crew and galley slaves enrapt in our battle royal, none noticed the natural tempest till it struck astern like the fist of a god, as if Father Zeus were counterpunching for smote Andromeda. All quarrels went by the board with mast and tiller; we were stove in a trice, sunk and drowned— all save my wife and me, who, still wrestling with the re-latched ruin of my chest, were washed with it the way of its contents. Empty, it floated; our grapple became a grip; the storm passed, the sharks were patient; two days the currents easted us, as in your picture, clutched and quarreling in the Sea of Candia; on the third, as if caught in a repeating dream, we were netted by a fine young fisherman, more the image of my golden youth than my own sons were. He congratulated us on our survival, complimented Andromeda on her brined beauty, introduced himself as Danaus Dictys's-son, and home-ported us with the rest of his catch to Seriphos."

Calyxa squeezed me. "When I drew that panel for the sculptor from your sister's sketches, I was afraid you and Andromeda were embracing over the sea-chest."

Embarrassed, she acknowledged under my amazed interrogation that all the murals in the temple were rendered from her drawings, after careful instructions delivered her from time to time over the years by couriers from Athene. She was not, then, merely maid, minister, and mistress of her deities, their temples, and devotees, but artful chronicler of their careers as well! I refrained from asking whether Sabazius and Ammon were similarly shrined, but praised her artistry to the skies.

"I'm no artist," she demurred. "Anyhow, I'm not interested in me."

But I would not let her off so modestly; with real appreciation I kissed her from crown to sole, which flexily she enjoyed, and pressed her tell me how far the murals went— for while I myself could predict, I thought, the next couple of panels, my memory of an odd dark passion in the desert just prior to my demise was still obscure to me, as was the manner of my death itself.

She shook her head. "Tomorrow, or the next night, maybe, I'll tell you, if you haven't guessed." Her tone grew graver. "What do you think the next panel will be?"

I supposed it would portray the famous "sculpture museum" at Seriphos, now the isle's chief tourist attraction, which we foursomed—Andromeda, Danaus, Dictys, and I —soon after, in what became the cycled dream's continuation. King Dictys himself was in declining age and health, but overjoyed to review the source and cause of his ascendancy. Andromeda, unsalted and refreshed, seemed to have lost five years and kilos in the sea; she basked in the gallantries of her yet-younger life preserver. The famous statues, of course, were no sculptured likenesses at all, but the stoned originals of Polydectes and his court, fixed forever in their postures of insult and abuse which I had countered with the Gorgon's head. There in the center sat the false king himself, still gloating at his declaration that my whole laborious adventure had been but his ruse for my riddance; that he had never intended to bed any but my gold-girt mother, whom presently he was starving from her sanctuary with Dictys in Athene's temple. Those had been his last words: fascinated, I pointed out to my companions that his tongue was still tipped to his teeth to make the theta of Ναῷ Αθήνης, to whose eta he would never come.

"Remarkable," young Danaus had agreed, and added with a trace of tease in his own teeth-tipped tongue: "If Uncle P. was forty when you froze him, and has been lisping that same theta for twenty years, you and he must be about the same age now."

Andromeda laughed, her first mirth in months; then the two of them went off at smart Danaus's suggestion to find something less boring to look at than his petrified progenitors. Dictys and I watched them go, my wife merrily accepting her escort's elbow, and then went round the remaining figures, pensively summoning names and patronymics from that glorious morning for half the afternoon. Returning at last to the now-cool shadow of Polydectes, we sipped from silver beakers of Hippocrene and traded troubles.

"I can't manage the boy," Dictys said; "it's because he never had a mother, and I was too busy running the government to be a proper father."

I sympathized, reflecting on my own sons' growing rebellion, and asked who was Dictys's queen; at his hem and haw I dropped the subject, inferring with some satisfaction that young Danaus was illicit. He suggested we ought to interrupt their tête-à-tête; but I asked for more wine instead, and two beakers later was confiding to him my domestic problems and my conviction I was petrifying.

Dictys shook his head. "Just ossifying, like the rest of us." Too bad about Andromeda, he said; he was just as pleased never to have wed the only woman he'd ever loved, seeing how seldom that sentiment withstood the years' attrition. For the rest, as there was no help for it, he advised me to resign myself to lovelessness and decline; he'd ship me off to Samos, Joppa, or wherever I wished—but all voyages, he reminded me, come soon or late to the same dark port.

"Better late, then," said I, and announced to the gathered company at dinner, I was determined to resume the retracement of my ancient route. If Andromeda would not retrace it with me . . .

Her eyes flashed. "Joppa, period."

"At least consult Athene," old Dictys implored me.

"I will," said I. "Where I did before, in her shrine in Samos."

"*Where he learned about life from art,*" Andromeda mocked me; "*for represented in her temple murals there were all three Gorgons—snakehaired, swinetoothed,* blah blah blah. I know it by heart. I'm staying here."

Young Danaus fiddled smiling with his flatware. "I've heard it said," he said, "that when you were done with

Medusa last time, Athene put her back together again, with a difference: nowadays she turns stone to flesh instead of vice-versa: makes old folks spry again. You and Dad should look her up."

At this impertinence there was a general pause, and general relief when I merely thanked him, level-voiced, for the report. If she declined to go with me, I told Andromeda next day, she must abide in Seriphos under Dictys's chaperonage until my return: I would not have her travel unescorted. She replied she was her own woman, would as she would. Very well, I countered, reminding her however that independence had its limits; that, given our particular tempers and past, the more she became her own woman, the less mine.

"Amen," Andromeda said, a Joppan expression.

"So I went it alone," I said to Calyxa, "and my guess is that tomorrow's mural shows us there in the hall of statues: Danaus grinning, Andromeda and I glaring at each other, Dictys shaking his head, and Polydectes still lisping Ναῷ Ἀθήνης."

I was mistaken, my artist informed me—not only about next day's scene (which pillared all I'd just rehearsed) but about the nature of parity between the sexes as well.

"I know," I sighed, mistaking her. "Andromeda was right."

"That's not what I mean!" Calyxa sprang to her nimble knees. "Look at *me*, for instance: would you call me dependent? I go my own way, lonely or not; that's why I've never married. But don't you get the point?"

"No."

She flipped my flunked phallus. "I swear, I'll have to draw you a picture."

Instead, she showed me one, next day: myself in conference already with the hooded woman in Athene's temple, beneath the familiar frieze of Gorgons, winged Pegasus grazing just outside.

"Remarkable!" I scrutinized my companion-in-relief. "The resemblance . . ."

"With the cowl it's hard to tell," Calyxa said; "but if that's Athene, then Athene's the one who's brought me the instructions for all these scenes over the years, and finally brought you here in person from the desert. She's always been very polite to me, but she never explains the pictures."

"I'll be glad to: at first I thought her a fellow-suppliant—"

But Calyxa reminded me of our little rule, explication only after forn. We went to bed early, I did better, fairly entered her, though for less than heroical time and space; I was chided for sighing; she held me between her pretty legs and said: "Aphrodite's a woman and so am I. Does that make me her equal?" Andromeda's fallacy, in her view, was an equivocation on the term *equality:* she Calyxa frankly regarded herself as superior in numerous ways to numerous men and women—

"I think you are too."

"Do don't flatter now; I'm serious." Her dark eyes were, past doubt; I'd have moved off-top, to beside her, better to manifest our parity, but she had extraordinary grip.

"I mean, they're mortals, and you're a nymph," I said limply.

"Never mind that." The point was, she asserted, it went without saying, in her opinion, that to say men and women were equal was to say nothing. She herself admired excellence wherever she found it; she was far from servile by nature, knew herself to be uncommonly intelligent, witty, healthy, athletical, articulate, brave, and a few other adjectives—

"*Pretty*," I suggested. "*Sexually adroit . . .*"

She stopped my mouth. "But I happen to know men and women quite superior to me in all these things, and not only wouldn't I dream of calling myself their equal, I happen to *prefer* them to myself and my equals. You reminded me once that you're a mythic hero, but you keep forgetting it yourself. Were you always psychosexually weak, or is that Andromeda's doing?"

Truly I wished to withdraw, and being at least her muscular match, managed to. She grinned and bussed my forearm.

"No man's a mythic hero to his wife," I said. But Calyxa took spirited issue: no woman remained a dream of nymphhood to her husband either, she daresaid, but real excellence in any particular should be excellent even qualified by comparison, long familiarity, and non-excellence in other particulars. That permanent relationship was fatal to passion was perhaps inevitable, and as she preferred to love passionately she would never marry; but having been more than once abused by those she loved, she knew for a fact that her admiration of their excellences was invulnerable. "Ammon's a real bastard, often as not," she said; "but I'd die for him tomorrow if he asked me too. I'm good, but he's great. Who does Andromeda think she is?"

I'd hear no more such criticism. "My question to Athene," I said, "was Who was *I*? I made proper sacrifices, prayed she'd appear and counsel me how not to turn to stone. If there was a new Medusa, let a new Perseus be resickled,

-shielded, -sandaled, and the rest, to reglorify himself by re-beheading her. It wasn't Mother Danaë wanted rescuing now, but Danaë's-son."

Calyxa snugged against me with a kind of fond exasperation. I went on to recount how, as I'd recounted to Athene my apprehensions, a hooded young woman had appeared beside me at the altar, whom I took to be a fellow-suppliant until from the corner of my eyes I saw a radiance from hers —which, however, like all her features, were cowled from view in the temple dusk. And when she said to me, "Your brother was right: there *is* a New Medusa," I recognized the voice as no mortal's: Athene had come to me, as was her wont, in suppliant's guise. I reminded her I had no mortal kin, only scores of divine half-siblings like herself, got by Zeus upon his scores of bedmates.

She touched my arm and softly undeceived me. "Dictys and Danaë were closeted a long while in the Seriphos temple before you rescued them. But think again, Perseus, what Polydectes was saying: it wasn't the theta of Ναῷ 'Αθήνης, but the sigma of Ναῷ 'Αφροδίτης. He really did lisp, and your mother's shelter was Love, not Wisdom . . ."

In short, she said, young Danaus my rescuer and current rival was half my brother! And fortunate it was—she went on at once, to check my flabbergasted ire—King Dictys and my mother had chosen Aphrodite's shrine instead of Athene's for their besieged amour, since Athene would have sorely punished them for sacrilege. Such exactly (I could not get in my outrage edgewise!) had been innocent Medusa's orig-inal sin: was I aware of the circumstances of her Gorgoniz-ing?

I surrendered.

"Me too," Calyxa said.

She'd been a pretty young girl, went on the cowled apparition: a daughter of the sea-god Phorcys and thus kid-sister to the grim Gray Ladies and cousin to the pretty Nereids. She'd been well brought up by her mother Ceto, was in fact as proper a sea-nymph as ever swam: discreet of her person, pretty as the April moon, a regular churchgoer and comforter of the drowned. Her only failing, if it could be so called, was a maiden's pride and interest in her budded beauty—in particular her naturally wavy hair, proof against sea-salt and so comely withal that it fired the passions of the admiralty-god himself, her Uncle Poseidon . . .

"Uncles, I swear," Calyxa said. "That's three in this story. And two hair-things. I'm glad I'm a crew-cut orphan."

"She came one morning to this temple, to sacrifice to Athene," Athene went on, oddly referring to herself in third-persons, "and catching sight of her reflection in the goddess's shield, left off her obsequies for a moment to pin up her hair. Next thing she knew, there was a smell of seaweed; wet lips pressed to her neck-nape, and Poseidon put her under. Shocked Athene turned away, Medusa did too, but my, her eyes were fastened on the shield's reflection: as the blue-eyed scallop resists the greedy star, but at length is pried and gobbled, so she saw herself shucked and forked by the mussled god. When he was done she redid through her tears her hair, to look more becomingly ravished, and called on Athene to avenge her. But that goddess, in her wisdom, punished the victim for the crime. Me—Medusa she banished to chilly Hyperborea with her sisters, whom she'd cursed into snake-haired frights; the very sight of them was enough to turn Medusa's suitors to stone when they approached her. It was a perfectly dreadful time."

"Just a minute," I interrupted.

"I was wondering too," Calyxa said.

"I know," said my sister's surrogate. "But Medusa didn't, back then. There were no mirrors, you see, in their stony cave, and her swinetoothed sisters could only grunt. After a few years of seeing her would-be boyfriends freeze in their tracks when she made eyes at them, she decided that if she was ever to have a lover she'd have to pretend in the cave what had been no pretense in the temple: not to know he was approaching. One day the seagulls on the statues of her bouldered beaux told her that Perseus himself was winging herward, a golden dream; she lulled her sisters to sleep with a snake-charm song she'd learned and then feigned sleep herself. Softly he crept up behind; her whole body glowed; his hand, strong as Poseidon's, grasped her hair above the nape. Her eyes still closed, she turned her neck to take his kiss . . ."

"O wow," Calyxa said. "Do you know what I think?"

"I know what I felt," said I. "But how was I to know?"

"I wish I'd known," I said shamefaced to the hooded one, who replied it was no matter: if she'd known herself to be as Gorgon as her sisters, Medusa would have begged to have her head cut off. In any case, when the Perseid tasks were done and the hero's gear returned (except the crescent scabbard, given Perseus as a souvenir, and the Graeae's eye, which unfortunately he'd dropped into Lake Triton on his Libyan overflight), Hermes had kept the adamantine sickle, restored their tooth to the aggrieved Graeae, and forwarded the helmet, sandals, and kibisis to the Stygian Nymphs; Athene retrieved her bright shield and affixed to its boss the Gorgon's scalp.

"Then there's no New Medusa? You said there was."

"There is," she said. "Athene reckoned she'd punished the girl nearly enough, so she rejoined her head to her body, revived her, and restored her original appearance. What's more, as a kind of compensation, she allows her some freedom of motion and took away her sculpting glance for the most part, as long as she abides by certain strict conditions . . ."

"Never mind those," I said. "Can she unstone me before I'm too far gone?"

The girl hesitated. "Perhaps. Under certain *very* strict conditions . . ."

But I would none of reservations and conditions; begged only to be outfitted as before and directed how to head off my recapped adversary. I paced about the temple, impatient to be off; already I felt younger, more Perseus than I'd been in a dozen years. No good her telling me things had changed; I was a new man; only regird me with shield and sickle, it was a decade's petrifaction in myself I'd cut off first, then Medusa's head to melt away another, then upstart Danaus's, and confront Andromeda with a better Perseus than had first unscarped her.

"That's really what you want?" the hooded lady asked then, and simultaneously later Calyxa: "That's really what you wanted?"

I yessed both; let there be no talk of past past capture, I was growing younger by the moment in both temples, hers with anticipation, mine with recapitulation.

Very well, then, said my coiffed counselor: she'd advise me as before. But the case was truly altered, and so must be both my equipage and my address. From beneath her mantle she produced a golden dagger the length and straightness of my phallus fairly drawn. I was dismayed, for what might never lose in love would never win in war.

"No adamantine sickle?"

"Just this," she said, "and your bare hands."

"I like your bare hands," Calyxa said. "But I see your point."

The point was, I was told, I must proceed this time with neither armor nor disguise. Why did I imagine Hades himself no longer used the helmet of his youth, if not that not it nor any other charm could work invisibility once one passed a certain point of fame? As for the polished shield, it itself was changed, aegissed with the former Gorgon's former power: hence its absence from the temple, lest self-reflection petrify its beholders.

"Magic wallet?" I asked, heartsunk.

"That may be useful," she said. "Not to put the New Medusa's head in, since you're not to cut it off—"

"Not cut it off!" But then I remembered and remarked that her deGorgonization made the kibisis unneeded. "All she has to do is look at me, then, and I'm twenty again? Or is it whoever looks at her? I was asked that question about the old Medusa, in a letter from a girl in Chemmis, Egypt—"

"It's not that simple, Perseus," my advisor warned, and my priestess: "You didn't answer the question."

Nor did she, I said, except to say that the New Medusa's probationary stipulations allowed for one special circumstance in which petrifaction might occur as of old, and one in which not only its contrary but a kind of immortality might be accomplished. As a possible safeguard against the former, I was advised to borrow once again the kibisis, to use not as a totebag but as a veil: Medusa herself would explain it when she came to me, "and I," I said to Calyxa, "when I come to her, in panel Six-A of your second series." What I asked Athene then was how to deal this time with the Gray Ladies, who though eyeless were not blind to my former strategy. Or might I skip them altogether and follow my own nose to the Nymphs' sour seat? In any case, surely I must borrow Hermes's sandals again as well, to fly to Hyperborea, or I'd die of old age before I ever reached Medusa.

The woman shook her head. "Athene said to remind you she has other relatives to look after too; that's why she couldn't speak to you here in person today. She's taken a great shine to a cousin of yours named Bellerophon—"

"Never heard of him," I said, and Calyxa: "I have; they say he's great." "Never mind him," I told her, and the hood-girl me: "You will, soon enough; your sister has big plans for him. Her exact words were: 'I'll always have a soft spot for dear old Perseus, but do remind him he's not the only golden hero in Greece.' I'm sorry."

"So am I," said Calyxa. "I see now why it upset you about Ammon and Sabazius. Let me ask you one question . . ."

"Hold on, I'm almost done." She did; the cowled messenger then summoned Pegasus from the court, stroked and purred to the pretty beast as to a favorite child, and set forth candidly, at times apologetically, Athene's new orders and instructions. I might borrow the winged horse, but strictly on a standby basis, since Bellerophon had first priority and could call for him at any moment. I should fly directly, not to Mount Atlas, but to the lakeshore of Libyan Triton. There I'd find the Graeae, helpless and cross enough to bite my head off; but I was to introduce myself plainly, endure with patience their threats and insults, and offer to skindive for their long-lost eye if they'd redirect me to the Stygian Nymphs. In general, she concluded, my mode of operation in this second enterprise must be contrary to my first's: on the one hand, direct instead of indirect—no circuities, circumlocutions, reflections, or ruses—on the other, rather passive than active: beyond a certain point I must permit things to come to me instead of adventuring to them.

Stung a bit still at being bumped by Bellerophon, I protested that direct passivity was not my style. It had grown by then as dark in that temple as now in this; I could discern my companion no more clearly than Calyxa. But a resonance in her reply—she observed that *before* the point aforementioned, initiative was mine to take—aroused me oddly through my new dismay and old-husband habit; I realized not merely that I was alone in the dark with a sympathetic and perhaps attractive young woman not after all Athene— but also that I hadn't put myself in the way of such realization for many years. Abruptly I embraced her; Pegasus skittered; she, too, was startled, and for some reason I when she neither protested nor pushed away. Simply she stiffened; I as well; thanked her for her counsel; prepared to unarm her with some mumble. She disarmed me with a murmur instead, how it had been long since she'd been embraced. Impetuously then I ran hand under habit; she drew off, not offended however, and from her bosom took a light gold bridle. "This is for Pegasus," she said, "to restrain him." Smiling, she led me therewith courtward, where she turned and straightway came to me, reminding me it wasn't Ναῷ Ἀφροδίτης we'd been in, but Ναῷ stern Ἀθήνης. She wouldn't uncowl, for modesty she said, but let me ground her and lift dun shift to white shoulders. It was an ample soft young body, wide-hipped and small-breasted; the night was warm, the empty court-flags also; but I, ay, I was cooled by the veiled allusion to Danaus—

"*And* by the novelty," Calyxa said, "*and* by your fear

you wouldn't get it up for her, which of course you didn't. No need to go on about ample young body wide-hipped et cetera; I get the picture." "Excuse me." "Don't apologize." "Sorry."

No more that night, Calyxa insisted, and turned away, pouting as it were with her very scapulae, her back's small small, pouting I declare with her lean little buttocks.

"No need to go on about small smalls and lean little buttocks."

Sorry, love, and good evening. I was sorry at once, reached to caress those same et ceteras and remarked, not ungently I hope, that just as Perseus was not the sole gold-skinned Greek hero, and the Calyxan religion not mono-theistic, so she might allow that lean small what-had-she's were not the only you-know's deserving admiration. She spun to me merry-faced and tear-eyed and kissed me hard enough to fetch me at last full-length into her precinct proper—if only for a moment, as I'd thresheld once again my offertory. But we were pleased.

"You're getting better," she said. "Now tell me how you know you'll meet Medusa in Series Two, Mural F, Panel One."

I replied, I thought I had the picture, but would with-hold hypotheses until next day—when, if I was not far wrong, II-D (using her system of enumeration) would show my ignominious Gray-Ladying at Lake Triton.

Calyxa smiled. "We'll see." I was not; we did: I fetched her couchward from the scene swiftly as Pegasus had me Lake Triton Samos and, lacking that splendid stone-horse's Bridle of Restraint, yet again fired surely but too soon. I was right, I told her eagerly: as the mural showed, I had been wrong to wrong the Gray Ladies in despite of the cowl-

girl's counsel. But old habit had died hard: even passing over
Seriphos, en route to North Africa at an altitude of forty
stadia, when it had occurred to me to drop in unexpectedly
and check on Andromeda, it had been my impulse I checked
instead, deciding to surprise her less directly by coming back
rejuvenated from Medusa. And when Pegasus touched
down at Triton, I could not bring myself to tell my old
victims straight out who I was. There they railed, craned,
and cooted on the beach, old past aging, and gummed their
breakfast; I altered my voice and asked crisply, "May I be
of service, ladies?" What flap, cackle, and plop ensued!
"Pah!" said Pemphredo; "Perseus!" said Enyo; "Puncture
him!" said Dino—vituperating serially as they took the
tooth.

"Not at all," said I, side-stepping their pecks. "Self-
centered Perseus is my enemy as much as yours. I understand
he dropped your eye somewhere hereabouts? I'll find it for
you if you'll tell me where the Styx-Nymphs are."

Pre-payment was my hope, for the lake though shallow
was wide, and I despaired of finding in it an eye lost twenty
years before. But "Pfui!" said Pemphredo, "Fool!" Enyo,
and Dino "Find it first!" So we coracled off in all directions,
the Graeae blindly paddling, I pondering, and Pegasus grazing back on shore.

"See it?" asked Pemphredo; "Sure he does!" Enyo; and
Dino, "Say something, silly!"

"I see it," I said. "But I won't dive for it till you tell me
where the nymphs are."

Alas, I was so banking on that desperate deceit I failed
to cloak my voice. "Tooth-thief!" Pemphredo cried at once;
"Eye-dropper!" Enyo added; and Dino, "Ditch him!" In a
jiffy they had me jettisoned; the air-waves were my medium,

not the sea-; I sank like a stone—and saw clearly, just before
I drowned, not my mere folly, but three eyes peering eerily
from the weedy bed, whereof one—useless miracle!—was
disembodied, the very Graeae's. Dropped from the high
point of my hubris, it winked now from the depths. I
clutched it, closed my own, and gave up hope, not knowing
my life was to be—

"Continued in the next installment," Calyxa put in. "Do
you remember now what happened then?"

"Three days ago," I said, "I'd've said I was fetched here
from my drowning in Two-D, if I'd remembered even that.
But One-E reminds me that I wasn't. Now answer me a
question: how far do these murals go?" For I'd seen, be-
latedly, how each in the second whorl echoed its counterpart
in the first, behind which it stood—yet no amount of examining the final panels in Series One called anything to mind
from my late mortality. Calyxa, however, declined reply:
I'd slept a night on *my* hypothesis; she demanded equal time.

And sleep she did, or feigned to, but I couldn't: like a
bard composing, who reviews each night his day's invention
in order to extend it on the morrow, I studied wide-eyed in
the dark my recollection of I-E (the acquisition of my gear
from the odorous nymphs) and imagined its correspondence
in next morning's scene.

We stood before it gravely, II-E, a relief as vast and
nearly empty as the desert and deserted shore it showed.
Owing to the spiral's grand proportion, the thirteen meters
of I-E were stretched to near two hundred; yet in all that
stadium but two things caught one's eye, even mine, who
had caught the Graeae's: Pegasus, winging off to the upper
left corner with Pemphredo astride his neck, grin-toothed
Enyo sidesaddle, and Dino leering backward over his

crupper; and, on the lakeshore far down right, myself looking mournfully up after, a drip-dry-hooded lady by my side.

"Same one as in the temple?" Calyxa asked. "Or a Styx-Nymph?"

I wondered how to tell her. "That's what *I* wondered when she rescued me," I said. "But don't forget our rule." We gazed awhile longer, until Calyxa let go my hand, said flat: "It was an easy picture to draw," and went back inside. I sneaked one preview over my shoulder of II-F-1, which quickened certain sluggish memories and dredged up others, then followed after, and found her not naveled on-center as usual, but briefed still and crosslegged on the couch, in her lap a gameboard.

"I'm bored with fucking," she announced. "Let's play chess."

"Are you jealous, Calyxa?"

"Whatever of?"

But she mated me in no time, four games straight, declaring frankly and frequently that I made stupid moves, rooking and queening me unmercifully until I put by board and pieces, bolstered her firmly by the shoulders, and ditto'd her. Dutifully she opened, but looked away the while, none of her usual frank inspection of our coupled parts. Therefore, perhaps, I did okay, if still briefly, even eliciting a minor moan of pleasure from her toward our pleasure's end. When we rolled, still a-clip, to rest sweating on our sides, she twirled a finger in my chest-hair and said, "I thought you said Styx-Nymphs stank."

"On the other hand," I retorted, "sea-nymphs douche with every stroke. You must remember how it was with Ammon, in the Nile?"

She apologized then for sulking and merely asked

whether, as she supposed, it was Medusa herself who'd salvaged me, and in whose embrace I would be stranded in the panel to come.

"That's putting it disagreeably."

Sorry—my words, not hers, but we know what she meant. No point in further false suspense; I told her it was, or turned out to be, the one I sought.

"All I knew at first was that she was a sea-nymph, that pair of green eyes down with the Graeae's gray. She must have beached and insufflated me; when I came to we were mouth to mouth under her cowl. I couldn't see a thing; when I opened my eyes she kept them covered with her hand till she'd moved off and veiled herself. Not a half-veil, mind, like some Joppa-girls wear, but a regular bag, with the hood over that."

"Hmp."

"When I thanked her, she reminded me I'd flouted Athene's orders, hence my dunking, and advised me to return the eye at once, unconditionally, to the Gray Ladies, by this time shoaled some way downshore. I did, beginning to wonder whether my lifeguard was perhaps amphibian, the same who'd briefed me in Athene's temple and bridled me in her court."

"Your horse-metaphor's ass-backward," Calyxa said dryly. "It's you who were in the saddle."

I was no poet, I reminded her; merely a man with a tale to tell. If I might get on with it? How, introducing myself to Pemphredo as Perseus, son of Zeus, I'd plunked the eye in her palm and pled to all three for triangulation; how, eyed, she'd eyed me, clapped for tooth from Dino, snarled "Nothing!" and taken off in a trice on Pegasus with her cronies, in the direction of Mount Atlas.

"So much for my sister's wisdom," I said to the hood-girl, excused myself, and waded into the lake, asking her please not to interrupt this time my drowning. No map no Styx-Nymph, no nymph no wallet, no wallet no Medusa, no Medusa no relief from calcifaction.

She waded behind. "Why do you want rejuvenating, Perseus? Do you really think you'll win back Andromeda?" I was in deep, couldn't think of a right reply. "Or is it simply to be able to do hero-work again?" "That too, mainly." "Then *wait!*" She clutched me by the tunic-top, now shoulder-deep.

"I wondered too," Calyxa said. "How can Being Perseus Again be your goal, when you have to be Perseus to reach it?"

I was twice fetched up, by the cowl-maid and Calyxa's question, which I'd not considered. I uncouched and considered her. "When you were mortal, Calyxa, did you write those seven letters?" Her lip-bite attested authorship; I could scarcely tell on, so many epistolary details came crowding on me. I repeated Athene's counsel, which the veiled one repeated to me: "Past a certain point sit tight, hang loose, stand fast, let things come." Don't fret about Pegasus, she advised me: Athene had recalled him for young Bellerophon, who was ready to commence now his own career. I should camp on the beach, at least for the night; since the Styx-girls were off the map and I seemed not to know where *I* was either, perhaps they were not far distant, might even come looking for me. She, at least, would return before morning to see; why not trust my nose for news and get some shut-eye?

I was certain then she was Athene's handmaid, the same I'd courted in Samos. I cloaked out on the shore and watched the stars wheel, not so many then as now, making stories from their silent signs and correspondences. The night was chill; I was stiffer than ever.

"Come on," Calyxa said: "she came."

"Right. It was a camper's wet-dream: she stole from the lake by starlight and slipped under my cloak, her own still sopping. She was all a-shiver; I helped her off with it, up to the cowl and veil, which she'd not remove. But I was right: I'd've known that body anywhere—"

"*Ample soft wide-hipped small-breasted* blah."

"You're being Andromeda," I chided Calyxa. "Sorry." "Don't apologize. She confessed she was the Styx-Nymph, her veil the kibisis, which she'd as leave keep on till morning if I didn't mind. We didn't get much done." "You said she was Stygian, I believe?" "Stop that. She was innocent, had had only one man before, Poseidon, he left his traces, never an orgasm." "*I* had orgasms long before I ever had a man." "She wasn't like you, for better and worse, but she was sweet, sweet, my lifesaver; I was grateful, she was impetuous and shy at once, I was flattered—but she *was* stiff with me, out of inexperience, and I limp with her . . ." "Out of practice." "You *did* write those letters! Anyhow, she was Athene's aide, I reminded myself, not Aphrodite's. I was eager to see her face, which she promised to unveil when the time was right; if her neck, which especially pleased me, was any indication . . ."

Calyxa sat up and requested a change of subject. She was past her pout, even teasy, but would not be touched by my retumescence, inspired as it was not altogether by herself. "We all know it was the New Medusa," she said. "Is that why she kept the bag over her head?"

"Don't be crude. Do I ask you what the point of Ammon's horns is, who put them on him?"

She turned sober. "I'm afraid of tomorrow, Perseus."

I was astounded, and explained that my Styx-Nymph, toward dawn, had said quite the same thing, which I'd explain in the morning. I comforted both: assured the sea-girl that I had more to fear than she, since without Pegasus to fly me to Hyperborean Medusa, the kibisis was useless; endeavored in Calyxa's case to change the subject to her Perseid letters, which could be said to be responsible for the narrative in hand, its source and omphalos. Had she died in Egyptian Chemmis—drowned while skindiving with Ammon in the Nile, perhaps, or been crocodiled in the deeps of love—and elevated posthumously? Or was her heavenhood a kind of prize for authorship, as Delphinus had been starred by Poseidon for his winning speeches? Speaking of Chemmis—

But she'd speak no more, only clung to me most close that night as Medusa, still mantled, was shown clinging to me on the beach in the morning's mural. II-F, like its counterpart, was septuple, but so grander in scale that its several panels were each broader than the broadest in the inner series and could be viewed only individually. I asked Calyxa whether, in Zeus's timetable, the whole of it might be seen that day, or we were obliged to give a week to its several panelets.

"Are you in such a hurry?"

"No no no," I assured her; "well, yes. For one thing I can't remember a thing after the week I spent with Medusa on Lake Triton, and I want to know exactly when and how I died. But what really interests me is the way this temple of mine is unfolding." What I meant, I explained when we returned to bed, was that given on the one hand my rate of exposition, as it were—one mural per day—and on the other the much rapider time-passage between the scenes themselves, we had in six days rehearsed my life from its gold-showered incept to the nearly last thing I remembered. It followed that soon—any day now, perhaps—the marmor history must arrive at the point of my death and overtake my present transfiguration. What was she drawing currently, I demanded of Calyxa, if not herself and me in spirate heaven, reviewing the very murals she was drawing?

After some pause she answered: "I'm not ready to answer that tonight." But she bid me consider two things: first, that, immortality being without end, one might infer that the temple was as well, from our couch unwinding infinitely through the heavens; on the other hand, it was to be observed that as the reliefs themselves grew longer, the time between their scenes grew shorter: from little I-B, for example (Dictys netting the tide-borne chest), to its neighbor I-C (my first visit to Samian Athene), was a pillared interval of nearly two decades; between their broad correspondents in the second series, as many more days; and from II-E to II-F-1, about the number of hours we ourselves had slept between beholdings. Mightn't it be, then, that like the *inward* turns of the spiral, my history would forever approach a present point but never reach it? Either way, it seemed to her, the story might be presumed to be endless.

"But it's all exposition! Where's the real-time drama? Where's the climax?"

Calyxa smiled seriously. "I think we'll come to it very soon. Together."

"Hmp."

You sound like her; please don't be critical. The evening was, I sensed: for one thing, Calyxa announced then, at first augustly, that next day, the ninth since the sun's entry into Leo, was the twenty-fifth anniversary of her birth and the twentieth of another red-letter day on the calendar of her life, which she'd tell me about tomorrow. By way of celebration, it being presently by her estimate an hour or so from midnight, she suggested we reverse our usual order and enjoy narration before copulation, so that she might arrive at the quarter-century mark in my arms. I was much touched—and troubled by another implication of her news—but I observed to her that the gloss on II-F-1 would be malapropos and anaphrodisiac in those circumstances, since, as she knew, that morning's scene had represented my tryst with Medusa. Should we not just skip it? Game of backgammon? Hour's nap?

"No," Calyxa said positively. "I'm okay now. I want to hear it."

"Okay, I guess she *is* okay. I'm still jealous, but I won't be critical any more."

Good. She *was* okay, certainly, that night, as I told the tale. I hope she's okay now. "It was in the morning," I told her, "Medusa told me she was Medusa. We'd tried again, not a whole lot better; she'd drawn up hind-to to me—please don't turn over—still wearing the kibisis alone, and bade me not turn her over till she'd told her tale. First came the story of her life, part of which she'd exposed to me in Samos: her pretty girlhood, Poseidon's rape, Athene's punishment, her ignorance of her Gorgonhood and mistaking me for her lover instead of her destroyer." Very difficult to tell this part, especially with you listening.

"But do, please. You owe it to me."

Very well: "Her eyes had been opened, she told me, by my sword at her neck, and her last sight had been her reflection in my shield—the same she'd set her hair by in Athene's temple. It so mortified her she was pleased to die; she knew

no more until Athene had scalped, rebodied, and revived her
—whereupon her first request was to redie at once if she was
Gorgon still. An odd thing was that, once brought back, she
could recall all her dead head's doings, and did so with mixed
feelings. To be perfectly frank, despite my having killed her
she still loved me, and had lived, during her death, for those
moments when I raised her by the hair and she withered my
enemies with a glance. This declaration moved me; I begged
her to unbag and let me kiss the pretty head—she *had* said it
was pretty?—I'd so ill-used to such good effect in its former
state.

"But she stayed my hand with a recital of the hard conditions of Athene's amnesty: first, should she ever again look
at her reflected image, she'd see a Gorgon, not a girl; second,
should she show her face to anyone, she'd instantly return
to Gorgonhood."

"That's not fair," Calyxa said. "For all she could tell—"

"Exactly. But there was one compensation and one
escape-clause. Athene granted her the power to juvenate or
depetrify, just once, whomever she gazed uncowled at or
whoever uncowled and gazed at her; but the conferral of
this boon on the beholder must be at her own cost, since by
the earlier stipulation she'd be reGorgoned."

"Ay," Calyxa said. "Your sister doesn't give anything
away free."

"She's not the goddess of justice. I asked Medusa what
the escape-clause was, but for a time she wouldn't say. I believe I mentioned she was shy; what I've told here in two
pages took me days to coax from her. Between confessions—
which I prompted by confiding my own troubles, at an exchange rate of seven to one—we strolled the beach, swam
and fished, talked about life in general."

"And made love," Calyxa said.

"And tried to make love. She was pleased enough; Poseidon, that time in the temple, had been rough on her; you know how gods are." "Yup." "Nobody'd ever done the forepleasures with her properly, or showed her what to do with herself . . ."

"I promise not to say anything critical," Calyxa said. "I kind of like Medusa now. But I thought most of those things were instinctive." "Nope." "Well . . . hadn't she *read* anything? You know."

"Reading was what she did most," I replied, "especially the old myths and legends; it was what we mainly talked about. However, as you may have noticed, myth isn't reality: it was agreeable to teach her how love is made, but her inexperience was as off-putting in its way as your expertise. What's more, I was naturally concerned over Athene's stipulations, as I learned them . . ."

"In short, you were impotent, like with me a few days ago." "Yes." "Not the whole time, I hope? I'm on Medusa's side now."

"Did she really say that, Perseus?"

She really did. "Just the first few times," I answered. "We got a bit better each night, just like us. It turned out she was afraid I wouldn't want her when I learned she'd been a Gorgon, and been raped by Poseidon, and given birth to Pegasus." "Hear me not saying anything?" "But I told her, honestly, that those things didn't bother me at all. The fact was—no other way to say it in a first-person narrative— Medusa really loved me, her first experience of that emotion, and I realized I hadn't been loved since the old days with Andromeda. What's more, she truly was a kindred spirit; we had jolly conversations . . ."

"Don't beat about the bush," Calyxa said. "Did you love her or not?"

I answered, forgive me, I was plagued by doubts about us both. "How could I be sure what was behind her veil?" I answered. "And wasn't it likely my attraction was mainly relief after all my troubles, or mere vanity at being loved?"

"What you *really* wanted," Calyxa said, "was to be twenty with Andromeda again. Can we get to the escape-clause?"

I was astounded by her insight. "That's what we got to, on the fifth night. We'd finally had a proper love-making; she'd learned to let herself go a little, even felt her first bit of orgasm; it was clear we'd be all right soon enough if we kept at it, just as *we'd* be; while we clung together in the dénouement, I declared I loved her and asked what Athene's last condition was, for I wanted very much to see the face that spoke in such a gentle voice and topped such a pretty neck, excuse me." Excuse me. "At last she got it out: if the man who uncowled her, and on whom she laid her one-shot grace, were her true lover, the two of them would turn age-less as the stars and be together forever. But since she hadn't known herself a Gorgon before, and couldn't view herself now, for all she or I could know she might be Gorgon still, and Athene's restoration a nasty trick. In short, whoever un-veiled and kissed her must do so open-eyed, prepared to risk petrifaction forever in a Gorgon's hug. 'I'm willing, Perseus,' she told me at the last, 'but *you'd* better think it over.'"

Calyxa shook her head. "I can't remember any analogues for that motif."

"I couldn't either. Next day she was quieter than usual, and that evening she told me very gently just what you said a while ago: in effect, that I loved her less than she me, and was still bound with half my heart to Andromeda. I wished then I'd had a kibisis for myself, to hide my shame; I swore I *did* love her, if anyone, as much as I could, not really knowing her and all—"

"O boy, Perseus."

"Yes, well. She wept a bit, near as I could tell; I was all cut up, yet at the same time stirred; lots of sex in this story: I touched her; she flowed at once, most womanly; I managed almost as well as with Andromeda. Medusa was in rapture; I don't say this out of vanity . . ."

"I know why you say it," Calyxa said. "But how about you, Perseus? Were you in rapture? I think about us, last night, on the very edge . . ."

I told her, what was true in the other case as well, I was still too preoccupied to feel rapture of the kind I'd been accustomed to with Andromeda in better days. Pleasure, yes, and some satisfaction, but as yet not rapture, quite, of the free transporting sort, nor would I likely, until we rose unfettered to the same high altitudes.

"If ever."

I shrugged. "In any case, Medusa came at last; there was the moment to discover her." "Yes."

"Yes."

Yes. "But I didn't, merely held her fast till I fell asleep. Next morning she was gone; I woke alone . . ."

"Perseus?" "Yes?" "It's after midnight. I'm twenty-five and scared. Will you make love to me?"

I did; she did; there *is* a surfeit of sex in the story; no help for it; we verged on much and didn't cross the verge. No more my merry priestess, Calyxa solemnly sat up and by the light of the altar-lamp watched me drip from her to the spiraled spread.

"I *like* my life," she said, as if addressing the little puddle. "I come and go as I please. It's a free, independent life. I wouldn't be tied down to any man. You and I don't really relate. I can't turn you on. We'd probably drive each other crazy if we stayed together. You're not in heaven, Perseus. Neither of us is."

One finger was permitted to touch her thigh. "Chemmis?"

She nodded.

"And alive, then." "Yes." "Pause. I wondered how it was you could have a birthday."

Pause. We both watched her flex to stop my flow from her, in vain for all her able musculature. "When you stopped here on your way to Joppa the first time, it was my fifth birthday," she said. "They let us out of summer kindergarten to see the gold-skinned flying hero who'd cut off the Gorgon's head. You only took a drink of water from the public fountain and flew off, but all through school we studied you and the other Greek heroes, along with Ammon and Sabazius and our native ones." She sat cross-legged on the spermy point, her tears running too. "I could stop this if I closed my eyes and legs," she declared, and didn't. "At first the town council put a little bronze plaque on the water fountain; Ammon and Sabazius were the local favorites. Later on, when I thought I might like to be a scholar, I wrote a thesis on the three of you: my heroes." She smiled, sniffed, fingered the pudlet. "In fact, that *was* my thesis: that since of the local heroes only Perseus was technically a hero, and a first-rank one at that, whereas the others were technically gods, but secondary ones, you were as deserving of a temple as they were. It was a stupid essay."

"I don't know."

She shook her head. "I can't do scholarship. Or write or draw or anything. I've got this great IQ and I can't do anything. I'd been working in Ammon's and Sabazius's temples to support my studies, and then Ammon screwed me, and I liked it, so I let Sabazius in too, and pretty soon I was in charge of all three temples. It's not bad work; I meet a lot of people; I just wonder sometimes if I'm *getting* anywhere that matters. The three of you are married; Ammon and Sabazius have loads of other girlfriends. In a way, I guess, you were my last hope; when Medusa brought you here, I couldn't help wishing . . ." Idly she flicked semen at the lamp-flame. Missed. "So it turns out even you've got a girl already."

"Not any more," I said. "Not even I." But I did, if I was alive, have a wife (I regarded her—young, naked, and lovely, chained to the cliff in I-F-3), to whom I'd better be getting back. "I *wondered* why Chemmis was the only scene missing. So tomorrow's mural—"

"Just the desert, as you'll see on your way out. But Perseus . . ." Suprisingly, for I thought her vexed, or self-sorrowing, or both, she slid over and put my head in her lap. "I might as well be the bastard who breaks the news: Andromeda's left you. For keeps."

I'd been enjoying close-up her lamplit navel. At this announcement my heart skipped as in poor poetry, and my eyes closed without my closing them.

"Medusa told me when she fetched you from the desert," Calyxa said. "Your wife's gone on to Joppa with Danaus."

I unlapped and found my missing voice. "I'll kill him."

But Calyxa observed, calmly, that killing Danaus would

change nothing; he meant no more to Andromeda than she
Calyxa me: a mere diversion, a refreshment. Andromeda
wanted rid of me, and that was that; if I examined my heart,
I must see that I was finished with her as well. Such things
happened. Wasn't that the case?
I spoke with difficulty, into her stomach. "I suppose."
Now my eyes were wet as well.
"Do you love Medusa?"
"I don't know."
Calyxa rubbed two fingertips in closing circles where
gold curls formerly grew. "If you wanted to stay on here . . .
I mean indefinitely . . . I'd like that."
We spent a sweet half-hour; then she slept imperiously
as a child while I tossed the night through, galed by emotions
sundry as the II-B winds. The image of Danaus abed with
Andromeda one moment made me retch and sweat with
rage; the next I was euphoric with relief to be at last un-
chained, free to be Perseus, starred or stoned as the issue
might prove, but my own man. Followed grief at the lost
past, my one young-manhood; then sympathy sharp as pain
for my Andromeda, mine no more—so fine and dainty in
the bed still (rerage at young Danaus! fresh fury!), un-
bearable as myself every other where. Toward dawn I went
round with the guttery lamp, reviewing for the last time the
first revolution of my story; lamp-oil, night, and heroic
youth ran out together; I came back to Calyxa, stroked her
out of dreams into drowsy liquefaction, here it comes again,
climbed with her to our first full fillment. She held my face
close for examination while we finished pulsing.
"I was sure you'd gone."
When I didn't answer she held fast yet a moment, blinked
once, then let go all and turned her face away.

"I may be back," I said. Further: "Thanks an awful lot, Calyxa. For *everything*." I might even have gone on to say, "I really mean it," had not a throat-lump spared her that final gaucherie. A tunic, prose-purple, hung in the passage behind I-A; I donned it, left my priestess leaking love, and tiptoed out, pausing just a moment at her final sketch (not yet graven), the second panelet of II-F. She'd blocked across it as on a billboard *PERSEUS LOVES*———, a slight inaccuracy. A few early tourists approached from the vast blank spaces which in time would be II-F-3 through 7 and II-G. Not having entered my story yet, they didn't recognize its hero; and I (I recognized an hour later, dhowing down the pea-green Nile) neglected in turn to notice whether any man among them looked deserving of its artful chronicler, and my gentle, cosmic jealousy.

"Do you still feel that way?"

I shall eternally; can't help it. Sorry.

"I didn't ask you to apologize."

I shall eternally; can't help it.   . "Joppa period," I told the boatman, who proposed a Memphis rest-stop and a tour of the river's seven mouths. On the beach at Pharos like a bearded beacon stood the Old Man of the Sea, but I had no need of navigation-aid: oriented, by falling-starlight I surely steered us east. Two-thirds of my tale was told, its whence and where; as to its whither, I knew only that I would once more and finally confront Andromeda: whether to kiss or kill, hello goodbye, her whomever, I'd know when I was II-F-3'd. Calyxa was behind; I assumed I was bereft of New Medusa too, despite her having yet again saved my life, since love and gratitude, in the clutch, had been kibisised by doubt. Don't say it, I'm not apologizing, I told myself it was just as

well: let my second tale be truly a second, not mere replica-
tion of my first; let a spell of monologue precede new
dialogue . . .

"Okay. I'll say no more."

Not till the epilogue; may its hour hasten. My scruffy
boatman, next morning when we landfell Joppa, pointed out
the cliff where fair Andromeda had been snacked for Cetus
till mighty Perseus et cetera. She wasn't fair, I corrected him.
One in every boatload, he rejoined, I having paid him in
advance for the night's sea-journey: had I been there, as he
had? To preserve my anonymity I let the seedy salt run on;
even when he described, in lewdest terms, my bride-to-be's
nakedness, to ogle which he claimed had been my motive for
going down, I didn't dagger him—only vowed to post Calyxa
this further hair-thing in my history, thitherto forgot: how
I'd thought Andromeda a marble statue till the sea breeze
stirred her hair. The seaman mistook my smile for smirk and
reported what he said was coastwise knowledge: that that
same Andromeda was currently whoring it in Joppa with a
new boyfriend; that one Galanthis, said to be Cassiopeia's
gigolo, was out to hump her as well; that the elder queen was
so smote with jealousy she'd hecatombed Ammon to send
another Cetus, which remonstration would permit her to re-
sacrifice her roundheel daughter; that—but that *that* was the
last he thatted: passivity be damned, I dirked and sharked
him, dhowed to port alone.

That day I prowled the town in hopes of reconnoiter,
hooded like my desert darling—till I recollected her advice,
near on to evening. I doffed my mantle then, went straight
to the palace gate, told the dusky guard I was King Perseus,
out of my way, strode into the court, where I sat on the

nearest bench to let come what would. Came, from behind the hedge behind me where old Cepheus grew his greens, his antique voice, I knew it.

"Good evening, good evening, I believe. I presume there's someone there? Eyes and ears aren't what they used to be . . ."

I went through the hedge. "It's I, old man." Much shrunk with years, Cepheus sat on the vegetable ground, not addressing me after all, but as it were the sprouts themselves, and went on as if I weren't beside him.

"Seems to me I've been here forever. I make a kind of circuit of our fields, I guess; rotate like my crops; after a while one's much like another. Pity, that. Caught me nap—"

I'd tapped his shoulder.

"I was about to say," he said, "you caught me napping, as one night Perseus will . . ."

"Sir, I *am* Perseus! Perseus?" My eyes welled up; his blanked on through me.

"But I wasn't really asleep, only drowsing. Old folks don't need much sleep; the night ahead keeps us awake. I, I'm always first one up, never really go to bed, prowl house and grounds the night through, napping and nibbling. O I fret about the wife and kids, national debt, salad garden; talk to myself, go round in circles . . ."

I squatted before him. "Old fellow, are you blind and deaf?"

"Excuse me," he said. I gripped his arm. "Used to be," he said, "I'd have a lackey do the introductions when I held an audience. No need now, I can start the story anywhere; it goes right along, you'll see, hangs together like a constellation if you know the stars, how to read them. My name's Cepheus—the Ethiopian king? My wife'll be along presently,

Cassiopeia; she's down washing her hair. Andromeda, too, Perseus, all the rest, they'll come by, you'll see them."

I moved my hand before his moveless eyes.

"To be king of Ethiopia, you know, it isn't easy; to be husband to a queen and father to a princess, that's harder yet; but to be father-in-law to a gold-haired conquering hero is hardest of all. Myself, all I ever craved was a quiet life: to mind the traffic, keep the books, pacify the gods, make a decent marriage for my daughter, tend my shrubbery, play with my grandchildren, leave Ethiopia no worse than I found it. Too long a list."

Except that her stonework never wept, I was fixed as by the first Medusa.

"But I never was a king," Cepheus said, "only consort to a queen. Cassiopeia, her majesty, that's the whole story; that's why we're all here, for better or worse. By heaven, she is beautiful! I can remember as if it were yesterday the first time—I forget. Andromeda? It was your mother! I forget." He frowned, seemed about to clear his head. "No, I remember, I remember! Zeus Ammon, it comes together!"

"You know where you are now, Cepheus?"

"Minding my business," he said, but in not just the right tone. "Out in the gardens, sure, late summer, grapes and tomatoes setting nicely, beans need another rain. I fret about Andromeda, why she and Perseus split up after all these years, what Cassiopeia's brewing." Now it was he took me by the shoulder, but blank as ever, confiding as if to a royal crony: "Children, I swear, you think you've got them settled at last and bang, home they come with a clutch of new grief. Not that I wasn't glad to see my girl, even with her new young man in tow—"

I groaned. "Where are they, Cepheus?"

"We've always got on, Andromeda and I, despite the Wife. I wish she'd brought the kiddies too, they'd like the beach this time of year. Don't forget, she's my only child: it left a hole in the house, I tell you, when Perseus fetched her off, happy as I was to see her saved. Just me and Cassiopeia then, in this big place. I don't know."

Hand on dagger I made to leave; but Cepheus held my robe for the moment it took to reinstruct myself in patience.

"It isn't the separation upsets me so," he declared.

"Oh?"

"They aren't kids any more; their kids aren't even kids; I keep forgetting. And often as Cassiopeia and I have wished we'd never met . . . Though even at the worst we've stuck together, marriage isn't what it used to be, youngsters nowadays. Faw! Andromeda's near forty, showing it too, eyelines mainly, all those worries, got that from me. It's like I told Perseus—"

"What'd you tell Perseus, Father?"

Again he frowned beside me. "You . . . you can't have two women in the same palace." "I believe it."

"So do I."

Love, please, we're a way from the epilogue. "That's what I told Perseus," Cepheus said, "right after the wedding. Taps me on the shoulder, wants to know how'd it all *really* start. I took him aside, put it to him straight: 'How does it always? Two women under one roof. Cass brags about her hair, natural curl, pretty as a goddess's, Andromeda's lucky to have it too, et cetera. Hundred times I'd told her: you got your natural curl, don't make waves. Sure enough, comes word from the oracle: Nereids in a pout, somebody's got to pay or it's Cetus forever—and you know, Perseus, place like

Joppa, once your fishery goes under, your whole economy goes.' Something like that."

I recalled the moment, sensed opportunity, quoted young Perseus: " 'Then how is it you cliffed Andromeda instead of your wife?' "

"There he had me," Cepheus replied. "All I could say was, 'It's a choice no man should ever have to make; anyhow, orders are orders.' But you put nothing over on Perseus, not in those days . . ."

I tried again. " 'Whose orders, Dad? Did Ammon speak to you personally, or did you take your wife's word for it?' "

Cepheus almost smiled. "Thank Zeus it was just then Phineus and company crashed the party! By the time they were stoned, you'd forgot what you'd been asking."

"I remember, I remember!" I resquatted, holding both his shoulders. "You do too, now?"

Cepheus shook his head ambiguously. "Twenty years later I'm still in a misery over it, weeding out my chickpeas and cursing myself for a coward, to let history repeat itself . . ."

"You never were a coward, Cepheus! I-F-5, the Battle in the Banquet Hall, remember?"

"No, by Zeus," he agreed, I hanging on his pronouns, "not quite a coward, just deadly henpecked, and there you are—"

"Perseus! This is Perseus!"

"Come to a man's fight, I always held my own." He let me help him to his feet; my own knees were scarcely less stiff. "I don't excuse myself," he said.

"Don't apologize! You know me now?"

"You can imagine how I felt when the time came, rambling in the bean hills, tapped once again, and there stands

Perseus, asking me what's Cass cooking up this time, and where's Andromeda, and what's she up to, as if twenty minutes had gone by instead of twenty years!"

I squeezed. "That's what I'm asking, Cepheus! Look at me!" His eyes were moving now, more like a frightened man's than a blind. I laughed and slapped my gut and pate. "See? It *has* been twenty years: I'm fortier than your daughter—stout and stiff, half turned to stone . . ."

Cepheus closed his eyes. "Perseus . . . stout, stiff, or ill . . ." He pursed a small smile. "Is Perseus still. Night air's bad for the arthritis. Let's go in, son."

Eyes cleared entirely, he confirmed as we limped palaceward that Andromeda and young Danaus were there shacked up; that Cassiopeia, furious at her own Galanthis's flirtations with her daughter, was nagging him Cepheus again with Ammon-oracles fishy as the first; that (what I hadn't heard before) it was she who'd set Phineus to disrupt my wedding, out of general jealousy.

I was stopped cold. "Why do you put up with her, Cepheus?"

He fingered an earlobe; glanced at me sidewise; declared he'd been of course long since distressed that he wasn't loved by the woman whose beauty he still so honored, but that he'd never reckoned himself especially lovable, and assumed it was not for no reason that women like his wife, who did not begin so, became what they became; concluded with a shrug: "You'll learn."

"I think not. Where's Andromeda?"

He chinned his beard at the house ahead. "In the banquet hall, waiting to say goodbye." By means he'd been unable to discover, he explained (certainly not his own intelligence department, always last to know anything, or the Royal

Ethiopian Post, which moved at sea-snail pace), reports of my arrival had preceded me to Joppa, caused general alarm in the palace, and brought on, he could only assume, his fearful trance. "But the reports were wrong; they said you'd lost ten years."

Wrong I replied was right: I'd lost twice ten, my wife as well, and felt ten older for the loss. We reached the banquet hall, Cepheus lagging some meters behind with vague complaints: damp ground, old bones. At the threshold I paused to let my eyes accommodate to the famous scene, I-F-5 in 3-D, an alabaster shambles. On the marble floor, in pools of marble blood, lay those done in before I'd fetched Medusa out to marble all: skewered Rhoetus, the first to die; Athis the mind-blown catamite pinned under Lycabas, the sickled Assyrian bugger; Phorbas and Amphimedon shishkabobbed on a single spear; granite Erytus, bonged by me to Hades with a sculptured drinking bowl; the sharp-tongued head of old Emathion, unaltered on the altar as if still hurling disembodied imprecations; Lampetides the minstrel, weddings and funerals a specialty, fingering forever on a limestone lyre the chord of his dying fall. Standing among these were those I'd rocked *in vivo:* Ampyx and Thescelus, cocked to spear me; false-mouthed Nileus; Aconteus my too-curious ally; and one hundred ninety-six others—chief among them Phineus, Andromeda's first-betrothed, whom I'd memorialized last in a posture of tunic-wetting terror to remind my wife how luckier she was to have me. Relocating him took some moments, in part because he was but one among so many, in part because—as I saw now when she smoothed her hair—the white-gowned woman standing before him, back turned meward, was not Exhibit 201 but live Andromeda.

"Nuisance to keep dusted, all this," Cepheus murmured behind me. I shushed him, not to miss the odd soliloquy my wife addressed to her uncle's statue:

"Poor Phineus. I'm as old as you are now, and Perseus is older. The man who stoned you's gone to seed; I'll soon go too; I don't scorn your last words to him any more." It was the cringer's seniority-over-merit plea she meant: that while I'd done more to deserve her, he'd known her longer. I considered wrath, but was touched instead by curiosity and complex jealousy: the timbre of her voice was so familiar I could not distinguish it for comparison with Medusa's, soft and throaty, or crisp Calyxa's; Cepheus perhaps was right about her harried face, but, dizzy at thought of Danaus, I remarked as I hadn't in years how slightly pregnancies and time had told on the rest of her—not much less trim than what I'd salvaged off the cliff.

"Trial enough," she went on to her skinflint uncle, "being life-partner to a Dream of Glory; but what a bad dream I woke up to! Thin-haired, paunchy, old before his time, dwelling in and on his past, less and less concerned with me and the family . . ." Her voice was hard-edged, a tone I winced from; now it softened. She touched the statue's averted cheek; had she ever touched mine so? "Thoughtful Phineus, gentle Phineus, weak-willed Phineus! With you I'd have been strong . . . and would have yearned, I guess, for somebody like—Perseus!"

Through this last she'd wept; my eyes stinging too, I'd drawn my dagger and called her name across the hall. At her cry it was as if the statues came to life, or shed live men from their dead encasements, and I saw too late the unnatural nature of her monologue: Danaus, armed and shielded, stepped from behind Phineus; half a dozen others in Seriphean garb from Astyages, Eryx, and the rest—and from a nearer door, a somewhat larger number of the palace guard, led by a rodent-faced young man and followed by grim-visaged Cassiopeia.

"O my," said Cepheus, "they've set a trap for you, Perseus. Sorry."

I moved to stick him as he to draw his antique sword, but was diverted by a fresher threat from Danaus, who roared upon me. Happy interruption! For Cepheus, in fact contrite, ordered the palace guard to kill my ambushers, except Cassiopeia and Andromeda. For a moment all were caught in the commands and countermands: Cassiopeia called on the guards to follow Galanthis in killing the lot of us, Andromeda and Cepheus included; Galanthis amended her directive with an order that Andromeda be spared; at the same time Danaus exhorted them to join the Seripheans in killing me, Galanthis, and their own king and queen, after which they themselves could govern Ethiopia by junta; Andromeda meanwhile screamed at everyone in general to kill no one, and at me in particular that she'd had no part in the conspiracy. Danaus's javelin whistled over my shoulder into the couch first speared by Phineus twenty years past, ending the suspension. Cepheus himself pulled it out and feebly hurled it at Galanthis; the gigolo side-stepped, a guard behind deflected it idly with his shield, and to all's surprise it punched into the Queen's décolletage. Dismayed, she sat down hard and died, drumming her heels upon the floor; Andromeda shrieked; Cepheus with a groan went at Galanthis, Danaus with a grin at me, the guards and Seripheans randomly at each other. Even shield-and-sworded I'd have had hard going, for I was out of practice, short of wind, and overweight; with Athene's mere dagger I had no chance

Danaus therefore took time to taunt: "Not a bad lay, old boy, your wife; plenty life in her yet; all she needed was reminding what beds are for."

I'd felt a moment of Phinean panic at my death to come, displaced next moment by red rage. But my helplessness itself gave me a third for self-collection. As Danaus jibed on— calling Danaë the mother of whoredom for having been first to spread her legs for coin, myself therefore the original whoreson and a paper drachma—I knew what I assumed would be my final satisfaction: that despite the inequity of our arms it was partly awe that hesitated him, inspired by the Perseus whose legend he'd cut his teeth on. My last chance to write a fit finale, however different in style, to that golden book came to me clear as Calyxa's art: declaring (what in another sense was true) that I preferred an even contest, I tossed away dagger and stalked him barehanded.

"Empty bravado," Danaus scoffed, and retreated one step. There was the only victory I could hope for, for (as I told him calmly above the din) we were born of one mother; mere inexperience of hero-murder delayed his hand. His pallor I knew was momentary; even as I spoke his color returned, his sword went up—"Ah, Andromeda (I can't say whether I said aloud or to my swoony self)! He *is* a fine lad, your lover; a young Perseus!" At this instant two things flew together from the free-for-all: a massive silver goblet, knocked from the altar-of-Emathion, spun to my feet; and Andromeda dashed between us to clutch her friend's knees. Shield? Stay? Embrace? Supplication? Frantic, Danaus pushed and shouted at her, slipped his helmet, got himself tangled and turned round. In moments fewer than these words I snatched up the great goblet, more welcome to my hand than its prototype beside long-smashed Erytus, and while my half-brother half-wept and swore at his handsome hobble, I fetched him such a clout aside his head that the goblet gonged.

As if at that bell, the fighting ceased. Danaus dropped dead. Stunned at my own salvation, I turned its instrument in my hand: of newer manufacture than the Erytus model, its reliefs depicted the earlier donnybrook in that same hall. Further, as though Calyxa herself had drawn the day, while distraught Andromeda lovingly cupped her late lad's head, I remarked that the wound she wept on, intaglio'd in his temple, was the image of his bowled foredropper. Now she stood, my wife, wild-eyed, to keen general grief: besides Cassiopeia and Danaus, all the Seripheans and sundry palace guards were slain—including Galanthis, whom Cepheus had had the satisfaction to dispatch and posthumously geld. Fresh flesh lay everywhere among the petrified. Slightly wounded, Cepheus wept by Cassiopeia's corpse; a guard tapped my shoulder and deferentially put himself and his surviving comrades at my orders: was it my pleasure that Cepheus and Andromeda be killed at once, or reserved for torture?

Before I could reply that they were on pain of flaying to obey henceforth no other than their ancient king, Cepheus entreated me to spare his daughter's life, but denied that any Ethiopian could take his, which was already flown to Hades with his black queen's shade. Fetching up Athene's dirk (scuffled himward as his cup had me-), he hilted it to heart, spat blood, rolled eyes, and died as he had lived, at Cassiopeia's feet. Andromeda wailed from her perished paramour dead-dadward, even washed with tears her hard mother's hair, root and follicle of our misfortunes. Then she rose above all, still regally herself, faced me from the fear-chased figure of chicken Phineus, and invited me to kill her as I had everything she prized.

"Sorry about your folks," I said. "Danaus too."

But she'd none of my apology: as I well knew, she declared, she hadn't loved my young half-brother, only consoled herself with him; it was I she'd loved—Perseus the man, not gold-skin hero or demigod—and wedded we, till I had by lack of heart-deep reciprocity murdered marriage and love alike. "You never *did* love me," she charged, "except as Mythics might mere mortals."

"She talks like you."

Two more pages? My soul winced from her words; the fact remained, however—*my* fact, felt first to the auricles in the heart of Calyxa's shrine—I *was*, ineluctably and for worse as much as better, one of the Zeusidae, a bloody mythic hero.

"You're free, Andromeda," I told her.

No thanks. "I've *always* been!" she cried. "Despite you! Even on the cliff I was free!" I couldn't follow her, let it go. Spear her or spare her, she declared, she wanted no more of me; would remain in Joppa if alive, fetch from Argos our younger children—

Unpleasant middle Perseus, who had dwelt stonily between the young Destroyer and the New-Medusa'd man, interrupted her to sneer, "And find another Phineus?"— his last words, as I put him to death promptly and forever on hearing me speak them. Therefore I didn't bother with apology when thereby Andromeda was inspired to perfect wrath. In the first place, she raged, her uncle had been a kind and tactful fellow, no doubt no hero, but a better man in other ways than myself; in the second, be me reminded I wasn't the only g-s'd hero in the book: she could if she chose most surely find another, even goldener; but (in the third place—and how her mother's regal eyes flashed in her face!) the last thing she cared to do was subject herself to another man, heroic or humble: no Cassiopeia she, all she wanted, in what years were left her, was to build as best she could a life of her own. What *I* craved, on the other hand, she dared say, was a votary, a mere adorer, not a fellow human; let me find one, then: the sea was shoaled with young girls on the make for established older men . . . "Like your girlfriend with the hood," she ended bitterly, pointing at the door behind me. "Do what you please; I've stopped caring; just leave me alone."

Till that last imperative she was in possession of herself; *alone* undid her: she threw her arms around Phineus's neck and salted his shoulder with fresh tears. My own flowed too, no want of eyewash in this episode. I unCepheus'd my dagger, considered which of us to kill. Motionless as her renditions on the walls of Chemmis, but in my tear-flood swimming as at my submarine first sight of her, gentle Medusa stood just beyond the threshold. Half the four chambers of my heart surged: one ventricle, perhaps, would stay forever vacant, like a dead child's chair, in memory of my mortal marriage and late young-manhood; one auricle, as yet unpledged, shilly-shallied on the verge of choice. If only she'd beckon, summon, relieve me of doubt, reach forth her hand! But of course she wouldn't, ever. For a pulseless moment I stood half-hearted in this transfixion, as if she were the simply baleful Old and not the paradoxic precious New Revised Medusa. Then (with this last, parenthetical, over-the-shoulder glance at Andromeda and my fond dream of rejuvenation: difficult dead once-darling, fare you well! Farewell! Farewell!) I chucked wise dagger, strode over sill, embraced eyes-shut the compound predications of commitment—hard choice! soft flesh!—slipped back mid-kiss her problematic cowl, opened eyes.

"Now may we talk?"

My heart: all night.

"The night's half done."

So was my life. *I.e.*:

"Okay. We've half a night ahead."

And ditto the next and next and next, till even our stars burn out. Half of each I'll unwind my tale to where it's ours, and half of every we'll talk. There's much to say.

"But much goes without saying."

And half of forever is forever. How long do you suppose we've been up here, love? Three nights? Three thousand years? Why do you imagine—

"You're asking all the questions. Shan't we take turns? I've seven."

I too. One:

"Least first. I love our story and the way it's told, but I wonder about one or two things. The alliteration, for example?"

No help for that; I'm high on letters. Look at II-F-2, my Saharan scribble, or the Perseid epistles posted between II-A and -B . . .

"*Basta.* One?"

We're not alone. Who else is here?

"Everyone who matters. No help for *that*, either. My eyes, you see . . . Athene's conditions . . . everyone I looked at in that last sentence turned to stars—except stone Phineus, who returned to flesh and blood. Don't ask me why."

I think I know, and thank you.

"Cepheus is overhead; he comes up first, talking to himself. Cassiopeia's with him; I put her a bit lower down . . ."

Good show. You needn't really have included my ex-in-laws, but I did like old Cepheus. I wonder whether he's repeating his monologue.

"Perhaps we all are. I thought you'd want the whole cast out. Even Cassiopeia has her bright spots, if you look for them. Pegasus is flying off upper-leftward—"

It's good you have custody.

"Perseus . . ."

I wonder what ours would have looked like. Not a question.

"I know. So. Andromeda's at his flank, just over my head, looking either at her father or at her mother's hair."

Above us . . .

"In chains again, too, but don't mistake my motives. She's on top only in the night's first half, and her chains are jewels —temples, nipples, loins, and shanks, if you want to know, where she *did* wear jewels when you first met her."

Ah.

"Don't be cross: those bonds she hated are what define her, from your story's point of view. I mean her immortal part, which can't be offended, whatever her mortal part might feel."

I'm not nettled; I thank you for the shining image, Medusa. What's her mortal part doing these days?

"You're out of turn. Cetus, finally, is below your left foot. Even she has a story, if one cared to tell it: it's a monstrous fate to be born beastly."

Now who's hung up on letters? Not a question.

"It's you I'm hung on. Shall I say how bright your stars are? N.Q."

Just *Delta Persei*, please. Its magnitude?

"That doesn't count."

Do answer, then. I haven't forgotten Calyxa's mistake in I-F-1. Who did the Chemmis stonework, by the way?

"If you want to make me happy, please forget both picture and artist. Her subject matter, anyhow, I remind you, came from me. As for the star you vulgarly inquire of: its magnitude is sufficient and fairly constant, you may take my word, as it stands directly in my line of sight all night long till the end of time. More than that you'd be in sorry taste to ask, since for all you know I may be with you from the neck up only."

Not even to be able to see you! Just from the corner of my eye I glimpse a twinkle now and then . . . You're not winking at someone out there?

"Really, Perseus, it *is* my turn! For your information— but I'm counting this, so I get to ask two in a row—my right eye, unlike your precious *Delta P.*, has a variable magnitude. If I'm winking at anyone, it's the whole wretched world down there, which I'm glad to be out of. Back to your story-telling now: much as I et cetera, isn't it just possible the style is too mannered?"

Excellent Medusa, sweet salvatrix: leave such questions. I don't mind sleeping with a critic now and then, but I wouldn't spend eternity with one. That's two. Three?

"*You're* the monster in this ménage! Do reflect, darling, that if the *Perseid* weren't my favorite fable I'd have starred us in a different one, with a more flattering role for me and a less for you. Now I *will* ask another literary question: that business just before the climax, where Andromeda flings herself between you and Danaus . . . You'll agree it's melodramatic?"

Heavens yes. In fact, from this perspective, a clumping *klitsch.* As is the whole story nowadays, I daresay. But that's

how it was, and at the time we were archetypes, not stereo
types; reality, not myth. Your own stonework, so realistic in
its day; I'll bet it's legendary now. So it goes.

"I yield."

And I pass, until you've done questioning my narrative
technique.

"I *do* have one more tiny one. The auricle-ventricle business at the story's climax? I'm not sure of that metaphor,
quite."

No more was I then of my heart.

"And now?"

Now it's my turn. Let's see. Why does Cassiopeia spend
half the night with her head in the ocean?

"If you could ask her, she'd say she's washing her hair;
Athene made me put her where she'd have to soak her head
now and then, to mollify the Nereids. Your heart's not in
that question."

Well. What ever happened to Cousin Bellerophon?

"That's another story. Look, I'm counting two half-
hearted questions as one whole. Do ask a real one; you've
only four left."

Calyxa?

"Must you, Perseus? No question."

Calyxa.

"It was brutal of you, darling! Brutal to jump from my
arms into hers, when I'd just rescued you; brutal again to
compare us in bed, as if my awkwardness were anything but
innocence, *loving* innocence, which you should have
treasured! Don't reply. And brutal finally to dwell on her
the way you did and do. Don't you think I have feelings?"

No question. I'm more or less contrite. But look here: in
the first instance, don't forget I thought I'd lost you . . .

"Your own fault."

Quite. In the second, although my friend Calyxa isn't at the heart of the story, it's her fate—her *immortal* part's fate—to spend eternity at its navel, where it and I both came to light. Have you done something dreadful with her?

"Sweetheart, you are a perfect prick!"

R.S.V.P.

"Only if you promise you'll never ask this question again for all eternity. One of the jewels, if you must know, in one of the manacles on one of Andromeda's wrists—make it her navel, you're such a fetishist—happens to be a spiral nebula, and that nebula happens to be your little friend. It also happens to be quite striking, I'm sorry to report, like fossil ammonite done in gold: in fact, a smasher. On the other hand, you may be sure I've seen to it she's simply oodles of light-years from us; out of our galaxy altogether."

Thank you, Medusa.

"Don't mention it. Now tell *me*, P.P.—"

"Prince Perseus?"

"A pretty presumption. How comes it to pass, sweet—what all this lit-crit's been building up to—that in a drama whose climax and dénouement consist ostensibly of your choice, however belated and three-quarter-hearted, of Yours Truly for eternity's second half, the two female leads are Andromeda and What's-Her-Name, that bit of fluff in your Egyptian omphalos? *That* strikes me as a weakness in your plotting, to say the least."

The less said the better: they're the ones I speak of; you're the one I chose.

"I withdraw all restrictions. Ask me anything."

How long *have* we been here, Medusa?

"Can't tell. What you're really asking me is—"

Yes. All this about mortal and immortal parts. Out there, in the world, are Andromeda and Phineus . . .

"Truly, Perseus, I don't know. And truly, do excuse me, that isn't our affair."

I withdraw the question.

"Sorry: you touched the piece. And my intuitions tell me you'd better ask your Number Seven before I my Six."

Beloved voice; sweet Medusa whom I cannot hold and couldn't see even when I could: not long since, you exhorted me to forget panel I-F-1 in a certain mural in some temple along the Nile, together with its first-draughtsman; but our arrangement here, whereof yourself are sole designer, suggests that that same scene may be still graved in your own imagination. What have you done to us? In what condition are we? Have you indulged yourself in a monstrous martyrdom to gratify what would be in me a perverse, unspeakable vanity? I retch, I gag at that idea! To see nothing; to feel nothing of you but your hair in my left hand! Why is it I look at empty space forever, a blank page, and not at the woman I love?

"Let me assume you mean myself . . ."

I'm not being clever, Medusa.

"No more am I. At that last moment in the banquet hall —it's not easy for me to say these words, Perseus—when you discovered me and kissed me open-eyed . . . what I saw reflected in your pupils was a Gorgon."

In the name of Athene, love, don't forget her conditions! Eyes are mirrors!

"I've forgotten nothing. Quite possibly it *was* a false reflection. Just as possibly your tricky sister never unGorgoned me at all . . ."

What an idea!

"I entertain it with deadly calm, let me assure you. But even assuming you'd abandoned your childish wish for rejuvenation—"

You know I had!

"—and granting a measure of vanity in my own wish— that you'd love me enough to throw everything overboard to have me . . ."

Please, please, please, please, please, please, please.

". . . it nonetheless remains a distinct and distinctly unpleasant third possibility that your kiss was in complete bad faith: an act not of love but of suicide, or a desperate impulse to immortality-by-petrifaction. In that event, I revealed my 'beauty' to the wrong man and *became* a Gorgon forever."

Pause. Hear how quietly, how calmly I reply. To give that unmentionable hypothesis one moment out of eternity, which is one more than it deserves: suppose it true. How would you feel?

"Sorry: your questions are all used up, and I haven't come to mine. When you opened your eyes, Perseus; when you saw me . . . what exactly did you see?"

My Medusa: I've thanked you for the pretty memory of Andromeda; for my own estellation; for all the selfless, supererogatory gifts you've showered on me, from bright Calyxa to a four-star likeness of my crescent blade. I even thank you for unstoning Phineus, and wish him and his companion well. Now listen and believe me, if there's any truth in words: it wasn't you who discovered your beauty to me, but I who finally unveiled it to myself. And what I saw, exactly, when I opened my eyes, were two things in instantaneous succession, reflected in yours: the first was a reasonably healthy, no-longer-heroic mortal with more than half his life behind him, less potent and less proud than he was at twenty but still vigorous after all, don't interrupt me, and grown too wise to wish his time turned back. The second, one second after, was the stars in your own eyes, reflected from mine and rereflected to infinity—stars of a quite miraculous, yes blinding love, which transfigured everything in view. Perhaps you find the image trite; I beg you not to say so.

"Pause. *Long* pause. I can't say anything."

You've one last question.

"It'll have to wait . . . I'm raining on half the zodiac . . . poor Cetus, swim again while you can . . ."

If *I* had one, I'd ask about your and my mortal parts.

"No use: those parts are private, like Andromeda's and Phineus's; not for publication. We didn't die down there at the climax, I can tell you that; simply we commenced our immortality here, where we talk together. Down there our mortal lives are living themselves out, or've long since done —together or apart, comic tragic, beautiful ugly. That's another story, another story; it can't be told to the characters in this."

So be it. Last question?

"Are you happy, Perseus, with the way this story ends?"

Infinite pause. My love, it's an epilogue, always ending, never ended, like (I don't apologize) II-G, which winds through universal space and time. My fate is to be able only to imagine boundless beauty from my experience of bound-less love—but I have a fair imagination to work with, and, to work from, one priceless piece of unimagined evidence: what I hold above *Beta Persei*, Medusa: not serpents, but lovely woman's hair. I'm content. So with this issue, our net estate: to have become, like the noted music of our tongue, these silent, visible signs; to *be* the tale I tell to those with eyes to see and understanding to interpret; to raise you up forever and know that our story will never be cut off, but nightly rehearsed as long as men and women read the stars . . . I'm content. Till tomorrow evening, love.

"Good night."

Good night. Good night.

Bellerophoniad

1

~~~~~~~~~

"Good night."
"Good night."
Some stories last longer than others. Now my wife's feelings were hurt, Philonoë's, and no wonder: for the occasion
she'd made ambrosia with her own hands, dismissed the
servants early, donned her best nightie; it should have been
one dessert after another. But Bellerophon, King of Lycia,
at sundown on the eve of his birthday found floating in the
marsh near his palace a Greek novella called *Perseid*, story

of his model hero; by the time he got to its last words he was forty and too tired.

Thus begins, so help me Muse, the tidewater tale of twin Bellerophon, mythic hero, cousin to constellated Perseus: how he flew and reflew Pegasus the winged horse; dealt double death to the three-part freak Chimera; twice loved, twice lost; twice aspired to, reached, and died to immortality —in short, how he rode the heroic cycle and was recycled. Loosed at last from mortal speech, he turned into written words: Bellerophonic letters afloat between two worlds, forever betraying, in combinations and recombinations, the man they forever represent.

"You never criticize," I go on to carp shortly at the bedroom ceiling, dark. "There's something wrong with a woman who never criticizes."

After a moment, pensive Philonoë beside me said: "Sometimes I criticize."

"No you don't. You're perfect; that's *your* trouble."

"My feelings are hurt, yes," Philonoë is represented here as having explained. "But there's no point in criticizing a person when he's obviously upset. Though *why* you're upset, I can't imagine."

"Upset upset. My life's a failure. I'm not a mythic hero. I never will be."

"You *are!*" Their dialogue conveys the general sense of our conversation, but neither establishes Philonoë's indomitable gentleness of spirit and body and her husband's punishing self-concern, nor achieves in proportion to its length enough simple exposition. Had I understood, when I consented at the end of this novella to be transformed by the seer Polyeidus into a version of Bellerophon's life, that I might be imperfectly, even ineptly narrated, I'd have cleaved to my original program: to fall from heaven into a thorn-bush, become a blind lame vatic figure, and float upon the marshy tide, reciting my history aloud, in my own voice, to Melanippe the Amazon—my moon, my muse, my final mortal love—as she ebbed and flooded me. And if Polyeidus the Seer had realized that his final and trickiest effort in the literary-metamorphosis way would be freckled and soiled with as it were self-criticism, he'd've let Bellerophon smack into the muck and bubble there forever, like Dante's Wrath-ful in the marshes of the Styx. Fenny father, old shape-shifter: here you are, then; even here. On with the story.

"It's perfectly obvious," Philonoë went on, her voice as gentle as her gentle body, whose beauty five-and-thirty years had scarcely scarred, "that Athene's still on your side. The Kingdom of Lycia is reasonably prosperous and politically stable despite our vexing military involvement with the Carians and their new alliance with the Solymians and Amazons. Our children are growing up satisfactorily, take it all in all—not like Proetus and Anteia's wayward daugh-ters. Your fame as a Chimeromach seems secure, judging by your fan mail; even the *Perseid*, I gather from the ex-cerpts you chose to read me, mentions you favorably a couple of times. Finally, our marriage (which, remember, is to me what your career as mythic hero is to you: my cardinal value and vindication, my raison d'être) is, if no longer fiery as Chimera's breath, affectionate, comfortable, and sexually steady, in the main. Certainly we've been spared the resent-ments that poisoned Perseus and Andromeda's relationship as they reached our age, and while we cannot be called innocent, surely we are rather experienced than guilty.

"Now, it may very well be that your most spectacular work is behind you—I've yet to read the *Perseid*, but what mythic hero isn't over the hill, as it were, by the time he's forty? However, it strikes me as at least as likely that your *best* work may not be your most spectacular, and that it may lie ahead, if not be actually in progress: I mean the orderly administration of your country, your family, and yourself over the long haul; the patient cultivation of understanding into wisdom; the accumulation of rich experience and its recycling in the form of enlightened policy, foreign, domestic, and personal—all those things, in brief, which make a man not merely celebrated, but great; not merely admired, but loved; et cetera."

I compare to this the rich prose of the *Perseid* and despair. Sleep with its author, then, if Melanippe's style won't do! No, no, my love, it's not your style; you merely set the words down as they come, or long since came: once-living creatures caught and fossiled in the clay; bones displaced by alien mineral, grown with crystals, hued with the oxides of old corrosion, heaved and worn and rearranged by the eons' ebb; shards; disjecta membra, from which the sleeping dragon is ever harder to infer. You said it. Anyhow I slept, and woke unhappy as before. As always, Philonoë ungrudgingly forgave—Melanippe is no Philonoë. I didn't mean to imply that she is—aroused and made love to me, then permitted me a post-coital nap while she prepared with her own hands a birthday breakfast: spinach pie and feta cheese. With this woman, Polyeidus wonders, the man was unhappy? He shouldn't wonder, Bellerophon believes (echoing for a moment, if lamely, the prancing rhythms and alliterations of the *Perseid*), as it was he who showed Bellerus as a boy the Pattern of Mythic Heroism, fourth quadrant of which calls for the mature hero's sudden and mysterious fall from the favor of gods and men; his departure, voluntary or otherwise, from the city of his own establishment; his mysterious apotheosis on a hilltop, symbolic counterpart of the place of his divine conception; et cetera.

Bellerophon is telling Polyeidus this? Whomever the buskin fits: Melanippe, too, perky priestess of his passions, shouldn't need reminding how the undauntable docility of the lady here featured as Philonoë, her absolute solicitude, her angelic, her invulnerable devotion—this is nauseating two-thirds of us—had long since made Bellerophon half-desperate, most particularly for the reason least appreciated by Philonoë herself in her reference to Andromeda, above. In a word, I was inescapably *content*— in my marriage, my children, my royal career—and because mythic heroes at that age and stage should become the opposite of content, my contentment made me wretched.

Pause. Melanippe the Amazon, let's say, is not at all sure she comprehends this sophistry. You were unhappy because you were happy?

The sophistry may be insufferable: the suffering was real. There was Perseus, risen from his misery and shining in the sky; here was Bellerophon, miserably content, holding his story in my hand.

For this you left your wife and family?

And my kingdom. And my empire. That's where my story starts, when I go wandering in the Aleïan marsh, "far from the paths of men, devouring my own soul," et cetera.

Wait while I write that plain: *wretched because nothing was wrong.*

Right.

Pause. It has been remarked that this state of spiritual affairs—the general malaise, I mean, not the specific etiology —is figured commonly in the myths by an objective correlative: one thinks of the miasma that hangs over Oedipus's Thebes, or Perseus's imagined petrifaction. Was there anything similar in Bellerophon's case?

I wonder how many voices are telling my tale. It seems to me that upon my first being transformed into the story of my life, at best a sorely qualified immortality, the narrative voice was clear and objective: in simple, disciplined prose it recounted my middle-aged distress, figured conveniently by Pegasus's inability to fly, voilà. Briefly it rehearsed my vain attempts to foment rebellion in my children over the question of which should succeed me to the Lycian throne; exasperation in my wife by endless repetitions of the tale of my youthful exploits, including my affair with her older sister Anteia; sedition in my subjects by continuing and escalating the unpopular Solymian war—my children were filially pious, my wife adored me, the silent majority of Lycians supported my administration. Beginning in the middle, on the eve of my fortieth birthday, this original or best *Bellerophoniad* proceeded with unostentatious skill to carry forward the present-time drama (my quest for literal immortality) while completing the plenteous exposition of my earlier adventures—a narrative difficulty resolved by the simple but inspired device of making the second half of my life recapitulate ironically the first, after the manner of the *Perseid*, but with the number five (i.e., threes and twos) rather than seven as the numerical basis of the structure, and a circle rather than a logarithmic spiral as its geometric motif. It commenced, moreover, with an echo not only of *Perseid*'s opening lines but of its dramatic construction as well: that is, not at the beginning of the hero's second series of adventures (Perseus's departure with cross Andromeda to revisit the scenes of his youthful triumphs in search of rejuvenation; cross Bellerophon's ditto with patient Philonoë in search of the magic herb hippomanes), but at their midpoint: Perseus, while always ultimately addressing the reader from heaven, tells most of his story immediately to his mistress Calyxa in Egypt; Bellerophon, it seems to me, while always ultimately addressing the reader from pages floating in the marshes of what has become Dorchester County, Maryland, U.S.A., used to begin by rehearsing his prior history to pretty Melanippe in the marshes of the river Thermodon, near Scythian Themiscyra. The narration was repeated daily and lasted all day: two tideslengths, to be exact, corresponding to the halves of my life and work. The First Flood, so to speak, covered my adventures from the death of my father and my brother, through the killing of the Chimera, to my marriage to Princess Philonoë—roughly, from my nineteenth through my twenty-seventh year; the First Ebb discovered my reign in Lycia and the establishment of my family, through my growing discontentment with my contentment, to Pegasus's inability to get off the ground, twenty-eighth through thirty-sixth year; the Second Flood covered my adventures from the time of my leaving Lycia to consult the Old Man of the Marsh (actually the prophet Polyeidus), through my travels in search of the horsenip herb hippomanes, to my idyll with Amazonian Melanippe, thirty-seventh through forty-fifth year; the Second Ebb discovered my attempted flight to Olympus, through my long free-fall from Pegasus, to the end of my chronological life, forty-sixth through fifty-fourth year. The thirty-six-year period, divided into eighteen-year cycles and nine-year quarters, was a compromise as I remember between the Polyeidic "solar" life-calendar, a seventy-two-year span based on a three-hundred-sixty-day year of twelve thirty-day months, and the Melanippic or Amazonian "lunar" life-calendar, based on four quarters of approximately fourteen years each (though Amazons do not acknowledge annual units), metaphorically correspondent to the phases of the moon and the four stages of female sexuality (birth to puberty, puberty to sexual maturity, sexual maturity to menopause, menopause to death—the life expectancy of Amazons, reckoned in Polyeidic terms, is fifty-six "years"; they begin menstruating at age "fourteen," on the average, and cease about age "forty-two"). It was, finally, a distinguishing feature of this ideal *Bellerophoniad* that while the length and periodicity of the narration were constant, the amplitude of the narrative varied like the range of the tides with the narrator's energy, itself a function of his concentration or distraction. Yes, yes, the tale was told to its fullest heights and depths twice per lunar month, when the pulls so to speak of Polyeidus and Melanippe were perfectly aligned; at the summer-solstitial full moon in particular, I recollect, my tale achieved a pitch of eloquence—a phenomenon no doubt to be accounted for by the latitude and longitude of tidewater Maryland. Contrariwise, twice each month the narration was unusually flat and shallow, especially in the neighborhood of the equinoxes—and distracted, as though the pure Bellerophonic voice were tugged and co-opted now by Polyeidus this way, now Melanippe that; not to the end of dramatic harmony and tension, but discordantly, to stalemate and stagnation.

In posing the question, I now observe, I or someone has answered it. Full knowledge of the five tidal "constants" (geographic location, mean water-depth, configuration of shoreline, speed of Earth-rotation, friction of sea-bottom), the four periodic variables (relative positions of Sun and

Moon to each other and to Earth, their respective distances from Earth, inclination of the lunar orbit to the Equator), and the three non-periodic variables (wind force, wind direction, barometric pressure) would doubtless afford a complete understanding of *Bellerophoniad*'s narrative processes —but such comprehension, difficult to acquire, is impossible to crave. All I sense is the current neapness! If Bellerophon might rebegin, unclogged, unsilted! Time and tide, however, et cetera.

For God's sake, Melanippe, put this down: *The winged horse won't fly!* Would not, wouldn't! Vehicle of my glory, from whose high back I bombed Solymian and Amazon alike, in better days, from Bronze Age back to Stone, sank the Carian pirates, did to death the unimaginable Chimera —Pegasus can't get off the ground! Could not, couldn't! Turned out to pasture since his master's marriage, fat and tame now, my sweet half-brother in time grew loath even to lift his moonshaped hooves, much less strike wellsprings with them for the Muses. Twenty years it had been my custom every morning, after breakfast, to take down from its place of honor over my throne the golden Bridle of Restraint, Athene's gift (Perseid reliefs, Series II, Panel 3), without which none can mount the steed sired by Poseidon on Medusa and foaled when Perseus beheaded her. My wife I'd perch athwart my pommel, and we'd make a high circuit of the empire, cheered by all we overlooked. Now, the *Perseid* under my belt, I burped to the paddock and was by lackeys boosted into place; applied the heel, laid on the crop; clucked and chucked and urged and whistled: the beast no longer giddyapped, much less went vaulting starward; only grazed in circles, trailing horsefeathers where his wings like doused sails dragged by the board.

This *Perseid* is that heavy? No, no, love, it's I was heavy, drag-hoofed as this telling of my tale. *Perseid* takes off like its hero. Hum. Did Bellerophon's grounding happen all at once or gradually, over the years of his marriage? You know the story. I wish I were dead.

Melanippe, as she is here called, being an Amazon, is not conversant with the niceties either of marriage or of narrative construction. In her position as Bellerophon's lover and alleged chronicler, however, she makes the following suggestion: the "present" action of this part of the story (you used the term "First Ebb," I believe), must cover your attempts to deteriorate three separate relations—with your late children, your late wife, and your late subjects—and at the same time accomplish, at least in a preliminary way, as much as possible of the earlier, "First Flood" exposition: the story of your former life. Then why not attempt to alienate your children with anecdotes of your own childhood, your wife with the Anteia episode, the citizenry with boring accounts of your later adventures? Isn't that the way you said it's done in that mythical "ideal" *Bellerophoniad?* Correlate these internal narratives and Pegasus's descending altitude, with an eye to ending the First Flood at the "climax" of the First Ebb: i.e., the morning you couldn't get Peg up at all and struck out for the swamp. At the same time, since First Flood, First Ebb, and Second Flood themselves comprise an internal narrative framed by our affair here on the Thermodon, punctuate them wherever convenient with conversation between Bellerophon and Melanippe, giving if possible a degree of dramatic development to our tidewater idyll. That is, unless *drama* and *development* on the one hand, *idyll* and *immortality* on the other, are not irreconcilable sets of notions. What do you think?

I think I'm dead. I think I'm spooked. I'm full of voices, all mine, none me; I can't keep straight who's speaking, as I used to. It's not my wish to be obscure or difficult; I'd hoped at least to entertain, if not inspire. But put it that one has had visions of an order complex unto madness: Now and again, like mazy marshways glimpsed from Pegasus at top-flight, the design is clear: one sees how the waters flow and why; what freight they bear and whither. Between, one's swamped; the craft goes on, but its way seems arbitrary, seems insane.

There, love: you flew. With Philonoë and the children? Yes, yes. Yes, yes, yes. From the time our first was born he flew too, nestled in his mother's breast as she in mine, and so loved the ride that to my discomfort she named him *Hippolochus:* "dropped from a mare." Soon little Isander took his place; sturdy Hippolochus hung on astern. Came Laodamia, gentle as her mom: the ladies rode before, the boys behind, never once squabbling which should sit next after me, and the royal family daily went sky-high.

But not.

But not so high as formerly, or far, or fast. For this Philonoë thanked me on the children's behalf and hers, thinking I reined us in on their account; at the same time she grounded herself thenceforward, lest the late infrequency of our flights beyond the Lycian border be a cause of the rumored new alliance between the Carians and Solymians, our ancient enemies. But even without her, though his range and altitude increased, Pegasus never quite regained his former heights; as the children grew, we found ourselves down again to the olive-tops. Not to buzz and turd my subjects into disaffection, I bumped in turn Hippolochus, Isander, and Laodamia, each time reclimbing to a lower peak, like waves on a foreshore as the tide runs out. I watched the new constellations wheel far over my head—Perseus, Medusa, Andromeda, Cepheus, Cassiopeia—and turned sour.

"It is remarkable," I'd remark to Philonoë in the royal boudoir, as she kindly tried to rouse me, "what a toll pregnancy takes on teeth and muscle tone." Her hand would pause—Melanippe's does, too—for just a moment. Then she'd agree, cheerfully adding varicosity, slacked breast and vaginal sphincter, striation of buttock and thigh, and loss of hair-sheen to the list of her biological expenses in the childbearing way—all which she counted as nothing, since for three such princelets she'd've died thrice over. But as I was at it I should add, she'd add, the psychological cost of parentage, to ourselves individually and to the marital relationship: fatigue, loss of spontaneity, diminishment of ardor, general heaviness—a kind of accelerated aging, the joint effect of passing years, increased responsibility, and accumulated familiarity—never altogether compensated for by deeper intimacy. For her part (she would go on—what a wife this was!), she took what she was pleased to term the Tragic View of Marriage and Parenthood: reckoning together their joys and griefs must inevitably show a net loss, if only because like life itself their attrition was constant and their term mortal. But one had only different ways of losing, and to eschew matrimony and childrearing for the delights of less serious relations was in her judgment to sustain a net loss even more considerable. Nor, mind, did she regard this perspective (which she applied as well to everything from vacation trips to historical movements) as spiritually negative or bleak: to affirm it was to affirm the antinomy of the cosmos, which antinomy she took to be not absurd contradiction but rich paradox, the pity and terror of the affirmation whereof effected in the human soul an ennobling catharsis. I can do it. Assuredly I can do it. That I can do it, I cannot doubt. That I cannot do it; that I can begin to imagine that I cannot do it; that I can begin to wonder whether perhaps after all I cannot do it; that I can begin to begin firmly to believe that I cannot do it; I cannot begin to imagine, I cannot begin to wonder, I cannot begin to begin. Beyond question I can do it. Can I do it? I cannot do it.

Do it.

Pegasus and I flew lower. "You are descended," I told the children on Hippolochus's thirteenth birthday, "from a line of half-breed horse traders reaching back through Sisyphus and Autolycus to the shifty centaurs."

They sat round-eyed; tutors and governesses fled to summon Philonoë, who entered with her knitting and watched their faces as I spoke, but neither protested nor interrupted.

"Your Grandmother Eurymede was a leading member of the Corinthian wild-mare cult," I declared to them. "She claimed that Poseidon the sea-horse-god had humped her stallionwise one night as she was skinnydipping in the surf during her organization's annual harvest-moon orgy. But Dad—your Grandpa Glaucus?—accused her of adultery with the stable-master, if not with one of the stallions themselves, and after dragging the former to death behind his racing chariot, he banished male grooms and stonehorses from our spread."

Hippolochus cried "Hooray!" Isander asked to be given, on *his* thirteenth birthday, a pony. Laodamia climbed into my lap and sucked her thumb. Out in the paddock Pegasus whinnied. Philonoë purled.

"Horses remain a conspicuous motif in my biography," I guess I said, "beginning with the circumstances of my birth

Assuming Poseidon to be my father, I've a deal of actual horse-blood in my veins, and you in yours. Insofar as we're human, the equine traits may be regarded as recessive, but the chance that one of you may foal a centaur or sire a literal colt, while admittedly small, had as well be acknowledged. My interest in the subject of heredity, which needs no further explanation, has led me to sponsor research in this area, certain findings of which I'll impart to each of you on your wedding day."

Laodamia asked where babies come from. Isander decided to have two each of sons, daughters, trotters, pacers. Hippolochus, displeased with his adolescent appearance, hoped he could make use of my research to give his own offspring black manes and tails instead of bay. Philonoë smiled and said, "Bay is beautiful." What I'm experiencing cannot be called an identity-crisis. In order to experience an identity-crisis, one must first have enjoyed some sense of identity. The tradition of the mad genius in literature. The tradition of the double in literature. The tradition of the story within the story, the tradition of the mad editor of the text, the tradition of the unreliable narrator. "I come now," how beautifully all this is managed in the *Perseid*, "to the twin-business, how I more or less killed my father and my brother." Polyeidus, old charlatan, this is your best? No answer. But I know you're here between the lines, among the letters' curls and crooks, spreading through me like the water through this marsh. Thank heaven I get to swat you at my peak!

"Bellerus and Deliades," I'm saying to the children, back in Lycia; "Deliades and Bellerus. From the day we were born, the country quarreled over which of us should succeed to the throne of Corinth, and my brother and I quarreled over it ourselves, for fun and profit, just as you boys will when you drive me out of town."

O Bellerophon! "Bellerus it was then, and do stop bawling." All of you. "Twins we were; twin brothers; look-alikes
and inner opposites; and Polyeidus was our tutor. Bellerus
from toddlerhood passionate, impetuous, Aphrodite's ardent
darling; Deliades circumspect, prudential, in all things moderate, a venerator of Athene. And Polyeidus was our tutor.
Everyone thought Deliades legitimate, as he shared the
famous gray-green eyes of Glaucus and his forebears; but
my earliest memory is of Mom and Dad squabbling in the
next bedroom over me, whether I was Poseidon's son or the
horse-groom's: a bastard to be exposed on the hillside or
a demigod destined for the stars."

Melanippe herself, though she loves her lover and is held
to be recording his history faithfully, can be of two minds on
this point when she hears him speaking to his children so. Yes,
well, even Bellerus had his doubts; but though we teased and
contested which was heir apparent, Deliades alone never
questioned which was mortal: I liked the kid well enough;
he worshipped me.

"*And Polyeidus was your tutor*," the children chorused.
I'm sending them supperless to bed: Isander has announced
that he hates this story because its words are too big and it
lasts too long. Hippolochus has kissed him and promised to
repeat it all in little words at naptime. My curly darling
Laodamia sleeps in my lap; Philonoë deftly replaces the
thumb with a pacifier. Dead now, all of them: dead and dead
and dead! Then do let them stay up awhile, Bellerophon, to
hear the Polyeidus part.

"Our tutor he became, Polyeidus, Polyeidus, after being
prophet laureate to the court of Corinth. Though featured
in several other myths, on the strength of which Dad had
hired him, he declared to us he had no memory of his pre-
Corinthian past, or any youth. Some said he'd been Proteus's

apprentice, others that he was some stranded version of The Old Man of the Sea himself. At such stories Polyeidus shrugged, saying only that all shape-shifters are revisions of tricky Proteus. But he dismissed the conventional Protean transformations—into animals, plants, and such—as mere vaudeville entertainment, and would never oblige us with a gryphon or a unicorn, say, howevermuch we pled, or stoop to such homely predictions as next day's weather. For this reason, among others, he was demoted to tutor; and he urged upon us, even as boys, a severer view of magic. By no means, he used to insist, did magicians necessarily understand their art, though experience had led him to a couple of general observations on it. For example, that each time he learned something new about his powers, those powers diminished, anyhow altered. Also, that what he "turned into" on those occasions when he transformed was not altogether within his governance. Under certain circumstances he would frown, give a kind of grunt, and turn into something, which might or might not resemble what if anything he'd had in mind. Sometimes his magic failed him when he called upon it; other times it seized him when he had no use for it; and the same was true of his prophesying. 'It will be alleged that Napoleon died on St. Helena in 1821,' he would announce, with no more notion than we of the man and place and date he meant, or the significance of the news; 'in fact he escaped to the Eastern Shore of Maryland, to establish his base for the Second Revolution.' Most disappointingly to Deliades and me, his transformations were generally into what he came to call 'historical personages from the future': this same Napoleon, for example, or Captain John Smith of the American plantation of Virginia: useless to our education. But no sooner did he see this pattern than he lost the capacity, and

changed thenceforward only into documents, mainly episto-
lary: Napoleon's imaginary letter from King Theodore to
Sir Robert Walpole, composed after the Emperor's sur-
render; Plato's Seventh Letter; the letter from Denmark to
England which Hamlet transferred to Rosencrantz and
Guildenstern; the Isidorian Decretals; the *Protocols of the
Elders of Zion;* Madame de Staël's *Lettres sur Jean-Jacques
Rousseau;* the 'Henry Letters' purchased for $50,000 by
President Madison's administration from the impostor
Compte de Crillon in 1811 to promote the War of 1812; the
letter from Vice Admiral Sir Alexander Cochrane, commander of the British fleet at Halifax, to that same president,
warning that unless reparations were made for the Americans' destruction of Newark and St. Davids in Canada, the
British would retaliate by burning Washington—a letter
said to be either antedated or intentionally delayed, as it
reached its address when the capital was in ashes; the false
letter describing mass movements of Indian and Canadian
forces against Detroit, planted by the Canadian General
Brock so that the U.S. General Hull would discover it, panic,
and surrender the city; a similar letter dated September 11,
1813, which purported to be from Colonel Fossett of Ver-
mont to General MacComb, advising him of massive reinforcements on the way to aid him against the Canadian General Prévost in the Battle of Plattsburg: it was entrusted to
an Irishwoman of Cumberland Head whom the U.S. Secret
Service, its actual author, knew to be loyal to the British;
Prévost, when she dutifully turned it over to him, took it to
be authentic and retreated into Canada, though no such
reinforcements existed. Et cetera. Doctored letters. My
brother and I were not very interested."

"Kill Granddad and Uncle Deliades, Daddy," Isander

begged. His brother shushed him. All dead now, and sent supperless to bed. Hippolochus giddyaps happily upstairs on a fancied flying-horse to do battle with imaginary dragons, declaring to Isander, who gallops beside, that what might seem to be arbitrary and excessive punishment is in fact the stern discipline of mythic herohood, to which I am as lovingly apprenticing them as did Polyeidus me. So their mother has explained to him. Dead.

I want sons, Bellerophon. I want my belly full. Don't withdraw. I'm tired of Amazoning.

A novel in the form of artificial fragments. A novel in diary form, in epistolary form, in notebook form, in the form of notes; a novel in the form of annotated text; a novel in the form of miscellaneous documents, a novel in the form of the novel. The tradition that no one who believes himself to be losing his mind is losing his mind. The tradition that people who speak much of committing suicide are talking themselves out of committing suicide, or is it into committing suicide. Kill Glaucus and Deliades.

"Our apprenticeship in herohood was real enough—all at Deliades's instigation, for Bellerus never took it seriously. My brother drew Polyeidus out upon the subject, from love of me, never presuming to the role himself." My dead son's candles gutter in the uncut cake; I sit in the palace dark; my wife clicks serenely on; I don't know who my audience is.

" 'Hurrah!' cried Deliades—the Corinthian equivalent of our *hooray*—after one of Polyeidus's lectures: 'We don't have to hate Daddy any more!' Using, as usual, Cousin Perseus as his example, Polyeidus had enounced the first several requisites and features of the heroic *vita:* that the circumstances of conception be unusual; that the child be born to royal parents but be alleged to be the son of a god;

that an attempt be made on his boyish life by either his maternal grandfather or his mother's spouse; et cetera. To Deliades, ever a peacemaker, this explained and excused Glaucus's jealous quarrels with Eurymede, which, as my brother loved us all, had been particularly painful for him to overhear.

" 'You merely have to fear him,' Polyeidus replied, 'your mother's father being already among the shades. At least Bellerus does, if we assume he's Poseidon's son.' I remember replying with a merry shrug that I feared no one. We were young men; Deliades was comely in a mortal way, but Bellerus, standing on the Isthmian strand, his copper curls lit by the descending sun—divine!

" 'We needn't fear him either,' Deliades maintained: 'You said yourself that the attempted murder never does more than leave a mark, usually on the hero's thigh or foot, by which he'll be recognized later in the cycle—and Perseus seems to've managed without even that. All we have to worry about is that Dad himself will get killed accidentally when the thing backfires'—as had been the would-be ancestral assassins of Perseus, Oedipus, and countless other heroes, some not to be born for generations yet, with whose biographies Polyeidus documented his point.

"Our tutor smiled. How describe a man who from semester to semester seldom resembled himself? That season, I believe, he was bald, shag-chinned, ill-odored, goatish; season before he'd been leonine; season to come—we'll come to that. He pointed out that to satisfy the prerequisites of herohood was not necessarily to be a hero; for every young Perseus or Moses boxed and shipped and rescued, scores of candidates must expire in their floating coffins, a menace to navigation and pollutant of the littoral. I hadn't *proved* I was the sea-god's son; Glaucus's attempt on my life might be successful. If it weren't, and I was a hero after all, the mythographical odds against *his* survival were great indeed: but he might, like Danaë's father Acrisius, live a long and useful life before retribution overtook him. For that matter, there was just a chance that the filicidal episode would be purely symbolic, a moment of peril in the company of my progenitor but not at his hands: young Odysseus's accidental goring by the boar while hunting with his Grandfather Autolycus would be a case in point when it came to pass. All the same, he said, one in my position did well to be wary—as did one in Glaucus's—especially as the attempt must be expected quite soon. We were well past puberty; actuarially speaking, it was overdue already.

" 'Tell us how it's going to turn out!' Deliades demanded, as would have little Isander had he heard this far. He would if he could, Polyeidus replied, but concentrate as he might, all he came up with were the images of two odd beasts: a lovely white winged stallion who had just that moment been born into the world, and a vague monstrosity in three parts, obscured from clearer view by the smoke of its own respiration. What these had to do with me and Glaucus, he couldn't say.

"Curling my lovely lip—how well I see me!—I said, 'A stallion would *have* to have wings to get into our stables!' Where, remember, there had been none since my conception —a policy I opposed as contrary to nature and conducive to nervousness in the mares. Deliades, as fond of horses as myself, was enchanted with the notion of a winged one; he wished Dad had it for the chariot events in the Argonauts' Funeral Stakes, to be run that night. Here I make a three-part digression . . ."

Over my dead body. Yes. We're *in* a three-part digression already, sinking in exposition as in quickmire! The Deterioration of the Literary Unit: yes, well, things are deteriorating right enough, deteriorating; everything is deteriorated; deterioration everywhere. God knows *I'm* not what I used to be; no help for that. But never for want of words! Too much to say, that's *my* complaint: everything to get said, and all at once or I'll forget it. Already I've forgotten half what I'd in mind to write; pen can't keep up; I make mad side-notes, notes of notes for notes; each phrase begets two more, four; I can't sleep for them; my joints are stiff; it's cold and damp here; this moment I should be lying with my warm young friend; instead it's scribble scribble the night through, red-eyed, dizzy: fine shape I'll be in at tide-turn, when the long ebb ends! What was I saying? There, gone. Digression from digression will not lead to the main stream; it's the wrong way out of the swamp. "Float with the tide," I'm told. By whom? My mistress? Monstrous. I know who sticks in my throat.

"The Corinthian succession," I press on: "Over that we teasily disputed, Bellerus and Deliades, mocking the arguments of the *polis*. Deliades had been born first, by an hour or so, but as we were twins, primogeniture struck most people as a technicality. The issue more often hassled in the Corinthian bars and byways was the issue of legitimacy. No one denied that we had different fathers, whether because they accepted it that all twins do, or because our demeanors were dissimilar, or because the royal quarrels on that point were common gossip. What one might call the conservative position was that since Glaucus was King of Corinth, his legitimate son was his legitimate heir, regardless of who had been born first; on this view, the only question was which of us was legitimate, and as was established pages ago, nearly

all inclined to Deliades by reason of his verdigris eyes. The more radical position was that if one of us had been sired by Poseidon, biological legitimacy and primogeniture were both superseded, or should be, and the proper problem was how to determine which if either of us was a demigod. Here the larger following was mine, though as the Glaucus–Deliades faction was fond of pointing out, popularity is not proof. Moreover, what was true in most such cases (Heracles and Iphicles, for instance)—that one twin was immortal and the other not—was not true in all; both might be either; therefore the experiment proposed in jest by Polyeidus and taken up seriously by others, of throwing us both into the Gulf of Corinth, say, and seeing who survived, was opposed as inconclusive as well as repugnant, since at best it would kill the King's legitimate son, and at worst terminate the dynasty without settling the dispute.

"These positions were fueled and complicated by political, historical, even logical considerations: the mare-cult itself, for example, was held to be a survival from a bygone matriarchal era, dating from the days before men realized that copulation, rather than magic, was the cause of pregnancy. The more militant votaries of the cult denied that even Glaucus had been the rightful king, and urged Eurymede to a coup d'état. Few favored an outright duumvirate of twins, but several groups called for joint rule by annual alternation, citing various actual and mythical precedents, as a peaceful resolution of the question. Even such apparently irrational expedients as the toss of a coin were seriously put forward: since only the gods knew whether one of us was a demigod and if so which, let the gods decide who should rule Corinth, et cetera.

"These arguments grew more heated every year, and

more inextricable from political power-alignments. Glaucus, though he took no open measures against me and made every show of treating us equally, could not conceal his jealousy and alarm, especially after Polyeidus, pressed, admitted the risks involved in 'fathering' a demigod. Eurymede, for her part, loved both her sons and took no stand on the issue of succession; even in the matter of my paternity she was shrug-shouldered by comparison to Deliades. But on one point she brooked no question: that it was Poseidon and no other who had climbed her in the surf.

" 'A woman knows,' she would say firmly, and Glaucus tear his hair.

"On our thirteenth birthday"—shades of my sons, forgive me!—"asked by our parents what we wanted in the present-way, I requested the usual hunting gear, racing mares, new tunics; Deliades, secretly coached by Polyeidus, surprised the court by demanding our pedigree-papers. Glaucus blushed: 'They're blank. You know why. Ask for something else.' 'I want Polyeidus to fill in the blanks,' Deliades declared: 'Bring out our papers and make him turn himself into the answers.' Glaucus glowered at his seer. Eurymede sharply asked Polyeidus whether he could in fact make such a transformation; if so, why hadn't he long since, to quiet the country? Glaucus protested that any such stunt would amount to no more than another man's opinion on the vexed question, which opinion, if Polyeidus had one, he could as well state plainly without recourse to the sort of circus tricks he famously disdained. Polyeidus nervously began a lecture on what he called the proto-existentialist view of ontological metamorphosis: within certain limits, everyone's identity was improvisable and responsible; man was free to create himself, et cetera. A willful lad, I drew my sword:

'Fill in the blanks or die.' Polyeidus blinked, grunted like a costive, disappeared. Deliades kissed me and showed gleefully to the court a scroll that popped from nowhere into his hands: *son of Glaucus and Eurymede*, it read beneath his name, and under mine: *out of Eurymede by Poseidon*.

"Thus ended, not the quarrel (which was fired additionally thenceforth by accusations of forgery and fraud), but Polyeidus's influence in the palace, at least with Glaucus; only the good offices of Eurymede, who was pleased with both her sons' behavior on this occasion, kept him on as our tutor. It was also the end, so far as anyone knew, of his 'animate' transformations, and the first of his documentary. It was not, however, as some allege, the invention of writing, though to Polyeidus rightly goes the credit for having introduced, some seasons earlier, that problematic medium to Corinth, where it never caught on. Writing itself, he told us in the Q & A after his act, would be invented some generations later by a stranded minstrel pissing in the sand of a deserted Aegean isle, making up endings to the Trojan War. It was the seer's limited capacity to read the future that enabled him to borrow certain ideas therefrom prior to their historical introduction. Why didn't he make use of this powerful ability to take over the world? Because knowledge, not power, was his vocation; he did not agree with Francis Bacon that the two are one; on the contrary, his own experience was that the more he understood, the less potent he became; the semantic and logical problems alone, to look no further, posed by such a stunt as stealing from the future, were a can of worms that no sane man would stir up unnecessarily. Et cetera. No one understood. 'Put it this way, then,' he grumbled: 'when I look back at the history of the future I see that Polyeidus in fact never capitalized on this

trick. Since I didn't, I can't; therefore I won't.' 'Thanks for
the present,' I said to my brother. 'Many happy returns,' he
replied—not knowing, as he couldn't see seerwise, there'd
be but five."

The eyes of Melanippe's lover are gray-green: explain.
Directly. Happy birthday, dead Hippolochus; happy birthday to you. Digression won't save them, dear Bellerophon;
do come to it: Your eighteenth birthday. Sibyl. Chariot-
race scene. The curse of God upon you, Polyeidus, snake
in the grass, whom even as I bored kind Philonoë decades
after with this tale I didn't know to be its villain!

"Eighteen, are we? On the beach? The horse race? Sibyl.
Polyeidus had a daughter, who knows by whom. Sibyl.
Younger than we. That summer she was our friend. Deliades
adored her, she me. I screwed her while he watched, in a little
grove down on the shore, by Aphrodite's sacred well.
Honey-locusts grew there, shrouded by rank creepers and
wild grape that spread amid a labyrinth of paths. There was
about that place a rich fetidity: gray rats and blackbirds de-
composed, by schoolboys done to death; suburban wild dogs
spoored the way; part the vines at the base of any tree and
you might find a strew of pellets and fieldmouse-bones dis-
gorged by feasting owls. It was the most exciting place we
knew; its queer smell retched us if we breathed too deeply,
but in measured inhalations it had a rich, a stirring savor.
There they played, Bellerus and Sibyl, while Dee-Dee
watched: no spite intended, but it cut him up. I told her to
let him in too; I didn't mind, and he was virgin. Nothing doing. I held her down for him to hump; he wouldn't even look.
The mad child offered to relinquish his claim to Corinth in
my favor if she'd marry him. No deal. 'Bellerus can have
Corinth the way he has me,' she would say sullenly: 'by

taking it, whenever he wants to.' I decided what to give my brother for his birthday gift that night. Now it's afternoon: Deliades has drawn Polyeidus out on the hero-business, above, brought him to preliminary images of Pegasus and Chimera, mentioned the Argonauts' Funeral Stakes, here we go. Ignore the myths that locate Glaucus's death at Iolchis or Theban Pontiae on the occasion of Jason's funeral games for Pelias: it happened at the regular Isthmian games, which in those days we called the Argonauts' Funeral Stakes in memory of the Pelian originals. It was a big day on the Isthmus, especially for Deliades: as many former Argonauts as could make it were there, and assorted other stars; strolling through the locker rooms was like touring a Hall of Fame; Dee-Dee, ecstatic, knew the program by heart, pointed out to me everyone from Acastus to Zetes, rattled off biographies and box scores like a sports announcer, urged me to help him catch the winged horse in time for us to race as a team next year, bet his whole allowance for the lunar month on Glaucus, a very long shot, to win the unlimited chariot event.

" 'Not a chance,' I said. 'Those mares are crazy.' Deliades agreed, but loyally put his drachmae on the line; it would break Dad's heart, he said, to lose the biggest race on the card, which he'd placed and showed in in the two years previous and trained for all that season. We pressed Polyeidus for prediction. 'Don't be impudent,' he replied. In those days I drew sword readily. 'Your father by a quarter-furlong,' he crossly volunteered, 'with hippomanes and your help. I see you're meeting my daughter tonight in the grove again, which also happens to be on the far side of the finish line.' By full-moon-light, he declared, near the lip of the well, grew the potent herb, which only a votary of the goddess could find and pluck: a mild aphrodisiac and hallucinogen to males of several species, it had a graver effect on mares, and for that reason, though its sale, possession, and use were prohibited by law, it was much favored by the mare-maids for their mysteries. Sibyl having shown some talent, even as a child, for sniffing it out, Polyeidus had apprenticed her to Aphrodite and become Eurymede's exclusive dealer in the weed—the supply of which, however, was so small that for some years he had been able to meet the cult's demands only by transforming himself into an amulet of concentrated 'hip,' as they called it, to be sniffed by the company in turn. In order to ingratiate himself with Glaucus, he confessed, what a story, he had offered to become that amulet that night: at post time Dad would give his team a toke; the mares, long starved for love, would go mad for more; in the grove, where according to Sibyl a rare new crop had sprouted, I was to pluck it at the signal, step forth and crush it in my hands; one whiff of the fresh and the Glaucan mares would finish first. 'Hurrah!' cried Deliades. 'Why me?' I asked. Because, Dee-Dee explained, it was a symbolic surrogate for the attempted filicide required to satisfy the Pattern: the turned-on mares, Dad at the reins, would fly as if at me, but I'd have ample time to take cover with him and Sibyl in the grove. No one would be hurt; Glaucus would win handily; his gratitude for our help must overcome any residue of fear in him of me or ill will toward our tutor. Polyeidus paled, then gave my brother on the spot an alpha-plus for the semester in Mythology I.

" 'I hate fixed races,' I complained to Dee-Dee in the grove. 'Me too,' said Sibyl. 'Yes, well,' said Deliades. Full moon, scattered clouds, balmy; couldn't see a thing when the moon was hid except for the beach-fires flaring from the

Argonautic cookout; then, between clouds, the grove glowed
phosphor-green. I made the most of each obscurity to deal
Dee-Dee in, preliminary to his birthday gift: with a hand
on one of Sibyl's breasts I would put his hand on the other,
or under her chiton, which she wore in the Amazonian
manner . . ."

Even then! exclaims Melanippe. Bellerophon wonders
where she's been these several pages? Long before Anteia
brought the style to Tiryns, we had real Amazons in Corinth
to mind the horses after Glaucus's decree, and the fashion
caught on with the younger women. That's why, when
Bellerophon saw Melanippe among Anteia's dykes and
falsies, he knew at once that she alone was the real thing.
Melanippe herself is less certain—but let it go. He begs her
pardon? No, please, let it go: go back to manhandling Sibyl;
you're telling this to Philonoë?

I talk to myself. Mad Sibyl's dead, sweet Philonoë—
everyone's dead except us cursed with immortality. Hum.
"In every case," I run on, "she knew at touch whose hand
was whose. Too bad for Dee-Dee. Now let's see. The chari-
ots assembled down the strand. I decided we'd play a prank
on Glaucus and not fix the race after all; Deliades objected;
Sibyl went round about the well on hands and knees to pluck
the herb, which we chewed till we were high as Helicon. I
set her after more, promising to climb her in our pet fashion,
stallionwise, when she was done, then whispered to Dee-Dee
what I had in mind: he was to declare impatiently, for Sibyl's
benefit, that he meant to take my place in Polyeidus's program, crushing hippomanes, while I dallied, to fetch the
mares on behalf of Glaucus and his own investment; but at
the moon's occlusion it was my place on Sibyl he'd take instead, humping her so ardently hind-to that she'd be nothing

wiser till too late. Stoned and love-starved as he was, the boy refused. I told him that only if he took her, as my gift, would I fix the race—which just then started with a roar. Let's see. Hum, that stuff was strong; things went awry; Glaucus gave the mares their dose of amulet and they went crazy; Dee-Dee —damn you, Polyeidus!—Dee-Dee, let's see, we were stoned and hot as rocks from Mount Chimera; who knew who was who. Our father—Polyeidus, viper whose wriggles these words are!—he'd, let's see, he'd tricked us all; we'd all tricked one another; Polyeidus hadn't mentioned that hippomanes would drive those mares carnivorous. He couldn't lose, God curse him, howevermany of us went. Dad's team charged crazily out front, snapping and frothing toward the grove; that hand-crushed business was a trick; we reeked hip to the heavens. All hid behind the well; stoned Sibyl, still on all fours, cried for love. I guess I—well, I guess I bared her butt just about when the horses turned on Glaucus, going for the amulet; spilled him at grove's-edge and went at him. Sibyl made to make rescue—mad mares eat only men—but I rammed her flat into the honeysuckle. At first bite Glaucus shouted. My brother sprang to save him in my stead. The moon came out; I drove in; Polyeidus, not to be gobbled, changed from amulet-'round-Glaucus's-neck to ditto-'round-his-daughter's (and straightway lost the power of such mere spatial relocation); Sibyl shrieked 'Bellerus!' as I pumped home and my brother went under the hooves. The whole team crashed into the creepers then, having gutted Glaucus and battered my brother past anyone's knowing. Sibyl, mad from that moment forward, rose up and calmed them, crooning 'Bellerus! Bellerus!' as they nuzzled the amulet between her breasts. But I leaped for my life into the well, so banging my head on its old oak bucket that I bear yet a crescent scar there and hear a roaring in my skull like wind or time. That blow, well, turned my eyes gray-green, let's see, impaired my memory, hear how I falter. If there are discrepancies or lacunae in this account, you must fill in the blanks yourself. All night I trembled in the well with frogs and crawlies, would've gone under but for the bucket-rope, heard hubbub overhead. Toward morning, when things stilled, as I miserably watched one star wink like Medusa down my hole, Polyeidus cranked me up, stone-stiff. We couldn't make each other out.

" 'You're either a comer or a goner,' he advised me. By holding back and humping Sibyl, he declared, I had in effect murdered my father and my brother. If he himself bore no grudge against me, it was because while the shock had left his daughter more or less deranged, it seemed also to have occasioned her first experience of second sight, on the basis of which he meant to recommend to Eurymede that she be made priestess of the grove for life. Moreover, though it went without saying that he hadn't exactly foreseen this debacle in detail, he couldn't say either that it came as a total surprise: it fit the Pattern, clearly, against which, it being preordained by an order of things transcending even Zeus's power much to alter, it were vain for a mere seer much to kick. Still and all, things were hot in town for both of us: my brother's supporters and Glaucus's—especially those who'd lost their tunics at the races—were crying Regicide and Crooked Track, and went so far as to accuse Polyeidus of engineering my succession. My heroic nature, he daresaid, impelled me straight through the waiting lynch mobs and sundry ambuscadoes to assert my claim; but the same Pattern which certified that kingly right (not to mention good diplomacy) required that I defer it. Just as Perseus, even as he spoke, was completing the exile trip from Seriphos through Egypt and Joppa, killing a Gorgon and picking up a bride before returning to rule Mycenae, so I, in my tutor's opinion, must beat it out of Corinth for the present. 'Leave it to me to calm the country and look after your mother. Take a new name. Make the grand tour. Discharge a few labors, dispatch a monster or two, et cetera. You'll know when it's time to come home; they always do. Questions?'

"I asked for a copy of the Pattern, by way of autobiographical road map. After some pause he said he hadn't one on him just then, but would forward it me as soon as he could envision my next mailing address. To what name would he send it? He paused again. '*Bellerophon*, of course. Is this a test?' We parted uncertainly in the dark. Let's see. I took off down the road. *Bellerophon* means Bellerus the Killer. Questions?"

But my dead darlings were abed long since; dead Philonoë was dropped off too in the drowsy dusk. Soon I'll wake and hurt her with the story of her sister. Questions?

Melanippe has several. Many, even, all disquieting. If she defers them, let's see, let's say it's because Medusa, in the *Perseid*, puts off hers till the epilogue. Not that a self-respecting Amazon in any respect resembles—but never mind. Wake her.

Let her rest in peace; let them all. O I wish—

How high now are Bellerophon and Pegasus? Gorse-top low. Wave-top low. All but sea-leveled.

Wake her then; hurt her now. The sooner begun, et cetera.

"Here's the full story of my sexual adventure with your sister," I'd wake my wife to announce. No. Aye. O. Done.

"I" On. "I believe I'm familiar with the several standard versions," let's say she'd say, rubbing her eyes. "A classical myth, however, is yawn excuse me infinitely retellable, and the connoisseur's pleasure is in those small variations, discrepancies, and lacunae that invariably yawn obtain among renditions. Add to that my love for both principals in this particular episode in the grander narrative of your career, and you will yawn see that no amount of pain occasioned by the events themselves can altogether spoil my pleasure in their rehearsal. I'll make coffee."

O. Nevertheless I gnash my teeth and proceeded. "For a year or two after dropping out of Corinth I hiked across the Peloponnese, doing odd jobs, seeing the sights, reconstructing as best I could from memory the Pattern. I felt I'd completed, in the main, its first quarter, the quadrant of Departure: my conception and birth certificate were in order; Glaucus was dead; I had the regulation scar, if not in quite the regular place, to mark what could pass as his attempt to kill me; I'd crossed a sort of threshold, in proper darkness, got my travel orders at a well in a sacred grove from a certified *Spielman*, set out to westward under pseudonym. When I reached Sandy Pylos, on the coast, I supposed that the correct thing to do was ship on as oarsman, say, aboard the next boat west, to commence my second quarter— Initiation—with a night-sea journey.

"But the more I combed the beach, the more I came to question whether I'd got off after all on just the right foot. Even allowing for some flexibility in the Pattern, I doubted whether any mythic hero could commence his principal tasks with blood-guilt, as we call it, on his hands: Odysseus and Aeneas, to name only two of Polyeidus's 'personages from the future,' would be obliged to retrace their steps laboriously in mid-career merely to bury a graveless shipmate lost by accident. Nor was it clear, as it seemed to me it should be, what exactly I was aiming *for*, even ostensibly: no hero of my acquaintance went west merely for the Pattern's sake; indeed, as many as not began by going *east*, in order to return to a westward home. Since I was to my knowledge homeless but for Corinth, to make it on my present course would require circumnavigation of the globe—and Polyeidus had prophesied to us years past that not for centuries would it be speculated, much less demonstrated, that the earth is round. Finally, as I stood making idle water one forenoon on the strand (like that nameless minstrel Polyeidus mentioned), I thought I saw a winged white horse flap past out on the horizon. Could've been a gull—the distance was far, and I was preoccupied with making my name in imaginary letters —but it put me in mind of magic Pegasus, of Perseus's fancy sandals, and of my own lack of any gear besides the tool in hand, which had got me only into trouble. In short, I came to feel that at least three things were wanting before I could proceed with my career: clearer counsel on the matter of absolution; a more definite course of hero-work, with specific adversaries, goals, and labors; and a magic weapon, vehicle, or secret with which to address that work. For all three I must apply either to the prophet or to the gods; not to lose more time I applied to both, making prayer-stops at every temple of Athene along the way back to Polyeidus."

"Athene?" Why not Aphrodite?

To entertain wife and mistress at the same time with the same tale is hard. "Dee-Dee, Athene's pet, died, Philonoë, there in Aphrodite's grove, right?" "Well." And I'd been marinated, Melanippe, overnight in the sex-queen's hole. So? "It wasn't love Bellerophon needed, but advice. Come Tiryns —as close to Corinth as I felt it safe to go—I got both."

"Um." Um.

Bellerophon wishes he had never begun this story. But he began it. Then he wishes he were dead. But he's not. Therefore he reconstructs it painfully for his darling Amazon, as he once pained with it patient Philonoë. Dee-Dee (dead) had daydreamed of riding that white horse till the night mares made hay of him, and on Polyeidus's advice had even fasted once five days and nights in Athene's Corinth temple, to find out how to find it. On the fifth—so he told me, right?— he thought he heard the goddess say: "Finding Pegasus is easy; he hangs around my sister's wells and bushes; I'm surprised you haven't seen him grazing down below. But to catch and ride him's another story: for that you need this." She fetched from around her tunic a fine gold bridle; even let him take it in his hand. But when he woke it was only his torpid tool he held, as I mine later—so he told me and Sibyl, stoned, next evening in the grove, right, the last of his life, when he let himself go, ran to Dad's rescue, got foddered. In the real *Bellerophoniad* this would be established in an earlier digression.

So: on the way to Tiryns it occurred to me to try again— i.e., Bellerophon decided to do what dead Dee-Dee'd done. The first two nights, nothing: those temples were roadside shrines, where all I could get was a fuzzy image in black and white of the horse himself, like that early one Polyeidus had picked up. On the third day I came to Tiryns, where King Proetus had a Ναῷ ᾿Αθήνης large enough for the greatest reception. There he and Queen Anteia received me as a suppliant;

over a five-course meal (but I was fasting) I told them the story of my life (First Flood, Part One) and asked permission to fast and sleep for the next three nights in the temple.

"There's room," said the King—a mild-mannered monarch, middle-aged, who fiddled with his flatware as I spoke. "And I imagine we can arrange a purification, if you really fault yourself for that fiasco on the beach—I must say I've heard more plausible accounts from my people up in Corinth. None of my business, I'm sure, but aren't you being a bit eager to take the blame?"

"I killed my brother," I insisted. "My dad too—I mean my foster father."

Proetus sighed. "O yes, the demigod thing."

I blushed, but held my tongue. Anteia—a sharp-featured woman somewhere between her husband's age and mine— said: "*I* think you've got a lot going for you in the hero way myself, Bellerophon. Here's hoping you get what you're after in Tiryns; we could use some excitement, God knows. And there's nothing wrong with a little ambition."

"Who's knocking ambition?" Proetus asked the company. "I was ambitious myself at his age: made war on my brother Acrisius; married me this beautiful Lycian princess here—the works. But I never went around telling people I was going to be a star, much less a constellation."

"Sour grapes," Anteia said.

"Nobody's satisfied nowadays to be a decent husband and father," the King went on, "or a reasonable administrator. It's hero or nothing."

Mortified, I replied, what was simply true, that in my opinion ambition had less to do than definition with my ends. Estellation—as the examples of Orion, Heracles, Castor, and Pollux testified or would testify—was as natural a fate for mythic heroes as coronation was for princes, death in battle for combat soldiers, oblivion for ordinary men. I had not "chosen" to kill Glaucus and my brother, any more than I had chosen to be sired by Poseidon or would choose to slay monsters and the rest. It was the Pattern . . .

"Ah-ah—" Proetus raised a finger. "You didn't choose your parents, obviously; and I'm glad to hear you admit that the mare-business was an accident, more or less. But nobody's obliging you to go after tnis winged horse, right? And you've acknowledged already that you're trying to decide what to do when you catch him."

The man was more tease than mock, but I couldn't readily refute him. I began to explain, reflecting on the matter for the first time myself, that in the case of heroes there seemed to be no choice of general destinies, they being foreordained as it were by the Pattern; but any given hero might at any point conceivably choose to turn his back on himself, so to speak, and sulk like Achilles in his tent instead of sallying forth to glory. Should he *persist* in such fecklessness, he'd become by definition no hero, just as a crown prince who declined accession would be no crown prince. Doubtless the point could be better put—

"But that's not Bellerophon's business," Anteia said shortly to her husband. "Logic is for your type; his job is to be a mythic hero, period."

I agreed, wishing I'd said less. Proetus shrugged. "He makes a good case for himself, all the same. Pleasant dreams, boy; let's hope it won't cost you many more people to get to heaven."

Troubled sleep. In fine-tuned black and white I saw

Pegasus grazing in the temple court; Athene, cowled, came up, belted with the famous bridle, and seemed to move her lips. At the sound of footfalls in the temple I lost the picture; woke to find a gray-cowled lady prowling in the precinct, near my pallet. My first theophany! I sprang up, dizzy at this evidence that I was on my way.

"Athene?" "Sorry." Anteia slipped back her hood and smiled. "Just checking to see if you're comfortable. Anything you need?" I thanked her, no. Couldn't sleep, she said, for thinking of my dinner tale. Spot of Metaxa? I groaned to get on with my dreamwork, but Queen was Queen. Neat? Bit of water in mine. "My husband's a coward," she said for openers; "no, not a coward, just minor league." "O?" We sat on a marble bench and sipped. "Time and again I've set him up to do something really big," she said. "Daddy loaned him half an army to knock off Acrisius—they were twins, like you-all? He blew it." "Ah." She smoothed her hair, swirled her liquor. "Half the fucking Lycian army. So I said Just up and *kill* the bastard, for god's sake—the way *you* did your brother? No thanks: too ballsy by half, that idea! Some seer, he claimed, told him *Perseus* is supposed to kill Acrisius as part of his hero-thing." "That figures, actually," I remarked, startled at her way of speaking and uncertain what to do. "Hmp. So I do a little homework on their famous feud, okay? And guess what I find out: it started in the first place when His Royal Highness slipped it to Acrisius's daughter! His own niece, right here in my palace! So okay, we weren't married at the time, but still. It's a wonder to me he ever got it up for the little twat; he doesn't exactly beat *me* to death with it. Even so he comes out a loser: Acrisius sticks Danaë in a tower where nobody can see her but the gods; she sits around bare-ass naked all day to get their attention—have you seen the pictures? Zeus himself puts it to her, and bingo —Perseus! Who it turns out is like as not to kill Proetus and Acrisius both and take over the country. I swear. That's why it riled him when you started on the hero business: he's petrified of mythic heroes. More juice?"

I guessed not. Anteia downed hers with a wink and declared her frank envy of women like Danaë who were smart or lucky enough to take up with gods and heroes, never mind the consequences. Being nothing but queen was so goddamn *boring*, especially in a two-bit city-state like Tiryns: one lousy amphitheater and half a dozen restaurants, all Greek. I thought her unfairly critical of her husband, but was interested all the same: my first experience of overtures from an older woman.

"I suppose this sort of thing happens to you all the time," she said, in a different tone.

"No, ma'am." I wished I had asked What.

"Hm." We sat awhile. Metaxa. "Read any good books lately, Killer?"

Really, Bellerophon? At least I'm certain she called me Killer, for though I'd not read Aristotle's *Nichomachean Ethics* or for that matter any other books—their invention being still far in the future and myself at that time unable to read—I explained to her at some length my position on the moral aspect of Glaucus's and my brother's deaths, which I'd reasoned out between Corinth and Pylos with the aid of terms from the aforementioned work, known to me in bits and pieces via Polyeidus. "Proetus," I declared, "says I'm innocent, and in the respect that my role in those deaths was not an example of *proairesis* (by which will be meant a voluntary act preceded by deliberation), I agree. Indeed, following Aristotle's classification of human actions according to the degree and nature of the agent's volition—

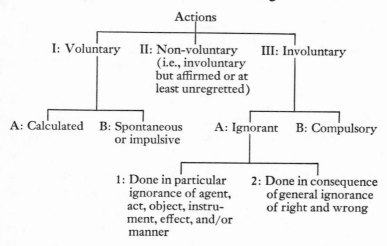

Actions

I: Voluntary   II: Non-voluntary   III: Involuntary
(i.e., involuntary
but affirmed or at
least unregretted)

A: Calculated   B: Spontaneous   A: Ignorant   B: Compulsory
or impulsive

1: Done in particular   2: Done in consequence
ignorance of agent,   of general ignorance
act, object, instru-   of right and wrong
ment, effect, and/or
manner

—my failure to spring to my kinsmen's aid and my preventing Sibyl from rescuing them might seem at first to share characteristics of both III-A-1 and III-B: on the one hand I was ignorant of the particular carnivorous effect of hippomanes on the mares and of Sibyl's ability to calm them; on the other hand I was 'compelled' in the sense of having no alternative, as I thought, but the futile sacrifice of Sibyl's life or my own. To the contrary it might be argued that my overmastering lust to cover Sibyl on the spot put my deed in the I-B category: psychologically voluntary but morally responsible. My own inclination, however, is to see it as a special variety of Category II, for while their death, particularly my role in it, breaks my heart and was half out of my hands, it fulfills the Pattern: I therefore affirm it, and *therefore* I'm culpable, morally if not legally, in the Aristotelian sense."

"You never got laid in your life," Anteia said, and left. The cock crew—

Melanippe too! But all that foregoing is in quotes: how did you speak the classificatory schema? Were there chalkboards in the Temple of Wisdom?

I'm writing. Melanippe is writing. Philonoë, Anteia, Sibyl —all mere Polyeidic inklings, written words.

"How'd you make out?" Proetus asked at breakfast. His children, three saucy little daughters, climbed all over us as I fasted and he ate. Dead now, who grew from frisky nymphlings into crazed wild whores, running mad and naked in the hills like gadflied Io. Don't start that. The Queen was sleeping in, Proetus said; but even as he said it she appeared, housecoat and curlers, hmping hmps. With any luck, I told him, a couple more nights should do it. Anteia hmped. "Most heroes I've heard of," Proetus remarked, "had a definite monster or task in mind when they set out. Doesn't your lack of one make you wonder whether you're really what you hope you are?" "Hmp," said Anteia, buttered a croissant, swatted a kid. Not at all, said I, though not so long before I'd have agreed with him: a review of the mythographic corpus would make clear that while the majority of demigods fit his description, a smaller but perhaps more interesting group did not: Aeneas, for example, would clarify gradually, by painful trial and error over a period of years, the details of his destiny and destination. And Perseus, if Polyeidus was correct, would in later life seek to overtake with understanding his present paragraph, as it were, by examining his paged past, and, thus pointed, proceed serene to the future's sentence, whatever those metaphors meant. Hmp.

"Little men talk," Anteia grumbled: "big men *do*." Proetus cocked an eyebrow at us. "I'm a young man with much to learn," I declared. "But never doubt I'll learn it." Assuming the half-tease tone of the day before, Proetus pointed out that my illustrations were drawn from the future and so lent substance to his own conviction that mythic heroes weren't what they used to be; that the present crop was small potatoes compared to the generation of their fathers— an age of gold, so to speak, succeeded by an age of brass. I denied this libel flatly: Cousin Perseus, I maintained, a man not many years my senior, would when all the returns were in be seen to be as dazzling a demigod as ever murdered monster . . .

"Or pronged princess," added Anteia, raising her morning drink. "Or slew slanderer, okay?"

Proetus paled. "Forgetting about this fellow Perseus," he said evenly after a moment, "would you go so far as to say about yourself that if you don't come up with your hypothetical winged horse in a couple of days, we may conclude that you're a fraud and execute you for misuse of Athene's temple?"

Anteia sipped and grinned. Sweating, I reminded him that I was as yet unpurified of blood-guilt. In the absence of instructions from my mentor Polyeidus, to whom I'd dispatched a messenger just the previous day, I was merely assuming that the old fast-and-vision method was the right one for corralling Pegasus; that Athene was the proper goddess to apply to for shriving as well; and that the two objectives were concurrently pursuable. The evidence thus far supported these assumptions more than not, but for all I knew, absolution might be prerequisite to theophany; or Athene, who was most certainly on the verge of speaking to me, might instruct me when I found her voice to clear myself with Aphrodite or my father Poseidon before bridling the winged horse. For that reason I'd prefer at present not to commit myself absolutely to a timetable. Et cetera.

"Hah," Anteia said.

"Word came this morning already from Corinth," Proetus informed me: "Your coach Polyeidus has disappeared from sight."

Trying to conceal my consternation, I observed that periodic disappearance was an occupational characteristic of shape-shifters; Polyeidus had doubtless turned into some document or other, as was his recent tendency—perhaps that copy of the Pattern which he'd promised to send me.

"Perhaps." Proetus patted his mouth with a napkin, brushed crumbs and daughters from his lap, rose from table. "Though there was no mail for you by either the Corinthian post or ours, as of this morning, and in fact your mother vowed to our messenger that both her sons were dead. It was the royal dungeon, by the way, that Polyeidus disappeared from: Eurymede had sentenced him to death for fraud, imposture, false counsel, and lese majesty. Good morning."

The Queen was entertained by my discomfiture. I sprang up, declaring that my mother's judgment was no doubt impaired by the sudden loss of husband and son and my own apparent defection (which plainly accounted for her calling me dead); what was more, Polyeidus himself had often pointed out to us that true shape-shifting resembled imposture as fiction resembled lies. If I must manage for the present without his advice, so be it, I said, not at all certain I could in fact; if my procedure was mistaken or my faith in Polyeidus misplaced, I would trust in Athene herself to correct and advise me, and to replace my dead half-brother with my living one. Tears, mine, started at this idea, which hadn't occurred to me till I heard myself give it voice: that sweet-winged Pegasus bore the same relation to me as Dee-Dee, say; could even be said to be his deathless spirit. The inspiration made me eloquent, and reckless: One way or another, I vowed, I'd be in the mythic saddle by my deadline; if not, I was theirs to dispose of as they saw fit (and at their own risk). Proetus apologized for baiting me and exited to the throne-room; Anteia hmped for coffee. I withdrew to the temple to fast and reflect all day on the bad news and my overboldness.

Famished nightfall, sound sleep and soundless images, for the first time now in living color: rose-pink Pegasus fed with the pigeons on the flags; off-white Wisdom held sternly forth one end of her waisted bridle, gold, and moved her lips in voiceless admonition. I snatched; she shook a free finger; I strained to learn her meaning; held fast but didn't dare the knot. "Let me," said nightied Anteia, perched on my bed-edge, and undid. I let her go with a cry: "My dream!"

"My hero," she said dryly. "Let's get on with it."

My stomach growled. "You don't understand!"

"So teach me." The Queen leaned on one elbow. "We're in Wisdom's temple, right?"

"Your Majesty, look here . . ." I grew dizzy with distress.

"Look here yourself, Bellerophon. I'm queen of this place, remember? How do you think I feel, coming after you like this?" I restrained my impatience and disappointment; attempted to explain that my reaction had nothing particularly to do with her. "Don't rub it in," she interrupted; "my being here has nothing particularly to do with *you*, either, as a matter of fact." She sat up and drew together her gown. "I don't give a particular goddam about you one way or the other; but I want what's under your tunic, and I want it now."

I remarked that even if I were willing to transgress the

rules of hospitality, as Proetus had done with Danaë, not I nor any man could erect himself on order.

"Excuses," said Anteia. "I'm not feminine enough for you, I suppose? Not seductive? Well, screw Feminine. Screw Seductive. Come on."

I begged for a moment to collect myself, at least.

"I hate this," Anteia said. "A man can always force a woman, but a woman can never force a man. Screw Nature. Screw Proetus. Screw you."

"If you feel like that," I asked, "why in the world should we make love?"

More calmly, as if in fact she found explanation as much of a relief as I, she declared herself misembodied: a heroical spirit trapped in a female frame. All her girlhood, she said, taking Artemis as her model, she had disdained passive feminine pursuits in favor of hunting, riding, wrestling; her ambition, in fact, had been to be a mythic hero; she scolded her mother for not having had adulterous relations with some passing god, to provide her with the right paternity; yet she adored her father, King Iobates, and went with him everywhere, even disguising herself as a boy to enlist in one of his perennial campaigns against the Solymians. The company captured a minor village, routinely sacked and burned it, put to the sword all but its younger female inhabitants, who were raped and enslaved. Shocked Anteia fled; hitching homeward, still disguised, she fell in with a young prince en route to Lycia to seek military aid from Iobates, and agreed to show him the way. Along the road she menstruated; pled diarrhea to explain her cramps and frequent disappearances into the bush. Fearing some trick, her companion followed her, saw she was female, jumped her; half an hour they grappled; then he pinned, bound, deflowered her, went his way to the court of Lycia. She appeared there next day, Iobates the day after. The suppliant, Proetus, recognized his victim, assumed he'd be put to death. Anteia married him instead.

"Since I couldn't be a hero," she told me, "I thought I'd be a hero's wife. Proetus seemed promising enough on paper: no demigod, but a bona-fide exiled prince out to reclaim his rightful kingdom, et cetera. By the time it was clear to me he'd never make it as a mythic figure, I'd borne him three kids and lost my own edge—too late to chuck it and start over. I even love him, believe it or not, much as I despise the rape-thing. He's as trapped in *his* role, as they say, as I am in mine, et cetera. But if I can't be a hero's wife, I'm damned well going to be a hero's mother, and since Proetus can't seem to turn out even an ordinary mortal son, I'm shopping around. Never mind what I've been reduced to to try to get Zeus or Poseidon to spend a night with me: obviously Danaë and company have something that I don't have. But I'm used by now to settling for less than Olympus: if I can't get a god to do me, a demigod'll do. Come on."

I replied: "I really sympathize with your story, ma'am. I really do. But as you know, only gods sire heroes every time on mortal women. If a demigod's what you're after in the mother way, another demigod like myself has only a fifty-fifty chance of turning one out."

"I'll take the chance!" Anteia cried. "Let the kid be a *semi*goddamndemigod; who cares? Even a one-eighth god's better than nothing!" She pounded the pallet. "Why can't men be raped by women? For pity's sake *bang* me, Bellerophon!"

But I could only point out to her, as Polyeidus had once to dead Dee-Dee when that child wondered whether he might qualify as quartergod, that semidemideities are genetically impossible: "Gods on gods breed only gods," I explained; "mortals mortals mortals; gods on mortals, demigods. As for gods on demigods, demigods on demigods, and demigods on mortals, the expectable results can be best represented by a diagram in which *gg* stands for god, *mm* mortal, *gm* (or *mg*) demigod, thus:

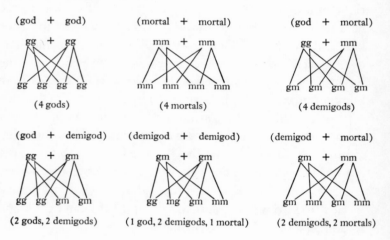

(god + god)
(4 gods)

(mortal + mortal)
(4 mortals)

(god + mortal)
(4 demigods)

(god + demigod)
(2 gods, 2 demigods)

(demigod + demigod)
(1 god, 2 demigods, 1 mortal)

(demigod + mortal)
(2 demigods, 2 mortals)

Semidemigodhood, as you see, doesn't happen. I presume you noted that while the issue of the first or upper group of pairings is absolutely certain, that of the second or lower group is a reckoning of probabilities, which over a very large number of instances takes on the force of natural law, but in individual cases is of less predictive value. For example, given the pairing you're interested in most immediately, demigod plus mortal, there's one chance in two that any child produced by such a union will be a demigod; but there's about the same likelihood of turning out four mortals and *no* demigods, say, as there is of you and Proetus having four daughters and no sons. In fact, since the diagram is drawn without respect to gender, if we correct for the fact that *gm* will mean demigoddess as often as demigod, the chances of your bearing a demi*god* to me go down to one in four. This on the assumption that both parties are fertile; that a demigod's embrace, like a god's, never fails to impregnate; and that the pregnancy is successfully brought to term. But inasmuch as none of these is invariably the case, the odds against your getting what you want from me should be more accurately put at eight or ten or even twelve to one. It interests *me* to notice, by the way, that a demigod and demigoddess can do together something that Zeus himself, with a mortal mate, can't do: namely, turn out a full-blooded deity—fullichored, I suppose one should say. Heh. That's also the only instance of genetical up-breeding in this scheme of possibilities—a child superior by nature to both parents—and the same pairing holds the only possibility of true *down*-breeding. Neither of these hypothetical possibilities, to my knowledge, has been realized in mythic history, but they make the coupling of a demigoddess and myself, for example, a good deal richer in geneticodramatic potential than the coupling of you and me, don't you think?"

Two women groaned from their utter bowels and fled: Anteia from the Tiryns temple, Philonoë from our Lycian boudoir. A third, groanwise these several pages their visceral sister, if she could set down what words she would would be said to have fled too, from this swampy nest of "love" and "narrative" on the Thermodon. Bellerophon, you were a bastard.

Q.E.D. But I remind the last-laid that that first-'s importunings imperiled my mortal life; the second-'s un- ditto my im-. If I could set down what words *I* would, would I speak

in diagrams and hyphens? Would I draw blanks on my own
account in ditto verse, ham-handeder than Heracles, tinner-
eared Lygeia, clubbeder-foot gimp Oedipus? Die, Polyeidus,
or let me!

Melanippe's here still, love; do indulge her; please go on.

"I'm back, love," Philonoë'd say some moments later.
"Do excuse my u.-b. groan; just a touch of catharsis, I
imagine: the purgation of my psyche through the emotions
of pity and terror effected in it by your narrative. Please go
on. My sister, I believe, comes back for more?"

"She'll come back," Proetus said at breakfast, after re-
porting to me that Anteia had disappeared during the night.
"She gets wild spells now and then, goes up in the hills with
her girlfriends for a day or so. I don't ask questions. Part of
being happily married is knowing when to be incurious. Any
luck with the horses?" As he spoke he cracked a soft-boiled
egg and spooned it onto bread for one of his daughters,
standing by. Another sat in his lap and played with his
whiskers; the third crawled about somewhere beneath the
table. Servants served and cleared the meal, but were apparently instructed to let the King feed the children himself.
I nibbled bread, sipped water, yawned, shook my head.

"Couldn't sleep."

Proetus seemed to consider this, wiping jam from the
sleeve of his purple robe, which the lap-child had used as a
napkin. Presently he sighed. "You're not the first state visitor
to complain that our temples aren't very private at night, and
I'll tell you frankly that you'd find the same thing true of our
guest-rooms here in the palace. I've learned to live with it.
But look here: forget about the deadline on that horse-thing,
if you're not sleeping nights; it's not good policy to kill a
suppliant. Sorry I even mentioned it yesterday. My advice

to you is to try another town, where you'll be left alone: there's a dandy acropolis over in Athens; if you're interested, my people will fetch you there."

Proetus's character wasn't clearly enough defined for me to judge how much he knew, or whether Anteia was really on a woodland spree or, for example, confined to quarters, or whether the proffered escort might be a murder-party. For want of a better tactic I asked permission to spend one night more in the temple, with a posted guard to insure my privacy. If I proved successful with Athene, I'd put myself and Pegasus at His Majesty's service for a reasonable term in the heroic-labor way; if not, I had no further business either in Tiryns or in the world at large, and was uninterested in my fate.

Again the King grew thoughtful. After some moments, breaking his custom, he had the children fetched away by their governess. When their bawling was sufficiently remote he said, "Look here, Bellerophon: you may think me a contemptible man, but I'm not an obtuse one. I'm perfectly aware that my wife's been going to you these past nights, as she's gone to others before you; judging from her temper, I gather you've turned her down, for one reason or another. Now let's not be naïve: suppliant or not, I could have you killed any time I wanted to and give your death out as accidental; about the gods I'm agnostic, but if they exist, their tolerance of injustice is high enough not to worry me overmuch: I have considerable credit in the obsequy and temple-building way. But as I remarked before, I've no particular interest in killing you, and wouldn't have even if you'd accommodated my wife. Who is Anteia? A girl I raped once, years ago, and married to get myself out of a tight spot. I'll keep her around for the kids' sake until her drinking and the rest get out of hand; then she goes. Meanwhile, if you want her, help yourself—I get my own amusement elsewhere. But don't get caught, or I'll have you killed for the usual public-relations reasons. In fact, given Mrs. Proetus's state of mind, I *advise* you to be nice to her if she shows up again. Insulting a First Lady is no joke: all she has to do is holler 'rape' and you're dead: I'd have no choice."

I sat dismayed.

"Nor would I have any particular compunction," Proetus went on. "Do you think it matters one fart to me whether you live or die? Now, let's look at this hero-thing. As you know, I once had aspirations in that line myself; so did my brother, and I think we might both have done fairly well if our feud hadn't eaten up our energies. Too late to bother about that now. But I've seen a couple of real winners in my time, and I must say you don't stack up very impressively against them, in my opinion. Sure, you're young and well put together, and I'll take your word for it you're Eurymede's boy (as for the demigod thing, that's never more than more or less metaphorical bullshit, right?): but you talk too much; you're not sure enough of yourself; you lack—I don't know, call it *charisma*. I can't imagine you doing in a real monster, for example, if there are such things.

"Still and all, as with the gods, I'm open-minded enough not to rule out the *possibility* that you're what you hope you are—you've got a kind of stubborn single-mindedness that seems to go unusually deep, and I've seen stubbornness get more results sometimes than intelligence, courage, talent, and self-confidence combined. It seems to me that some people choose their vocations by a sort of inspired default, you know? A passionate lack of alternatives. That's how you strike me: not so much an absolute apprentice hero as absolutely nothing else instead, if you see what I mean.

"So okay, I'll take a chance; what have I got to lose? Stay as long as you want; use all the temples you need; prong my wife if you care to—maybe it'll keep her off *my* back for a while. If Athene doesn't come across for you, be a good sport: get lost and keep your mouth shut. If she does, never mind the monster-princess-treasure rigmarole; just do me one small favor in the assassination way, okay?"

Thinking I knew what he had in mind, I observed that routine murder-for-hire, even of royalty, was not a feature of the heroical curriculum so far as I knew; in any case, killing Acrisius, so I understood, had been held by Proetus himself to be *Perseus*'s destined business, not mine.

The King waved off this suggestion disdainfully. "Who cares about Acrisius? He grabbed the old man's kingdom; I grabbed half of it back with my father-in-law's lousy mercenaries. I fucked his daughter once, as I'm sure Anteia told you; he'll do the same to one of mine if he can still get it up when they're old enough. We bushwhack each other's shepherds and rustle sheep back and forth across the border. It's a way of life by now; neither of us takes it seriously any more. Never mind my brother; it's a certain bastard son of mine I want killed." He winked. "By little Danaë herself, believe it or not. Don't swallow that line about a rain of gold in a brass tower: Acrisius locked her up because I'd knocked her up, and he had to invent some cover-story for the reporters. Kill Perseus for me, friend: I'll give you Acrisius's kingdom and your choice of my daughters."

Appalled, I asked him why he wanted Perseus killed.

"Why in Hades d'you think?" Proetus said impatiently. "You call yourself a hero, and you never heard of oracles? The bastard's scheduled to kill me and Acrisius both! With t22tty2tyityity2222

his goddamn Gorgon's-head! Father and maternal grandfather, right? You think I want to be a frigging statue?"

"I understand your concern, sir," I said carefully. "But believe me, I've done considerable homework in the oracle field, and if yours was the usual You-will-be-killed-by-your-own-son thing, it seems to me you don't have much to worry about from my cousin. If he really *were* your son by Danaë, he wouldn't be a bona-fide mythic hero; however, the fact that he tricked the Gray Ladies and killed Medusa, et cetera, proves he *is* a mythic hero; therefore he can't be your son—he has to be the son of a god. But if he's not your son, the oracle doesn't apply. It's a simple sorites, actually."

The King's face set. "You won't kill him?"

"Not unless Athene tells me to. But as she's Perseus's advisor also, I can't imagine her doing that."

"And yet you expect me to let you use my temple, diddle my wife . . ."

I replied that I expected nothing. If Pegasus should be granted me, I stood still ready to perform for my host any legitimate extraordinary services up to the number of, say, five; if in return for such services he chose to enrich me with half a kingdom and, upon her arrival at nubility, one of his daughters, I had no objection, that being the customary honorarium for hero-work. But my real objective and true reward was immortality, which was not Proetus's to bestow. As for the unhappy Queen, I'd be doubly obliged if he'd post a guard to prevent another interruption of my vision from that quarter. Finally, it was no doubt disagreeable to realize that one was fated to be killed by one's own son, legitimate, illegitimate, or putative: the overwhelming evidence, unfortunately, argued that such fates, once oracled, were inescapable—indeed (witness Glaucus), that attempts to avert them by homicidal or other means were as likely to precipitate as to delay their fulfillment. But except for that tiny minority of us destined for the stars, we must all expire in any case, and surely there must be some small compensation in dying at the hands of such a splendid chap as Perseus. That was itself a kind of immortality: were not the adversaries, human and monstrous, of great heroes almost as celebrated as the heroes themselves? Petrifaction, particularly, struck me as a far from miserable end, assuming it overtook one reasonably well along in years: it was reported to be quick and apparently painless; it was in no way disfiguring; it spared the survivors the expense of an elaborate funeral-barrow, not to mention embalmment, and it furnished them and the general citizenry, free of charge, with an accurate and touching memorial of their late lord—provided the subject be not overtaken in an expression of panic, or eating, defecating, picking his nose, et cetera, which embarrassment a moderate alertness should render unlikely. Next to outright estellation, take it all in all, petrifaction by the Gorgon's gaze in a dignified position toward the evening of an honorable reign seemed to me as near an approach to immortality as any merely mortal monarch could be blessed with.

By my speech's end, speechless Proetus sat fixed and glassy, as if the anticipation of Medusa did for half her glance. I excused myself, strolled the city to kill the day, fed lucky pigeons peanuts from park benches when faintness overtook me from my fasting, turned in early and unsuppered.

Flicker, focus, fine-tune; a little bit of the old scratch and static; then a high hum and bright Athene, clear, appeared in the form of Polyeidus's daughter. But she was Sibyl with a difference! Gray-eyed, calm, reproachless, tall, she stood chastely off some meters from my bed and spoke more plainly than ever in Aphrodite's grove:

"That took a while. So it's *Bellerophon* now, is it?"

I strove to speak, for although it was quite clear in my vision that Sibyl was the goddess in disguise, I understood also that such masks had their own reality—Polyeidus, in manuscript form, could be read, revised, annotated—and I much desired to apologize for my past behavior and its distressing consequences. But my own voice failed as Athene's came clear.

"Poor Anteia," Sibyl said: "she's doing hippomanes up on the hill, out of desperation. Too bad she wasn't in the grove that night, instead of me. But you've certainly exercised restraint, if not human sympathy, and Restraint seems to be the name of this particular game. Here's the bridle." She tossed me the light gold chain. "You'll find Pegasus out back. I don't envy you your life to come: I'd rather be dead, like your brother. One day you'll wish that too. 'Bye."

"No!" I found my voice, sat up to implore her to stay, I had so many things to ask, explain.

"Neigh!" Anteia whinnied madly about the pallet, full-moon-dappled, her weighty body bare; finally came at me hind-foremost and bent over, waggling her buttocks. The bridle was in my hand; I fled.

Why? What? Why. Why? So Philonoë sometimes asked, when I'd pained her to this point. "You had what you needed, and my poor sister was strung out. Why'd you run?" And being Philonoë, she'd offer reasons: respect for Proetus and the rules of hospitality; reluctance to offend Athene; concern that precious Pegasus might fly off; overwhelmment by the memory of those wild mares in the grove . . . Well? Well, in keeping with my ongoing project to disaffect

Philonoë I'd say, "Who could make it with a forty-year-old pickup? Especially one going to fat?" To which, herself late-thirtyish, she'd reply, "Some people can't admit to an honorable motive. You were shy with me too at first, remember?"

Being Amazon, Melanippe is torn between admiration for her lover's dead wife's large-heartedness and a great desire to bark her submissive shins. At least Anteia had spirit enough to call you a gelding, holler Rape, and do her best to have you killed; in Amazonia you'd have lost your balls for Sexual Refusal of the Needy. It's a serious offense.

Bellerophon had his reasons—which you must know, if you know what happened before I tell it.

Why were you timid at first with Philonoë? You said you were a lusty youngster, Aphrodite's pet, but for the past three dozen pages you've been cunt-shy.

You *don't* see, then; I feared you were becoming Polyeidus, as people in this telling tend to do. All of Philonoë's reasons applied; others also; but mainly, I swear, I was out to be on with it: Anteia had no place in my hero-work, the only thing that mattered. If she'd been Melanippe herself, I'd've done the same thing.

You know how to disarm an Amazon. When you raped "Melanippe," then, a few months later, that was hero-work?

It was true rape, in any case, of a true Amazon, which even this *Bellerophoniad* will sog its way to sooner or later. As for the false rape of the false, Anteia cried it to the temple-tops; the palace guards, never there when I needed them, appeared now everywhere: some I directed in to aid the Queen, others to the rear of the temple, where I said I'd seen someone run, others off to summon Proetus. Thus for one moment I was alone in the marble forecourt, by a chuckling fountain: at once vast wingbeats came, and the horse of heaven. Heart near bursting, I lightly slipped the bridle over Brother, seized his great (near) pinion, swung astride, was off before the guards reswarmed.

What a thing it is, to fly! His white wings spread and coursing easily, Pegasus drew up his legs and soared between the streetlamps and the stars. All fell into correct perspective: ships' lanterns, shepherds' watchfires, palace, temples, harbors, hills. Cold wind and dizzy altitude, night-loneliness— they were nothing: for the first time in my life I felt at home; I wanted never to come down. We lit on Athene's pediment after a splendid shakedown circuit of the suburbs.

"Proetus!" I called down to the plaza. Torched guards drew back amazed; the King came out with his sheeted wife. "Anteia's hipped out of her mind!" I cried. "Hallucinating! Don't believe her! Hi yo, half-brother! Away!"

"Poor dear sister!" Philonoë would lament. "Honestly, honey, for all it hurts to imagine you with another woman, I guess I like your other versions of this story better." For in some I had Anteia be a lovely woman, skin fragrant with sun, hair with sea-salt, as if she'd been day-sailing; she steals into the temple, where I lie dreaming lecherously of her cool brown thighs; suddenly her hand caresses my stomach; all my insides contract violently; I fairly explode awake; "Good Zeus!" I croak, and grab her—naked, unbelievable!—when she sits on my pallet-edge; I bury my face in her, so startled am I; pull her down with me, that electrifying skin against mine, and mirabile dictu! at the sheer enormous lust of it do indeed explode, so wholly that I'm certain liver, spleen, guts, lungs, heart, brains, and all have blown from me, and I lie a hollow shell without sense or strength, et cetera, until she restores me and we make repeated love; complaisant Proetus smiles on the ménage; Anteia is pleased when I lie to her that I was thitherto a virgin, but grows subject to fits of jealousy when I tell her later that I've raped an Amazon between our trysts, and breaks off the affair when she finds herself pregnant, but reinstitutes it some years later, I forget why, but breaks it off finally when she and Proetus go vacationing in Italy, et cetera, I forget. In another telling our initial intercourse is a paradigm of assumed inevitability: wittol Proetus leaves the polis on state business and bids me keep Anteia company in his absence; I spend the afternoon playing ball with their daughters in the palace, then stay to drink ale with Anteia during the evening; we talk impersonally and sporadically—mutual silences are neither unusual nor uncomfortable with that woman; on the face of it there is no overt word or deed that unambiguously indicates desire on the part of either of us; the Queen's manner, which I find attractive, is of exhausted strength: throughout the afternoon her movements have been heavy and deliberate, like those of a helot after two straight shifts; in the evening she sits mostly without moving, and frequently upon blinking her eyes keeps them shut for a full half-minute, opening them at last with a wide stare and a heavy expiration of breath; all this I admire, but really rather abstractly, and any sexual desire that I feel is also more or less abstract; at nine-thirty or thereabouts Anteia says, "I'm going to take a shower and go to bed, Bellerophon," and I say, "All right"; to reach the palace baths she has to go through a little corridor off the ale-room where we sit; to reach Athene's temple I must pass through this same corridor, and so it is still not quite necessary to raise eyebrows at our going to the corridor together; there, if she pauses to face me for a moment at the turning to the baths, who's to say confidently that good nights are not on the tips of tongues? It happens that we embrace instead before we go our separate ways, and further (but I would not say *consequently*) that our separate ways lead to the same bed, where we spend a wordless, tumultuous night together, full of tumblings and flexings and shudders and such, exciting enough to experience but boring to describe; for the subjects' sakes I leave before sunrise, weatherless, et cetera; remorseful, Anteia soon declares to Proetus that I've seduced her; he obliges her, out of some mad craving for moral clarification, to repeat the adultery; presently she conceives, and fearful that the child will prove a parentslaying demigod, considers suicide and abortion; I leave town on Pegasus and never see them again, but learn from my spies in Tiryns that the misadventure has produced a normal son and improved the marriage, et cetera. Yet another version—

Which was the truth?

"I quite understand," Philonoë used to say, "that the very concept of objective truth, especially as regards the historical past, is problematical; also that narrative art, particularly of the mythopoeic or at least mythographic variety, has structures and rhythms, values and demands, not the same as those of reportage or historiography. Finally, as between variants among the myths themselves, it's in their contradictions that one may seek their sense. All the same— not to say *therefore*—I'd be interested to know whether in fact you made love to my sister and wish you hadn't, or didn't and wish you had."

"What a horse!" I invariably replied. "I spent the whole night learning how to fly him and unstarving myself with moussaka at all-night restaurants. By morning I was able to make a perfect four-point landing atop the statue of Abas,

Proetus's father, which stood in the breakfast-terrace of the palace. The children were delighted; Proetus blushed; Anteia flushed, hushed the kids, and hmped off with them from the table, giving her husband a last sharp look.

" 'We're at your service, sir,' I said. He bade me park my brother elsewhere, the pigeons were bad enough, then told me frankly that his wife, per program, was holding to her accusations and agitating for my life, motivated no doubt in part by some final urge, such as comes sometimes on ladies at her age and stage, to inspire jealous anger in her husband and prompt him to dramatic if not heroic action in her behalf. For himself, Q.E.D., if he believed her accusation and gave a damn, he'd arrange to have me done in quietly, with minimal fuss. But he was indifferent, except for the sake of public appearances. He therefore requested simply that I disappear. 'At the same time she's hollering for your head,' he said with a sigh, 'she's giving out already that she's eight hours pregnant with a semidemigod.' Doubly impossible, I told him. He raised his hand wearily: if I would not do him the service of assassinating Perseus, at least I might leave the Queen her delusions: fact was, she did show signs of being a couple months gone again, by himself or whomever, and that condition, which given her age et cetera might as possibly be menopause, perhaps accounted for her late irrationality. His p.r. people would do their best to minimize the gossip, but as Anteia was insisting that she'd been divinely raped (half-ravished, anyhow, by a demideity), the best thing I could do for him was not deny the child's paternity should she bring it to term, and in the meanwhile go and *be* a mythic hero—somewhere else.

"I shrugged. 'Set me a task.' 'Kill Perseus!' he whispered. 'Nope.' So he gave me a sealed letter to Iobates—diplomatic business, he declared—and asked me to deliver it to Lycia, air mail special, no peeking, no reply or return necessary, okay? 'Okay.' I took off, came back: 'Which way is Lycia?' He covered his eyes, pointed east-southeast-by-east; here I am"; there it is. Philonoë'd say "Thanks for the story; you tell it better all the time." Those were the days. And "When can we visit my sister, Bellerophon? It's a pity the kids have never met their own cousins. Better get off to your lecture now; here's your notes. Kiss goodbye?" I'd tear my hair then, do now, one digression still to go, Zeus Almighty, half a hundred pages in and only launched. How does one write a novella? How find the channel, bewildered in these creeks and crannies? Storytelling isn't my cup of wine; isn't somebody's; my plot doesn't rise and fall in meaningful stages but winds upon itself like a whelk-shell or the snakes on Hermes's caduceus: digresses, retreats, hesitates, groans from its utter et cetera, collapses, dies.

Q: "What about the purification of your blood-guilt, sir?"

A: "Granted Pegasus, I inferred I was clear with Athene, who, Deliades having been her particular votary, I presumed to be the only god concerned."

Q: "How far up did Pegasus get this morning, sir?"

A: "Not above a meter. Our investigation of this problem, to which my administration gives the highest priority, continues, and you may expect a full report after the present digression."

Q: "In one of the earlier meetings of this course of lectures on the First Flood of the Distinguished History of Bellerophon the Mythic Hero, required of all members of the court of Bellerophon the King in hopes of alienating them from him in partial fulfillment of the fourth quadrant

(Reign and Death) of the mythobiographic Pattern, describing your recent systematic abuse of Queen Philonoë, the Princes Hippolochus and Isander, and Princess Laodamia by prolix and tactless rehearsals of your childhood, you mentioned that writing—as a means of ordinary communication as opposed to a mode of magic—will not be introduced into Hellenic culture for some centuries yet except as borrowed in isolated instances from the future by seers like Polyeidus. Yet the 'labor' imposed on you by King Proetus was the delivery to your late father-in-law of a diplomatic message in epistolary form. Moreover, the lecture in which you made the aforementioned mention was itself, we recall with excitement, read from a written text, at least delivered from written notes, as have been all the lectures in this thrilling course—the very word *lecture*, I believe, comes from a barbaric root-verb meaning 'to read,' and reading, a priori, implies writing. Finally, our presence here in the University of Lycia's newly established Department of Classical Mythology, your stimulating requirement from us of term papers on The Story of Your Life Thus Far, et cetera, all suggest that we are, if not a literate society, at least a society to which reading and writing are not unknown. Is there not some discrepancy here?"

A: "Yes."

Q: "Several other things also perplex us, sir, researchers after truth that we are and in no way disaffected from our country, our king, or our university by, respectively, your prolongation of the Carian–Solymian war, your mistreatment of good King Iobates's gentle younger daughter, and your unseemly perversion of professorial privilege to the ends of self-aggrandizement and/or -abasement—all which we readily accept as the self-imposed rigors of the above-alluded-to Pattern. Are you not inclined, as we are, to see a seerly hand, perhaps Polyeidus's, in such apparent lapses of authorial control, even narrative coherence, as the presentation, before we've even heard today's lecture, of these Q's and A's, which in fact *follow* that lecture? Or the mysterious, to us very nearly unintelligible, text of the lecture itself, which reads:

"*Good evening. On behalf of the mythic hero Bellerophon of Corinth, I would like to thank* [supply name of university, publisher, sponsor of reading, et cetera] *for this opportunity to put straight a number of discrepancies and problematical details in the standard accounts of his life and work; to lay to rest certain items of disagreeable gossip concerning both his public and his private life; and to respond to any questions you may wish to put concerning his fabulous career.*

"*My general interest in the wandering-hero myth dates from my thirtieth year, when reviewers of my novel* The Sot-Weed Factor (*1960*) *remarked that the vicissitudes of its hero—Ebenezer Cooke, Gentleman, Poet and Laureate of Maryland—follow in some detail the pattern of mythical heroic adventure as described by Lord Raglan, Joseph Campbell, and other comparative mythologists. The suggestion was that I had used this pattern as the basis for the novel's plot. In fact I'd been till then unaware of the pattern's existence; once apprised of it, I was struck enough by the coincidence (which I later came to regard as more inevitable than remarkable) to examine those works by which I'd allegedly been influenced, and my next novel,* Giles Goat-Boy (*1966*), *was for better or worse the conscious and ironic orchestration of the Ur-Myth which its predecessor had been represented as being. Several of my subsequent fictions—the long short-story* Menelaiad *and the novella* Perseid, *for example—deal directly with particular manifestations of the myth of the wandering hero and address as well a number of their author's more current thematic concerns: the mortal desire for immortality, for instance, and its ironically qualified fulfillment—especially by the mythic hero's transformation, in the latter stages of his career, into the sound of his own voice, or the story of his life, or both. I am forty.*

"*Since myths themselves are among other things poetic distillations of our ordinary psychic experience and therefore point always to daily reality, to write realistic fictions which point always to mythic archetypes is in my opinion to take the wrong end of the mythopoeic stick, however meritorious such fictions may be in other respects. Better to address the archetypes directly. To the objection that classical mythology, like the Bible, is no longer a staple of the average reader's education, and that, consequently, the old agonies of Oedipus or Antigone are without effect on contemporary sensibility, I reply, hum, I forget what, something about comedy and self-explanatory context. Anyhow, when I had completed the* Perseid *novella, my research after further classical examples of the aforementioned themes led me to the minor mythic hero Bellerophon of Corinth.*

"*As it was among other things the very unfamiliarity of Bellerophon's story, even to those acquainted with the myths of Menelaus and Helen or Perseus and Andromeda, that I found appropriate to my purposes, a brief summary might be helpful. Here is Robert Graves's excellent account in* The Greek Myths, *itself a collation of the texts of Antoninus Liberalis, Apollodorus, Eustathius, Hesiod, Homer, Hy-*

ginus, Ovid, Pindar, Plutarch, the Scholiast on the Iliad, *and*
Tzetzes:

"*a*. Bellerophon, son of Glaucus . . . left Corinth under a cloud, having first killed one Bellerus—which
earned him his nickname Bellerophontes, shortened to
Bellerophon—and then his own brother, whose name
is usually given as Deliades. He fled as a suppliant to
Proetus, King of Tiryns; but . . . Anteia, Proetus's wife
. . . fell in love with him at sight. When he rejected her
advances, she accused him of having tried to seduce her,
and Proetus, who believed the story, grew incensed. Yet
he dared not risk the Furies' vengeance by the direct
murder of a suppliant, and therefore sent him to Anteia's father Iobates, King of Lycia, carrying a sealed
letter, which read: 'Pray remove the bearer from this
world; he has tried to violate my wife, your daughter.'

"*b*. Iobates, equally loth to ill-treat a royal guest,
asked Bellerophon to do him the service of destroying
the Chimaera, a fire-breathing she-monster with lion's
head, goat's body, and serpent's tail . . . Before setting
about the task, Bellerophon consulted the seer Polyeidus, and was advised to catch and tame the winged
horse Pegasus, beloved by the Muses of Mount Helicon,
for whom he had created the well Hippocrene by
stamping his moon-shaped hoof.

"*c*. . . . Bellerophon found [Pegasus] drinking at
Peirene . . . another of his wells, and threw over his
head a golden bridle, Athene's timely present. But some
say that Athene gave Pegasus already bridled to Bellerophon; and others that Poseidon, who was really Bellerophon's father, did so. Be that as it may, Bellerophon
overcame the Chimaera by flying above her on Pegasus's
back, riddling her with arrows, and then thrusting between her jaws a lump of lead which he had fixed to the
point of his spear. The Chimaera's fiery breath melted

the lead, which trickled down her throat, searing her vitals.

"*d*. Iobates, however, far from rewarding Bellerophon for this daring feat, sent him at once against the warlike Solymians and their allies, the Amazons; both of whom he conquered by soaring above them, well out of bowshot, and dropping large boulders on their heads. Next, in the Lycian plain of Xanthus, he beat off a band of Carian pirates led by one Cheimarrhus, a fiery and boastful warrior, who sailed in a ship adorned with a lion figurehead and a serpent stern. When Iobates showed no gratitude even then but, on the contrary, sent the palace guards to ambush him on his return, Bellerophon dismounted and prayed that while he advanced on foot, Poseidon would flood the Xanthian Plain behind him. Poseidon heard his prayer, and sent great waves rolling slowly forward as Bellerophon approached Iobates's palace; and, because no man could persuade him to retire, the Xanthian women hoisted their skirts to the waist and came rushing towards him full butt, offering themselves to him one and all, if only he would relent. Bellerophon's modesty was such that he turned tail and ran; and the waves retreated with him.

"*e*. Convinced now that Proetus must have been mistaken about the attempt on Anteia's virtue, Iobates produced the letter, and demanded an exact account of the affair. On learning the truth, he implored Bellerophon's forgiveness, gave him his daughter Philonoë in marriage, and made him heir to the Lycian throne. He also praised the Xanthian women for their resourcefulness and ordered that, in future, all Xanthians should reckon descent from the mother, not the father. . . .

"*Those familiar with my fiction will recognize in this account several pet motifs of mine: the sibling rivalry, the hero's naïveté, the accomplishment of labors by their trans-*

*cension (here literal), and the final termination of all tasks
by the extermination (here figurative) of the taskmaster; the
Protean counselor (Polyeidus means 'many forms'); the ro-
mantic triangle; et cetera. But it was the two central images
—Pegasus and the Chimera—which appealed to me most
profoundly. I envisioned a comic novella based on the myth;
a companion-piece to* Perseid, *perhaps. To compose it I set
aside a much larger and more complicated project, a novel
called* Letters—*it seemed anyway to have become a vast
morass of plans, notes, false starts, in which I grew more
mired with every attempt to extricate myself. Hopefully I
turned to the lesser project, labored at it unremittingly for
a full year and a half—alas, it, too, metamorphosed into
quicksand, not before much good spiritual money had been
thrown after the bad. Followed my first real affliction by the
celebrated ailment Writer's Block, a malady from which, in
the hubris of my twenties and thirties, I had fancied myself
immune; I examined it as one might a malignant growth, with
sharp interest and dull fright. For a long time I could not
understand it—though I did come to understand, to the heart,
the lamentations of those mystics to whom Grace had been
once vouchsafed and then withdrawn. To the world it is a
small matter, rightly, whether any particular artist finds his
powers sustained or drained from one year to the next; to
the artist himself, however minor his talent, imaginative potency is as crucial to the daily life of his spirit as sexual
potency—to which, in the male at least, it is an analogue as
irresistible as that of Grace, and as dangerous.*

*"Eventually I did come to understand what was ailing
me, so I believe; in any case the ailment passed—for little
better or worse from the world's point of view, but much to
my own relief—and I found myself composing as busily as*

ever. What I composed is another story, of no concern to us here; I recount this little personal episode by way of introducing the subject of this afternoon's lecture: an altogether impersonal principle of literary aesthetics, the understanding of the nature of which illuminated for me my difficulty with Bellerophon's story and, so I must presume, set me free of both the mire and the myth.

"*The general principle, I believe, has no name in our ordinary critical vocabulary; I think of it as the Principle of Metaphoric Means, by which I intend the investiture by the writer of as many of the elements and aspects of his fiction as possible with emblematic as well as dramatic value: not only the 'form' of the story, the narrative viewpoint, the tone, and such, but, where manageable, the particular genre, the mode and medium, the very process of narration—even the fact of the artifact itself. Let me illustrate:?*"

A: "I am."

Q: "Sir?"

A: "I *am* inclined, with you, to sniff in this a certain particular seer, the full history and scope of whose treachery, however, I'm still in no position to appreciate at this point in this rendition of this *Bellerophoniad*. The writer's language is not Greek; the literary works referred to do not exist—wouldn't I, of all people, know that *Perseid* if there were one? As for that farrago of misstatements purporting to be the story of my life, the kindest thing to be said about its first three paragraphs is that they're fiction: the brothers are too many and miscast; my name is mishistoried (though 'Bellerus the Killer' is not its only meaning); my acquisition of Pegasus is mislocated as to both time and place; the Bellerophonic missive read simply 'Pray remove the bearer of these letters from this world'; et cetera. *d* and *e*, perhaps, are slightly less inaccurate, if no less incomplete, and their events are out of order. I call your attention, earnestly, to the suspension-points following the fifth paragraph: that's where we are, have been, have languished since the first good night. There's the sink; there's the quag; there's the slough of my despond. Drive me out."

Q: "No, sir."

A: "That's a question?" The document disappointed me as much as my students' unwillingness to follow the Pattern. We're to the day before my fortieth birthday now, page before Page 1: this particular lecture-scroll I'd pinned great fresh hope upon: sealed with an impression of the Chimera, it was inscribed *For B from P: Begin in the Middle of the Road of Our Life*; I'd first come across it twenty years previously, in circumstances about to be set forth at length; newlywed Philonoë had taken it to be a posthumous wedding gift from newly dead Polyeidus, who'd expired in circumstances about to be et cetera, and interpreted its legend to mean either Open at the Midpoint of My Life or Open Halfway Through Our Married Life. Either way, reckoning from the Polyeidic calendar, it meant age thirty-six—four years too late already! I'd put the thing aside many years ago; forgot it existed; then it turned up accountably in my scroll-case this morning in place of my text for this final lecture in the First-Flood series. Crushing, to find it such a mishmash! "Drive me out, sirs, as you love me; exile me from the city; make me wander far from the paths of men, devouring my own soul, et cetera, till I meet my apotheosis in some counterpart of the Axis Mundi or World Navel: in a riven grove, say, where one oak stands in a rock cleft by the first spring of the last freshet on the highest rise of some hill or other." This is your best, Polyeidus?

"Here's how it was. As I came in on the glide-path over Halicarnassus into Lycia, Pegasus swept into a sudden curve and went whinnying around what I took to be the plume of a small volcano, in ever-diminishing circles like a moth around a candle, till I feared we must disappear up our own fundaments. When we finally touched down and the world quit wheeling, I found us inside the crater itself, not active after all except for smoke issuing from one small cave; there an old beardless chap in a snakeskin coat, that's right, was lighting papers one at a time and tossing them into the hole, where they combusted with enormous disproportion of smoke to flame. At sight of Pegasus the fellow panicked, and no wonder: willy-nilly we charged, and Peg nipped him up by the neck-nape. Better to grasp the bridle, I'd been holding Proetus's letter in my mouth; lost it when I hollered whoa; next instant the man was gone and it was that letter in the horse's mouth; instant after, when I snatched it from there, I found myself holding sidesaddle the same old man, himself holding the letter. 'I'm an unsuccessful novelist,' he muttered hastily: 'life's work, five-volume *roman fleuve*—goddamn *ocean*, more like it; agent won't touch it; I'm reading it aloud to the wild animals and burning it up a page at a time. Never attracted a winged horse before; mountain lions, mostly, at this elevation; few odd goats from lower down, et cetera. Dee dee dum dee dee.'

"What Pegasus held now instead, and chewed on placidly till I took it from him, was the amulet. 'Passing prophet hung that on me,' Polyeidus lied; 'said I ought to try something in the myth way, very big nowadays, three novellas in one volume, say: one about Perseus and Medusa, one about Bellerophon and the Chimera, one about—' I squeezed him. 'Polyeidus!' 'That was his name, all right,' Polyeidus said:

'had a daughter very high on this Bellerophon fellow, said she goes around hollering Bellerus Bellerus all day, that sort of thing. You're Bellerophon, are you? Told me I should hang that gadget around my neck, fetch me better ideas. What do you hear from your mother?' When he saw it was for joy I pounded him, he admitted he was Polyeidus and congratulated me on my achievement of Pegasus, which he was pleased to take for a sign that his petitions to Athene on my behalf had not been inefficacious. The fatal amulet virtually *was*, these days—it was the smell of wild mares on it, more than hippomanes, that had attracted Pegasus—and if I'd oblige him with a lift back to the Lycian capital, where he was now employed by King Iobates, he'd be happy to discard it against future impediment to navigation.

" 'You've heard nothing from Corinth, you say?' 'Only that Mother had you arrested. What for?' 'Ugly business, that,' Polyeidus said, and pitched the amulet into the cave. The smoke diminished. 'Poor woman's quite out of her tree, I fear. I told her you'd be back one day to reclaim the kingdom; thought that would cheer her up? Not a bit of it! Patriarchal plot, she said: sexual imperialism, et cetera. Clapped me in the keep. I decided to turn into the vaulted cell itself so that the guards would think I'd escaped and leave the door open, whereupon I *would* escape. But something went wrong: I turned into a fierce she-monster here on this mountain, and all but ate myself alive before I could switch back. I just don't have it any more in the three-dimensional way.' His best explanation of the phenomenon, he went on to say as we winged off to the Lycian capital, was that Hermes, famous trickster and inventor of the alphabet, must be as well a lover of puns and practical jokes: in keeping with his recent tendency to turn into documents, Polyeidus had changed not directly into his dungeon cell but, intermediately, into a magic message spelling out that objective: *I am a chamber.* Finding himself instead a fire-breathing monster with lion's head, goat's body, and serpent's tail, dwelling in a cave in a dormant volcano called Mount Chimera on the Lycian–Carian border, he could only infer that the god had sported with the proximity of the names *kamara/Chimera.* But being nearly lost in translation was not the end of the difficulty: so violently had Polyeidus dissociated with the monster, his resumption of human form (sans hair and twenty kilos) had left the *Chimera,* as he now called his accidental creation, intact: the first such case in the history of magical transformation, so far as he knew, and he regarded it with mixed feelings. On the one hand, foreseeing that Amisidoros, the Carian king, would attempt to exploit the beast as a new secret weapon to guard the long-disputed boundary, he was able to forewarn Iobates and establish himself in the Lycian court as a special defense-minister; on the other hand, he was obliged not only to conceal his own responsibility for Chimera's existence, but to make periodic secret field trips to the crater to feed the beast a ream or so of specially composed tranquilizing spells, until he could devise a better way to neutralize her.

" 'So here we are,' he concluded; 'you keep my little secret, I'll keep yours'—by which he meant, you understand, my responsibility for the death of Glaucus and my brother. 'You've learned to read and write, I see?' He indicated the letter. I confessed I had not, except for an odd half-dozen alphabetical characters. 'Just as well,' he said; 'only mischief in letters—Q.E.D.! Look where the birth-certificate trick got us! I'll deliver this for you. Any idea what's in it?'

"I shook my head and, for shame, volunteered only that

I was doing a kind of purificatory labor for King Proetus, perhaps unnecessary, but a good trial run in any case for whatever true labors lay ahead. At his suggestion we landed here in the main square of Telmissus, for maximum effect. A crowd assembled, also the court, to admire Pegasus; Polyeidus took several bows and introduced us to Iobates, describing me as a former protégé and an up-and-coming mythic hero. The King was cordial, inquired after Anteia and his granddaughters, thanked me for the letter, insisted on feasting me for nine days before opening it. He introduced me to his younger daughter, Philonoë, at age sixteen an undergraduate mythology major here at the University (though we had no department then, only a couple of course-offerings), who shyly asked me to autograph her syllabus. I drew a careful upper-case Beta, best I could do, with her curious writing tool, a lead-pointed stick Polyeidus had given her that made marks on things. A charming girl, by turns demure and bold, she sat next me at dinner; told me her father's nine-day custom drove her buggy—she always tore into *her* mail the second it arrived; bade me describe in detail her little nieces, whom she was dying to visit; confessed an absolute passion for the study of mythology; asked me would I visit her senior seminar if she okayed it with her professor —no need to prepare anything, just rap with the kids, et cetera; pressed me particularly for anecdotes about Perseus, her favorite among contemporaries in the field.

"In the days that followed we became great friends. My intellectual superior, she nonetheless deferred to me as an example of what she called 'the imaginative embodiment of otherwise merely intellectual conceptions, you know?' What I saw as small embarrassments—my then illiteracy, for example—she was pleased to interpret as marks of authenticity, though she volunteered to tutor me in writing if I'd give her flying lessons. Indeed, she told me frankly that the only thing that bothered her about me, hero-wise, was my articulateness and apparent gentleness of manner: heroes, she fancied, should be rougher-edged and less ready of speech. But she soon had it reasoned out that her preconceptions in this regard were no doubt due to the stylizing nature of the mythopoeic process itself, which simplified character and motive just as it compressed time and space, so that one imagined Perseus to be speeding tirelessly and thoughtlessly from action to bravura action, when in fact he must have weeks of idleness, hours of indecision, et cetera. Besides, who could stroll the palace gardens, play catch, sing duets, and have long talks with a *mere* Golden Destroyer?

"At her coaxing, King Iobates shortened the feasting period from nine days to seven, seven to five, in case the letter contained news from Anteia. But as it was after all government business, on the fifth evening he gave it to Polyeidus, his official state-message reader (Iobates shared my limitation), to read to him. The seer opened it, paled, glanced at me sharply, pled for a moment to consider the accurate Lycian equivalents of a few Tirynish idioms, then read what amounted to a note of introduction from Proetus in my behalf: *Pray remove the bearer of these letters from the world of blood-guilt which he fancies himself to carry in consequence of his innocent role in the deaths of his father and brother; kindly permit him to do for you some heroic service, the more hazardous the better. Yrs, P.* I had been anxious that the letter might allude to my contretemps with Philonoë's sister; at the news I smiled, thought better of Proetus, affirmed my willingness to attempt whatever Iobates wished. The company drank my health; Philonoë glowed; Polyeidus smiled, quite in command of himself now, and held a whispered conference with Iobates, who at first flushed angrily and seemed about to rise from table, then—on further whispers from the seer—composed himself and coolly requested me to rid the coast, if I would, of a band of Carian pirates lately infesting it. Perhaps I could set out immediately after dinner?

"His sudden change of mood perplexed me, but I took off on Pegasus without waiting for dessert, spent the night and morning talking with fishermen and merchant-skippers, located the chief pirate vessel by aerial reconnaissance with the aid of their descriptions, sank ship and company by bombardment with big rocks, knocked off the paddlers with low-level hoofing, returned to the palace by cocktail time. The King and Polyeidus, celebrating, seemed surprised; Philonoë kissed me. 'Nothing to it,' I said, hanging up my bridle: 'Captain's name was Chimarrhus, which I believe means goat? Red-bearded chap. Real fire-breather, judging from the way he hissed and gurgled going under. Their rig had a lion figurehead, serpentine taffrail: a nautical monstrosity. I wasted them. No big deal.'

" 'Hmp,' Iobates said, his elder daughter's father, glaring at Polyeidus, who rapidly declared that the great similarity between the old Carian pirate outfit and the new border-monster should not be taken as evidence that my testimony was fanciful: in his opinion it corroborated his opinion that the Chimera, while newly embodied up in the hills and a great fresh threat to Lycia, was a monster of long-standing Carian tradition: his genealogical visions and researches inclined him to believe her the offspring of Typhon and

Echidne. The former, son of Earth and Tartarus, had been the largest monster ever: a serpent from the waist down, he featured hundred-league arms with serpent-heads for hands, an ass-head that touched the stars, sun-darkening wings, flaming eyes, and live-lava breath—hence Chimera's volcanic habitat. The latter, half lovely woman and half speckled serpent, a man-eater killed by hundred-eyed Argus, was one of the Phorcids, sister to the Gorgons and Graeae of Persean fame. Thus Chimera, interestingly, was in fact Medusa's niece, Pegasus's cousin, and, since the winged horse was my half-sibling, not altogether unrelated to me.

"Iobates rehmped, and with not so much as a congratulatory word to me, said he wondered now and then what was in some people's drinks. 'I take it you can back up this claim?' he asked me incordially. Surprised, I retorted that the numberless sharks had been my only body-counters; Philonoë protested to her dad that while trophy-fetching was a common enough feature of heroic expeditions, to put the burden of proof on the hero was unprecedented and discourteous. Polyeidus diplomatically suggested that just as I was still a novice at performing hero-tasks, the King was a novice at taskmastering; why not both of us try another? Detachments of the Solymian and Amazon military, he understood, were once again bivouacked along the border on opposite sides of Mount Chimera, a clear and present danger to our territorial integrity. How about a twin wonder, the single-handed repulse of both armies?

"Iobates made the family noise, but seemed interested. Philonoë showed alarm. 'Of course, if you think that's beyond you . . .' Polyeidus offered. 'Nothing's beyond me,' I said. Then the King, all smiles, bade me have a nice dinner first, at which he specified, in the trophy way, a good-looking Amazon captive not older than twenty-five Polyeidic years or below the rank of first lieutenant, sufficiently intact for concubinage.

" 'That's *disgusting,* Daddy!' Philonoë said. 'Besides, any Amazon would *die* before she'd be a slave; we learned that in fourth grade.' Iobates chuckled and declared he'd take the chance. I remarked that while serial labors were not unusual for heroes, I knew of none whose tasks were imposed without so much as a night's sleep between. Polyeidus agreed, but seconded the King's timetable on the grounds that just as no literary classic is quite like any other literary classic, so no classical hero's biography exactly duplicated any other's; one attained such generality as the Pattern only by ignoring enough particular differences. This notion oddly troubled me. The Princess kissed my brow and said, 'Daddy's afraid to have you around because he sees I have a crush on you. Lots of kings are like that.' Iobates hmped; I took off blear-eyed but much aroused.

"I was, remember, a prime and healthy fellow, so pre-occupied with my career that except for occasional chamber-maids or temple-prostitutes I'd had no women since Sibyl-in-the-grove. All the while I drowsily wrecked the Solymians (saturation-bombing of their encampment by moonlight with boulders from Mount Chimera—where I saw this time neither smoke nor monster—and sporadic high-level horse dung), I had ardent fantasies about Philonoë, so much more fetching than Anteia or Polyeidus's distracted daughter. At dawn, when I landed sleepily to verify the rout, I could scarcely concentrate on trampling the wounded for imagining the perky Princess (in Position One) on my temple pallet or among the creepers of the sacred grove. The camp was empty; indeed, the old chap I was absent-mindedly hoofing to death was the only sign of life; had I been less full of Philonoë I might have heard in time his protests that he was not Solymian but Carian, a goatherd whose flock the Solymian raiding party, taking him for a Lycian, had made off with at my first bomb-run from the hilltop. Declaring that he would have fled after them in hopes of stealing back his goats had he not slipped on a Pegasus-turd and turned his ankle, he cursed warriors in general and mythic heroes in particular, who in his opinion were worse than mercenaries in that we had not even the excuse of getting our daily bread by doing hired hurt to others, but performed our lethal offices for mere self-aggrandizement. This point I would have debated with him readily had he not expired upon making it; just as well, I reflected, recalling Philonoë's attitude toward overmuch rationality on the part of heroes. The recollection of her earnest face and dainty neck too aroused me for discourse anyhow; marveling tumescently at how my image of her worked to turn me into her image of me, I flew off to find the Amazons.

"Their rout was easily effected, for all their famous battle-courage, inasmuch as they were strictly horse soldiers, and their mounts, trained not to shy from the most clangorous conventional combat, bolted unmanageably at first sight of swooping Pegasus. The 'war party' reported by Lycian intelligence numbered no more than two dozen, mostly middle-aged: I learned later from Melanippe that they were in fact scouts sent to investigate the Chimera, distorted reports of whose existence and possible usefulness had come to Themiscyra from Lycian operatives. They were lightly armed and, far from home, more concerned with preserving their horses than doing battle with me, whom they took to be the monster. A few passes scattered them; had I been in their territory, they'd have regrouped, blindfolded their mounts, and come back to dispatch me at whatever cost. As I wasn't, they returned to their base with reports (corroborated, so our own intelligence people subsequently confirmed, by the Solymian scouting and foraging party) that Chimera was a flying centaur in Iobates's service, not a fire-breathing dragon in Amisidoros's, and recommended withdrawal from the Carian alliance, as did the Solymians —Amisidoros, it turns out, knew nothing at all of the treble beast alleged to be his house pet and secret weapon.

"But they returned, the Amazons, minus one, the youngest-looking, whom I buzzed and harried several kilometers from the rest until her horse fell. She was pitched hard to the rocky ground; the horse, a black mare, sprang up and, less fearful now that Pegasus was landed, stood nervously by. The Amazon lay still. I fetched up her brazen bow and half-moon shield to club her with if she happened to be alive, and rolled her over with my foot. She seemed more dazed than dead, but required no further blows. I tied her wrists and ankles with her bowstring as she stirred, and stanched enough blood to try to judge her age and rank. She was very young, Philonoë's age at most, dark-skinned, short-haired, wiry, the most attractive of her kind I'd seen. Back in Corinth I'd heard the usual Amazon stories—that they burned their left breasts off to clear the bowstring; that they were actually men, a kind of Spartans in drag—and with my brother had teased in vain our Themiscyran horse-grooms for confirmation. Now, as my prisoner began to regain her senses, I did my own research: both breasts were there when I pulled her shirt open; little pomegranates by comparison with Philonoë's ripe pears or Sibyl's honeydews, but no less appetizing. I unbuckled her chiton and pulled down her spotted tights, ripped and dirtied from her fall: despite bruise and brush-burn, her thighs were lean and smooth to touch, her parts altogether female: neat and dainty, lightly fleeced. As I poked to learn whether she still had her hymen, she thrashed about and swore military oaths.

" 'Are you by any chance an officer?' I asked her.

" 'Lance Corporal Melanippe, Fifth Light Cavalry,' she answered furiously. 'Get your filthy hands off me!'

" 'That's under First Lieutenant, I suppose? No matter. Are you a virgin?'

"She replied, in a tighter voice, though still as if at least as angry with herself as with me, that the Second Rule for Amazonian Prisoners of War forbade her to give any information beyond her name, rank, and unit. I cordially pointed out that inasmuch as I'd been ignorant of that rule, she'd broken it already by informing me of its existence. Amazons do not weep, but their voices tremble. She requested that I kill her first.

" 'Before what?' Then I realized, rather to my own surprise, not only that I'd been totally erect ever since dismounting from Pegasus (who grazed and nuzzled peacefully with the black mare), but that I really did mean forcibly to have her. She put up a formidable resistance, particularly for one bound hand and foot and barely sensible after her fall: certain Amazons, I was to learn later, especially those named Melanippe or Leaping Myrine, have a kind of limited Protean capacity when sexually in extremis: my lance corporal, before I stuck her, turned briefly but unmistakably into a stone crab, a water snake, a hind, and a squid, in that order. Her undoing was that, frenzied, she could think only of what she hoped were frightening or swift beasts (and, at that, happened not to think of wild mares, which would

have undone me), not realizing, what I knew from Polyeidus, that anything limbed she might turn into would be
bound as she was—and that my acquaintance with shape-
shifters somewhat immunized me to her effects. Had she
turned into a cloud, say, or a stream of water, she might've
got clear; as it was, I merely backed off from the crab and
held it by a backfin against scuttling off on its other legs;
seized the viper safely behind the head (my brother and I
were great early terrifiers of little girls with snakes we caught
in the grove); and actually entered, a tergo, the lassoed hind,
knowing it must soon rebecome what I lusted for. Squealing,
it turned squid, only two of whose five pairs of tentacles
were tied: I'd've got out fast—that beak, you know, down
by the sex-parts?—but the free six suckered me, not bad
actually, from the same squiddy instinct which then inked
the penis it might have bitten off. A moment later she was
unmaidened Melanippe, held by the hair and howling under
me as I gave her squirt for squirt. Once come, I was at once
appalled at having twice been so overmastered by desire,
this time replacing with unkindest force my kindless deception in the grove. I withdrew, contrite; squid ink, mixed
with cherry-bright blood, smeared from my shrinking tool
onto her hams and cheeks, still fiercely squeezed, initialing
my shame in the strokes and diacritics of a barbarous alphabet.

" 'Pig! Pig!' she spat, choking with outrage. I saw no
point in pointing out to her that that transformation, had
she thought of it in time, would have been spitted as her
hind.

" 'Awfully sorry,' I panted. 'Long time between women;
got carried away. Say, that squid was a crackerjack!'

" 'Cut my throat,' she requested, speaking into the dirt.

" 'Don't be silly.'

" 'Disembowel me.'

" 'Nonsense.'

" 'I'd kill you if I could, you sexist swine.'

"There we lay. 'I shouldn't blame you,' I said. 'I've never deflowered anybody before, you know, much less committed rape. I'm thoroughly ashamed of myself. What shall I do to make it up to you?' Her suggestions were ill-humored and impossible to carry out without ending my career. We were still for a while.

" 'In my country,' she said presently, 'we'd cut your rapist cock off and choke you on it. We'd impale you up the ass on a hot stake. We'd make you eat your own balls. O! O! O!'

"A third time I apologized for having forced her; despite her oaths, spits, and thrashes, then, I cleaned her up and put her clothes in order, saving only the armored chiton as evidence for Iobates. As I worked I recounted sympathetically Anteia's rape-story; her frustration at unfair nature's one-sidedness in this area; my admiration of the excellent horsemanship of the Amazons on our palace staff in Corinth, and her own fine fighting spirit; my resolve to see her back to her outfit instead of enslaving her to my taskmaster, for whom I had no particular affection, et cetera. Putting by the Second Rule for Prisoners, Melanippe then informed me, more calmly but still in a cool fury, of the First—to die in battle rather than be taken prisoner, since Amazons must expect to be raped by their Sexist Pig Captors—and the Third—if captured by surprise, to kill oneself as soon as possible, not to afford more gratification than necessary to those same SPC's. I reminded her that I had no intention of repeating that shameful violation, of her and of my own better nature. She spat at me, unimpressed, and said that as a point of honor no Amazon, once captured and sexually assaulted, ever returned to Amazonia unless with her assailant's severed parts strung on a lanyard, for though her people, contrary to popular belief, had a high regard for heterosexual as well as homosexual connections, and copulated vigorously and freely on their own initiative with males, they abhorred above all things being forced. Their moral education, their religion, their art, even their history and mythology, turned on this point: they traced their descent, for example, from a company of some two thousand virgins forcibly deflowered by an Asian despot who then transported them en masse to Scythia, bidding them remember him kindly as having relented in his vow to kill each one after raping her; instead, those who found themselves pregnant by him killed their children, and they established a militant gynocracy to oppose the forcible suppression of their sex. *Amazon*, she said, had a higher meaning than the vulgar one: though a zealous leader might literally lop one breast off for symbolic reasons—Melanippe herself had considered doing so—the single-breastedness implied by the name was metaphorical and positive: one half pure woman, one half pure warrior, et cetera. In consequence of all this, if as sometimes happened a raped Amazon had no chance to take revenge on her defiler before he released her, she was not obliged to kill herself, but she must live in exile, raising the consciousness of foreign women to the facts of their exploitation—hence the isolated instances of Melanippe's countrywomen in such places as Corinth, where, while doing yeoman service, they quietly subverted the patriarchy.

"But my victim herself, ambitious in her way as I, had aspired from earliest girlhood to the grand objective of leading her sisters victoriously back to the country of their legendary origin, Samarkand; deposing and castrating the male sexist pig despot, whoever that luckless fellow might be, and making the ancestral motherland a matriarchy. From this destiny, toward which her precocious attainment of lance-corporalship was a promising first step, one fall of her horse and thrust of my yard had barred her forever; as her whole heart and mind and soul was in Themiscyra, she would not live in exile; if I was too cowardly to follow up rape with murder, she would kill herself.

"I had been penitent; hearing my victim's most touching account and imagining how *I'd* have felt, even without the extra moral and historical resonances, if some bitter mischance (such as befell my brother) had nipped my career in the bud, I was inconsolable. I dared not turn her loose; neither could I leave her where she was or fly her to Themiscyra or back to Telmissus (where, perhaps, Philonoë's friendship would have soothed her, if not mine—but I did not trust Iobates); on the other hand, contrite as I was, I was not willing to emasculate myself for penance. Melanippe rejected angrily my offer to supply her with the genitalia of a certain dead goatherd over the hill, which she could represent back home as her violator's. At length, for want of better, though I was perishing for sleep I flew her across the Sporades and Cyclades, all the way to Corinth, binding her tightly across Pegasus's back to prevent her jumping off: we landed by night atop the royal horse-barns, astonishing two owls and the Amazon on watch—whom I recognized as fat Hippolyta, a friend of my youth, and saluted by name.

" 'No, not Prince Bellerus any longer,' I called down to her: *'Bellerophon. The Killer?* I have a young sister of yours here: Lance Corporal Melanippe, Fifth Light Cavalry, a valiant soldier shamefully raped in Lycia while unconscious after a bad fall from her horse. So. Please see she doesn't harm herself, okay? And commend her to my mother and your comrades, et cetera. Also, tell Mom I'm fine and will come back to claim Corinth sooner or later. Also, that she was wrong about Polyeidus. I think. Thanks.' While amazed Hippolyta went to fetch a ladder and her comrades, I deposited Melanippe, too despondent to speak, gently on the roof; kissed her hair; reapologized. 'Best I could think of,' I said; 'you're among friends, anyhow. Subvert all you want to. Anything else I can do for you?' Why, yes, she responded: matter of fact she desired urgently to perform fellatio upon me then and there, on the roof, out of her vast gratitude for my not having killed as well as raped her. The voice was odd; and the particular phrasing of her motive . . . I declined, embarrassed, and leaned over to unbind her wrists. Instantly she seized my legs and bit fiercely into my crotch; I jumped, slipped on the roof-tiles, very nearly tumbled off; she was after me, lunging as best she could with ankles still tied, clawing at my privates; I leaped clumsily onto Pegasus and dug in my heels; left her shrieking curses at me from the ridgepole.

"Shaken, I returned to the foothills of Mount Chimera, spent three days resting and recomposing myself. The blood-and-ink-stains on the lining of Melanippe's chiton were indelible, a ciphered execration. I had bad dreams. Every time I saw a snake (the woods there are infested), I imagined it a fleeing Amazon. When Solymian or Carian border scouts approached, I flew off with the jays and blackbirds; I searched out another patrol of Amazons and tried to tell them of Melanippe's courage and current circumstances; obliged to hover out of bowshot-range, I couldn't make myself heard. Much of the time I merely soared in high circles over the dead volcano like a misbegotten hawk, thinking dark thoughts about myself. Finally I returned to the plain of Xanthus and Iobates's city.

"The King was even more surprised than before, and openly displeased to see me. Polyeidus, too, appeared distressed. But Philonoë cried out for joy, hung on my neck, covered me with kisses, until she saw what black humor I was in and drew away.

" 'That took a while,' Iobates said sourly. 'Where's my Amazon?' I displayed the ruined chiton and gave it to Philonoë, whose delicate beauty and girlish ways seemed to me suddenly bizarre, affected, as if she were imitating a Phrygian faggot. 'Amazons don't permit themselves to be slaves,' I said. Iobates chuckled: 'But they're dandy captives while they last, eh?' Philonoë threw the chiton down and ran from the room; her displeasure with me put the King at once in brighter spirits. '*Seduction is for sissies,*' he said; '*the he-man wants his rape.* Heh heh. We used to prong 'em and then watch them kill themselves. How about lunch before you knock off King Amisidoros for me?' My repulse of the Solymians and the Amazons, he declared, counted as but a single labor, especially since I'd brought him no proof at all of the former and only ambiguous evidence of the latter. Moreover, his spies in Caria reported that while Amisidoros was alarmed by the 'flying centaur' stories and the consequent weakening of his Solymian–Amazon alliance, and perhaps amenable therefore to a negotiated settlement of the boundary dispute, he was by no means frightened to the point of mere capitulation. My next task, then, proposed by Polyeidus in keeping with the classic pattern of ascending unlikelihood, was to fly directly to the Carian court, land before Amisidoros in broad daylight, and offer to destroy the capital city with everyone in it unless he ceded half of Caria to Lycia.

" 'Take the whole weekend if you need it,' he concluded. 'And save Amisidoros's queen for my Sanitation Workers' Brothel. Toodle-oo.'

"I responded: 'Nope. I'll do you one more labor—you call it the third; it's Number Five in my book, counting that special-delivery from Proetus—but it's got to be something extraordinary, not like those others. Pirates and outlaws, maybe, if they aren't in fact protesting injustices in the Lycian socioeconomic system—I wish I'd had a chat with Chimarrhus about that before I sank him. Rebels ditto, if they're mere adventurists making a power-grab. Invading armies sure. Et cetera. But no more imperialist aggression, okay? You'll have to come up with something better, or I quit. I've had my consciousness raised.'

"From the wings of the throne-room came the sound of two hands clapping. Philonoë returned, and looking at me levelly, told her father to stop pussyfooting around and send me after Chimera.

"I tried to gauge her feelings. '*The* Chimera?' Polyeidus declared nervously that the definite article was optional.

" 'That's not a bad idea, Phillie,' her father said. 'Not bad at all. Then we'd still have our Flying Centaur, and Amisidoros wouldn't have his counter-monster. You say this Chimera's a sure killer, Polyeidus?'

" '*I* never heard of its hurting anybody,' I said. 'For all I know, it may be minding its own business up there in the crater. Am I supposed to kill it just because it's monstrous? Besides, it's female. No more sexist aggression.'

"Polyeidus defended the monster's deadliness on genealogical grounds—both of its parents had been legendary man-killers—but acknowledged that the creature had not left its lair in Amisidoros's deadly service at least since tranquil-ized by the Polyeidic magic papers, and so could be said to be a threat only to vulcanologists or ignorant spelunkers, whom a posted guard could easily warn off. He agreed with me therefore that there was no particular need to kill it—or her, if I preferred.

" 'He's a chicken and you're a hustler,' Iobates hmped. 'If he wastes the Chimera you're out of the protection racket, right?'

" 'Don't kill her, then,' Philonoë suggested in a gentler tone. 'Bring her back alive for the University's Zoology De-partment. Okay, Bellerophon?' She grew excited at the idea: we could build Chimera an asbestos cage; her breath could be used to heat the whole zoo free of charge, maybe the poorer sections of the polis as well. 'You wouldn't have to hurt her,' she insisted, and added, blushing: 'But don't *you* get hurt, either.'

" 'Capital idea!' Iobates cried. 'Steal Amisidoros's secret weapon and make a public show of it for the hoi polloi, keep their minds off their troubles. Go to it, Bellerophon! If you get her, no more tasks; if she gets you—no more tasks! You can't lose. Of course, if you're afraid . . .'

"I reflected for a moment, then declared I'd go after Chimera—with great reluctance, not on account of my per-sonal safety, but because for all I knew, in my lately aug-mented awareness, monsters might have an important eco-logical function, be some crucial link in the food-chain, et cetera. Only the essential *appropriateness* of the labor, which it astonished me I'd not recognized two thousand words ear-lier, its perfect conformity to the Pattern, induced me to undertake it—and that same Pattern prescribed that she must be not captured, but slain. No mythic hero ever brought back *anything* alive, except his glorious self and an occasional beleaguered princess.

"Now Philonoë was at my arm, her late vexation passed, rationalizing for the both of us that in view of Chimera's famous respiration we could perhaps regard the monstermachy as an antipollution measure. What did Polyeidus think?

" 'Never mind what *he* thinks,' Iobates said happily: 'I'm still king around here, and I say go to it. May the better gladiator emerge victorious, et cetera. Dead or alive, it's all one to me—but no hearsay or half-measures this time: fetch the carcass back here, so I can see it with my own two eyes.'

" 'Impossible,' Polyeidus put in.

" 'So much the better.'

"But the seer explained, more confident now, that while dispatching Chimera was at least imaginable for a mythic hero of my stature, and so obviously appropriate that it went without saying he'd had it in mind from the beginning as my climactic labor—had even had previsions of it back in Corinth, as I might recall—no souvenir whatever of the monster would be salvageable, much less the whole carcass: it was the nature of the beast, as a fire expirer, on expiration to go up in smoke. What was needed, for purposes of verification, was an expert witness—who would, however, in the ordinary case be in greater peril than the Chimeromach himself, with his special equipage and prerequisite dispensation from Olympus. Only a witness with extrahuman powers of his own stood even a moderate chance of surviving the fury of a mortally smitten external-combustion monster . . .

" 'You're elected,' Iobates said. 'If you both get wrecked,

we'll put up a little plaque for you somewhere, okay?' He frowned. 'But if you both come back claiming the Chimera's done in—I'm supposed to take your word for it?'

" 'I'll prove it by going into the cave myself,' Philonoë said quickly, nor could any amount of paternal threat or expostulation dissuade her.

" 'I want to have a long talk with you when I come back,' I told her happily, and promised to return by dinnertime. Polyeidus asked for an hour to pack a few things and prepare the special spear he said I'd need to dispatch Chimera. Iobates, frowning still, went off to a meeting of the Lycian Home Defense Council. I ate lamb kabobs and olives with the Princess; told her a few things I'd learned about Amazons (to which she listened pensively but closely, saying such things as 'You seem to admire them very much'); asked her why her father, after his original welcome, had seemed to take so sudden a dislike of me upon the reading of Proetus's innocuous letter, at a time when she and I were no more than pleasant friends. Philonoë brightened up immediately and promised to check the letter, which, especially in Polyeidus's absence, she believed she had ways of getting access to. Why check the letter, I asked, whose contents had been plainly read to us?

"She smiled and said, 'Call it Woman's Intuition,' a term and phenomenon I was unacquainted with but had no time to inquire further about. We fondly kissed goodbye, she bade me take care of myself, I bridled pretty Pegasus, picked up Polyeidus, winged northwestward in high spirits.

"En route I chattered on about my excitement at confronting what according to the Pattern must be as glorious a moment as any in my career; I praised Philonoë's courage in volunteering to prove the Chimera's elimination, and her loyal resolve to find out what had turned her father against me. Surely my Sacred Marriage, which, if I remembered the Pattern rightly, followed hard upon completion of my labors, must be destined to be with her; I did hope so; her affectionate docility, now I reflected on it, was much more in keeping with the notion of a *cunjunctio oppositorum* at the Axis Mundi than would be, say, the more active mettle of that Amazon lance corporal whom I'd left in Eurymede's keeping some days past. Et cetera. Didn't he agree?

" 'I hate flying,' the seer said sourly, and gave me my instructions: we were not to attempt to sneak up on the monster, who could not be fooled, but rather fly directly to the crater's rim; at noon the Chimera regularly retired to her cave for a long siesta—doubtless that was why I hadn't seen her in my recent overflights—and the trick was to trap her there, where she lacked maneuvering-room. The late absence of smoke from the crater, which I had remarked, indicated that her breath was temporarily less fiery than usual (such things happened); but given her triple ferocity, this was small advantage. Just as Perseus, vis-à-vis Medusa, had made his enemy his ally, so I like a cunning wrestler must enlist my adversary's strengths against her. Hence the special spear he'd brought along, a larger version of the writing-tool he'd given Philonoë, which instead of a sharp bronze point had a dull one of lead. Depositing Polyeidus behind the cover of a rim-rock, I was to blindfold Pegasus, put upon my speartip several sheets of paper from the prophet's briefcase impregnated with a magical calorific, and thrust my spear deep into the cave. Chimera would attack it; the calorific would superheat her breath (I was to shut my eyes and hold my own breath against the noxious smoke) and melt the lead, which then would burn through her vitals and kill her. 'Got it?'

" 'I don't get to see her?'

" 'You'll see her,' Polyeidus promised. 'But do it my way, or you're cooked. No need for your girlfriend to check out the cave tomorrow, incidentally; there'll be other evidence.' We landed on the rim, no monster in sight, only a bit of steam rising from one smallish hole, which Polyeidus identified as one of her vents and thus as good as any to attack her through. 'So have a nice battle,' he said when the spear and blindfold were prepared, 'and marry your princess and like that. I'm sure your brother would be pleased to know what a great success you turned out to be. Don't trust your father-in-law too much; he'd've put you away before now if I hadn't invoked the hospitality laws and set him up as your taskmaster instead. See you around, hero.'

"Well, so, I did all that, wondering why he spoke so curiously. Pegasus couldn't fly blind; I walked him to the hole, popped in the old spear, hit something anyhow: whoosh came the smoke, black billows, a certain stink, a sound like a horn-call. No thrash or struggle. I peeked to see whether I'd missed; withdrew my charred spear, its tip half-molten, and apprehensively rethrust, waiting for the bite. Instead, a kind of flapping came; I jumped back, slipped, very nearly fell from Pegasus as in the pall around us something large and obscure appeared to rise, rolling and spreading like the smoke itself, and buffet across the crater toward my prophet's perch. I unblinkered Pegasus and took off after, eyes running from the vapors, but before we overhauled the rim there was a whump: the mountain shook, and a smokeball rose from the spot upon its own black column. No sign of Polyeidus; only, on the rock-face, a blurred silhouette in soot of what I took to be the beast herself. With my cindered spear I sadly traced it, lion's head to serpent's tail, as down

upon us gentle ashes—whose, if not my imperfectly combusted tutor's?—commenced to fall. I yearned to spell out
his name there for the generations he had glimpsed ahead;
would not have minded subscribing my own for those same
readers, had I known one letter from another. I headed
sadly back on slightly smutty Pegasus, resolved to learn from
Philonoë how to write.

"I spied her on a beach not far from town, wearing of
all things Melanippe's chiton and waving a flag at me. I
landed, dismounted, kissed her, and said: 'Hi. I killed the
Chimera. But she killed Polyeidus. What's up? Why are you
wearing that? You don't look right in it.'

"She answered: 'Hi. Good. Good. An ambush. Because
it's time to make war, not love. I thought you liked Amazons;
no matter; I'll take it off after the battle.' She had an excellent
memory, even as a teen-ager. What battle? Rapidly she
opined that Polyeidus had been a traitor: according to her
father, from whom she had demanded an explanation of his
inhospitality on pain of eloping with me, the message from
Proetus had been *Pray remove the bearer of these letters
from this world; he has tried to violate my wife, your daughter*. But when, heartbroken, she had examined the document
itself, she found it to contain in fact only the first of those
two clauses. In any case, it made no mention of purificatory
tasks, which Iobates freely admitted having imposed, on
Polyeidus's advice, to get rid of me. Anteia's husband, he had
declared to her, was no hero, but except in the area of his
feud with Acrisius he was a reasonable man: whether or not
I'd tried to rape Anteia, I must have mortally offended him
in *some* way; therefore Philonoë was neither to see me again
nor to interfere with the ambuscade of palace guards waiting
to slaughter me should I return. Surely she had no use for a

man who had murdered his father and brother, abandoned his mother, tried to rape her own sister, and in fact raped and murdered a helpless Amazon prisoner-of-war? Heh heh, et cetera.

" 'You might be right about Polyeidus,' I admitted. 'Sometimes I've wondered about him myself. But there *is* another way to read his role in all this. Proetus knows the truth about his wife and me. False letters! You'll have to teach me how to read and write. Thanks for warning me about the ambush. I didn't kill that Amazon; I took her home to Mother. The rest is pretty much true, and I admit it makes me look bad, at least on paper. There. How come you're here?'

"Philonoë answered: 'Because I love you with all my heart and mind and soul. And body. My sister always wanted to be a mythic hero. I always wanted to be loved by one.' She fingered the chiton. 'Did you rape this poor girl?'

"I said: 'Yep. I was sorry afterward, but as my deed wasn't involuntary, that fact scarcely matters.' She shuddered; murmured something about Rough Edges; inquired whether, we being alone there in a secluded spot and she unable to call for help, I intended to ravish her as well.

" 'I guess not. I say let's fly off to Corinth and take over the kingdom.'

"Philonoë considered. 'I don't think you tried to attack my sister. You wouldn't've *had* to; I know how she is. Did you sleep with her?' When I shook my head she squeezed me, wiped soot from Pegasus's muzzle, confessed happily that she'd have gone off with me, albeit unhappily, in any case, and as wife or mistress, even if my love for her didn't measure up to hers for me. Her late mother's advice—never to wed a man whom she loved more than he her—Philonoë regarded as sensible enough if it meant love should be equal, basely self-gratifying if it meant the opposite inequality; what it lacked in either case was the dimension of Tragedy, which in her view—but there'd be time enough for her view, and my rape-tale, and Corinth too, when we'd deposed her dad and taken charge of Lycia—which we could do by nightfall if we played our cards right.

" 'What are cards?'

" 'Figure of speech. While you were doing hero-work up on the hill, I wasn't sitting on my hands. My roommate at U.L. is a meteorology major and vulcanology minor: she predicts that this afternoon's tremors from Mount Chimera, together with the recently prevailing south winds, the time of day (almost low water), month (full moon), and year (vernal equinox), will produce an extraordinary flood tide a few pages from now. Interviews conducted by her and me a couple hours ago with certain Xanthian fishermen (my contact with whom I'll explain presently) confirm this prediction. Here's what I suggest: I'll fly home on Pegasus now, for effect, and announce to Daddy that unless he comes off it and does the daughter's-hand-and-half-my-kingdom thing, you'll come on like Poseidon and drown the city. You pray to your father (whom I really look forward to meeting after we're engaged) (your mother too) to lend us a hand, or at least excuse the trick. I believe we can count on the palace guard to fold: they're mostly uplanders, scared to death of water. At a certain point, when you and the tide are up over the Xanthian plain, a delegation of women from the fishing towns approaches Daddy and offers him politically to offer themselves to you sexually in return for your sparing the city, in return for his granting matriarchal home rule to the Xanthians, which their women's groups have

agitated for for years. Got that? The minute I stepped out
this afternoon with this chiton on, you see, their lobbyists approached me as a convert, and we worked all this out.
Daddy'll go for the idea because he thinks *you'll* go for the
idea because he thinks you're this horny rapist, okay? And
I act as though I'm very upset at the prospect of my fiancé's
laying all those women, which I am. But what you do, you
chastely decline, just as you did with my sister, and I point
out to Daddy that that proves the whole thing was forged
by your former tutor, who's out to get you for some mysterious reason, which I think he is. Daddy agrees to everybody's conditions; you hold out till the moon's just overhead,
that'll be tide-turn; then you agree not to flood the city and
you ask Poseidon out loud to make the water go down. The
point of walking up with the tide instead of flying on Pegasus, I forgot to mention, is to demonstrate Change of Pace
—the way Perseus did when he rescued Andromeda without
using the Gorgon's head? In my senior thesis I argue that
mythic heroes do this now and then to show that it's the
general favor of the gods that gives them their clout, rather
than some particular item of gear, which could be lost,
stolen, or neutralized. It's a debatable generalization, I know,
but I had to get a prospectus in by mid-semester. I hope
you'll take a look at my list of examples and counter-ex-
amples. All set? How do you make Pegasus go up and
down? But maybe you don't *want* to do all this . . .'

"I proposed marriage to her, she cried 'Hooray!' and accepted, we did all that, it worked and then some. Philonoë
hadn't mentioned that the Xanthian women's-liberationists
were the wild-mare kind; I cocked my spear and came up
nicely before a beautiful surf that the hillbillies took hook
line and sinker: then a great whinny came from the wall,

and in the failing light I saw what looked like a dozen full moons or mad medusa-jellies charging toward me across the flat—the skirts-up tail-first business, paragraph *d* of the text-within-the-text et cetera. It was Corinth and Tiryns together; I dropped my spear and hit the breakers; we'd've lost the evening if salty Pegasus hadn't whiffed hippomanes on those prevailing southerlies, swooped unbridled from the battlement like a five-legged dragon, and cuckolded two Xanthian haulseiners before he realized that their fleeing wives were only playing horsie.

" 'My daughter's hand and safe passage to Corinth,' Iobates offered me.

" 'Don't be silly,' Philonoë said: 'he can have all of Lycia the way he can have me, just by taking it, whenever he wants to.'

" 'Her plus half the kingdom outright, okay? You can't ask for a better deal than that. Or her plus heirship to the whole operation, whichever you want.'

"I tipped tongue to make the theta of 'That's just fine,' but Philonoë spoke faster: 'We'll take both.'

" 'Both!' Iobates whistled for his landlubbers up on the roof; I for Pegasus down on the beach; Philonoë for her prospective father-in-law out in the surf. 'You mean all three, don't you?' the King asked weakly, putting his daughter's hand in mine. 'Enjoy them in good health.' Philonoë kissed him, tossed away the chiton, leaned her head demurely on my arm. Our engagement was declared at once (together with matrilineal-but-patriarchal home rule for the Xanthians, a compromise grudgingly accepted by the shaken mare-cultists), the wedding to be held as soon as Iobates and the Home Defense Council returned from a verification-trip to Mount Chimera. Regrettably, the party was intercepted

on their descent through the goat-slopes by a troop of venge-
ful Amazons, possibly acting on information leaked by the
haulseiners: half a dozen high Lycian officials fell in the
skirmish; half a dozen more, the King included, were taken
captive and, one at a time, given a knife and their choice of
relieving themselves therewith of either their lives or their
intromittent organs. Of this latter six, the one who took the
latter option (Chairman of the H.D.C.) was set free to report—with tears in his eyes, but not, as some vulgar his-
torians have it, in a high voice—that eleven Lycian matrons
were dishusbanded; that Philonoë was now orphaned and
queened, myself defatherinlawed, uncabineted, and kinged;
that the Chimera was to all appearances no more, and my
account of its traces correct in all particulars except that no
sooty silhouette was on the rock-face, only a sooty outline,
beneath which was found (and here delivered to me by the
valiant old officer) a sooty scroll sealed with a wax impression of Chimera rampant and inscribed on the outside (in
soot) *For B from P: Begin in the Middle of the Road of Our
Life.* It pleased me to conclude that Polyeidus was not dead,
only transmogrified. Philonoë taught me how to read and
write; I put the scroll away and forgot about it until this
morning. Drive me out. We were married and crowned, and
lived happily ever after. Drive me out. Exile me from the
city. Pegasus was put to pasture and now can scarcely clear
the clover.

"In conclusion, I call your attention to the ambiguity
of my official mythic history. I was never formally purified
of my guilt in the matter of Glaucus and my brother. My
behavior in Tiryns was at best questionable. Of the sinking
of Chimarrhus and his Carian pirates, no observers save myself survived. To the rout of the Solymians and Amazons,

the only possible witnesses were by me respectively stomped to death and raped-and-deported—I've never even bothered to inquire after that Amazon lance corporal in Corinth, a fact which also attests my apparent indifference to the welfare of my mother and my motherland. Not even that chiton is producible, since Philonoë took it off for keeps. Of the Chimera, no trace of either her existence or her demise except my tracing, which any schoolboy could duplicate on any wall. Of Polyeidus, the only other witness to the monstermachy, no further sign except the tedious text of this lecture. My only demonstrated wonder, the rising tide, I've shown to be more stratagem than miracle. Pegasus, unquestionably a marvel, was midwifed by Cousin Perseus, not by me, and merely lent me by Athene; moreover, he's not what he used to be. But the final proof, if any is needed, of my fraudulent nature is that on the eve of my fortieth birthday, when your typical authentic mythic hero finds himself suddenly fallen from the favor of gods and men, I enjoy the devotion of my wife, the respect of my children, the esteem of my subjects, the admiration of my friends, and the fear of my enemies—all which argues the protection of Olympus. Throw me out."

Q: "That's an answer?"

A: "Pardon?"

Q: "We're pleased to announce, sir, that in recognition of this brilliant lecture series in particular, and in general appreciation of your patronage of the University and your distinguished contributions to the fields of heroical genetics and automythography, a committee of students, faculty, and administrators of the University of Lycia has voted unanimously to name you to the Iobates Memorial Throne of Applied Mythology, the most coveted chair in the University, newly established and funded by Queen Philonoë. Many happy returns, sir."

I fled to the marsh, heaved my breakfast and lecture-scroll into the spartina grass, remembered the handsome Chimera-seal on the latter, waded in to find and retrieve it from the ebbing tide, couldn't, slogged about till sunset, found then in its place, high and dry at low water, *Perseid,* which I fetched back dismally to Page One, read, "Good night" "Good night," et cetera, next A.M. fetched down the bridle after breakfast, burped to the horse-barns, was by lackeys boosted et cetera, clucked chucked et cetera: Pegasus flapped down on the tanbark like a fallen stork, here we are. In time Queen Philonoë, sitting pityingly by the paddock, read the *Perseid* and proposed:

"Let's take a trip! To all the places where you did your famous things? We'll start in Corinth: Eurymede won't *believe* how the kids have grown! Then Tiryns: I'll tease my sister about her old crush on you and that disagreeable trick with the Bellerophontic letters, which you call *Bellerophonic.* Cyprian Salamis is out, since the Solymians seem to be acting up again, but we can tour the Carian–Pirate Museum at Pharmacusa and make a state visit to the Amazons at Themiscyra. I maintain a friendly interest in the Women's Liberation Movement, though I've no particular desire to be 'emancipated' myself, as my neglect, since marriage, of intellectual activity, formerly a passion with me, unhappily testifies. Finally, what I guess I'd rather do than anything else in the world besides be embraced by you: we'll stand together on the exact spot where you killed the Chimera! It's disgraceful that I've spent my whole life not a hundred kilometers from that mountain and never once gone up to see your celebrated drawing, now a leading Lycian tourist attraction—one more sad bit of testimony to the way we women are apt to let everything else slide in our preoccupation with child-bearing and -rearing, till we find ourselves grown dull and uninteresting people indeed, just at the time when our husbands and marriages may most need a spot of perking up. We'll come home by way of the beach where I flagged you down and you proposed marriage to me and I accepted—the happiest moment of my nearly twoscore years. And so to bed.

"Now, it goes without saying that this is merely a suggestion—both the general idea of a sentimental journey and the specific itinerary I've proposed. Possibly it strikes you as too directly imitative of the *Perseid*? However, it seems to me that surely no *harm* could come of such a trip, and perhaps some real good might, since, as you once remarked informally to my Senior Mythology Seminar, the archetypal pattern of mythic adventure is as it is and not otherwise: while we may not comprehend it, we cannot deny it, and heroes will-they nill-they follow it. What perhaps *doesn't* go without saying is that if in fact your adventure with Anteia, to name only one example, was less innocent than the official version maintains, and you feel it necessary to rehearse your past absolutely, you may depend on me as always to understand, even to honor, your decision: I count my own feelings as nothing beside my love for you and the importance of your career as mythic hero, et cetera."

Bellerophon senses, not for the first time, that this picture of his late lamented, distorted for accuracy like a caricature, is being drawn with jealous pen, and wonders by whom. Why should, for example, Polyeidus the Seer be jealous of Philonoë? But the hero of this story is no longer confident that Polyeidus is its author. Polyeidus reminds him that

Polyeidus never pretended authorship: Polyeidus *is* the story, more or less, in any case its marks and spaces: the author could be Antoninus Liberalis, for example, Hesiod, Homer, Hyginus, Ovid, Pindar, Plutarch, the Scholiast on the *Iliad*, Tzetzes, Robert Graves, Edith Hamilton, Lord Raglan, Joseph Campbell, the author of the *Perseid*, someone imitating that author—anyone, in short, who has ever written or will write about the myth of Bellerophon and Chimera. That's not easy to comprehend, or agreeable, and I'm working toward you, viper, toward you, gnat, and will swat you without fail. Could it be Amazonian Melanippe?

Melanippe, who has copied silently and without comment these many, these innumerable pages, imitates no one, except the honorable line whereof she is the namesake, dating back forever And she is not not *not* any kind of author, sculptor, painter, nor even a student of classical mythology: please understand that, Bellerophon! In a word she is *not* Perseus's Calyxa, not not not, and will not imitate that odd, proud, vulnerable girl. She is at most an Amazon: i.e., she'll lend herself no further than to that imposture.

Imposture! Cute Melanippe was the only true Amazon in a courtful of falsies! See Second Flood, Second Phase!

When she says imposture, what she means of course is that in fact she is—she doesn't know exactly how to say it; even the phrase "human being, female" puts her already into two categories from which her self feels more or less distinct; *herself* itself puts her into one. In any event, while certainly an Amazon and pleased to be, she feels herself to be by no means comprehended by that epithet. A fringe benefit, she believes, of the Amazonian custom of doing without surnames and assigning to each newborn girl one of a dozen-odd given names is that beneath the apparent confusion which results (there are by her estimate six hundred Melanippes of all ages in Themiscyra at any given time, who regard one another as sisters, and a similar number of Leaping Myrines, Penthesileas, Hippolytas, et cetera), is an actual clarification of identity. For distinct from her "Melanippe-self," immortal because impersonal, Melanippe knows a private, uncategorizable self impossible for her ever to confuse with the name *Melanippe*—as Perseus, she believes, confused himself with the mythical persona *Perseus*, Bellerophon *Bellerophon*...

Bellerophon acknowledges this wise, well-taken point, kisses its taker, but begs her pardon: for reasons to be discovered by Phase Three of the Second Ebb, my identification with "Bellerophon" is clear and systematic policy, not confusion—even as is, was, or imaginably could be the apparent chaos of this tale. Look me in the eyes. You know what I mean.

His mistress Melanippe, official recorder of this portion of his history, interrupts it for the last time in this telling to stand tenderly corrected on that point and to declare to whoever reads these words (of hers) that wherever they may lead and however end, she loves her lover to distraction.

He her ditto! And pernicious Polyeidus—not impossibly because we approach his re-entry—seems less obstructive now of the narrative channel. I feel my tale's tide flowing strong from the ocean of story; the magic feedbag is hung on: my winged half-brother can refly at last!

Aweigh?

Neigh. Slackwatered, back in Lycia, I climbed off foundered Pegasus, looked in the eye my rail-perched wife, said: "Okay, we'll do all that. You pack. I'm going to take a stroll

out in the marsh; devour my own soul a bit, et cetera. If I'm
not back in five days, go without me."

"Entendu, Green-eyes," Philonoë replied, and kissed my
forehead. "Take this along in case you get bored between
meals." She returned my cousin's history. "When I was into
the myths and legends thing," she went on, "I found a sort of
analogue to the shape-shifter motif in our Lycian folklore:
the Xanthian muskrat-trappers and mussel-fishermen speak
of an Old Man of the Marsh, a tidewater Proteus, more or
less, who takes the form of any of the common species of
wetland fauna and works mischief with their boats and gear;
but if they happen to catch him accidentally in a crayfish-
pot or a clam-rake—one chance in a million—he's at their
service till the tide turns, et cetera. For generations this was
no more than a pleasant little folk-belief, which the folk
themselves pretended to believe in only for the sake of their
grandchildren or tourists and eager students like myself.
Since our marriage, however, reports of the O.M. of the M.
have come in more frequently and seriously from the outly-
ing districts, especially from the Aleïan marshes. Now, given
the uncanny reappearance yesterday of that missing lecture-
scroll and its apparent transformation last evening into this
floating opus, I can't help making the obvious association
with Polyeidus. I believe you quoted him once to the effect
that all shape-shifters are versions of the Old Man of the Sea?
It seems at least possible to me that Polyeidus foresaw our
discovery of his double-cross of you and Daddy and took
advantage of the Chimera episode to turn into that image on
the rock, thence into the lecture-scroll, and thence into the
dormant tradition of the Old Man of the Marsh, to lie relatively low until the next turn of your career. In sum, and
not having seen myself this capital-Pi Pattern you always

allude to, I read all the events of the last few days as exciting portents: the scroll, the *Perseid*, Pegasus's final grounding, the absolute peaking of your obnoxiousness to the children and myself and your tedious, boastfully self-critical harangues to your audiences, all coincident with your passing the midpoint of your life. Everything says it's time—past time!—for another conference with your Advisor, and that Polyeidus is about to turn up. My private conviction is that you're holding him in your hand, but inasmuch as his recent form seems to have been that of the Marsh Man, my intuition is that you're likelier to get through to him if you take the *Perseid* to the Aleïan swamp and go through the motions of looking through the snails and soft-crabs. Maybe cast the manuscript upon the waters? Remembering further what you've said and resaid about his documentary tendencies, especially that intermediate transformation into the *kamara*-message in his Corinthian prison cell, I hope you'll be able to persuade him to turn into the Pattern itself, for you to check out, before or after he takes 'human' form for you. Finally, when and if you do confer with him, I trust you'll be at least cognizant of my own skepticism regarding his good faith, whether or not you've come to share it. In any event, since the bring-down of Pegasus has been the principal image of what you're pleased to call your First Ebb, I'm sure we agree that finding out how to get him up again is your first order of business with Polyeidus. In addition, however, I'd be very interested to hear his opinion on the question whether, once the metaphorical tide has turned and you're airborne again, it's okay for you to be sweet to me and the children the way you used to be. That would make me happy enough to die, since, despite all, I love you as much now as I did the night we first went to bed together, and you gently deflowered me, and we slept in each other's arms till sunrise, et . . . et cetera. Also give him my regards. 'Bye."

" 'Bye." I did all that, went slogging out among the Littorinas and Melampuses, the Medusae drifting in like fallen moons; of mosquito, frog, and fiddler-crab I sought counsel, how to open my life's closed circuit into an ascending spiral, like the sand-collars on the beach, like the Moonshells that I put to my ear for answers—keeping one eye always on the document in hand. I bedded down under a pine on a point of high ground between two creeklets; the sun set and rose a time or two; I considered Philonoë and the course of life, wished I were dead a bit. Hippolochus and Isander hiked out with a box-lunch; I shooed them home but chewed meditatively the chicken, deviled eggs, Greek salad. The marsh ticked, bubbled, soughed, cheeped, hummed, twittered: Polyeidus was in the neighborhood, all right. I put *Perseid* in the little wine-jug that came with lunch and, full of doubt, let the tide take it. Twelve hours fifty minutes later its like washed back with an odd but plainly Polyeidic letter:

On board the Gadfly, *Lake Chautauqua, New York, 14 July 1971*

To His Majesty George III of England
Tidewater Farms, Redman's Neck, Maryland 21612

Your Royal Highness,
    On June 22, 1815, in order to establish a new and sounder base of empire, I abdicated the throne of France and withdrew to the port of Rochefort, where two of my frigates—new, fast, well-manned and -gunned—lay ready to run Your

*Majesty's blockade of the harbour and carry me to America.
Captain Ponée of the* Méduse *planned to engage on the night
of July 10 the principal English vessel,* H.M.S. Bellerophon,
a 74-gunner but old and slow, against which he estimated the
Méduse *could hold out for two hours while her sister ship,
with my party aboard, outran the lesser blockading craft.
The plan was audacious but certain of success; reluctant,
however, to sacrifice* Méduse, *I resolved instead like a cunning wrestler to turn my adversary's strength to my advantage; to reach my goal by means of rather than despite Your
Majesty's navy; and so I addressed to your son the Prince
Regent the following:*

Isle of Aix, 12 July 1815

In view of the factions that divide my country and
of the enmity of the greatest powers in Europe I have
brought my political career to a close and am going like
Themistocles to seat myself on the hearthstone of the
British people. I put myself under the protection of
English law and request that Protection of Your Royal
Highness, as the most powerful, the most trustworthy,
and the most generous of my enemies.

*Having sent my aide-de-camp before me with this mes-
sage and instructions to request from the Prince Regent pass-
ports to America, on Bastille Day I put myself and my en-
tourage in the hands of Commander Maitland aboard the*
Bellerophon *and left France. Alas, Your Majesty's own betrayal and confinement on the mischievous charge of insanity
should have taught me that my confidence in your son and
his ministers was ill-placed, more especially as it is with the
Muse of the Past that I have ever gone to school for present
direction. When therefore I learned that my destination was*

*to be, not London and Baltimore, but St. Helena, like a dere-
lict student I applied in vain to my old schoolmistress for
vindication:*

On board the *Bellerophon,* at Sea

. . .I appeal to history. History will say that an
enemy who waged war for twenty years against the
English people came of his own free will, in his mis-
fortune, to seek asylum under her laws. What more
striking proof could he give of his esteem and his trust?
But what reply was made in England to such magnanimity? There was a pretence of extending a hospitable
hand to that enemy, and when he had yielded himself
up in good faith, he was sacrificed.

*My maroonment on that desolated rock I need not de-
scribe to one so long and even more ignobly gaoled. I, at
least, had the consolation that my exile was both temporary
and as it were voluntary; I needed no Perseus to save me; I
could have escaped at any time, and waited seven years only
because that period was needed for me to exploit to best
advantage my martyrdom, complete the development of that
stage of my political philosophy set down in the* Memorial of
St. Helena, *and execute convincingly the fiction of my death
in 1821; also for my brother Joseph in Point Breeze, New
Jersey, my officers at Champ d'Asile in the Gulf of Mexico,
and my agents in Philadelphia, Baltimore, New Orleans,
Bloodsworth Island, and Rio de Janeiro to complete the
groundwork for my American operations.
By means I will not here disclose (but which must bear
some correspondence to those by which Your Majesty
effected his own escape from Windsor), I departed St.
Helena in 1822 for my American headquarters—first in a*

*house not far from your own in the Maryland marshes, ulti-
mately in western New York—an area to which my attention had been directed during my First Consulship by Mme
de Staël (who owned 23,000 acres of St. Lawrence County)
in the days before that person, like Anteia or the wife of
Potiphar, turned against me. Here, for the last century-and-
a-half, I have directed my operatives in the slow elaboration
of my grand strategy, first conceived aboard the* Bellerophon, *whereof the time has now arrived to commence the
execution: a project beside which Jena, Austerlitz, Ulm,
Marengo, the 18th Brumaire, even the original Revolution,
are as our ancient 18-Pounders to an H-bomb, or my old
field-glass to the Mount Palomar reflector: I mean the New,
the* Second *Revolution, an utterly novel revolution.*

"*There will be no innovations in my time,*" *Your Majesty declared to Chancellor Eldon. But the truly revolutionary nature of my project, as examination of the "Bellerophonic" prospectus (en route to you under separate cover)
will show, is that, as the first genuinely scientific model of the
genre, it will of necessity contain* nothing original whatever,
*but be the quintessence, the absolute type, as it were the
Platonic Form expressed.*

*The plan is audacious but certain of Reset Nothing now
is wanting for the immediate implementation of its first phase
save sufficient funding for construction of a more versatile
computer facility at my Lilydale base, and while such funding is available to me from several sources, the voice of History directs me to Your Royal Highness, as the most powerful, the most trustworthy, and the most generous of my
Reset Adversaries, we shook the world; as allies, who could
withstand us? What might we not accomplish?*

In 1789 Your Majesty "recovered" from the strait-waist-

coat of your first "madness," put to rout those intriguing with your son to establish his Regency, and until your second and "final" betrayal by those same intriguers in 1811, enjoyed an unparalleled popularity with your subjects—as did I between Elba and St. Helena. Then let us together, from our Second Exiles, make a Second Return, as more glorious than our First as its coming, to a world impatient to be transfigured, has been longer. To the once-King of the Seas, the once-Monarch of the Shore once again extends his hand. Only grasp it and, companions-in-arms such as this planet has not seen, we shall be Emperours of the World.

N.

Of this obscurely touching epistle, its several familiar names glinting from their dark context like those shepherds' fires I'd seen on my first flight, I asked a few trial questions—Who am I? et cetera—and receiving no reply, sent it out with mixed feelings on the next tide. I hopefully presumed Polyeidus to be following a classic pattern himself, the pattern of graduated approach, as had Athene on my appeals to her (I mean Deliades's and mine) and Iobates in the matter of opening Proetus's letter; as three days had elapsed already of the five I'd bid Philonoë wait, I called after the departing amphora to please do its trick if possible in two more steps rather than, say, four, six, or eight. All that night I swatted bugs, studied stars, listened to my heart beat, wondered what a Bellerophonic prospectus was. My name, from endless repetition, lost its sense. Toward dawn a ship sailed by, unless I dreamed it. By and by the pot-red jug bobbed back, barnacled now and sea-grown as if from long voyaging, et cetera. I watched impassive till it fetched up at my feet, fished out its contents, the script in places run, et cetera.

To: *Mr. Todd Andrews, Executive Secretary*
       Tidewater Foundation, Tower Hall
       Marshyhope State University
       Redman's Neck, Maryland, 21612

From: Jerome B. Bray
       Lilydale, New York, 14752
       July 4, 1974

Re: *Reapplication for Renewal of Tidewater Foundation*
       Grant for Reconstruction of Lilydale Computer
       Facility for Second Phase of Composition of Revolu-
       tionary Novel NOTES

Sir:

Inasmuch as concepts, including the concepts fiction *and* necessity, *are more or less necessary fictions, fiction is more or less necessary.* Butterflies *exist in our imaginations, along with* existence, imagination, *and the rest. Archimedeses, we lever reality by conceiving ourselves apart from its other things, them from one another, the whole from unreality. Thus Art is as natural an artifice as Nature; the truth of fiction is that Fact is fantasy; the made-up story is a model of the world.*

Yet the empire of the novel, vaster once than those combined of France and England, is shrunk now to a Luxembourg, a San Marino. Its popular base usurped, fiction has become a pleasure for special tastes, like poetry, archery, churchgoing. What is wanted to restore its ancient dominion is nothing less than a revolution; indeed the Revolution is waiting in the wings, the Second Revolution, and will not stay for the bicentennial of the First, than which it bids to

be as more glorious as its coming, to a world impatient to be
Reset Now of "science fiction" there is a surfeit; of scientific *fiction none . . .*

Another blank. The sheaf of papers was more bulky than
Perseid itself, but though my reading skill was by that time
fair enough, and I pored and repored through them, I comprehended most imperfectly what they signified, and despite
a number of tantalizing references, could make no use of
of what I could make sense. Overall, the document seemed to
set forth its author's plan for completing a project that sometimes appeared to be a written work of some heroically un-
orthodox sort, at other times a political revolution; but inter-
spersed with Bray's description of the project, the history
of its first three years, and his prospectus for its completion,
were literary polemics, political diatribes, autobiographical
anecdotes and complaints, threats to sue a certain fellow-
author for plagiarism, and pages of charts, mathematical cal-
culations, diagrams, and notes of every sort. The hero described himself as descended "originally" from Jerome
Bonaparte (brother of that Emperor so recurrent in Polyeidus's accidents) and a "Maryland" lady named Betsy Pat-
terson to whom Jerome was briefly married; more immediately from a princess by the name of Ky-You-Ha-Ha Bray
who claimed marriage "in the eyes of God and the Iroquois"
to Charles Joseph Bonaparte, grandson of Jerome and Betsy,
during his tenure as "U.S. Indian Commissioner under Theodore Roosevelt in 1902." There being alive at the time of his
writing no "bona-fide Bonapartes" more closely related to
the original Napoleon (whose name and honeybee insignia,
even whose identity, he seemed sometimes to assume, as in

the previous letter), Bray regarded himself as legitimate heir to the throne of "France"—whence his sobriquet "J.B. the Pretender." But for all his noble lineage, Bray's fortunes had been adverse as my own: the impostor rulers of the country France ignored his claims; like Polyeidus he was reduced to teaching, in a post far humbler than my honorary one at the U. of L., and to writing out for public sale a kind of myths called *novels*. His political enemies conspired to prevent publication of at least two of these latter, entitled *The Seeker* and *The Amateur*; worse, when he was visited (as was I by Athene) by a kind of deity—a minor goat-god named Stoker Giles or Giles Stoker—and vouchsafed, not a winged horse, but a sacred scripture called *Revised New Syllabus*, publication of which should have made him immortal, those same enemies contrived to plagiarize it entire, bring it out under a name with the same initials as its true editor's, and—most insulting of all—not only represent the *R.N.S.* as "fiction" but allege that Bray's touching foreword, which they pirated verbatim, was also fictitious, the work of a hypothetical author!

Disillusioned, Bray resigned his instructorship and left his family to "become as a kindergartener again," dedicating his energies to the solitary task of making a concordance to the writings of the goat-god George Giles, who is to our Pan as, say, Polyeidus to Proteus. Packing his few belongings into a sort of mechanical Pegasus named V. W. Beetle, he retreated to the Lilydale community of his letterhead, an entire polis of seers and sibyls; there he established himself in a sub-group called Remobilization Farm, supported by the eccentric Maryland millionaire Harrison Mack II, who either also was or at times fancied himself to be "George III, the mad monarch of England." (Noting that Mack II, mad, imagined himself not as George III sane, but as a George III mad who in *his* madness imagined himself Mack II sane, Bray uses our word *paradox*.) When the group, "dishonored as are all prophets in their own country," later moved to "Canada," Bray stayed on, supported in part by the conscience-stricken author who had basely lent his name to the plagiarism plot, in part by side-efforts of his own as goat-farmer, fudge-maker, and skipper of the Lake Chautauqua excursion boat *Gadfly*, but principally by George III via Mack II's philanthropic organization, the Tidewater Foundation. As best I could make out, the Five-Year Plan for the ambiguous "Second Revolution" was conceived not by Bray directly but by a second ingenious machine, an automatic Polyeidus called Computer which Bray was using in his scholarly endeavors; it suggested to him one day that he might better vindicate himself to the world and attain his rightful place among its immortals by putting aside the tedious concordance in favor of a Revolutionary Novel— the "scientific fiction" aforementioned, which in Bray's letters to Mack II, perhaps also in his own mind, was either confused with or had aspects of a Novel Revolution.

In "Year *N*" of the project (ciphered 1971/2), having "called [his] enemy [George III] to [his] aid," Bray used the Tidewater Foundation grant to reconstruct his machine in such a way that, once a number of works by a particular author were fed into it, it could compose hypothetical new works in that author's manner. The results of his first experiments were in themselves more or less inept parodies of the writings of the plagiarist aforementioned, upon whom Bray thus cleverly revenged himself: they bore such titles as *The*

*End of the Road Continued; Sot-Weed Redivivus; Son of
Giles, or, The Revised New Revised New Syllabus*—in
Bray's own cryptic words, "novels which mimic the form of
the novel, by an author who mimics the role of Reset"; but
they demonstrated satisfactorily the machine's potential.
Most of the rest of the year Bray spent recuperating from
a nervous disorder, the effect of a poisonous gas sprayed
about the area by his enemies on the pretext of eliminating
lake-flies; nevertheless he seems to have acquired a mistress—
"a tough little Amazon" (how my heart leaped at that!)
named Merope, whose initial distrust of him as a "White
Anglo-Saxon Protestant" must have been overcome by the
revolutionary nature of his work and his ardor in such causes
as "the fight against DDT"—and to have altered radically
his conception of that work itself. For in Year O (code
#1972/3) he began programming his machine to compose,
not hypothetical fictions, but the "Complete," the "Final
Fiction." Into its maw (more voracious if less deadly than
Chimera's) he fed all the 50,000-odd entries in "Thompson's
Motif-Index of Folk-Literature," the entire stacks of Lilydale's Marion Skidmore Library plus a reference work called
Masterplots, elements of magical mathematics with such
names as Golden Ratio and Fibonacci Series, and (I could
not tell why; it seemed his mistress's suggestion) a list of
everything in the world that came in sevens. Thus equipped,
the machine was to analyze the corpus of existing fiction as
might an Aristotelian lepidopterist the existing varieties of
butterfly, induce the perfect form from its "natural" ap-
proximations, and reduce that ideal to a mathematical model,
preliminary to composing its verbal embodiment. Such was
Bray's genius, his machine began the year by producing

such simple diagrams as this *schema* for the typical rise and
fall of dramatic action—

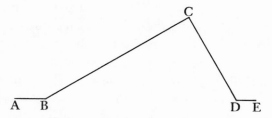

—and ended it with such "perfected" alternatives as the
"Right-Triangular Freitag"—

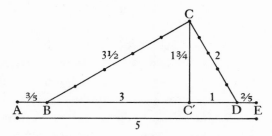

—and the "Golden-Triangular Freitag"—

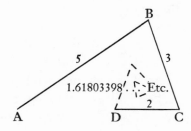

—which prescribed exactly the relative proportions of exposition, rising action, and dénouement, the precise location
and pitch of complications and climaxes, the relation of in-

ternal to framing narratives, et cetera. Little wonder he describes himself as humming happily as the machine all summer, eager for the first trial print-out in the fall: I myself was as involved by this time in his quest as if it had been my own, and searched vainly, heart-in-mouth, among his technical appendices and catalogues to see whether they might include the Pattern for Heroes, which surely Polyeidus must have plagiarized from him—unless, as seemed ever less implausible, Computer itself was some future version of my seer.

But my disappointment was as nothing beside poor Bray's, in Year T, "the midpoint of [his] life," at that long-awaited print-out. The title, *NUMBERS*, bid fair enough: its seven capitals, ranged fore and aft of his central initial, reflected promisingly Bray's mathematical preoccupations, his friend Merope's own special contributions (two "ancient" literary-numerological traditions of her tribe, called *gematria* and *notarikon*), and "such literary precedents as the fourth book of the Pentateuch, held by the Kabbalists to have been originally a heptateuch, of which one book had disappeared entirely and another been reduced to two verses, *Numbers* 10:35,36." But alas, as he himself was obliged to acknowledge, he "had not got all the bugs out of [his] machine"; what followed was no masterwork but an alphabetical chaos, a mere prodigious jumble of letters! These quires of nonsense "shocked [Bray] numb"—another sense of the title? To make matters worse, that very evening, thinking to divert him, Merope took him into the parlor of a group of militant radical students drawn to Lilydale by rumors that it was the hot center of a grand revolutionary conspiracy. When at one point in the conversation they brandished spray-guns filled with a chemical with which they planned to "defoliate the Ivy League," Bray in his distracted anguish mistook them for his poisonous enemies and "narrowly escaped" (this part of the narrative is unclear) by means of a horrifying disguise, a venomous barb with which he struck down and temporarily paralyzed "[his] beautiful betrayer," and a mad flight on V. W. Beetle. Merope, upon her recovery, left him to join the revolutionaries in their obscure immediate project of "filling the office water-coolers of certain large corporations with Lake Erie water"; Bray, convinced now that she was responsible for the *NUMBERS* fiasco, sat for a long while despondent in the ruins of his project—for which, shortly after, the Tidewater Foundation withdrew its support. He describes himself as "rudderless as a ship whose T has been crossed"; as "without weather"; as "stung." "Christmas, bah!" he snarls at the celebrants of Lilydale's principal religious festival; at Year *T*'s end ("July 3, 1974"), in a startling allusion to Medusa, he surveys the debris of his grand ambitions and writes: "My scrambled notes are turned to stone."

But the very next night, while steering the steamboat numbly around the lake, he is vouchsafed, whether by Computer or by V. W. Beetle, an astounding insight. Mourning the loss of Merope, he remembers her comparison of the *NUMBERS* print-out to the primordial lawbook of her tribe: according to some commentators, this *Torah* was originally a chaos of scrambled letters, which arranged themselves into words and sentences only as the events described by those sentences came to pass. At the same time he idly notes that *notes* is an anagram for *stone* and vice-versa, and is thus ("by this mild *gematria*") re-reminded of his former mistress. On the occasion of her reading out those thousands of narrative motifs for him to feed in enciphered form to

Computer—quite as Polyeidus had fed the magic spells to Chimera—she had remarked: "Hey, they missed one: The Key to the Treasure. This fellow's born into this family where all the men for centuries have worn themselves out looking for this particular Secret Treasure, okay? So when he grows up, instead of chasing all over the world like they did, he reads all the books in the library about Quests and stuff and decides that the Treasure's probably somewhere in his own house—the Maeterlinck *L'Oiseau Bleu* thing, et cetera. That same night he dreams that there's this big apartment of rooms right in his basement, that he'd never suspected, and for some reason or other, in the dream, this news doesn't especially surprise him. When he wakes up he realizes that there isn't any such apartment, but there *is* an old toolshed or storage closet down there that he's never looked into, because the door's all blocked with piles of junk left by his ancestors, and he's absolutely certain that's where the Treasure must be. So with no sweat at all he gets further than the others did after years of adventures and dangers and such. But to locate the Treasure's one thing; to get it's something else: when he clears the junk away he finds the door locked like a bank vault. The lock's not jammed or rusty—in fact it's very well lubricated—but it positively can't be opened without the key, even by the best locksmith around. So he ends up having to search all over the world after all, right? But for the key instead of the treasure. He goes through the usual riddles and battles and monsters and clues and false trails and stuff and finally rescues this princess et cetera, and on their wedding night she finds this real pretty key in his own pants pocket. She thinks they ought to let it go at that, but he leaves her, rushes back to his own country and his old house, dashes down to the basement, unlocks the door, and finds the closet empty. Once he's left the girl and her country he can't go back, I forget why, so he throws the key away in despair and lives the rest of his life as a sour old hermit. On his deathbed, thinking about his adventures and his lost girlfriend and all, he sees that the Key to the Treasure *was* the Treasure, et cetera. It's a piece of male chauvinist phallus-worship, but not a bad story." At once, on his remembering this tale, everything is illumined for Bray in a series of flashes "like the fireworks reflected in Chautauqua Lake": not *NUMBERS* but *NOTES* is his novel's true title; 5, not 7, is its correct numerical base; what he'd thought a fiasco was the proper culmination of the first three-fifths of the project: a Five-Year Plan, so he realizes now, at whose "*Phi*-point" he presently stands ("*NOT* is to *ES* as *NOTES* is to *NOT*"). Those reams of random letters are a monstrous anagram for the Revolutionary Novel, to unscramble which will require no more than the "reprogramming" of Computer with these new insights.

To test his theory he feeds it a simple impromptu list of "fives": the fingers, toes, senses, and wits of Homo sapiens, the feet of pentametric verse and "Dr. Eliot's shelf of classics," the tones (Computer hiccoughed happily at this word) of pentatonic music, the great books and blessings of "China," the bloods of "Ireland," the nations of "Iroquois" and divisions of "the British Empire," the aforementioned Pentateuch, the days of the week, the vowels of the alphabet, the ages of man, the months of Odysseus's last voyage, the stories framed by "Scheherazade's *Tale of the Porter and the Three Ladies of Baghdad*," the letters of the word *novel* (three-fifths of which et cetera), and a few non-serial odds and ends such as *quincunx, pentagon, quintile, pentacle, quinquennium, quintuplet,* and *E-string*. These are as noth-

ing beside the hundred-odd "sevens" already in the machine;
yet with that meager priming, valiant Computer belches
forth two remarkable observations: On the one hand, inasmuch as "character," "plot," and for that matter "content,"
"subject," and "meaning," are attributes of particular novels, the Revolutionary Novel *NOTES* is to dispense with
all of them in order to transcend the limitations of particu-
larity; like the coded *NUMBERS* it will represent nothing
beyond itself, have no content except its own form, no subject but its own processes. Language itself it will perhaps
eschew (in favor of what, is not clear). On the other hand,
at its "*Phi*-point" ("point six one eight et cetera of the total
length, as the navel is of the total height of human women")
there is to occur a single anecdote, a perfect model of a
text-within-the-text, a microcosm or paradigm of the work
as a whole: not (what I anticipated) the "Key to the Treasure" story, but (what fetched me bolt upright in the Spartina alterniflora) "a history of the Greek mythic hero Bellerophon; his attempt to fly on Pegasus to Olympus like
Apollo's crew to the Moon; his sting; his free downfall to
Earth like ditto's to the *U.S.S. Hornet*; his wandering alone
in the marsh, far from the paths of men, devouring his own
Reset."

Never mind that the events in this "quintessential fiction," as Bray called it, were out of order and somewhat
fanciful, like those in the lecture-scroll synopsis; they bespoke the presence of Polyeidus, Polyeidus, whose name I
called and recalled, without effect. All his original conviction restored, Jerome Bonaparte Bray heroically concludes
his appeal to the Executive Secretary of the Tidewater Foundation with a prospectus of the task ahead: In Year *E*
(#1974/5), assuming the Foundation renews its support, he

will reconstruct and reprogram Computer to compose *Bellerophoniad*, which he now describes as "that exquisite stain on the pure nothingness of *NOTES*; the crucial flaw which perfects my imitation of that imperfect genre the novel, as the artful Schizura unicornis larva mimes not the flawless hickory leaf (never found in fact), but, flawlessly, the flawed and insect-bitten truth of real hickory leaves." In Year *S*, Computer will make the final print-out of the complete novel; the Second American Revolution will ensue at once upon its publication, and, like the First, trigger others, this time everywhere; J. B. Bray and H. Mack II will reassume their rightful names and thrones—the monarchies at first of France and England respectively, but eventually the emperorships of West and East; all existing stocks of DDT, pyrethrin, rotenone, and similar barbarous poisons will be destroyed, their manufacture prohibited forever; and the world will be restored to a New Golden Age.

I shivered with sympathy for the vision, loftier than my own in its redemption, not of a man, but of mankind—and for pity of the poor misfortunate visionary, his dreams struck down by a hand-scrawled cover-note to the application as lightly as the humming marsh-gnats I swatted with it:

File. Forget. Throw back in the river. No need to prosecute (or reply). T. A.

There was no aiding J. B. B. (as I thought then) across the eons—though he, perhaps, had aided me. Sadly I reposted Bray's prospectus on the tide and spent the buggy night considering my own history and objectives. In the morning, impatient for the next high tide to bring its message, I strolled the beach, sun-dried, sea-salted, and skipped shells across the water. When I rereached my starting point I found in the wrack along the high-tide line where sandfleas jumped not my familiar jug but, amazingly, a clear glass bottle, unlike any I'd ever seen, wreathed in eelgrass full of sand and tiny mussels. Around the outside, in letters raised in the glass itself, a cryptic message: *NO DEPOSIT NO RETURN*; inside, a folded paper. Trembling, I removed the cap and tipped the bottle down; the note wouldn't pass through the neck. I cast about for a straight twig and fished in the bottle with it, grunting at each near-catch.

"For pity's sake bust it!" cried a small voice from inside. Seizing the neck, I banged the bottle on a mossed and barnacled rock. Not hard enough. My face perspired. On the third swing the glass smashed and the note fell out: half a sheet of coarse ruled stuff, folded thrice. On its top line, when I uncreased it, I found penned in deep red ink:

TO WHOM IT MAY CONCERN

On the next-to-bottom:

YOURS TRULY

The lines between were blank, as was the space beneath the complimentary close. In a number of places, owing to the coarseness of the paper, ink spread from the letters in fibrous blots. Heartsick, I flung the blank paper down—whereupon it turned at once into a repellent little person, oddly dressed, with a sty in his eye and a smell of urine and stale cakes.

"I swear," Polyeidus said, surveying himself with a sniff: "I tried your cousin Perseus—thought it would be appropriate? And look what I end up. I should stick to letters. How are things? Never mind; I know."

"My life's a failure," I told him matter-of-factly. "I'm not a mythic hero. I never will be. I'm forty years old already. I'm going to die and be forgotten, like the rest."

"Like your brother?"

"Never mind that. How do I get to be immortal fast?"

Polyeidus squinted. "You sure you trust me? Your wife seemed to think I was out to get you last time around."

"Maybe you were. But you didn't."

"Why should I go on helping you whenever you get stuck? You think it's been fun being Old Man of the Marsh all these years?" He swatted his arm. "Goddamn mosquitoes. And seafood makes me break out."

"Evidently you had no choice," I replied. "Zeus stuck you with the job, right? So it's to your interest to get me constellated like Perseus. Who remembers the helper if the hero doesn't make it?"

"Skip the arguments," Polyeidus said. "I already know how the story ends."

I pressed him urgently for that knowledge.

"Never mind. In this part I advise you, that's enough. You want to be a mythic hero, you follow the Pattern. You want to follow the Pattern, you leave town in the Fourth Quadrant, et cetera. You want to leave town and do the second-cycle thing like Perseus, you got to get Pegasus off the ground. You want Pegasus to fly like before, you're wasting your time with me and Athene." Whether I knew it or not, he declared, riding the winged horse had always involved the goodwill of two goddesses, not one, manifested in the beneficences appropriate to each. Athene's bridle was what reined him in and steered him; but what put him in the sky was Aphrodite's sacred herb

"Hippomanes!"

"What else? As a young man you didn't need to think of that; what you had to go looking for was the bridle. Now you're all bridle and no hip, and believe me, at your age it's not easy to find."

How so? Didn't it grow by full moonlight at the lip of Aphrodite's well, et cetera?

Polyeidus winked. "Those were the days, eh?"

In the Stygian marsh, then, where Perseus had got his gear? Ought I to shut my eyes and follow my nose, not opening the former till I was obliged to—

"Reset. Don't be naïve; it's right *under* your nose— which doesn't mean you'll sniff it."

I scrabbled in the reeds and rushes.

"O boy," Polyeidus said. "I tell you what: forget about revisiting the places where you did your tricks, okay? This isn't the *Perseid*. Instead, look up all the women you've ever loved, in order; that's the sort of thing Aphrodite goes for. Somewhere along the line you'll come across the big H. I envy you. When you get the pattern, stick to it. See you in heaven."

I had more to ask: Once refueled, where ought Pegasus and I to fly? Assuming Corinth to be my first searching-place, ought Philonoë to accompany me there, or should I avoid her until her turn came in the series? For that matter, how many women comprised the series, and which ones? I could think offhand of only two—his daughter Sibyl and my wife —for whom I'd felt a considerable degree of passion for any length of time; but there were others—the Amazon lance corporal, for example—who had attracted me powerfully for a short while, and still others with whom I'd disported for an hour or a weekend. Which counted? But Polyeidus was transformed already from that nasty-looking little person to the precious Pattern—

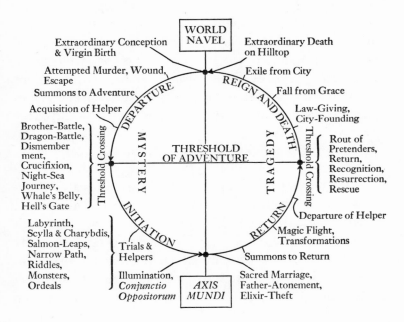

—which I snatched from the mudflat, folded in the manner of the water-message, and fetched home.

"All aboard," I said to Philonoë, and lining up our children and cabinet ministers on the dock, declared: "No telling when or whether we'll be back. Here's my wedding ring, Laodamia: hang it on a string around your neck. If you boys should start to quarreling over which should usurp the kingdom in my absence, settle the question by seeing who can shoot an arrow through this ring. Heh heh. Got that, ministers?"

"We'll try to be good adolescent children," responded

Hippolochus, Isander, and Laodamia in imperfect unison, more their mother's blood than mine, "avoiding the pitfall of rebelliousness for its own sake, to which the incompletely schooled passions of youth naturally incline, and honoring the accumulated experience of our forebears as embodied in cultural traditions and existing institutions, while at the same time always reviewing those traditions and institutions from the fresh perspective of our youth, with an eye, not to their destruction, but to their ongoing development. Have fun."

"Thanks for the ring, Dad," Laodamia added, bussing my cheek.

"If the royal traveling-account doesn't cover your expenses," my chancellor of the exchequer said discreetly, "don't forget that your endowed throne at the University includes an expense fund too. The Lycian economy's in excellent shape, thanks mainly to the combination of a considerable defense industry to protect us from the Carian–Solymian–Amazon conspiracy and little or no actual fighting with them. The tourist business at Mount Chimera National Park doesn't hurt, either. For these plums, a grateful citizenry and affluent ministry thank you. Bon voyage."

A horseshoe wreath of flowers was hung about my neck, another about Pegasus's who drooped between me and weeping Philonoë on the quarterdeck. Off we went. Polyeidus's observations to the contrary notwithstanding, I looked for a tempest to wreck our ship as in that remarkable sentence in *Perseid* where the *t*'s of the approaching storm trip through the humming *n*'s of inattention and are joined by furious *s*'s to strike the vessel as Perseus struck Andromeda. But the wind held fair through the Sporades and Cyclades, and Philonoë, grieved as she was to leave Lycia and children for the first time, could not be quarreled with. The boat ride, the prospective reunion with her older sister, her excitement at my having secured Pattern and direction from Polyeidus—all kept her sunny as the weather. She praised my stratagem for averting faction between the boys (who, however, she was sure would not only rule in harmonious tandem should any accident befall us, but share the throne with their sister, all three loved one another so), kissed the white indented ring on my finger where the gold one had been for so many years, and removed (but carefully stored) her own wedding band, to give our second honeymoon, as she gaily called it, the air of an elopement. For she was convinced, and found the idea enchanting, that my search for hippomanes must lead ultimately to her and the rejuvenation of our love. Anon we ran up the Saronic Sea and ashore on the famous Isthmus. I said: "Here's where I leave you. The boat will take you back around the point to Tiryns and Anteia."

In a small voice, for she had been eager to meet my mother, she replied: "Well. Okay."

I saddled up. "No saying just when I'll see you again, Philonoë. You've been a very good wife and mother. And queen. Friend, too. I like your taste in music, food, myths. Clothes and furniture, so-so. You're very bright and, of course, extraordinarily gentle-spirited. Also, you've maintained your physical youthfulness fairly well, considering. And are noble-charactered. Let's see. O: I wish I were good at loving people, which it seems I'm not. So. In addition, it's too bad I wasn't a regular king and husband, without this immortality thing. You'd've been a lot happier, and you deserve that. Goodbye."

She wept again, not noisily, and as she couldn't reach my mouth (I was on Pegasus already), kissed the ring-place again, where I held the gold bridle, and disagreed with me as on the night before my birthday, when I'd said I was no hero. My heart was full of love, she declared; more than I wanted to admit: love for her and the children over many pleasant years; love above all for my late twin, who though I seldom mentioned him must have been a most extraordinary person, so driven was I by devotion to his memory.

I might have questioned this surprising observation, but Pegasus, less alert than in younger days, mistook my uneasy hmpf for giddyap and plodded down the gangway. Corinthians wondered as I hoofed into the old hometown. Nothing much was changed: some stores were different; couple of new schoolhouses. The palace seemed smaller, needed paint; shrubbery in the yard was overgrown; one tree we used to climb still stood—I went up it with my eye, limb by limb, a great catalpa rich in caterpillars and long seed-pods which we dried and smoked behind the stables. Another favorite was gone, as was my best-remembered of the outbuildings: a whitewashed combination toolshed/torture-chamber between the woodhouse and the privy in the slaves' quarters, where in my tenth year a laureled, loose-toga'd lady, my music teacher, whom I'd threatened to punish for cracking my knuckles with a ruler, had led me, put aside her five-stringed lyre among the rakes and dusty amphorae, knelt sweating to embrace my knees, and—while bees droned in the lattice as if on an ordinary summer afternoon—purchased clemency at a surprising price set by herself. I checked around: no sign of hippomanes there; anyhow the wench was doubtless dead. Some old dog woofed a warning from the dungheap near our hives, back among the hollyhock and mimosa. Steering clear, I espied a shrunk old Amazon, gone in the chest and toothless, whom I took to be my childhood friend or ancient nurse, I forget which, Hippolyta. I gave her Pegasus to stable, waiting with a smile for her to remember that night on the rooftop and recognize me; but she shuffled him off to a stall with no sign of having noticed even the great white wings. When I asked her, on her return, whether a former lance corporal named Melanippe was still among the stable-hands, she grumbled, "Help nowadays isn't worth a drachma; got to do every blessed thing my own self," and I recognized Mother's voice.

"I can't believe it!" I told Sibyl in the grove that night. "Her health is good, but she's simply shrunk; and her memory's so poor, it's a wonder she can manage the palace, much less the polis. Heh. For a long time she didn't recognize me; one minute she'd say she'd never had any sons, the next minute that they'd been dead for years. Later on, when she told me that she'd established matrilineal descent in Corinth after her menfolk had deserted her, I realized that either she was being bitter or the shock had affected her mind on this particular subject—she seemed clear enough on other matters —so I admitted I'd been a poor son in some respects and apologized for not getting in touch with her for twenty years. I'd assumed your father had explained to her what happened here in the grove that night; he was supposed to let her know about the mythic-hero business, how I had labors to do, et cetera, and would probably come from the east to reclaim the kingdom when I got the right sign, which I haven't yet, unless this hippomanes-trip is it, which I wonder. But I gather that that bastard, excuse me, never did *any* of these things, and I'm really beginning to think that my wife might be right about him, because wow, when I mentioned

his name, Mom came out with this wild story, how after the
funeral-games for Glaucus and my brother, Polyeidus took
her aside, asked her to marry him, and confessed that out of
his love for her and his ambition to be king of Corinth he'd
promoted the quarrels between her and Glaucus, Glaucus
and me, me and my brother, et cetera, and set up the horse-
race trick so that some or all of us would get killed, and made
up this Pattern thing as a way to get me out of town in case
I were a mythic hero—though at the same time he claimed I
was actually *his* son, because it hadn't been Poseidon in the
form of a horse who'd made love to her in the surf that night,
but himself in the form of Poseidon in the form of a horse.
Got that? Now Polyeidus, when I picked him up off Mount
Chimera that first time, told me *she* was crazy, and had had
him arrested because she was imagining all this stuff; but I
swear, Sib, she said it all perfectly calmly, and it was especially convincing that she hadn't even been incredulous or
angry when your dad told her these things, just contemp-
tuous, and had him locked up as a vulgar nut rather than as a
dangerous traitor and murderer. What she says explains a
lot about the things he's done since, too, you know? Like
trying to kill me with one hand and hanging onto my coat-
tails with the other. Yet Mom's obviously *not* quite right in
the head: she had to admit, for example, considering the
above, that she *had* had sons after all, and that only one of
them had been killed along with her husband; but she
couldn't keep straight which one of us it was; kept calling
me by the wrong name; and pretty soon she was back to her
first line: that Bellerus was dead to the world and Deliades
dead to her (she got it backward), and that this Bellerophon
who claimed to be the killer of Bellerus (she meant Bellerus
the Killer) was a total stranger; not a mythic hero but a

myth. Well, I was all cut up. I said, 'Don't you recognize my voice, Ma?' and explained that as far as I was concerned, *Bellerophon* meant 'Bellerus's voice,' you follow me? And wasn't she pleased to know her son Bellerus was going to be immortal, et cetera? She looked me in the eye and said sorry, her whole family was dead, kindly leave her alone or she'd call the guards. I thought of mentioning her grandchildren, but since she's never met them, and I left them back in Lycia, I doubted it would help. What a day. It's a pity how people get old. Hi, there. I guess you're pretty excited to see your childhood sweetheart Bellerus again, right? Look at this scar where the well-bucket hit me and turned my eyes green; you can see it plainer now my hair's going. How's the sibylling business? Heh."

She squinted at me through the moonlight with glassy eyes and shook her frowsled head. "Bellerus. O wow." Sibyl too had changed in twenty years, not apparently for the better. Granted that her vocation as sacred prostitute and prophetess involved considerable orgiastic activity, characteristically cryptic speech, the use of laurel and other mantic drugs, and a certain abandon in costume and coiffure, I saw no good reason why she couldn't come off it a bit with an old friend, especially as my own address to her was so informal and confiding. A far cry from my vision of her in Athene's temple, she was in my estimation not so much disheveled as wrecked, her hair wild, her clothes filthy and torn from the abuse of her current lover, who I was distressed to learn was not even a man, much less a deity or demigod, but the "boss dyke of the horsebarns," according to Sibyl: one of the few of our Amazons who had not drifted south to Tiryns, "where the action's at." At forty, the dream of my adolescence was overbreasted and underwashed, thick-thighed and -waisted, hairy of leg, lip, armpit; even when not officially entranced she swallowed, sniffed, and smoked large doses of her sundry herbals and talked seldom more than half-intelligibly; feast-day or not, she took on all comers to Aphrodite's well, regardless of number, rank, or gender, drew the line at no perversion, masturbated casually between visitors when not comatose. She also burped a lot. On the other hand, she was generous with her scanty means, let all sorts of bums and drifters share her stuffed grape-leaves as well as her pallet, seldom stole from drunks, and gave without charge to needy suppliants oracles neither more nor less enigmatic than those she dispensed to me.

I told her what I was in search of. "One stud's hippomanes is another's saltpeter," she declared. "But the first dose is free. Let's see what you've got under your toga these days."

When it became (relatively) clear that I must make love to her in exchange for a sample of the herb, I reluctantly did so—stallion-fashion at her insistence, "for old time's sake" —though the combination of her appearance and the memory of that old time was anaphrodisiac. Sibyl knew her trade: though I never saw the hippomanes itself, as I came I heard a whinny overhead and saw Pegasus erratically circling the grove, his first real flight in several seasons.

"Hooray!" I cried as he crashed into the creepers.

"Plus ça change," Sibyl incanted dryly. "Bellerus my ass. Again."

Crude as was the invitation, after a spell I managed to remount her briefly, and Pegasus briefly reflew. Overjoyed to have found so quickly what I sought, and eager to lay hold of it for good and learn its use, I stayed with Sibyl the night through, and the next and next, as had Perseus with cowled Medusa on the lakeshore, II-F-1, but with opposite effect: instead of flying higher and farther each time we coupled, Pegasus rehearsed in four nights his pattern of four times four years, and my own potency diminished as rapidly.

"Dum dee dee," said Sibyl on the fifth, "heroes aren't what they used to be."

"Neither is hippomanes. Don't you have the kind that grew here in the old days?"

"One toke of the good stuff left," she said, tapping an amulet like the one her shifty father used to use. "Secret of my success in the whore and oracle way. When this is gone I'm out of business."

"Can it take me where I want to go, Sib? Where is that, anyway?"

It was a palpable hit, she replied in her fashion, and would send a man like me skyhigh enough before his downfall to drop him into another world.

"Olympus? Olympus?" I asked excitedly. "That's a swell idea! But do I become immortal just by flying there?"

Sibyl scratched her rump and shrugged. "Not many immortals among my customers, you know? Anyhow, I don't remember saying I was going to make you a present of my last good high. What did you ever do for me?"

I agreed there was nothing for her in my apotheosis except what satisfaction she might derive from having been party to it—a reflected glory, to be sure, but apparently one not to be sneezed at: look how it had driven her father; look how (the late lamented) Deliades, in time past, had thriven in the glow of his twin's predestination; look how she herself, when we three disported in that grove in the bright mid-morning of our lives, had said, "Bellerus can have Corinth the way he has me: by taking it, whenever he wants to." "Let's have it, Sib," I said

"Are you kidding?"

"Please?"

She hooted. "You're self-centered enough to be a hero, at least! Don't you give a fart what happens to me? Or to your wife and kids when you go flapping off to heaven? You don't even remember that your mother's name is Eurynome, not Eurymede! And Jesus, it's not as if you're benefiting *mankind*! What good does it do anybody in this world if you make it to another one?"

"You're the sibyl," I said: "Figuring out things like that is not my line. My business is to be a Mythic Hero, period, and to do it I need the hippomanes in that amulet, so I guess I'll threaten you with this sword. I can show you the Pattern, if you want to see it; it was your dad who drew it up. Now please do the heart-of-gold thing and help your former boyfriend Bellerus become immortal, at whatever sacrifice to yourself. I'll appreciate it. As to Mom's name: some accounts give it as Eurymede, some Eurynome; that's a not-uncommon discrepancy in the case of accessory characters in a myth, for that matter, the hero himself will often have variant names: Deliades, for example, was also called *Alcimedes*, which I believe means 'big genitals,' and *Alcmenes*—'mighty as the moon'? Also *Peiren*, after the Muses' well on our acropolis. So. I just call her *Mom*. Please?"

"A hero that says please," Sibyl said, but handed over the amulet with a yawn.

I kissed her (pocked) cheek. "Thanks a lot. I really mean it."

"Sure. Here's an airmail special for your hostess at the next stop. No peeking. Fuck off, now, and leave me to my dykes and winos."

It wasn't exactly Perseus's farewell to Medusa, but I

thanked her again, promised to intercede in her behalf with Aphrodite when I got to heaven and delivered the letter (which was addressed simply with an upper-case Alpha), just as I meant to apply gratefully to Athene to do what she could for Eurymede/-nome and Philonoë. " 'Bye."

Sibyl brushed away the cloud of fruitflies that often as not hovered around her head and said: "Drop dead twice." Whether this most terrible of curses was directed at them or me I chose and will ever choose not to wonder; I broke open the amulet, swung a leg over Pegasus, put it to him, and hung onto the bridle for dear life while he bounced all over the vault of heaven like a mad moth in a closed room. First and last time I was ever airsick; Zeus knows where Sibyl came across that crop. I lost my bearings with my breakfast, commenced hallucinating, wow. Nowhere back in my flying youth did I ever have such a bring-down as when Pegasus now tailspun with a whinny into a lemon orchard just outside some town.

Not Olympus. I woke up bruised, headachy, sore; no sign of Pegasus, much less a cute Calyxa to priestess me back to life with love and egg-lemon soup. I was in the same rocky grove, bleeding mortal blood from half a dozen scrapes; even for the five minutes till I recognized the walls of Tiryns, I could not imagine my crashing place to be other-where than Earth. I groaned and, not to be suckered more than one-and-six-tenths times by the same device, tore open Sibyl's note. *Pray bring the bearer of this letter to life,* read its mean first clause; never mind the second till my Second Ebb. A pale dandy with limp-wristed shortsword and high-fashion armor stepped from behind a tree and lisped: "My name ith Megapentheth the themidemigod, thon of Queen Ththeneboeia by the demigod Bellerophon and thlayer of the falth mythic hero Pertheuth. I order you to thurrender on pain of death—and thtop tearing up thothe thecret methageth, pleathe."

I groaned again. "Good grief!"

"Yeth, well. You think I'm homothecthual jutht becauthe I have a bad lithp. Let me tell you alpha that while it'th true that thome queenth affect thith impediment, ethpethially in vulgar joketh, in my cathe ath in many otherth the defect ith congenital and hath nothing to do one way or the other with mathculinity; beta, neither thpeech defecth nor thecthual proclivitith thtrike me ath very rithible ecthept to the coarthetht thenthibilitith. And gamma, while it happenth that I *am* in fact homoerotic, tho are the warlike Thpartanth, tho there. Quit your thmirking: I may be gay, but I'm awfully handy with thith thyortthword."

Perhaps he was, but as I advanced to inflict on him, fairly or not, the full measure of my frustration, banged-up Pegasus staggered to me from where he'd wandered, favoring his near wing and off hind leg and shaking his head dizzily—a sight to make the fiercest faggot falter. I sprang on as a platoon of Amazons, one behind every bush, stepped forth fully armed to Megapenthes's rescue, but Peg went down under my weight as if back in Lycia. Remembering what Amazons do to rapists and fearing that my former victim might have immigrated to Tiryns with her just complaint, I drew my sword and prepared to fall on it rather than do battle with them or be taken alive, neither of which options I had taste for.

"Thtop!" Megapenthes cried, to the Amazon guard as well as to me. "That'th my father Bellerophon! You can tell by the winged horth. Do the Xthanthuth trick!"

Sure enough and woe was me, like the fishermen's wives

on the plain of Xanthus all but one of the Amazons spun round, flipped up her chiton and down her tights, mooned meward. The dissenter, a crop-haired youngster, sheathed her sword and stalked off, disgusted. Me too: looking more closely, I doubted they were even real Amazons: their skins were too white; their hams and buttocks too soft-looking, their voices too feminine, their costumes too chic. Even Pegasus took one sniff and lost interest.

"I give up," I announced. "Everything's out of order. Tell King Proetus he's got company. And tell my wife that if this is her idea of a joke, I'm not amused."

Neither were my captors, as they proved after all to be. "Quiet, pig," their leader said, and ordered her company to bind my wrists and lead me by a rope around my neck to Queen Stheneboeia. "No funny stuff," she warned me, "or I'll kick you in the nuts."

"Take it eathy," Megapenthes complained in my behalf. "He'th my father the demigod. Hi, Dad."

"Be damned if I am," I said. "I don't even *know* anybody named Sthenewhatsername. Besides, semidemigodhood doesn't happen. Where's Proetus? Let go my tunic, damn you!"

"Our orders are not to geld you unless we're provoked," said the captain of the guard, who though I was convinced now she was no Amazon, was formidable enough. "Frankly, the pleasure will be mine. Come along home now, Prince, and tell your mother we've caught her old boyfriend. We'll show him Proetus on the way."

Megapenthes pouted. Puzzled and distraught, but after all helpless, I was stripped and led into town. Shopkeepers and sidewalk-loiterers, all women, whistled and made coarse remarks about my manly parts. A few men peered with shy curiosity from behind half-drawn window hangings. Some others, young and heavily painted, smirked on the arms of their middle-aged female escorts or feigned embarrassment and hid their faces with their fans.

"Where's Anteia?" I demanded. "What's happened to this town?"

"The Queen will ask the questions," said my captor, thumbing the edge of her blade. "You shut up and listen."

Led into the familiar throne-room, I gasped at a sight straight out of *Perseid:* an armed (male) palace guard, a conference table of (male) ministers and advisors, various (male) tablewaiters, busboys, attendants, pages, musicians, and chamber-flunkies, three naked (female) dancers on the table, and, at its head, King Proetus himself, all gazed in our direction, frozen in postures of attack or alarm. I'd've thought them cunning statuary, but that their stances (save for that of one dancing girl, who shielded her breasts with one arm, her shame with the other) were not classical, and their eyes, unlike the eyes of our good Greek statues, were pupiled, gazing not on eternity but on the terrible intruder who must once have stood in my place. Poor Proetus had ignored my counsel and been petrified for posterity half off his throne, wiping his mouth with a stone napkin and spilling alabaster wine from his granite glass.

"Perseus was here?" I asked Megapenthes.

"Shut your pig mouth and curtsy fast," said the guard-captain. "Here comes the Queen."

Megapenthes, curtsying beside me (I'd never made that form of obeisance and was obliged to hold his elbow or fall), nodded and whispered: "The year I wath born. Then, a few yearth ago, he came back, like you, and I killed him to prove I wath a themidemigod."

"Nonsense!" The guard redrew her sword, but when I recognized the entering Queen (now about fifty, heavy-set and light-mustached, tricked out in armor and accompanied by the same young Amazon who'd left the scene of my capture), I stood up and cried, "Anteia! What's all this silliness?"

"Call me Stheneboeia," she said imperiously, taking the empty throne beside her stoned late spouse. "Anteia was my slave-name."

"Make them give me my clothes back, Anteia!"

"Not till we've had a look." She inspected me with a disdainful smile. "My my, we do age, don't we?"

"Never mind. Where's Philonoë?"

"Does it matter?"

"Of course it matters; it will always matter! Just because a man deserts a woman, it doesn't follow that he doesn't love her a lot. Especially if he's a—"

"Cut his cock off," she idly instructed the guards. "For impudence. Heh. You can use this famous conference table as a chopping block. Some conferences *they* used to be!" She permitted them to force me trembling to the table edge, draw out my edgeless tool, and raise their edged before she bade them wait. For the rest of our conversation I remained in this dreadful position. "Stheneboeia," returning to her throne, coldly informed me that not long after my flight from Tiryns twenty years before, she had found herself pregnant; inasmuch as she'd long since ceased to have intercourse with Proetus and was between established lovers at the time, it could be only my "repeated rape" of her in Athene's temple that had inspired her condition. While this "outrage, even by a demigod," still outraged her, and she looked forward to punishing me for it in the fashion of the

Amazons, she had nonetheless spared "its issue, the semi-demigod Megapenthes," not to offend "his grandfather Poseidon" and the goddess in whose temple he'd been "brutally engendered." But Proetus, "in his sexist pig way," had abused her as if the child were sprung from a love affair rather than a rape, and she was not displeased when Perseus, in fulfillment of his destiny, had come through town with his bride Andromeda and the Gorgon's head not long afterward, broken in on one of her husband's "swinish revels" —from which she'd been fortuitously absent out of disgust for them—and turned the whole court and elite guard to stone when panicked Proetus gave the order to attack.

"Not that Perseus wasn't a pig like all the rest of you," she made clear, "with his swaggering hubris and his babydoll bride—as if he didn't owe everything to Athene and the poor woman whose head he'd cut off! But as pig heroes go, he was better hung than most, god knows, and had a decent streak. They stayed on a few months; I tried to raise Andromeda's consciousness on the subject of marriage as a sexist institution; we had a little fun *à trois;* and he let me do whatever I wanted to with the polis—not that he had any right to take it from me, but a pig is a pig."

What she'd done, I learned next, was seize the opportunity of the court's petrifaction to install all the ministers' wives in their late husbands' places, train a female palace guard with the help of Amazon military advisors, reverse the genders of every law on the statute books and every custom in the city having to do with relations between the sexes, and convert Tiryns into an absolute matriarchy. That her success (like that of Mother's milder programs in Corinth, I now surmised) was owing to Perseus's benevolent hegemony over all of Argolis had rather rankled her than made her grateful, and when she'd heard he was retracing the course of his earlier adventures, she'd laid a simple trap for him with her son's help. Knowing that no pig chivalrist would challenge a woman, she had arranged for Megapenthes to challenge him, wait until he brandished Medusa's head and Athene's shield, and then counter with a mirrored shield of his own: caught in compounded reflection, Perseus's flesh had turned to stone, the stone into diamonds, the diamonds ultimately into stars, which the women of Tiryns nightly cheered the setting of. Too bad that Medusa herself—and Andromeda, Cassiopeia, and a few others—had had to go too, but one could not make souvlakia without killing lambs.

"That's all preposterous!" I cried. The guard looked to the Queen for leave to lop; was stayed with a head-shake; gave my *glans* a nasty pinch. Fingernails. I pointed out the discrepancy between this sordid account of Perseus's estellation and the glorious one I'd read in the document upon which I was modeling my own life story.

"My unliberated little house-mouse of a sister told me all about that," Anteia replied (I could not call her Stheneboeia). "It's a lie. An utter fiction. It says that Pegasus is a constellation in Medusa's custody, for example: so who's the nag you flew in on?" Seeing me taken aback by this consideration, she went on to deride the male-supremist character of the great body of our classic myths, with which she revealed a fairly extensive acquaintance—Philonoë's influence, no doubt—and which she held to be the fabulated record of a bloody overthrow, by male pig patriarchs in ages past, of the original and natural matriarchy of the world. "Mythology is the propaganda of the winners," she declared, adding that the grand myth supported by all those particular mythlets was the myth of heroic maleness—not importantly in the matter of brute strength, where man's unquestionable superiority to woman was as nothing beside the dumb ox's to man, but in such virtues as courage, cunning, and sexual prowess, and most especially in the aspect of divine dispensation to greatness and immortality. "You're a lie!" she fiercely concluded: "We're going to rewrite you!"

Though I shivered for my organ's sake, I could not help remarking that she'd done much rewriting already, of Perseus's history and our own. I didn't doubt that my idol had been there: petrified Proetus attested to that, and though the specific event was not recorded in *Perseid*, I recalled its noble narrator's "ending, by the death of both, the twinly old feud between Acrisius and Proetus," et cetera; moreover, the physics of the estellatory process as Anteia described it was similar to what transpired between the lovers' eyes at that story's climax. But as anyone not blindly hostile to the very concept of herohood must acknowledge, my version had the ring of authentic mythopoeia, hers the clatter of mere scurrilous iconoclasm. For the Pegasus discrepancy I could not account; for the subordinate role of women in mythic and actual history I did not feel particularly accountable; for my own contributions, voluntary and involuntary, to their cumulative exploitation and felt degradation, I was heartily sorry (perhaps she recalled the Aristotelian diagram?); about complex questions of nature versus nurture in the matter of sex and temperament, distinction versus valuation, or customary roles versus personal inclinations, and the rest, I had some curiosity but no firm opinion. But of my vocation as mythic hero and demideity I had no doubt whatever, whatever one might choose to make of it, any more than I had of Megapenthes's disqualification for that calling, and I would pursue it like my skyborne cousin until I was either dead or deathless.

"People's memories improve things, Anteia. Proetus ended up believing he'd fathered Perseus on Danaë. My old tutor Polyeidus claims now that it was himself and not Poseidon who sired me on Eurymede. I never once made love to you, and you know it."

The guard confidently raised her sword.

"Pig rhetoric," Anteia growled. "In Tiryns a man doesn't 'sire a child on a woman'; she conceives it on a man. Position One in this polis is with the man underneath. You admit you've committed the crime of rape?"

"Not on you. On an Amazon lance corporal, twenty years ago, and I hated myself afterward. She was a dead ringer for your young attendant there: astonishing coincidence."

"Put him away," the Queen ordered. "You're not going to the sky, Bellerophon. You're going to Tartarus with your bloody prick stuffed down your lying throat."

"Thorry, Dad," Megapenthes said as they led me out. "Why not 'feth up and be Mom'th thecthual thlave forever? Aunt Philonoë wouldn't mind, if it thaved your life. We're raithing her conthiouthneth."

Anteia told him to be a good boy and stop nattering and go fetch her a glass of Phaedra. I was led down to a dungeon to wait my fate, burdened as much by the thwart of my ambition as by the prospect of torture, mutilation, death. An examination of my cell suggested no way either to escape or to kill myself. I spent a dreadful day under the eyes of my warden, Anteia's attendant, who watched impassively as I sighed, paced the bare room, tried to nap, ate and drank, pissed and shat. Her resemblance to my lance corporal was truly remarkable: cropped dark hair, wiry build, brown skin and eyes, small breasts and buttocks—I wished I weren't about to die, so that I might explore the coincidence undistracted, inquire whether her mother was perhaps an Amazon refugee in Corinth, et cetera. I did indeed ask whether her name was by any chance Melanippe: she neither replied nor turned away, but regarded me steadily while the footfalls of my executioner, as I supposed, came down the stair.

But Anteia merely bid the girl unlock my cell and entered, without visible instruments of emasculation or execution.

"Hi," she said, standing just inside the closed door. Her tone was mild.

"Hello," I answered carefully, and got up from the floor. "Have a seat."

She smiled quickly and came over to the tiny barred window where I stood, but—as the floor was filthy and there was no bench or pallet—declined my invitation. Her breath was vinous. I kept my eyes on her face, trying to assess the situation. She mostly looked down, as if at my flaccid parts.

"You have to understand everything at once," she declared. "I'm not able to talk about anything just now."

"I understand nothing. Where's Philonoë?"

"I didn't want to come down here," she said tersely. "I didn't want to see you again at all, Bellerophon."

"Same here. What's up?"

"You're not helping me," she complained, whipping her head from side to side. "You're not saying any of the right things."

"Megapenthes isn't my son," I said. "And there's no such thing as semidemigods. My only offense was not making love to you when you wanted me to, and that's not against the law except in Themiscyra. Besides, I was trying to get through to Athene, to get my work done, and you kept interrupting. What's more, Athene doesn't like people making love in her temples: look at Medusa. You might be a Gorgon right now if I'd let you seduce me."

"The way you turn away from me," she complained, "you'd think I *was* a Gorgon."

I explored this attitude. "That's not so, Anteia. In the temple, that first night, you really excited me; I'm sure you saw it. But I was an ambitious young man, trying to become a mythic hero and purify myself at the same time, and worrying about the laws of hospitality. It was just the wrong place and the wrong time. I'm sorry about that."

"Hmp." But she went on, her voice still more injured than belligerent. "My sister worships you. It's criminal the way she takes all your double-standardist crap with a smile. She should kick you in the balls."

I made no reply; began restlessly to wonder about the pattern of incremental revelation in my case, whether it was going to follow sexual intercourse with a succession of women rather than, as in *Perseid*, successive nights with the same woman, and whether I was obliged to include Anteia in the lot or might proceed directly to Philonoë. But now, her tone gradually hardening, the Queen observed that she was about to enter what the Amazons called Last Quarter: her menses came only infrequently, soon would cease. Her daughters had turned out to be whores and freaks: one was dead of an overdose; the other two, after years of madness and scandalous behavior, had made bad marriages. Running the polis after Proetus's death had been no picnic: like all wealthy widows, she'd been preyed upon by false seers and con-men of every description, until out of anger and desperation she'd founded the matriarchy. There was little in her life that gave her pleasure to recollect; it was a catalogue of abuses at the hands of men, from her coarse father Iobates through her rapist debauché of a husband to her cruel and faithless lovers—none more false than I.

"Megapenthes was the last straw," she concluded bitterly. "When I saw how he was, I knew you were an impostor. But I stuck to the quarter-godhood story, for my own pride's sake. Now you try to take *that* away from me. Damn you for coming back into my life!"

I despaired of setting right the wrong-headed inconsistencies of her complaint; only repeated, like Melanippe her name and unit, that I was no impostor, and that she and I had never been lovers.

Anteia's manner grew broadly cunning: "We're two of a kind, Bellerophon," she chuckled. "Do you think I *believe* that nonsense about the Chimera? Even Philonoë admits there's no proof that it wasn't something you and Polyeidus dreamed up: another pig fantasy, killing the imaginary female monster. Nobody ever saw her, even! You conned Iobates the way Polyeidus tried to con your mother—and the worst-conned of all is Philonoë, who's known all along you were a fake and loved you anyhow."

"I *did* kill the Chimera," I protested, much dismayed. "It was very real, Anteia: I saw the smoke and flame . . ."

"Who can't make a little smoke in an old volcano?"

"I felt it bite my lance! I saw it flying in the smoke!"

"Which has wings?" Anteia pressed. "Lion, goat, or snake?"

"It left a perfect imprint on the rock!"

"Which nobody saw but you. Come off it, Bellerophon. Philonoë says you want to improve on your first achieve-

ments, like Perseus; I think you never achieved them in the
first place. It wasn't this phony Pattern that made you tell
the Lycians to throw you out—" She flung at me the Polyeidic paper, confiscated earlier by the palace guard. "It was
bad conscience. Your life is a fiction."

Shaken, I shook my head. "I can see how it might seem
that way to you. But there's one thing even Philonoë doesn't
know about me . . ."

"She knows more than you think," Anteia said contemp-
tuously. "When she got word recently from the goatherds
on Mount Chimera that the monster was back in business
again up in the crater, she killed the story to cover up for
you. Why do you suppose she was so anxious to get you out
of town?"

"You're lying! You keep contradicting yourself! I *did*
sink the Carian pirates; I *did* drive off the Solymians and
Amazons, and rape that poor lance corporal who had such
high ambitions for herself and her people. And I did did *did*
kill the Chimera! The high-tide thing was Philonoë's trick,
I admit, but it was a trick the gods favored and helped me
with, just as Athene helped me bridle Pegasus. There's proof
enough that I'm for real: what about Pegasus?"

Anteia smiled triumphantly. "A fake, just like his master.
Philonoë told me your cock-and-bull story about hippomanes: she even believed it! Well, I just happened to have
some in the house, and to show her how blind she was to
your phoniness I climbed aboard that sexist pig horse this
afternoon and fed him my whole bag. Some stud! He keeled
over dead."

Sick at heart, helpless to tell what in her harangue were
lies, what misapprehensions, what distressing truths, I argued
no more, only leaned miserably against the stone wall of my

cell, laid hold of my swinging yard, and said: "*Real* Amazons give a man his choice between death or emasculation. If you're going to do both to me, please kill me first. For your sister's sake, okay?"

"For her chicken-hearted sake," Anteia said, "I'm going to let you both go back to Lycia, as a matter of fact—cock and balls, impostures, and all. On one condition."

I looked at her suspiciously. She smiled.

"Make me pregnant."

"Don't be silly."

"Draw your sword," she said coolly to the Amazon, and to startled me, as she undid her chiton: "Never mind the odds against conceiving at my age, or all those diagrams you insulted me with before, or the fact that you find me unattractive. I'll tell our son the demigod it was your last heroic labor, and you're bloody well going to keep at it till it's accomplished. Down on the floor, please."

I shook my head. "We've had this conversation before, Anteia. A man can't get it up just because he's threatened."

"So we'll play awhile. Do you want Melanippe here for a teaser? I'm not proud."

"You *are* Melanippe!" I cried to the guard, who stood by as expressionless as ever. "That's a miracle!"

"Fuck or die, Bellerophon," Anteia said. "We'll do it any way you like; you can even be on top. But frig we must."

I repeated, in plain honesty, that I could not, with her, under any circumstances. No personal slight or sexist snobbery intended: the phallus had a will of its own, as imperfectly harmonious with mine as Polyeidus's magic was with his. See how it hung now, and no wonder, when so much hung on it . . .

Anteia refastened her armored placket and left the cell. "I want it cut off and broiled for dinner, Melanippe. I'll send down some help." She gave me a final scornful look. "And a little hors d'oeuvre tray."

When she was gone I appealed desperately to the poker-faced young guard, who waited outside for her reinforcements. I could not plead innocent, I declared, to the charge of not having risen to the Queen's original need (though surely there were mitigating circumstances); or of having sacrificed my family to my heroic ambition (but ditto); or of having relegated the women in my life to supportive roles (but how many people of either gender had transcendent callings? and how could Philonoë be said to have been coerced?). Certainly I was guilty of having blindly assaulted the only woman I'd ever met who *did* have such a calling: her proud, incredible self, not a day older than when, overcome with self-loathing at my late bestiality and later enlightenment, I'd flown her to Corinth and Hippolyta's care. It was true, then, that certain Amazons had not only metamorphic but rejuvenating powers! For all my transgressions against womankind—not least my apparent inability to treasure one of their number above all else in life, as did many so-called sexist pigs—I was contrite, and did not expect absolution. If I was fated not to die, the gods would preserve me willy-nilly; otherwise I had misconstrued myself and had no wish to live, since my heroic vocation, not my life, was what I valued. But before she and the counterfeit Amazons with whom she consorted there in Anteia's travesty of true Amazonia (for I knew authenticity from its opposite, both among those who called themselves Amazons and among the values they espoused) made a gelded corpse of me, I begged leave to say goodbye to (and ask a few questions of) my patient wife, who had loved me better than herself.

"Okay," Melanippe said, and unlocked the door briskly, and strode off in a different direction from the Queen's. When I recovered my wits, I followed, whispering loud thanks; she paused a moment to look back at me, still neutrally, then strode on. I could not assimilate the string of miracles: the coincidence of remeeting her, her apparent forgiveness of my crime against her person and her aspirations, her absolute agelessness. How trim her waist and hips were, shapely her legs (she eschewed the dotted-lozenge tights most Amazons wore), fine her shoulders in that fetching sleeveless chainmail blouse! We wound through corridors and back alleys; the night was still, dark, balmy—but I was goosefleshed in my nakedness and sundry emotions, and my scrotum shrank from its imminent leave-taking.

Turning a corner, we came upon the palace garbage-dump, at sight of which, despite the crying need for silence, a wail of grief escaped me: atop the peels and potsherds lit by the gibbous moon lay poor dead Pegasus, belly-up and wings aspread like a great shot gull, all four legs stuck straight toward the heaven he would never take me to. I swarmed through the crud to hug his neck, curse his poisoner, keen his praises: old soarer, stout companion of my hero-works, high-flown half-brother! Ah, he was not dead, only dying: one white primary-feather wiggled, and I heard a horsy heart throb faintly in my ear.

"Hippomanes!" I hissed to Melanippe, who (horse-lover herself like all Amazons) had put away her sword and rushed with me to check his pulse at the fetlock, peel back one eyelid (the white shone pupilless as a statue's, or a minor moon), and even attempt mouth-to-mouth resuscitation. "Never mind Philonoë, I guess," I guess I said: "we've got to get this horse some real hippomanes before you kill me, or he's a goner!"

Melanippe sat back on her heels, wiped her mouth on her war-scarred forearm, mused a moment, handed me her sword. "I have some on me. All Amazons do, especially in their First Quarter. Why not kill me for it and escape?"

The voice was the same. I hesitated no longer than she'd mused, put my hands behind me. "Nope."

"Rape me and escape?"

I closed my eyes, shook my head.

"Take it from me by force?"

I paused again. "No. I'm done with all that, Melanippe I'll just say please."

She put down the sword and squinted up at me. "Are you really impotent?"

"Of course not."

"I hate this town," she said, suddenly loquacious. "Every Amazon does. It's not just the misanthropy, which isn't really Amazonian at all. Our prophets say that a woman of Tiryns whose name begins with Alpha will give birth to the greatest lady-killer of all time: Heracles the Amazonomach. That's why I'm stationed here: my assignment was to check out Megapenthes and kill him if he was really a semidemigod, which I saw he wasn't. I knew what Stheneboeia's real name was, and what her ambitions had always been; if you or any other god or demigod had made her pregnant, I'd have killed her. But I don't think she'll ever conceive now."

I agreed, and informed her further (what I happened conveniently to know from Polyeidus) that the woman's name would be Alcmene ("mighty as the et cetera"), her lover Zeus himself, their tryst some generations yet to come. I hadn't heart to add that their son's bloody rendezvous in Themiscyra—as represented on an Attic black-figured amphiphoreus Polyeidus had once turned into when he was trying for *Amphitryon* by way of *amphigouri* back in our schooldays—was already a matter of the history of the future.

"Can you bring Pegasus back to life?" I pleaded.

She grinned. "Sure. You too. Stand back." With a quick modest motion, quite feminine in fact, she took from under her chiton a single tiny leaflet of the magic herb and bent to hold it to the horse's muzzle. Almost involuntarily—I was so close behind her, and moved, and curious—I rested my hands lightly on her hips. She smiled back up at me. "Be ready to jump on."

O, I was—and even as she surely felt it, Pegasus exploded to his feet in a whinnying swirl of feathers. I snatched the bridle, had as much as I could do to hold him down while she scrambled on and helped me get up before her. Time only for the fleetingest thought of Philonoë, sacrificed once more: Melanippe laughed merrily, hugged me about the waist to keep from falling as I dug my bare heels in and we rocketed from the dreck, even seized my grand standing phallus when we cleared Argolis at an altitude of five kilometers, Attica, Euboea—and boldly steered me with it across the black Aegean, under moon and stars too near, it seemed, to envy, toward Scythia, Themiscyra, the warm reedy banks of Thermodon.

There, let's see, she and Bellerophon live happily ever after. She got the lead out of Pegasus and put it in her lover's Polyeidic pencil. These are her words; this is his life. Her hippomanes is out of sight; they fly three times a day. She

will not explain the nature of her immortality (which, however, he infers to have a Lethe-like component, as she remembers few details of the ancient rape, fewer of her girlhood and early exploits in the Fifth Light Cavalry), but he
feels bathed in it, younger by a dozen "years" at least, his
tide reflooded. Let's see. She's an amazing lover, Melanippe
—frisky, uninhibited, imaginative, lean and tight. They
wrestle a lot. She likes to bite, usually not so it hurts. Bellerophon's okay too, though that quarter-hour on Anteia's chopping block took its toll on his genital self-confidence. He
wonders sometimes how Philonoë and the kids are getting
along, also his mother, and old Sibyl, and whatever happened
to Polyeidus. But he comforts himself with that business at
the end of *Perseid* about mortal and immortal parts; look
it up.

What else. They go into Themiscyra on weekends, to do
the restaurants and theaters and museums and such; week-
days they spend in a little rented cottage out in the marsh,
writing this story. Melanippe's return-from-exile visa, Bellerophon gathers, and his own status as former rapist and
former king of their principal former enemy, impose these
after all modest restrictions on their movement. Dum dee
dee. O yes: he is altogether impressed with life among the
Amazons: a truly emancipated people, they no more resemble their caricatures in Tiryns than a male passive-pederast
resembles a woman. Lesbianism is not uncommon among
them; bisexuality is commoner yet; but the majority are vigorous heterosexuals, and man-haters are rare. Males themselves are welcomed as visitors and treated cordially, though
their visits are carefully supervised, and only in exceptional
circumstances are they permitted to live and work in the
polis. Bellerophon has made notes toward an anthropological

treatise on the relations between the Amazons and their counterparts, the all-male society of Gargarensians, which with Melanippe's help he will no doubt write sometime in their timeless future: members of the two societies mate freely, for example, during two months every spring in the wooded mountains along their border, the impregnated Amazons returning home to bear their children; male babies are not killed or emasculated, but nursed lovingly, weaned, and turned over to the Gargarensians. As no one knows her parents (the Amazon collective and indefinite pronouns are feminine), the incest-taboo is foreign to them: when Bellerophon recounted to Melanippe the story of a certain future king of Thebes, she was distressed that he will accidentally kill his father, but thought it only right for him to marry his mother in recompense. Though marriage is forbidden (and very difficult for Amazon schoolteachers to explain to their tittering charges), love between women and men, even "permanent" relationships, are punished only by the stipulation that the lovers relinquish whatever positions they hold in their respective societies and live outside the city, as during mating season—indeed they regard such connections as a kind of permanent mating season, therefore a permanent daftness, and make gently deprecating jokes about the lovers' overappetitiveness, underimaginativeness, and irresponsibility. That mistress of Jerome B. Bray's, by the way, like the ladies of Anteia's court, must have been merely mimicking an Amazon: neither Melanippe nor anyone else hereabouts has ever heard of *Torah*, *Pentateuch*, *Gematria*, and the rest.

Et cetera. All that's another story, of no great concern to the characters in this, which Melanippe will wind up now, seal in an amphora, Bellerophon supposes, and run down the

Thermodon on the tide, into the Black Sea, Propontis, Aegean, past fell Heracles's pillars, across Oceanus, et cetera. He likes to imagine it drifting age after age, nudged by great and little fishes, under strange constellations bobbing, bobbing, while the generations fight, sing, love, expire, et cetera. While towns and statues fall, gods come and go, new worlds and tongues swim into light, old perish, stuff like that. Let's see. Then it too must perish, with all things deciphered and undeciphered—no no, scratch that: it *mustn't* perish, no indeed; it's going to live forever, sure, the voice of Bellerus, the immortal Bellerophon, that's the whole point.

So, well: their love, Bellerophon's and Melanippe's, winds through universal space and time and all; noted music of our tongue, silent visible signs, et cetera; Bellerophon's content; he really is; good night.

2

~~~~~~~~~~

"Good night is right," Melanippe said when she read Part One. "I can't believe you wrote this mess."

I asked her, hurt, how so; I thought it not half bad, considering.

"*Because*," she cried. "It's a lie! It's false! It's full of holes! I didn't write any of it; *you* did, every word. And you make out that I'm all emancipated and no hang-ups and immortal and stuff, and that's crazy. *Content* my ass! *Content* is a death-word in my book; if I were Medusa and I asked Perseus if he was happy to spend eternity with me and he said he was *content*, I'd spit in his eye! Okay, you got the Amazon business pretty straight, but I'm amazed at your picture of me: you know very well I'm not immortal except in that special way I told you about: the 'Melanippe-self' way. I'm on the verge of my Full Moon, and I feel every lunar month of it: just in the time it's taken you to write these pages I've gained ten kilos and aged five 'years.' That very first night in Tiryns, I told you how my nurse Hippolyta in Corinth told *me* that my mother was a crazy Amazon deaf-mute who killed herself when I was born, and my father a hero on a white horse who'd left her on the stable roof one night. Why pussyfoot around about it? I not only *look* young enough to be your daughter; just possibly I *am* your daughter, and if that doesn't bother me, it shouldn't bother you. I never held a grudge against you; I took it for granted you didn't know you'd made my mother pregnant. Even when I learned (from you) that she'd been the hottest prospect in Amazonia until you raped her, and I decided that that was what drove her crazy and made her kill herself, I excused you. But I don't fool myself about my reasons: I'd heard a lot about you in Argolis; I admire heroes and had never met one; I was disgusted with Stheneboeia, and I wanted out of Tiryns. I don't mean anything vulgar like screwing my way to the top (I never let Stheneboeia sleep with me); I really did fall for you, in a hurry. I honor and respect you, as you know. I even love you; you're the gentlest, sweetest lover I ever had, if not the most passionate, and the difference in our ages doesn't matter to me at all except when it takes the edge off your enthusiasm because you've done everything once already. Like getting married and having a family and building a house and buying furniture and stuff. If you want to know the truth, I think we're bogged down more than immortalized: you scribble scribble scribble all day, morning noon and night, and honestly, I believe it must be the greatest thing in the world to be a mythic hero and be immortalized in the story of your life and so forth—I really do appreciate that—but I love *activity*, you know? Philonoë was more your type—I mean that perfectly kindly. She liked books and myths and needlework and all; I'm used to an *active* life, and we never *do* anything! I'd sort of hoped we'd go down to Lycia after you'd got yourself together, not that I'm eager to be a queen, but just so we'd be *doing* stuff. It drives me crackers that we've got this winged horse right here to take us anywhere in the world, and all we do is spin around the saltmarsh after mealtimes— then back to your scribbling scribbling while I make dinner and twiddle my thumbs. I hate to say this, but I guess I'd be happier with less of a hero and more of a regular man. I don't mean that sarcastically. I'm tired of Amazoning; I'm tired of being a demigod's girlfriend, too, if it means hanging around this cottage till I die. But I'm also tired of bopping about with different lovers; what I want is a plain ordinary groovy husband and ten children, nine of them boys. Call me a cop-out if you want to; I ought to find some swinging young Gargarensian M.D. or lawyer next mating season who'll think I'm the greatest thing that ever happened to him, instead of just the recentest, you know? I might not love him as much, but I bet I'd be happier. I don't want to be around when my hippomanes doesn't work for you any more, Bellerophon; either you'll leave me like the rest or we'll both sit around wishing we were dead. You thought that that Pattern Polyeidus gave you for your Second Flood predicted three women, but by my count I'm the fourth: Sibyl, my mother, Philonoë, and me, right? But you said yourself that everything comes in fives in the *Bellerophoniad*, so maybe you ought to start looking for that next one and get on with your career. Maybe this Chimera has turned into a pretty girl again, like Medusa in the *Perseid*. You should check and see if she's It, and if she isn't, kill her for real this time and see if *that* gets you where you want to go. Anyhow I know *I'm* not It for you, and you know it too, only you don't want to admit it. You're not getting any younger; neither am I: lots of Amazons look younger than they are because we don't count years, and it's the distinctions people acknowledge and condition themselves to look for that usually show, in my opinion. But the more I think about it, the more I'm *sure* that tonight's full moon is going to end my First Quarter, and you'll think I've aged fourteen years in one night. Will you still say I'm 'frisky and lean and tight' and so forth? I get tired too, you know; dead tired; sometimes I feel *Last* Quarter! Maybe I shouldn't go on like this; I know it's getting near my period, and that always makes me blue and a little bitchy. But I swear, this isn't immortality: it's suspended animation. Which brings me back to your story: despite all those clever things you have me say in it, the truth is I know zero about writing; but if *I* were to find this washed up on the beach and read it through, just as a plain story, I'd sure be pissed off that you never tell what happened to Polyeidus and Philonoë and Anteia and your mother and your kids, especially that ring business when you left home; and you don't say what the rest of Sibyl's letter said, or clear up that episode with the Chimera— whether she was real in the first place and whether she's back again—or explain all that fudging about your brother's death, et cetera. You even call it 'Part One,' but I don't see any Part Two. There are nice things in it, sure, a lot of nice things, once you get past that heavy beginning and move along; but if your immortality depends on this piece of writing, you're a dead pigeon."

A bad night. I couldn't speak to explain the difference between lies and myth, which I was but beginning to comprehend myself; how the latter could be so much realer and more important than particular men that perhaps I must cease to be the hero of my own, cease even to exist, cease somehow even to have existed. In fact I couldn't speak at all. Melanippe either, having spoken. Sadly and fiercely we made love: Medusa winked down at us; Pegasus snorted; my darling came as never in her life, sure sign of her passage. Me too. She slept; by full-moon light I wrote Part Two; just before dawn, as Perseus and company sank over Asia Minor, we gently made love again; she gave me the last of her First-Quarter hippomanes, an enormous stash, and bade me go kill Chimera for real.

"Are you sure you're not Polyeidus?" I asked her, and she responded: "Are you sure you're Bellerophon?"

Heh. I wrapped up in the prophet's Pattern the story thus far—which if less than *Perseid*-perfect was anyhow clear, straightforward, and uncorrupted at that time—hauled up on sleepy Pegasus, slipped him his quid of hip, winged west.

3

~~~~~~~~~~

Polyeidus here: shape-shifting, general prophecy.

No one who sees entire the scope and variety of the world can rest content with a single form. Gods and seers have such sight; hence our propensity for metamorphosis. Yet Zeus in all his guises is still Zeus, "presiding god of classic Greek mythology"; I in mine only Polyeidus, advisor to, perhaps father of, a minor hero in that same local corpus. Being Old Man of the Marsh was irksome. I grew bored to death with Bellerophon. What Zeus sees I don't know, but *I* saw (in bits and pieces, to be sure, like runes on my scattered daughter's oak leaves or scrambled bits of satellite photography) the fore and aft of the whole vessel of human history; as I swatted spiders and pulled leeches off me there in the Aleïan flats, I came understandably to wish myself not only out of that particular swamp, but out of Greek myth altogether—that tiresome catalogue of rapes, petty jealousies, power grabs; that marble-columned ghetto of immortals. Why couldn't I turn myself, I wondered, not into another personage-*from*-the-future (no more than a disquieting anachronism), but into Scheherazade, "Henry Burlingame III," or Napoleon in his *own* time and place? Recollecting the odd document I'd briefly been on Bellerophon's second try (a happy chance; I don't by any means always read the pages I turn into), I petitioned Zeus himself to give me a hand (promising the customary quid pro quo, to spread his fame in the new world), concentrated as one must on a single image—that verbo-visual pun of a honeybee which appears on Napoleonic flags and, stitched in gold, on the violet pall of the casket that transported his alleged remains from St. Helena back to Paris—and grunted hard.

I woke up at the back door of heaven, an odious large insect, Tabanus atratus perhaps, with noisy wings and wicked mandibles, buzzing about a mound of godshit. Great Zeus (from my perspective) towered over me disdainfully and thundered: "You're a shape-shifter: think of it as transmogrified ambrosia. Heh heh."

Until one is beyond their reach, the Olympians' whims are our directives. I tried; no luck. No matter, either: my newly compound eyes showed me more aspects of the future —mine, Bellerophon's, the world's—than I'd ever seen. I tried to groan; Zeus grinned.

"Now you see it, eh, Heironymous? By imitating perfectly the Pattern of Mythic Heroism, your man Bellerophon has become a perfect imitation of a mythic hero. That sort of thing amuses us. But look again at your famous Pattern. It says *Mystery* and *Tragedy:* Mystery in the hero's journey to the other world, his illumination, his transcension of categories, his special dispensation; Tragedy in his return to daily reality, the necessary loss in his translation of the ineffable into sentences and cities, his fall from the favor of gods and men, his exile, and the rest. Now look at Bellerophon's story thus far: it's not Mystery and Tragedy, but confusion and fiasco, d'accord?"

A gadfly (so I was, Heironymous hight, imperfectly magicked once again, into a name without initial in our alphabet) doesn't quibble with the god of gods. I buzzed neutrally, shrugged some shoulders.

"All which is as it should be, in his case," Zeus rumbled on. "But see what's coming up! I've had Amazons in my time; take it from me, that girl Melanippe's hippomanes is the real thing. Look at Bellerophon climbing on that crazy horse, straight for heaven, a kilometer a minute! He's high enough already to see Mystery and Tragedy plain; give him a few more pages and he'll rise above both and be a star boarder here forever! That's the sort of thing we're *not* amused by, and there'll be no bugging out for you until it's taken care of."

"Mm."

He tested the zigzag edge of a thunderbolt with his thumb. "Pegasus, on the other hand, is my natural nephew and a pretty piece of horseflesh, just what I need for packing these bolts from the Cyclops' smithy when somebody's hubris wants a bit of smiting. But if I shoot down your Bellerophon with one of these babies, there'll be nothing left of the winged horse except a few hundred kilos of viande de cheval bien cuit. You follow me?"

"Mm."

"Okay: if you want an exit visa out of that pile, wait till your boy gets this far and then give Pegasus a bite in the crupper. The rest will take care of itself: new country, new language, new myths—three millennia from here. It's that or eat shit forever. Done?"

I readily M-hmm'd.

"Good. Then you only need to eat it while you wait. Mortals, I swear."

I swore too, in available nasals, as he left, rubbed my wings furiously with two back legs, and looked with all my eyes for ways to turn the letter of his law to my advantage, like a cunning wrestler his adversary's Reset But there were none, and lunchtime came, and I was famished, but dared not leave the sill for better fare. Presently the Queen of Heaven herself came out, under pretext of emptying the royal thundermug. As best one can in mm's and hm's I buzzed for pity.

"Don't worry," Hera said, breathing through her mouth. She set the pot aside and pointed down to Corinth. "See that sexy little white heifer grazing near Nemea? How'd you like to have *her* for lunch?" It was, I saw, Io, her husband's latest mistress, by him disguised: in my then condition (and by contrast with my doorsill menu) an appetizing morsel, the more so for its relish of revenge on my tormentor. "Bellerophon won't be here for a while yet, as you know," the Queen went on. "I'll cover for you. Go to it."

I did, made a long lunch of squealing Io from Dodona to the sea since named after her, across the Bosphorus ditto, up into the Caucasus (where Big Z's buzzards made *their* lunch of foie Prométhe), back to Colchis, off to Joppa (crashing through *Perseid* I-F-5 like a bull through a china shop), as far east as Bactria and India, then west through Arabia Deserta with a caravan of stories picked up along the way, to Ethiopia and down the Nile. At Chemmis, gorged, I let her go, paused to wash my mandibles at a drinking fountain near the empty temple, then sped burping up to Olympus just in time to see, with my left eyes, wrathful Zeus, thunderbolt in hand, sitting on the sill among the shit and shards of the celestial chamberpot, smashed either by himself in anger or by his overtaken wife in fright; and with my right, bold Bellerophon casting away the golden bridle, feeding Pegasus the final leaves of Melanippe's herb, and with the scroll-rolled Pattern for his riding crop, whipping the grand beast up those thin last leagues to heaven.

"Just in time!" I tried to call to both. "Let me give you a little goose there, Bell-boy! Heh! Sorry about Miss Io, Zeus, sir: your missus had me sort of cornered. But I saw to it she got to Egypt safely in time to have your child; she's in a nice little spiral temple down in Chemmis: pretty pictures on the wall, et cetera. I didn't bite her hard; just a tickle, really; not the way I'm going to bite this horse here, to put him over the old finish-line for you! Heh. Here goes!"

I dived in and gave Pegasus a good one under the tail, bleh, as Zeus raised his bolt and Bellerophon his Pattern-scroll. The god stayed his hand when the winged horse bucked and whinnied; not so the hero, who in the instant before he pitched from that seat forever let me have it, then let go all. Pegasus bolted to his final ditto'd master; I changed, postswatly, into a fading copy of the Greek seer Polyeidus, falling with his fallen son to death. Zeus laughed down after us (the drop from heaven takes a dizzy while):

"A hundred eyes, a hundred blind-spots, Polyeidus! We gods can't break our vows, but we can make you wish we could. One way or another, in that new world you're dropping in on, you'll be Old Man of the Marsh for keeps. And unless your son forgives the tricks you've played on him, you'll always be some version or other of his story. God knows why. Heh. 'Bye."

Spread-eagled Bellerophon sailed over and called: "When he said I was your son, you sonofabitch, which twin did he take me for?"

I was too busy dying and plotting to answer directly: dying forever to the form of Polyeidus; plotting to my best interest this dénouement—how I might begin by becoming the terminal interview which follows; grow thence into all of Part Three and ultimately permeate (at least when the moon was on my side) the whole *Bellerophoniad*; grow narratively on in death like hair and fingernails until I comprehended the entire Bellerophonic corpus and related literature; con my son the imitation hero, as Admetus conned his wife Alcestis, into taking my place, or part of it, in death's company by becoming his own life story, the myth of Bellerophon. One way or another, if I was obliged to be Old Man of the Marsh, I would make the world my oyster. With an expiratory grunt I changed, for openers, into these fluttering final pages, written (so help me Muse) in "American":

Polyeidus: Ah so. As you see, our stars are falling fast. In the manner of the *Perseid*, mutatis mutandis, would you care to end this tale by answering freely as we fall five questions for posterity?

Bellerophon: Perseid may be your model; I have none any longer. That's one for you. *My* first is the last I asked before you changed format: when Zeus called me your son, whom did he take me for?

P.: Bellerophon, of course. Who else? N.Q. When you swatted me with the Pattern, you fulfilled the prophecy first laid on me as I humped your mother in the surf: that I would die by my son's hand unless he agreed to take my place, et cetera. The usual. And I scarcely expect you to do that, even though you'll die anyway when you make your hard landing a few questions from now, whereas a paginated form like mine can expect a certain low-impact afterlife. So what've you been up to since you left Themiscyra at the end of Part Two? Please speak directly into the page.

B.: A funny thing happened on the way to Mount Chimera. Melanippe's hip sent me higher than I've ever been, and I saw the ends of all the supporting characters in my

story. I saw my mother in Corinth, bitter and senile, dying
at the graves of Glaucus and Bellerus, cursing Poseidon for
not taking better care of his by-blows and Bellerophon for
not taking better care of her. There was your daughter, out
of her head altogether, wrecked by the goddess who
should've honored her: in a mantic stupor in the grove she
was crying "Bellerus! Bellerus!" while her lover sold her
frowsy favors to frightened fourteen-year-olds at a drachma
per. Worse yet, that lover, Sibyl's last, was Melanippe, the
first Melanippe: not a suicide after all, but a gross and bitter
bull-dyke who had taken Hippolyta's name and place to
raise her daughter, Melanippe Two. Whether I was that
daughter's father, my second sight was kindly blind to: once
I'd deflowered Melanippe mère and nipped the bud of her
career, she'd turned promiscuous as Sibyl, but out of self-
spite: a predator with heart of flint. Over in Tiryns I saw
her bitter bullish like, Anteia, forcing docile girls into tribad-
ism while Megapenthes plotted coup d'état and double-
theta'd sodomocracy. I saw Philonoë: heartbroken but gentle still after brief romances with other men and suicide, she
had withdrawn to a lonely Lycian retreat-house to live out
her days in bookish solitude and infrequent masturbation. Of
the high-altitude kisses I showered on her head, she was as
mercifully unaware as of the wreckage of our children and
our state. Those former were grown not into semidemideities
(an impossibility) but into commonplace adults, grasping,
doomed. The boys, per program, had taken the ring-bait,
quarreled over whose child should be shot through it to
determine my successor, and been finessed by their clever
sister, who volunteered her own child Sarpedon; this was
her son by a high-school dropout who'd seduced her in the
guise of Zeus-disguised-as-a-high-school-dropout, oldest

trick in the book: it duped her brothers into relinquishing their claims in her favor as easily as it had her into relinquishing her favors to the dropout's claims. Zeus himself, unduped and unamused, then commissioned Artemis to cut my dear daughter down for this imposture, and Ares (count on Z for overkill) to dispatch my sons in the ten-millionth bloody skirmish of our endless war with the Carians and Solymians. Dead, dead, dead. The kingdom, then, was ruled by greedy viceroys, my former students, in the infancy of Sarpedon, who will himself grow up to die on the losing side in the Trojan War.

This latter vision was my first clear evidence that I was flying now above mere panorama, into prescience: fearfully therefore I turned my eyes to the banks of the Thermodon, and beheld the final horror: straightforward as always, my dauntless darling had put me through the ordeal of Part Two by way of testing her conviction that it was not her mortal self I loved, so much as some dream of immortality of which I fancied her the cute incorporation; not one to toy with either life or death, upon my flight she'd washed face and hands, brushed teeth, combed hair, made up our bed, lain down upon it, and passed the time by singing to herself as many Amazon campfire songs as she could remember from her girlhood until, as she'd expected, her first Full-Moon menstrual flow commenced, about midafternoon; at that evidence that she was after all not pregnant by me, without expression or hesitation she drove her knife hilt-deep into her perfect little left brown breast. Whatever blinders I still steered with thereupon fell from me, and I saw the chimera of my life. By imitating perfectly the Pattern of Mythic Heroism, I'd become, not a mythic hero, but a perfect Reset I was no Perseus, my tale no *Perseid*—even had we been, I and it, so what? Not mortal me, but immortality, was the myth.

P.: That asks and answers your second question.

B.: Who cares?

P.: Come come. You've wrecked a certain number of good women, my daughter by who knows whom included, and you're heroically chastened by the wreckage—small comfort to them! But you admit you're new at second sight, which at its clearest is foggier than first: what if I told you that your view was strictly from your viewpoint? That in her "mortal part" at least (per *Perseid*), Philonoë remembers you with much affection and some gentle amusement as her first real lover, regrets (but no longer bitterly) your deserting her for Melanippe, but has come rather to enjoy and even prefer her more or less solitary life? And that while Melanippe, a more demonstrative young woman, did indeed stick herself with that dagger, she was saved from Hades by a passing Gargarensian, a handsome young visiting surgeon of promise who heard her cries, rushed to the rescue, took her with him on a tour of the Mediterranean to cheer her up, subsequently married her, and made her the happy mother of ten beautiful children, nine of them sons?

B.: I'd like it fine, god damn you. So much for your third, fourth, and fifth. Is it true?

P.: Who knows? All I see when I look in that direction is their (relatively) immortal part, this endless story of yours. So let's not count rhetorical questions. What about Chimera, my greatest invention? I hope you don't think you've killed an image like that with the line "I saw the chimera of my life."

B.: Not at all. What I saw was that it's *not* a great invention: there's nothing original in it; it neither hurt nor helped anyone; it's preposterous, not monstrous, and compared to Medusa or the Sphinx, for example, even its metaphoric power is slight. That's why, up there in the crater, it cooperated in its own destruction by melting the lead on my lance-point: its death was the only mythopoeic thing about it. Needless to say, the moment I understood *that* was the moment I really killed Chimera. No need to go to Lycia then; I changed course, chucked Athene's bridle, dug in my heels, and made straight for Olympus.

P.: Whatever for, your dying father asks obligingly, inasmuch as you'd already decided that immortality is a bad trip? Megalomania? Ambitious affirmation of the absurd?

B.: Certainly I was ambitious, all along; but to call ambition on that epic scale mere vanity is a double error. For while it's true that Bellerophon's aspiration to immortality was without social relevance, for example, and thoroughly elitist—in fact, of benefit to no one but himself—it should be observed that it didn't glorify "him," either, since the name he's called by is not his actual name, but a fictitious one. His fame, then, such as it was, is, and might have been, is as it were anonymous. Moreover, he does not, like an exiled tyrant or absconder, enjoy his fortune incognito; even had his crazy flight succeeded, he'd not have known it: there'd be another constellation in the sky, bearing the name he'd assumed—but *Perseid* to the contrary notwithstanding, it's hardly to be imagined that those patterns we call "Perseus," "Medusa," "Pegasus" (There he is! Sweet steed, fly on, with better riders than myself!) are aware of their existences, any more than are their lettered counterparts on the page. Or, if by some mystery they are, that they enjoy their fixed, frigidified careers. Got that, Dad? For you *are* my dad—old pard, old buck, old worm!—I don't question that: only Polyeidus's son could have mimed a life so well, so long.

P.: So. Well. *So long* is right. And so much for Poseidon's name on your birth certificate.

B.: False letters spell out my life from first to last. But not Bellerus's.

P.: Here it comes. You down there: wake up for the anagnoresis!

B.: What marsh did you say we're falling into? Do the people speak my language?

P.: Forget it. The present tenants are red-skinned, speak Algonkian, and have a mythology but no literature. At the rate we're falling, by the time we land they'll be white and black, speak more or less in English, and have a literature (which no one reads) but no mythology. On with the story: even in Greek it's muddy enough, but I've known what's coming for two hundred pages. In any language, it's Sibyl's Letter's Second Clause.

B.: Right: *POSEIDON'S SON HE ISN'T*. I'm not starbound Bellerus, but starstruck Deliades. Bellerus died in the grove that night, in my place, while I humped (halfsister!) Sibyl in holy his. I was his mortal killer; therefore I became his immortal voice: Deliades I buried in Bellerophon, to live out in selfless counterfeit, from that hour to this, my brother's demigoddish life. It's not *my* story; never was. *I* never killed Chimarrhus or Chimera, or rode the winged horse, or slept with Philonoë, or laid my head between Melanippe's thighs: the voice that spoke to them all those nights was Bellerus's voice. And the story it tells isn't a lie, but something larger than fact . . .

P.: In a word, a myth. Philonoë guessed all this, you know, back in First-Ebb days. And Melanippe long before she wrote the horse-race episode. As for me, it goes without saying that this and everything else you say goes without saying. I knew it before it was true, and if I'm astonished now it's because seers see past and future but not et cetera—everything takes your true prophet by surprise. So, you blew your big scene. That's no Elysium rushing up at us: it's Dorchester County, Maryland, Upsilon Sigma Alpha, and will be for several generations yet. When you hit it, you'll go deeper underground than your brother.

B.: How many questions left?

P.: One for me, two for you. Now that I've answered you, one apiece.

B.: Can you turn me into this story, Polyeidus? Let me be Bellerus's voice forever, an immortal *Bellerophoniad.*

P.: Out of the question.

B.: It's what you've tried to trick me into for half a dozen pages! I'm offering to take your place! Don't tell me it's impossible!

P.: Quite impossible—in the naïve way you mean. I can't turn anybody but myself into anything.

B.: Then I'm dead. Good night, Bellerus. Good night, all.

P.: What I *might* manage—not because I owe you any favors, but for reasons of my own—is to turn *myself* from this interview into you-in-*Bellerophoniad*-form: a certain number of printed pages in a language not untouched by Greek, to be read by a limited number of "Americans," not all of whom will finish or enjoy them. Regrettably, I'll have to have a certain role in the thing also—no beating Zeus out on that. But since I'll be there as an aspect of *you,* so to speak, I'll be free enough to operate in a few aspects of my own: "Harold Bray," perhaps, or his nonfictional counterpart, the legitimate heir to the throne of France and impresario of the Second Revolution, an utterly novel Reset No *Perseid*, I grant you, but it's the best I can do in what time we have left. That tidewater's coming up fast.

B.: I don't like the sound of it. I'd rather fall into a thornbush; become a blind lame vatic figure; avoid the paths of men; float upon the marshy tide forever, reciting my Reset

P.: Stop gnashing your teeth. Take it or leave it.

B.: I'll take it.

P.: Done. Heh. Any last words to the world at large? Quickly.

B.: I hate this, World! It's not at all what I had in mind for Bellerophon. It's a beastly fiction, ill-proportioned, full of longueurs, lumps, lacunae, a kind of monstrous mixed metaphor—

P.: Five more.

B.: It's no *Bellerophoniad*. It's a

ABOUT THE AUTHOR

John Barth's other works of fiction include
four novels—*The Floating Opera, The End
of the Road, The Sot-Weed Factor,* and
Giles Goat-Boy—and *Lost in the Funhouse:
Fiction for Print, Tape, Live Voice.*
He is currently Edward H. Butler Professor
of English at the State University of
New York at Buffalo.